Martha Louise Rayne

What Can A Woman Do

Her Position In The Business And Literary World

I0592421

Martha Louise Rayne

What Can A Woman Do
Her Position In The Business And Literary World

ISBN/EAN: 9783742812476

Manufactured in Europe, USA, Canada, Australia, Japa

Cover: Foto ©Andreas Hilbeck / pixelio.de

Manufactured and distributed by brebook publishing software
(www.brebook.com)

Martha Louise Rayne

What Can A Woman Do

WHAT CAN A WOMAN DO

OR,

HER POSITION IN THE

Business and Literary World

By

Mrs. M. L. Rayne

ILLUSTRATED

The fleet foot and the feeble foot,
Both seek the self-same goal.
The weakest soldier's name is writ
On the great army roll.

SUSAN COOLIDGE.

EAGLE PUBLISHING CO.

PUBLISHERS,

PETERSBURGH, N.Y.

→❧PREFATORY.❧←

THE belief that a book whose scope is suggested by the title of the present volume will be of great value and interest to all, is the reason why this work has been given to the public. It is not the effort of one individual, but of many gleaners in the field which it explores. It has been compiled from various reliable sources, and treats wholly upon facts. It is believed that it is the only book of its kind that has been published, and the compiler trusts that it will be found helpful to those who are seeking positions of usefulness, and valuable to those who are already established, while to those fortunate ones who do not need to step beyond the horizon of home, it will give a deeper interest in "Woman's Work," and cause them to feel a personal pride in her labor and achievements.

"What can a woman do?" Fifty-three or fifty-four years ago Miss Harriet Martineau is reported to have said that, in Massachusetts, one of the most highly civilized and advanced communities in the world, there were but seven industries open to women who wanted to work. They might keep boarders, or set type, or teach needlework, or tend looms in cotton mills, or fold and stitch in book binderies. This statement was rather too restrictive, because there were other forms of labor open to, them, especially those of the needle. But there is no doubt that the opportunities of self-support for women by honest industry in some other way than that of domestic service were very few and very limited. In the State of Massachusetts, which was the scene of Miss Martineau's reputed observation, it is now announced that there are more than three hundred occupations open to women, instead of seven, and that 300,000 women are earning their own living in these occupations, receiving from $150 to $3,000 every year. This computation does not include amateurs, or mothers and daughters in the household, and of course excludes domestic service.

As new occupations for women are continually becoming available, some well known professions are omitted from this volume to make room for newer and more responsible ones. The writer has endeavored to illustrate the many employments given, by facts and curious incidents gathered from various sources and from personal observation, thus making the work peculiarly interesting, instructive, and amusing.

In "Women as Poets," will be found some of the rarest and choicest poems in the English language, and in many instances the biographical note was contributed especially for this volume by the author of the poem selected, thus furnishing much reliable information not to be found elsewhere. So many pure and beautiful thoughts in rhyme, which have echoed and re-echoed throughout the world, making it better for their being, must add to the value of the book. The kingdom of home has not been overlooked; the aim of the writer—indeed the great object of the work—is to elevate and glorify the humblest home, and it is her earnest wish that "What Can a Woman Do" may be found a welcome visitor into every home in the land, there to accomplish its mission of usefulness and instruction.

CONTENTS.

Women in the Business World.

Women in the Literary World.

POEMS.

⟶CHAPTER I.⟷

Woman's Work.

"The hand that rocks the cradle moves the world."

A woman cannot do the thing she ought.
Which means, whatever perfect thing she can
In life, in art, in science, but she fears
To let the perfect action take her part
And rest there; she must prove what she can do
Before she does it."—AURORA LEIGH.

LESSED, says Carlyle, "blessed is he who has found his work; let him seek no other blessedness." Equally blessed is the woman who has found her work. Life is, indeed, a burden to one who, day after day, must plod for a mere existence at some work for which there is no special adaptation, but it is peculiarly trying and discouraging to a woman, who cannot choose for herself the profession or vocation in life which will give her the most pleasure to follow in the toilsome effort of winning her own bread. "We all know," says a popular writer on these topics, "how much happier that woman is, who can cheerfully take up the work she likes, than the one who toils daily at uncongenial employment." The only remedy for this evil is to choose when youth, free hearts and minds, leisure and means are all within demand, yielding their best to educate these young women in some specialty, by which they may support themselves when it is necessary. It is a great mistake in the management of children when the boys only are educated to become self-helpers, while the girls are taught to write gracefully, acquire various accomplishments, do a little light housework, and fit themselves to live as merely ornamental members of society. A girl is not expected to earn anything, while a boy, even if he already has a fortune, must be proficient in some trade or profession, or he is not considered of much account. At least he must know enough to be able to invest his own money with prudence.

Now take the world as we find it. Are not the majority of the women in a community in great need of some money-making talent? How many do we know in the average society of even a prosperous village who have a competency provided for them, with no thought or care of their own except to spend it prudently. Would not a great deal of the small pinching and distressing privation be done away with, if every woman had her own private purse, with which to supplement the money supplied to her for household expenses, and which is often so inadequate? Or if, when thrown suddenly on her own resources, she has the faculty of doing one thing well, shall she hesitate between the honest labor of her own hands, and the doled-out bread of charitable relatives? The day has gone by when a woman who enters any pursuit of industry loses caste. If our great grandfathers could revisit the earth, what would astonish them quite as much as the telegraph, railroads, telephone, and the electric lights, is the position that woman has taken and is so nobly sustaining under all these difficulties of non-fitness and lack of business education. It might not surprise them so much to find lady cashiers, lady bankers, lady clerks, but what would they say to women lecturing in public and filling great halls, to women preaching in the pulpit and filling pastorates, to women as school commissioners, women appointed by governors to responsible positions on commissions of charities, prisons and reformatory institutions, to women as practicing physicians, counseling with the wisest of the faculty of the opposite sex. If they could see these facts as they are, the results would not astonish them so much as the indomitable courage and perseverance which led them through difficulties which were almost insurmountable.

THE INITIATIVE STEP.

How to educate young girls so that they can become efficient co-workers with their brothers in the commercial walks of life, is a question that must interest every mother in the country to-day. It is a perplexing question, because every mother naturally dreads the ordeal of a business experience for the young girl just budding into womanhood, who has no idea of the hardships of life. If the mother has been a woman of broad experience there will be little for the daughter to unlearn; she will not be hampered at every step by a dread of Mrs. Grundy, and even though her field of observation has been limited to the happy circumscribed walls of

home, she will have no narrow prejudices or small bigo-
tries of character to overcome; a brilliant coterie of women
has led the way into new fields, where a woman working
for her daily bread need feel no shame or embarrassment,
or trammel herself unnecessarily with the set formulas
of a dead past.   The world is full of women who must
work or starve, and it is for these women particularly
that a liberal education is desired—one that will lead to
their advancement in a pecuniary way.   There are true
womanly women, who may not have another opportunity of making themselves a home, for whom providence
has furnished no mate—women who are denied marriage,
or who prefer a life of single independence to taking up
with one lame offer; or, it may be, they are already married, but have no taste or strength for domestic work,
and prefer to bear the mutual burden in their own way.
There are other women who have time from the duties
and obligations of housework to earn a little pin money,
and turn an honest penny, for their own profit.   There
are several hundred different methods by which a woman
can earn her own livelihood, and she should study them
at her leisure, and educate herself in that one for which
she is the best adapted.   She does not require the genius
of a Napoleon to succeed in any one of them; very ordinary qualities can be grafted and improved on the tree
of knowledge; much depends on the earnestness of purpose and power of concentration which she brings to her
work.

BUSINESS EDUCATION.

It is an established truth, that a woman who is competent in any one branch of business will always find a

situation open to her, if she seeks it. In a contest, skilled labor will always succeed, against the assumptions and pretences of ignorance.

"He is thrice armed who has his quarrel just;" so she, who can demand work in return for a diploma of merit, is the most likely to succeed in the struggle for place. The experience of education in any sphere of labor gives preparatory strength to achieve laudable results. True, it involves much arduous and patient endeavor to attain such a position, but once there half the battle is fought.

Among the many female applicants for work, there is no class more dreaded than that of reduced ladies. Why? Because they have no specialty. The higher education and many accomplishments of the poor gentlewoman only add to her embarrassments and leave her but one profession—that of teacher. It may be of music or embroidery, or an infant school, for any of which she is unfitted by either nature or inclination. The number of incompetent women who attempt to conduct a business they know absolutely nothing about, is almost incredible, and they work harder, to make ignominious failures, than the educated woman does to succeed. But in one sense they are themselves educators; they are many of them pioneers in the work they have chosen, and their mistakes serve as warnings to other women who, armed with their energy, added to a practical knowledge of business in its many details, will accomplish all that they failed to do.

TRAINING SCHOOLS.

There are colleges now in nearly all States, where girls

are educated in all the important branches which young
men study before entering upon the profession of a life-
time, such as book-keeping, stenography, telegraphy,
and other branches, where she learns to calculate with
rapidity; to write a plain business hand; to concentrate
her thoughts on useful, instead of ornamental work; to
understand many of the intricate theories involved in
commercial life, which, to the average woman, are problems unsolved and unsolvable. The young men who are
her associates may at first feel bored over this new
assumption of knowledge, and miss the more frivolous
part of her nature, which served them as recreation, but
they will soon understand that her development of
strength need not detract from her womanliness or make
her one degree less lovable. She will be less dependent
but more companionable. Her work itself is becoming
more and more adapted to her own tastes and her ability
to perform it, and it is a duty imposed on all who have
the power to advance her interests to unite by word and
deed in clearing away all false ideas of the true woman's
position in the world. The working woman of the
future will have one great advantage over her prototype
of the past—she will have the advantage of thorough
training schools and industrial colleges, such as the trustees of the late John Simmons of Boston are pledged to
build, for which purpose Mr. Simmons bequeathed one
million of dollars. What Canon Kingsley calls the
lower education of women has been shamefully neglected. and the fault is largely due to themselves. They
have cultivated accomplishments at the expense of valuable knowledge. Accomplishments are good in their

place, but if half the girls who spend hours every day in thrumming the piano, with no taste or capacity for music, would invest the same time and money in one practical study, they would realize a much better profit on their capital, and would never come to be regarded as dependent incumbrances by their friends and relatives. "What shall I do to be saved?" is literally the cry of thousands of young women, who without friends or protectors, find themselves facing the world—the severe, critical world—that is so kind and flattering to the successful, so cruel and pitiless to the helpless and improvident of either sex. The financial test is a strong argument of success, for employers are slow to part with their money for inferior work, and this is an age of competition. One inefficient worker brings to naught, theoretically, the practical services of a dozen competent ones. The employers judge other women by her isolated case, and refuse to give occupation to one whom they must first educate, and who gives them plainly to understand that she has no interest in her work, is driven to it by necessity, performs it grudgingly, and will abandon it at the first opportunity for something more congenial.

CHAPTER II

Average • Wages • in • New • York • and • Elsewhere.

T is a common wish among young and inexperienced women about to enter the arena of public labor to find situations in a large city such as New York, Boston or Chicago, but they must remember that while there are many situations in a large town, there are also many competitors, and these always out-rate the positions in the ratio of fifty applicants to one appointment. This is the case in business situations for men, as well, only on a still more discouraging scale, there being frequently a hundred applicants to one vacancy. With this excess of demand on the wrong side prices must be low, but there are always exceptions to every rule, and there may be fortunate circumstances to give the last new comer immediate compensation, and if that is not possible, months of waiting may bear good fruit in an added experience, a knowledge of the city, and other beneficial results.

In answer to enquiries in a New York paper, whether there is any position open to a woman except that of a teacher, where she can earn more than $800 a year, the

18

following list of prices is furnished, with the comment'
that women, as a rule, received from twenty to thirty per
centum less than men for the same or equivalent services. Just here I would say that no woman need feel
aggrieved or discouraged by this statement, or imagine
that it is an injury which she must avenge by recourse
to the ballot. It is one of the barriers which men themselves erected to defend women, from behind which they
purposed to earn bread for both, unforeseeing the coming
army of women who have no one to work for them, and
who must of necessity work not only for themselves but
for those dependent on them. But even with this statement, a canvass of our large stores and city business
houses would show a large percentage of men working
for eight or ten persons against single women clerks who
are working for themselves only. The adjustment of
false averages in wages, even in these cases, may be a
wrong one, but it is one which time and justice will
remedy. The woman must console herself as Whittier
did, under a national evil—

> " I only know that God is just,
> And every wrong shall die."

Meanwhile, whatever her hand finds to do, let her do it
with her might.

These, then, are the average prices paid at the present
time in large cities for certain positions. Good sales-
men, for example, get from $6 to $10 a week; some few
who have worked a long time receive $12, and occasion-
ally a salary as high as $15 is paid. But the latter are
exceptional cases. Heads of departments, such as the

leading saleswomen in the glove or lace departments, or in the dressmaking, who command a large influential custom, receive as high as $20 or $30 a week, in exceptional cases, and there are not fifty such positions in New York city to-day.

Lady cashiers receive, on an average, a little more than good saleswomen. But $15 a week is a large stipend for a cashier, and it requires a guaranteed ability, the best of references, and sometimes good security, to obtain such a position. The employment of book-keeper commands as high as $20 a week, but the majority of good bookkeepers get from $10 to $12, and many women well trained in the business think themselves fortunate if they obtain $8. In the Employment Bureau of the Young Women's Christian Association, whose proteges obtain, as a rule, better positions and better wages than the subscribers to ordinary employment agencies, $15 per week is stated as the maximum that a woman can hope for, exclusive of the professions. The Superintendent of the Bureau says it is rare that a woman obtains more than $15 per week as a teacher, and that $800 per annum would be regarded as a very large salary. In the position of housekeeper $1,000 a year is occasionally paid to an experienced woman, trustworthy and capable of assuming the entire management of a first-class establishment. Such instances are very rare, and can only be commanded by experienced women, well trained theoretically. On piece work, in artificial manufacture and occupations approximating to the artistic, it is stated that wages as high as $18 are occasionally earned by first-class hands; but, in ordinary industries, from $8 to $12 per week represents the average earnings of women in occupations requiring some training, and from $3 to $6 is the common price in the lower industrial walks.

WOMEN AS HOTEL CLERKS.

At the Palmer House, Chicago, the head cashier, who is a woman, receives a salary of $2,000 a year and board, which is equivalent to $500 more. Two other lady clerks have $1,500 each a year and board, and a stenographer receives $1,500 and board per year. Mr. Palmer, the proprietor, announced some years ago that the change from men clerks was so satisfactory that he would employ them in the hotel as substitutes for male help whenever practicable, and he has been consistent in carrying out this policy ever since. There is a popular hotel in Michigan where the manager, clerk, bookkeeper and steward are all women. For these services they receive the same salaries that men do. It might appear at first thought, derogatory to the dignity of a lady to fill such positions, but it is in such places that true ladyhood is needed, and the very fact that the position is difficult and in public places, should inspire the bread winner to maintain and assert, at all hazards, her principles of womanly honor. It is because of woman's moral superiority that she is given the position, and the surety her employer has that the interests of the public, as well as his own, will be safe in her hands. She will not embezzle his money in gambling or in late suppers. She will not smoke his cigars, or bestow them on her impecunious friends; she will not be insolent to one person and cringing to another; and, if she is a true woman, the very trials and stumbling blocks of her position will only form for her a St. Augustine ladder, to raise her above ignoble things.

DEPARTMENTS OF BUSINESS IN WHICH WOMEN ARE ENGAGED.

As a forceful illustration of the extent to which women are now invading the fields of labor which have hitherto been occupied in the main by men, we append the following list which offers an interesting study. There are a great many branches not included in this list into which women are making their way, and to which reference is made elsewhere in the book.

Bankers and brokers, clergy, teachers, lawyers, physicians and surgeons, dentists, nurses, poets, dramatists, artists, journalists, editors, reporters, printers and typesetters, proof-readers, stenographers and type-writers, telegraphers, musicians, elocutionists, piano tuners, teachers of dancing, photographers, retouchers of photographs, government clerks and officials, dressmakers, professional cooks, hotel and boarding-house keepers, restaurateurs, inventors, electricians, lecturers, pilots, bookkeepers, commercial travelers, canvassers, engravers, wood turners and carvers, carriage trimmers, bell foundry operators, brass founders, gun and locksmiths, tinners, architects, auctioneers, clockmakers, agricultural laborers, gardeners, bee-keepers, poultry raisers, stock herders and stock raisers, barbers and hair dressers, cigarmakers, brewers, ı shers, distillers, curriers and tanners, weavers.

It is now almost impossible to find any business in which a woman is not engaged, if not as principal, as

assistant; in which position she pays the penalty of a
lack of business knowledge and experience, by receiving
a lower rate of remuneration than a man would for doing
exactly the same work; but she must patiently bide her
time and learn what it is that she can do best, and not
be spasmodic in her work or in her business relations.

FALSE PRIDE.

When a young girl selects some money-making business she will naturally aspire to one of the professions,
such as teaching, because of the desirable associations
which surround it. School influences are all good, and
a teacher is fitted to appear in the best society, as the
result of association with the cultured and refined educators of youth. But all can not be teachers, nor are
they adapted to the work if they could secure situations. What then? The shop, cashiers, bookkeepers
or clerks? The training for any of these positions must
be such that they can compete with the male clerk who
began by sweeping out the store, and not only learned
to cast up accounts with accuracy and precision, but to
understand and take an interest in the fundamental laws
upon which business is based. The girl who was playing with dolls when her fellow-clerk began his apprenticeship expects to pick it up in a few months, and earn
as much as he! She will learn in a few lessons that she
is mistaken, and if she is wise will pocket her pride and
go down to the bottom of things as he did, learning the
science as well as the routine of what she is doing. She
need not abate a particle of her dignity of character, or
grow hard and commonplace through the service of life,

any more than she need ape the manners or don the garb
of her male co-worker.   It is not necessary that she lose
that essential charm of womanhood, which is her natural
heritage, because she turns the pages of a ledger.   The
whole tendency of her being is to grow in womanly
strength, not to develop into some kind of a masculine
nondescript.

⟶✧CHAPTER III.✧⟵·

HE author of the first modern novel was a woman — Miss Burney — and concerning it Macaulay said: "It was a tale in which both the fashionable and vulgar side of London might be exhibited with great force and with broad comic humor. Most of the novels which preceded Evelina were such as no lady could have written, and many of them were such as no lady could, without confusion, own that she had read. The very name of novel was held in horror among religious people. Miss Burney took away the reproach which lay on a most useful and delightful species of composition."

This was over a century ago. Miss Burney was the daughter of a London music teacher and lady in waiting to Queen Charlotte, consort of George III., in whose service she nearly expended her life. She had for her friends such men as Dr. Johnson, Sheridan, Burke, Warren Hastings, and others of that period, who were shining lights in literature. Before Dr. Johnson knew who the author of Evelina was he had publicly praised

the book, and in her humility and total lack of self-con-
sciousness she records in her diary:

"Dr. Johnson's approbation almost crazed me with
agreeable surprise; it gave me such a flow of spirits that
I danced a jig to Daddy Crisp.   I think I should love
Dr. Johnson for such lenity to a poor, mere worm in literature, even if I were not myself the identical grub he
has obliged."

It was in the midst of this delicious atmosphere of
flattery, Dr. Johnson praising her; Edmund Burke
desiring to make her acquaintance, after sitting up all
night to read her book; Sheridan offering to take, without first seeing it, any play that she would write; that
she lived and wrote another novel, Cecilia.   Although
not so simple in style, it was a more effective piece of
work, and was received with great excitement.   It is said
to have brought the author a remuneration of two thousand pounds.

Both of these novels are now unread and have passed
out of fashion, but her letters and diary, as Madame
D'Arblay, are on sale in new revised form, and are valuable as faithful, piquant chroniclers of a past literature, and a graphic reproduction of the minds and
manners of the eighteenth century.

WOMEN FAMOUS IN LITERATURE.

A modern writer says: In English literature there is
hardly a department which woman does not adorn.   In
history, biography, poetry and fiction, she seems equally
at home, presenting a versatility and comprehensiveness,
a grasp of deep and intricate questions, a delicacy and

faithfulness of treatment, a logical force and clearness, seldom equaled or surpassed by the stronger sex. The writer then alludes to that remarkable woman Harriet Martineau, who popularized the principles of political economy, defined the phenomena of mesmerism, wrote histories, biographies, manuals of statesmanship and treatises on the condition of the laboring classes, while herself a suffering invalid. Her "Life in a Sick Room" has cheered and strengthened thousands of invalids by teaching them occupation and diversion for the dreary hours of solitude and suffering which no external aid can altogether relieve. The story of her "Farm of Four Acres" has been read and studied with profit by hundreds of practical agriculturists, and the history of her life, written by herself, and bearing in every line the impress of her independence and originality is, notwithstanding its negation of that hope which is the light and life of the Christian, one of the most valuable and instructive of studies.

Marian Evans, better known as "George Eliot," has made an enduring fame through her novels, which are justly considered the best works of modern fiction, those which she first gave to the world being considered superior as domestic literature to the more elaborate and powerful works of her mature years. The fireside favorites are "Adam Bede" and the "Mill on the Floss." The classic romances of her later years were "Romola" and "Daniel Deronda," standard novels, full of a rich, ripe, intellectual vigor, but demanding an equal breadth of understanding to enjoy them, consequently less popular with the great class of people who do not enjoy abstruse reading. But they are wonderful monuments to the genius of the writer; albeit they have neither the pathos of Dickens or the brilliant sarcasm of Thackeray, but are worthy of comparison with either.

Mrs. Oliphant, Mrs. Gaskell, and Mrs. Henry Wood, are all well known as novelists, and have made handsome fortunes out of their writings. Agnes Strickland has given us the " Queens of England," the most charmingly written history in existence. Mrs. Gaskell wrote the Life of Charlotte Brontė, the gifted author of "Jane Eyre," so delightfully that the critics said it ranked next in interest to the novel whose writer it depicted, and it stands unrivaled as a biography, just as Mrs. Anna Cora Ritchie's autobiography surpasses all others.

In poetry the names of Felicia Hemans and Elizabeth Barret Browning, the author of that rare poem for women, "Aurora Leigh," stand pre-eminent. Mrs. Hemans was the poet of the affections and of sentiment. Mrs. Browning wrote heroic epics, and stands acknowledged the crowned queen of song. England's poets of the gentler sex have led unhappy lives of repression and non-appreciation, or have been helpless invalids, with a few notable exceptions. As the bird whose eyes have been put out sings the sweetest song in its blindness and captivity, so these wounded spirits, such as Mrs. Hemans, L. E. L., Mrs Caroline Norton, Adelaide Proctor, and Mrs. Browning, have given us the divinest strains of sorrow through their suffering souls. Take a glance at any collection of poets and see the women's names there inscribed: Jean Ingelow, Dinah Maria Mulock, Adelaide Proctor, Mary Howitt, Eliza Cook, Christina Rosetti, and hosts of others as well known and as popular. Our own country has Harriet Beecher Stowe, whose "Uncle Tom's Cabin" not only made her famous but independently rich; Margaret Fuller Ossoli, whose unhappy death took her from us in the flower of her genius, and who was the first American writer in the ranks of women to produce essays of clearness and vigor, which were in the highest sense intellectual and educational; Mrs. E. D. E. N. Southworth, a popular novelist; Lucy Larcom, whose graceful poetry is much admired; "Gail Hamilton," Miss Abigail Dodge, who has written several sparkling books, and a host of women who write books, write for the newspapers and for the periodicals, and whose work is well paid for. There are women whose names do not become widely known who have made valuable contributions to the literature of the day. The bookstores are filled with new books, and on the handsome covers the names of female writers are inscribed. There are industrious workers who produce a new volume every year, the labor pays them pecuniarily, and the people are the critics who read and accept what they write.

HOW TO GET A MANUSCRIPT PUBLISHED.

If there is merit in the work it will be discovered by some publisher to whom it may be submitted, and the manuscript will be given to a reader, and if it is accepted, a certain price will be paid for it; or it may be published on a royalty to the author, which is usually ten per cent. To ensure attention the writing should be legible, written only on one side of the paper, the manuscript smooth and easily handled, and everything made

as plain to the reader as possible. Stamps for its
return, in case it is not used, should be enclosed. No
rules can be given to ensure success. If there is merit
and originality in the story, and it is well told and
pleasantly written, it will take. "Cape Cod Folks" was
a first novel by an anonymous writer, and it had a sudden local success. It was written by a bright young girl
who taught school a season among a lot of quaint characters whom she mimicked in such a brilliant manner that
the work had a novelty and dash that made it sell. "An
Earnest Trifler," another popular society novel, was written by an Ohio girl, and has been in demand for several
seasons. "One Summer," by Blanche Howard, has been
a very successful book for light summer reading. It is
not likely that these books will be remembered after a
dozen years. They will hardly enjoy the popularity of
"Queechy;" and "The Wide, Wide World," by Miss
Warner. It is doubtful if the writers made very much
out of them—perhaps what it would have taken them
three years to earn at school teaching. Books written
under difficulties are nearly always the most successful,
as the friction of adverse circumstances brings out more
freely the sparks of genius. It will do amateur writers
good to study the habits of successful authors, to read
successful books, and analyze their contents. The home
life of the Bronté family has always possessed a great
interest for those who are engaged in literary pursuits.
An old family servant says that the famous sisters had
very regular habits of indoor life. At nine o'clock precisely every evening all domestic work was laid aside and
literary tasks were begun. They talked over the stories

they were engaged upon, and described their plots. Apparently there was some writing during the day, for, according to the servant: "Many's the time that I have seen Miss Emily put down the tally iron, as she was ironing the clothes, to scribble something on a piece of paper. Whatever she was doing, ironing or baking, she had her pencil and paper by her. I know now she was writing 'Wuthering Heights.'"

HOW THE AUTHOR OF "WE GIRLS" WRITES HER BOOKS.

Apropos of the home life of writers, a few words about one of our own fireside authors may not be amiss here. There are few persons who read the lighter class of literature who do not admire the sweet, pure, wholesome works of Mrs. A. D. T. Whitney, and who would not be glad to know something about her personal and private life. She lives in a quaint, old-fashioned brown house, with a rotunda running across the front, supported by pillars, over which are trailing vines. It is hard to imagine a more homelike place. Everything shows the work of hands at home, from the pretty parlor curtains of an unbleached muslin, bordered with red and black, to the combination of the shades of brown in the furniture covering. In the parlor hang photographs which bring to mind "Sights and Insights." Two or three exquisite panels of pansies, which must have been suggested by the book of "thoughts that have blossomed into words;" two fine outline engravings of Fra Angelica's "Angels;" Raphael's "Madonna of the Goldfinch;" Delanche's beautiful "Moses in the Bulrushes," and some pretty little chromos. Wherever one happens to be there is a book to pick up, and it is always sure to be interesting. Macdonald is a very great favorite with Mrs. Whitney. His picture hangs in her room. And Mrs. Whitney herself? She is a quiet, sweet little woman, dressed in black and gray.

She has no special place for writing when hay-lofts are out of the question. Her "Odd and Even" was mostly written in a hay-loft on summer days. She keeps her few books of reference in a music rack, which she rolls around where fancy leads her, writing generally on a board or book placed on her lap. She copies all the manuscript with a type-writer.

One singular thing in Mrs. Whitney's books is, that those circumstances which seem most immaterial are founded on fact. The black cat in "Zerub Throop's Experiment" was taken from life. The whole solution of the plot in "Odd or Even" hung upon a sneeze. In writing she generally has an idea from which some life lesson can be taken, which she calls the core of her story. "It comes first," she says, "and I build around it. I sit as a spectator and let my people come upon the stage, not knowing what they are to be myself, but I never take a portrait. If I find one coming unawares I immediately change the features." If a house or room is to be described, Mrs. Whitney puts her idea first in the form of a pencil sketch and keeps the drawing with her to be sure of consistency. One of her very best books for the home is "We Girls," in which so many beautiful, graceful features of domestic life are drawn,

MRS. ROSA HARTWICK THORPE.

while a simple story is charmingly told in her wise and gracious way.

MRS. ROSA HARTWICK THORPE,

Author of "Curfew Must Not Ring To-Night."

Mrs. Rosa Hartwick Thorpe is the author of one poem which has made a world-wide and enduring fame for her, such as other writers have spent a life-time in vainly trying to acquire. It was written for the Detroit Commercial Advertiser, and the writer did not probably receive any compensation for it. It was copied in all other papers throughout the Union, and was reproduced in English journals, and translated into the German language in Germany. Mrs. Thorpe was but seventeen years old when she wrote this famous poem. As a child she was a thinker and reader, and in her school days her delightful essays and composition were the admiration of teachers and classmates. She has never made a profession of writing, but has jotted down her thoughts during her household exercises, or in seasons of ill-health, as a sort of mental recreation. Mrs. Thorpe has furnished many short poems to the newspapers, heroic or sentimental incidents of history furnishing her with themes. There is no doubt she might have acquired wealth and fame both with her pen had she made literature a profession.

A magnificent tribute to Mrs. Thorpe has been contributed by the women of Michigan for the Michigan building at the World's Fair. It is a large banner with her portrait, life-size, emblazoned on it.

3

→✲CHAPTER IV.✲←

The ✲ Profession ✲ of ✲ Journalism.

THIRTY years ago a woman who wrote for the papers was looked upon as a great curiosity—a sort of nondescript who occupied a purely ideal position, and whose name was veiled from the contaminating gaze of the public under initial letters or some graceful nom-de-plume of the Lydia Languish school. The term blue stocking was still in vogue for any woman who dared let her proclivity for writing stories or poetry be known, and the vulgar taste dictated such verses as the following specimen as a means of ridicule:

> "To see a lady of such taste
>   So slatternly is shocking,
> Your pen and poetry lay by
>   And learn to darn your stockings."

In spite of these discouragements many daring women did manage to add a respectable sum to their otherwise meagre purses every year, by writing poetry, essays and stories for the papers. Among these was Emily C. Chubbuck, who, under the alliterative name of Fanny Forrester, wrote very acceptable poems and stories,

84

which were the means of introducing her to her future
husband, the distinguished missionary Adoniram Jud-
son. She is long since dead, but her poems and her
book, Alderbrook, etc., are found still in old libraries. Miss Sarah Clarke, who used to write as Grace
Greenwood, was also of that period. She wrote for the
columns of various papers, and edited a child's magazine, the Little Pilgrim. Mrs. Hale was then the editor
of Godey's Lady's Book, and continued to be for forty
years. Mrs. Sigourney had written sweet verses, which
had given her both name and fame. The Boston Olive
Branch had a number of ladies employed in its office
as editors, readers, story-writers, and editorial writers in
those days. Mrs. M. A. Denison, author of "That Husband of Mine," edited the "Ladies Enterprise," a
paper issued under the management of the Olive Branch
Company. Fanny Fern came into that office one day,
and handed Mr. Norris a "little piece." He referred it
to Mrs. Denison, who read it and passed it along to Mrs.
Gerry, who wrote something on the margin. It was
this: "A very readable sketch, bright and sparkling."
Mr. Norris said: "You can leave it; if it is used we
will pay you at the rate of $1.50 per column of our
paper. Afterwards Robert Bonner paid her one hundred dollars a column. Every line she wrote was a
satire on some pet folly, and her articles became
immensely popular. It is recorded of her, that she
wrote once a week for the Ledger for fourteen years, and
in all that time was never once late with her manuscript
or missed a paper. I mention these as representative
women. There were many others who wrote then and

have won for themselves an honorable competence in newspaper writing, if not as public a fame.

But the style of writing has changed. The pretty love stories in which romantic names and pastoral scenes are blended are no longer in favor. Even the genius of Margaret Fuller might not get her a situation on the public press to-day as an editorial writer, for the newspapers no longer publish literary essays, however learned and well written; it wants a quick and comprehensive digest of the news—a tender and pathetic sketch in which are all the elements of a first-class drama, a poem worthy of Longfellow or Bryant, or a description of a dog fight or local disturbance, written in rhetorical English, and a style that will compare with Ruskin.

THE LADY JOURNALIST.

No work is more strangely and more curiously misunderstood than that required by journalism. It not only requires special talent of a high order, but the greatest amount of technical discipline, general information, adaptability, quickness of diction, and fertility of resources. With all this it requires, too, what is almost a sixth sense, the mental habit of keen analysis and swift combination. While these qualifications are in their perfection, the result of experience, they must also be natural gifts. The journalist, even as the poet, is born, not made. The young woman who aspires to do "critical literary work" would, upon trial, be found incompetent to write a local paragraph satisfactorily. If she is in earnest in her desire to enter journalism, she must be content to begin at the beginning. She must realize the importance of that sympathetic perception, graphic delineation, and power of representation that characterize the able reporter. It is a department whose discipline is invaluable, and whose scope it may well be a young woman's aspiration to ably fill; and there is not the slightest danger of her work being too good for it. The anxiety should be to have it sufficiently good. If the aspiring young woman is ready to begin in the simplest manner, and bring her best abilities to whatever she is set to do, she may in time grow to other work. That depends wholly on innate ability and her power of perseverance.

Again, the professional journalist is as often amazed over the attitude taken by the young woman whose contributions he rejects. Now, it is an unwritten law, well understood in journalism, that no editor is under the slightest obligation to give a reason for his acceptance or non-acceptance of a manuscript. He is not called upon to write a private critique on the article to the author of it. His acceptance or rejection is an absolute and unquestionable fact. Among amateur writers this does not appear to be understood. "The article is hardly available for the columns of this paper," writes the editor of the journal. Now, that should be sufficient, and end the matter. The article may be better in some respects than a dozen others he accepts; but if he is in any sense worthy of his place, he has an innate intuition of subtle fitness and intellectual acquirements which he could no more communicate than he could put his mental life on exhibition. Moreover, there is not the slightest necessity of his convincing them. But his contribu-

tor can not let the matter rest.   Perhaps she has written
a book and is not pleased with his review of it.   She
must write him a letter deprecating his judgment.   She
wants to know if he has read her book carefully.   She tells
him the critical connoisseur gave two columns of extracts
from it, and she thinks it too bad that he referred to it
so unkindly.   She favors him with nine pages of her
views on his conduct.   All sub-editors and reporters
understand that it is an unjustifiable impertinence to
ask the managing editor his reason for publishing or not
publishing any matter submitted to his judgment.   Outside writers and aspiring amateurs rarely seem to comprehend this truth, and their transgressions are largely
from ignorance, rather than intention.   The nature of
editorial work requires absolute power of decision in
order to preserve the unities of the journal the editor
conducts, and the amateur contributor should not permit his *amour proprè* to incite him to open any discussion regarding the justice of the editorial judgment.

ETHICS OF JOURNALISM.

The above statements are strictly true, but how are
young writers to know this?   There is no school in
which journalism is taught as any other profession is,
and an amateur in newspaper work must therefore learn
the etiquette of the occasion from actual experience.
The editor of a daily journal, for example, has no time
to instruct callers with manuscript they wish him to
peruse, in the ethics of journalism.   He may frown and
look bored, and consult his watch, as he frequently does
on such an occasion; and if his visitor has the intuitions

which the situation demands she will leave her manu·
script and go away, without another word. It is not
necessary that she explain how she came to write it,
what her necessities are, where she was born, and if she
is married or single. The editor is not personally interested in her history, and his time is money to him.
Now, if she would reach his notice in a business way, let
her present her manuscript, ask him if he will please
look it over when he has time, and either leave her
address and stamps for its return, or state that she will
call again at such a time. Then she will bow pleasantly
and retire. A lady who has won name and money as a
newspaper writer, took her first effort to a weekly journal in Boston. The editor was amusing himself with a
pet dog when she entered the office, and he merely
inclined his head toward a chair, and went on feeding
the dog lumps of sugar. The lady at last became so
indignant at such neglect that she rose to go. Then the
editor asked what he could do for her, and extended his
hand for the roll of manuscript she carried, telling her
that if it was used it would be paid for at the rate of $2
a column. The columns were very long, and the lady
left the office feeling much discouraged. The next week
she bought the paper and saw her sketch. When she
visited the office the editor handed her $1.50, and said
he would like a long story, complete in one issue. She
wrote it and it measured nine columns, for which she
received eighteen dollars, and from that hour she has
continued to earn money freely with her pen; yet, the
editor candidly told her that if she had not called in person he would not have used her contributions. "It was

the magnetism of your presence, your quick, decided manner, and the few words you expressed your business in, that led me to examine the manuscript in which I found the merit suggested.''

There can be no possible reason why a woman who has manuscript to sell should not seek a market for her literary wares as she would for needle work or pictures; but she must be competent to write a poem or prose article, just as she must be to sew well, or paint a satisfactory picture. And there will be grades of merit, too, in the writings as in the material products. She need no more expect that her first articles will be accepted by Harper or the New York World, or Tribune, than that her first picture will find a place in the Academy of Arts, unless, indeed, she has exceptional genius or inspiration amounting to it. ''But how am I to know whether my articles will be worth publishing unless I submit them to the editor of some paper?'' That is very true; but you will need wings before you can soar. A brief and well written communication on some topic of interest—not yourself or your family affairs—but a bright, attractive half-column sketch, written in a bold, free hand, on one side of clean, unwrinkled paper—something that will strike the eye and the understanding at the same time, and demand attention—this is what a newspaper wants. Use concise terms; have a choice of words; be anything but commonplace. If you attempt to describe a horse-race, put motion into the article; make it so picturesque and full of life that your readers can see the flying animal, the crowd of spectators, and hear the loud cheers that announce the winning heat. Give strength

and beauty to the simplest things you describe; use a lead
pencil and eraser, and strike out any sentence that is not
a picture.   Some of the strongest journalistic work in the
world has been done by women.   Miss Middy Morgan
was before her death the live stock reporter for a number
of New York daily papers.   It was rather a strange occupation for a woman perhaps.   Miss Morgan commanded
respect, and she was an earnest, honest worker, who loved
her somewhat bizarre occupation, and brought to it practical knowledge which few men possess.   She was of Irish
birth, a descendant of one of the oldest families of Irish gen-
try, had from childhood been devoted to out-door sports,
and could ride horseback better than any boy of her
native country.   She was thoroughly educated, and was
a sort of Lady Clancarty in elegance and grace of manner.   Domestic reverses found her in this country, in New
York city, proud and penniless.   It seemed as if she
could not find any field in which to exercise her talent.
At last she went to the old white-haired philosopher,
Horace Greeley, for advice.   During their chat he
alluded to the need of a reporter of cattle sales, and jok-
ingly suggested that she try the occupation.

"I will do it," she exclaimed, and rising to her full
height, six feet two inches, she looked a veritable young
Amazon, as she grandly stalked from the room.   But
she was an Amazon in height and intellect only, for otherwise she was not at all masculine, and had a dainty complexion, despite her constant exposure to wind and sun.
Her eyes of bright Irish blue—"celestial blue," as Mr. Mc-
Gowan describes them—were very expressive.   She was

a bright, intelligent talker, full of anecdote and adventure. She believed that, if she behaves herself, a woman can earn her living wherever she develops most aptitude. In short, Miss Morgan said: "It is the woman who makes the occupation." She had purchased horses in France for the King of Italy's stables, and no one has ever called Middy Morgan unwomanly, or done anything but commend her for her fearless pluck and her excellent journalism.

LADY REPORTERS.

A lady reporter has been employed for years on the New York Daily Sun. She writes up everything that comes in her way, in the shape of local news; is here, there, and everywhere that an item can be collected, and gives it to the public in an easy, readable style. One used to attend Mr. Beecher's church on Sunday, and report the sermon, from a little stand placed under and in front of the pulpit platform. There is a large number of women in New York who support themselves by writing for the newspapers, daily or weekly; some are local; some write short sketches; others furnish long serial stories; many are book reviewers. There are publishing houses which pay liberally for children's stories, biographies, and compilations from different sources, which are brought out in book form.

Household departments, fashion letters, such as Jenny June furnishes to a dozen papers simultaneously; children's column, market articles, art criticisms, book reviews—these are nearly always the work of women. Mrs. Fanny B. Ward writes for the Burlington Hawkeye,

Frank Leslie's and other journals; Miss Mary H. Krout is at the head of the Woman's Kingdom, in the Chicago Inter-Ocean; Miss Jennie Starkey is editor of the Puzzler, Fair Woman's "World," "Society," and the " Letter-Box" departments of the Detroit Free Press; Nellie Hutchinson is a valued member of the editorial staff of the New York Daily Tribune. Indeed the papers to which women do not contribute, and on whose pages they are not employed, are exceptions to the rule. And there is always room for more. People with brains, talent, and capability for using them, will open all doors. She who writes a poem will find some paper to publish and pay for it. But it must be a poem in the true sense—not " lines," "verses," dull and commonplace—but a harmony of mind, thought and execution. Offering mental wares to the public and asking it to buy, is much like soliciting patronage for a new cook stove or ironing board. If it is better than any in the market it will have an enormous sale; if as good, it will have its share, and if inferior will not be wanted at any price.

Just here I recall the case of a good woman who was an excellent housekeeper, and set such a good table that her house during the summer months—she lived in the country—was the resort of guests who paid liberally for the privilege. But in an unlucky hour, a little woman boarded there who wrote for the papers—was a paid contributor. The woman who had hitherto been content to toil in her kitchen, making premium bread, butter, and pickles, saw how well her boarder dressed, how easily she appeared to earn her money, and she. too. longed to

write.   As soon as she was alone she neglected her house
duties, and wrote "pieces," as she called them, and sent
them off, badly written, ill-spelled, to half the editors in
the country.   I have seen one of these scrawls, and it
began as follows:

dear Mr editur

"I stop my moping"—she was washing the
floor at the time and meant mopping—"to Inform yurc
reeders how to keap yung Childreen from geting into
Hot water."   She then tells them to have the water
"torpit;" she probably meant "tepid," and if the child
falls in, it will not be "scalt."   For this very valuable
information she demanded the modest sum of five dollars !

This is why I urge women to be sure of their·ability
before they enter the flinty paths of journalism, where
it is a sin to be ignorant, and where you are expected to
be wise, witty, sensible, poetical, and versatile for very
moderate pay.   An attaché of a newspaper must be
ready to take up the pen on all occasions, at a moment's
notice, to write a column or a paragraph, for either of
which a hint from the managing editor must suffice, and
to be versatile enough to write grave to-day and gay
to-morrow.   Nor must such a one ask the why or wherefore of what is to be written.

> "Theirs not to make reply;
> Theirs but to do—and die."

It is agreeable, wide-awake work, with no more drudgery than there is in other professions, and with many
compensations.   I refer particularly now to women as

newspaper reporters or members of the local staff. There are not many women who can do such work, but there are some who have made it successful. The New York Sun, the Cincinnati Commercial, the Chicago Inter-Ocean, and other daily papers of prominence have always had a lady reporter, who is "assigned" to certain work, such as attending meetings of a political or public nature, and giving reports of them; writing up weddings, social gatherings, openings and markets. An Iowa daily paper had a lady base ball reporter—Mrs. Sallie Van Pelt, who was then on the Dubuque Times. Mrs. Fitzgerald, of the Chicago Inter-Ocean, went on that paper as night reporter, and would go into the office at midnight with police news. No one molested her, and she retained her position until something more desirable offered itself. The salary for such work averages about $10 a week. It requires energy, courage, and, above all, promptness. The expected articles must be on hand at the moment. The pages of a great newspaper can not be dependent on the caprices of an employe. Harper's Bazar, published by Harper Brothers, New York, and formerly edited by Miss Mary Booth, is always desirous of receiving good short stories—something bright and original—and pays from fifteen to twenty dollars for them, sending the money as soon as the story is read and accepted, but publishing it at the convenience of the editor. There are a number of papers in New York that pay small sums, ranging from fifty cents up to five dollars for short, pleasant, readable sketches, topics of the time written up attractively, and short love stories. Style must be cultivated in all writing. At the present time a terse, practical, brilliant style is in favor. No one writes now in the sentimental manner of the author of the "Children of the Abbey;" nor is Lord Macauley a criterion even for the editorial writer. New words are in use, sentences are short and crisp, writing is a more ephemeral thing, and is expected to have the glow and sparkle of champagne while it lasts. The world moves rapidly, and no one wants to stop to read dull platitudes; nor will your success be ensured with the publication of one article. You will need to go on **pruning**, cultivating, and acquiring all the time, in order to keep up the ever-increasing demand for new things.

AN OPEN LETTER.

"I want you to tell me how to begin newspaper correspondence," modestly demands an aspiring young woman. "I live in a small town where there is nothing but sewing for women to do—for pay. I believe I would make a good newspaper correspondent. My stories, the few I have sent to magazines and papers, are generally accepted and paid for. I want to go to Florida, but can not afford to, unless I can get an engagement as correspondent."

Now, the person who regards newspaper correspondence as a trade by means of which she may be able to "go to Florida," or anywhere else, has not the faintest element of capacity for it. It requires a certain creative type of talent to be an acceptable newspaper writer, whether in correspondence or any other line, and the woman who wants to turn from sewing, because it doesn't pay, to writing, because it does pay, shows herself utterly unappreciative of the work. Newspaper correspondence is not a trade, a mechanism, an industrial pursuit to be chosen on the ground of its being a remunerative vocation. Like all forms of literary work, it chooses its votaries, to a large degree, rather than waits to be chosen by them. If a woman is born with a talent to write she will write—there is no possible doubt about that. That she "lives in a small town" has nothing to do with it. The size of one's native village does not necessarily determine the size of one's intellectual capacity. The person who feels a conviction of a certain destiny does not require to have that conviction propped up by admiring and miscellaneous encouragement. If a woman "believes she would make a good newspaper correspondent," let her proceed to business forthwith. What's to hinder? There isn't a newspaper in the country that wouldn't welcome the fresh writer who had anything to say. If she has any ideas, there is every possible opportunity for expressing them. And if she has anything to express, she will quietly do so, and not inundate strangers with a nine-page letter, written on both sides of the thinnest possible paper, soliciting their approval or admiration. Worth is proved alone by work. What can one do? Probably she does not know herself till she tries, and how can she expect an entire stranger to cast her horoscope? The successful people are those who, if they feel a conviction of a certain line of talent, follow that line and make of it an art; not a trade, a religion; not an industrial pursuit. The girl who begins newspaper correspondence because she loves it, because it is to her a joy, an expression, an intellectual necessity, will very likely in time work it up to a remunerative pursuit. But it will undoubtedly require some time. The one who seizes it to relieve the emptiness of her pocket instead of the fullness of her mind, had far better save her postage stamps. If this should appear unsympathetic, the reason lies in the fact that the miscellaneous desire to earn money is not an affair that enlists profound sympathy. Newspaper correspondence, rightly viewed, is an art. The special correspondent of a journal has an influence and a place second only to that of the editorial page. If she does not hold her work above the level of mere local chronicle, of the exclusive narration of transient and trifling events; if she does not bring to bear on it, her best work, and refresh her resources from the finest thought and widest suggestion of the day, then is she unfit for the responsibility that is entrusted to her. Newspaper correspondence should be a work of significance, and the woman who regards it as an easy way of earning money has of its scope too little comprehension to invite further discussion.

A WOMAN'S SUCCESS AS MANAGER OF A NEWSPAPER.

A prominent German newspaper, published in New York city, called Der Staats Zeitung, has made an almost phenomenal success in the hands of a woman. Some years ago its present owner was left a widow with several small children and a little newspaper, which she tried to dispose of without avail. Prevailing on the man employed as its editor to remain and fulfill his duties, she herself attended to the business, and in a few months there was a marked improvement, the editor doing his share in making its columns of value to the public, and finally the widow decided to keep the paper and married the editor. She purchased the paper on which the publication was printed, employed the work-people, managed the funds, and, at the same time, educated her boys and girls. After a time she grew rich, and instead of walking to the office, drove there daily in a handsome carriage. The office itself was now a fine modern establishment. From 10 to 3 o'clock the proprietor attended to business, after which she returned to her elegant home, the fruit of her own labor.

She built one of the finest blocks in New York city, and has donated fifty thousand dollars to the Old Ladies' (German) Home. During these years of toil and public life, she has commanded the respect of all who knew her, and has never ceased to be a lady of high breeding and sweet womanly sympathies. Der Staats Zeitung is the leading German newspaper, and Der Zeitung building is a most beautiful monument of woman's capacity to do the very best bread-winning work in the world, provided she gives her mind, heart, and enthusiasm to its accomplishment.

THE FIRST NEWSPAPER CONDUCTED BY WOMEN.

The first paper in the country of which any record is made of ownership or personal connection on the part of women, was the paper printed in Rhode Island, at Newport, in 1732. It was printed by James Franklin, brother of Dr. Benjamin Franklin, and at his death by his two daughters and a servant girl. The daughters, it is said,

4

did the type setting; the servant girl worked the press.
Their business was printing and publishing; not writing
or editing.

THE FIRST MAGAZINE EDITED BY WOMEN.

The first magazine in this country which was managed
and edited solely by women was the Lowell Offering. It
originated in an "Improvement Circle," in one of the
churches in Lowell, Mass. Operators in the Lowell mills
were its first editors, from 1842 to 1849. Its first motto
was:

> "The worm on the earth
> May look up to the star."

The articles were all written by factory girls, and
printed as written. Miss Lucy Larcom was then an
operative, and one of the magazine's frequent contribu-
tors. This was when American girls of good parentage
were employed in the Lowell mills, and the factory community was inspired with the ideas of self-culture and a
better education. But when foreign born operatives
came in, the whole tone of factory society was changed,
and the Offering had to be abandoned, but it was a
marked power for good while it lasted.

PIONEER WOMEN IN JOURNALISM.

The first daily newspaper printed in the world was
established and edited by a woman—Elizabeth Mallet,
in London, 1702—almost two hundred years ago. In
her salutatory she said she had established a newspaper
"to spare the public half the impertinences which the
ordinary papers contain." Woman-like, her paper was
reformatory.

The first newspaper published in America, of which we have any record, was in Massachusetts. It was called the Massachusetts Gazette and News-Letter. After the death of the editor, the widow edited it in the most spirited manner for two or three years. It was the only paper that did not suspend publication when Boston was besieged by the British. The widow's name was Margaret Craper.

In 1732 Rhode Island issued its first newspaper. It was owned and edited by Anna Franklin. She and her two daughters did the printing, and their servants worked the printing press. History tells us that for her quickness and correctness she was appointed printer to the colony, supplying pamphlets, etc., to the colonial officers. She also printed an edition of the Colonial Laws of 340 pages.

In 1776 Sarah Goddard printed a paper in Newport, R. I., ably conducting it, afterward associating with her John Carter. The firm was announced Sarah Goddard & Co., taking the partnership precedence, as was proper and right.

In 1772 Clementine Reid published a paper in Virginia, favoring the colonial cause, and greatly offending the royalists; and two years after another paper was started in the interests of the Crown, by Mrs. H. Boyle, borrowing the name of Mrs. Reid's paper, which was the Virginia Gazette, but which was short lived. Both of these papers were published in the town of Williamsburg. The colonial paper was the first newspaper in which the Declaration of Independence was printed.

In 1773 Elizabeth Timothy published and edited a

paper in Charleston, S. C. After the Revolution Anna Timothy became its editor, and was appointed State Printer, which position she held seventeen years. Mary Crouch published a paper in Charleston about the same time, in special opposition to the stamp act. She afterwards removed her paper to Salem, Mass., and continued its publication there for years.

LUCY LARCOM.

Lucy Larcom has written a great many tender and touching poems, for all of which she has been well paid. She was for years a regular contributor to the Atlantic Monthly Magazine, and in that journal she gave a sketch of the factory girls of the Lowell Mills, and of the social life which existed there when she was one of the operatives and a writer for the Lowell Offering, which was published during the years inclusive of 1842 to 1849. Miss Larcom said :

"The home life of the mill girls, as I remember it in my mother's family, was nearly like this: Work began at 5 o'clock on summer mornings, and at daylight in the winter; breakfast was eaten by lamp-light during the cold weather; in summer an interval of half an hour was allowed for it between 7 and 8 o'clock. The time given for the noon meal was from a half to three-quarters of an hour. The only hours of leisure were from half-past 7 or 8 to 10 in the evenings, the mills closing a little earlier on Saturdays. It was an imperative regulation that lights should be out at 10. During that two evening hours when it was too cold for the girls to sit in their own rooms, the dining-room was used as a sitting room, where they gathered around the tables and sewed or read, wrote and studied. It seems a wonder to look back upon it and see how they accomplished so much as they did in their limited allowance of time. They made and mended their own clothing, often doing a good deal of unnecessary fancy work besides; they subscribed for periodicals, took books from the libraries, went to singing school, conference meetings, concerts and lectures, watched at night beside a sick girl's bedside, and did double work for her in the mill if necessary; and on Sundays they were at church, not differing in appearance from other well-dressed and decorous young women. Strangers who had been sitting beside them in a house of worship were often heard to ask, on coming out: 'But where were the factory girls ?' "

Lucy Larcom was a factory girl when she wrote the beautiful pathetic poem which first brought her to the notice of the public, and which we publish elsewhere. It is a labor song, one of the plain, homely occupations which are now controlled principally by machinery which neither suffers nor thinks.

❖CHAPTER V.❖

The Profession of Law.

It often falls in course of common life,
  That right long time is overborne of wrong,
Through avarice, or power, or guile, or strife
  That weakens her and makes her party strong,
But justice, though her doom she do prolong,
Yet at the last she will her own cause right.

HERE are some ninety practicing women lawyers in the United States, a large majority of whom are graduates of the University of Michigan, which was the first university in the United States to open its law department to women, placing them on an equal plane with men. Nearly all law schools in the United States have now women matriculates. There are two lady lawyers in Tiffin, O., but none in Cincinnati. Half a dozen ladies have been admitted to practice in the United States Circuit Court, and among these Mrs. Belva Lockwood stands the highest for real legal acumen and ability. The newspapers thus describe Mrs. Lockwood's appearance and characteristics when she was admitted to the bar: "Supported on either side by

MRS. BELVA LOCKWOOD.

Judge Shellabarger and Hon. Jeremiah Wilson, and accompanied by friends and admirers outside of the legal profession, sat Mrs. Belva A. Lockwood within the sacred precincts of the bar of the Supreme Court of the United States, from high noon Monday until after 4 o'clock, waiting, not for a verdict, but for an opportunity to present herself, under the new law for admission to the bar. She was dressed neatly in a plain black velvet dress, with satin vest and cloth coat, cut à l'homme, and with gold buttons, a neat white ruffle round the neck and cuffs, black kid gloves, a tiny bouquet on the right lapel of the coat, the well-known gold thimble, with the addition of a miniature pair of scissors in gold, suspended at the throat, completed the costume; the head was uncovered, the hair being rolled back from the face and fastened in a knot by a comb at the back." Mrs. Lockwood was duly admitted, and has won a large and successful practice.

Miss Kate Kane has the honor of being the first lady lawyer to whom permission has been granted to practice in a Milwaukee court. The lady studied at the Ann Arbor University of Michigan, and completed her legal education at a law office at Janesville, Wis. It is said of her that she is a bright, spirited, and fine looking woman of unimpeachable moral character and indomitable will. Her reception in court almost partook of an ovation, being invited inside of the bar and introduced to the judge, sheriff, clerk, and principal lawyers, by all of whom she was warmly welcomed.

Judge Albion W. Tourgee, the accomplished jurist and author, bestowed a legal diploma at Raleigh, North

Carolina, upon the first lady lawyer of that State, making, as he did so, a grand and thrilling speech in recognition of the divine right of woman to succeed in any
work she fitted herself for.

Mrs. Myra Bradwell, of Illinois, the editor of the Chicago Legal News, demonstrates what a quick-witted,
energetic woman can accomplish in business. Not only
does she edit and publish one of the most valuable and
successful periodicals devoted to the interests of the
legal fraternity, but as soon as the Illinois Legislature
adjourns, she goes to Springfield personally, makes a
careful copy of all the enactments of the session, and
publishes them in a well-bound volume. Although a
pioneer in legal work, Mrs. Bradwell has never been
admitted to the bar, a State law preventing the admission of a married woman.

Any of the ladies whose names are here mentioned
would, no doubt, answer the questions of others of
their sex anxious to learn the preparatory steps of a
legal education, if corresponded with on the subject;
but let the questions be briefly and lucidly stated, and
at least three two-cent postage stamps enclosed for an
answer, thus covering the expense of paper and postage,
the more valuable time being a free contribution. As
time is money with professional women as well as men,
make your communication so short that a few strokes of
the pen will answer it. For the better guidance of young
ladies not accustomed to business letters, a brief form is
appended:

WEST BRANCH, Penn.

M..

DEAR MADAM:

Will you kindly inform me what steps to take preparatory to a course of instruction in the law; what books to buy; what college is the best and cheapest for a woman student? Hoping this will not demand too much of your valuable time, I remain,

Gratefully yours,

SUSAN SHARPE.

The next thing is to have town or postoffice address, county and State, plainly recorded. It is unnecessary to give any other reason, than the one implied for asking the advice of the person written to, as it is evident you had heard of her standing, and the letter suggests a compliment to her position and authority. You will not write again after receiving the answer, except a brief line of thanks, unless the lady herself specifies her willingness to be of service to you. There should be a natural Freemasonry among women as among men, to assist each other by voluntary contributions of help; but sometimes success hardens the finer feelings, and the woman who has reached an eminence, is only too willing to forget the helping hand that was extended to her; still, there are plenty who will give generously of their prosperity, by helping others to the isolated plateaus of success.

The Michigan University at Ann Arbor, Mich., and the Boston University Law School, are popular institutions for ladies to study law in.

A LAW FOR THE MARRIED WOMAN—INDIANA LEGIS-
LATION.

Previous to the enactment of the following statutes, a married woman of Indiana, doing business in her own name, with the consent and co-operation of the husband, could not collect a single bill of money owed her, by law. Section 4 seems to need a little elucidation, but time will probably make that as just as the rest:

SECTION 1. Be it enacted by the general assembly of the State of Indiana, a married woman may bargain, sell, assign, and transfer her separate personal property the same as if she were sole.

SEC. 2. A married woman may carry on any trade or business, and perform any labor or service on her sole and separate account. The earnings and profits of any married woman, accruing from her trade, business, service of labor, other than labor for her husband or family, shall be her sole and separate property.

SEC. 3. A married woman may enter into any contract in reference to her separate personal estate, trade, business, labor, or service, and the management and improvement of her separate real property, the same as if she were sole, and her separate estate, real and personal, shall be liable therefor on execution or other judicial process.

SEC. 4. No conveyance or contract made by a married woman, for the sale of her land or any interest therein, other than leases for a term not exceeding three years, and mortgages on lands, to secure the purchase money of such lands, shall be valid, unless her husband shall join therein.

SEC. 5. A married woman shall be bound by the covenants of title in deed of conveyance of her real property.

SEC. 6. A married woman may bring and maintain an action in her own name against any person or body corporate for damages for any injury to her person or character, the same as if she were sole; and the money recovered shall be her separate property, and her husband, in such cases, shall not be liable for costs.

SEC. 7. Whenever the husband causes repairs or improvements to be made on the real property of the wife, with her knowledge and consent thereto in writing delivered to the contractor or person performing labor or furnishing material, she alone shall be liable for materials furnished or labor done.

SEC. 8. A husband shall not be liable for any debts contracted by the wife in carrying on any trade, labor or business on her sole and separate account, nor for improvements made by her authority on her separate real property.

SEC. 9. Whenever a judgment is recovered against a married woman, her separate property may be sold on execution to satisfy the same, as in other cases. Provided, however, that her wearing apparel and articles of personal adornment purchased by her, not exceeding $200 in value, and all such jewelry, ornaments, books, works of art and *vertu*, and other effects for personal or household use as may have been given to her as presents, gifts, and keepsakes, shall not be subject to execution; and, provided further, that she shall hold as exempt, except for the purchase money therefor, other property to the amount of $300, to be set apart and appraised in the manner provided by law for exemption of property.

SEC. 10. A married woman shall not mortgage or in any manner encumber her separate property acquired by descent, devise, or gift, as a security for the debt or liability of her husband or any other person.

HOW THE LAW PROTECTS WOMEN IN MICHIGAN.

An examination into the laws of the State of Michigan will show that woman has more privileges than man, and that there at least the latter may be safely trusted to legislate for his mother, sister, wife, and daughter. The State gives each sex equal educational advantages. A woman can obtain not only as broad a literary and scientific training at the University as man, but she can also obtain a special education in the several professional departments. She is not precluded from obtaining a livelihood in any of the avenues of industry. Men can be imprisoned in all personal actions for damages, except those arising from open contract, and even in these where there has been fraud or breach of trust, or where moneys have been collected in any professional employment. Women can not be imprisoned in any civil action. Women are allowed an attorney fee where judgment not exceeding twenty-five dollars for personal services are obtained before a justice of the peace. A woman's honor is protected by the most stringent provisions. A wife has a life interest in all the real estate which her husband has owned during her marriage. He can not deed or will this away from her; he can not sell or mortgage his homestead without her consent; but she can do both, or either, without his consent. After he dies she is entitled to the rents and profits of his homestead, if there are no children, during her widowhood, unless she is the owner of a homestead in her own right. A wife who signs a note for money loaned her husband, can not be compelled to pay it, but a husband who gives a note

for money loaned his wife, is not correspondingly privileged.

A woman can obtain a divorce from her husband who
is able to support her but does not, and the husband is
compelled to pay his wife's counsel fees and other legal
expenses in contesting the suit; in short, a wife has full,
complete and absolute control over all her own property,
real and personal, whether acquired before or after her
marriage, and she may contract, sell, transfer, mortgage,
convey, devise and bequeath the same without any control on the part of her husband. There are several other
particulars which could be specified wherein the law of
the state discriminates in favor of women, but enough
has been mentioned to show that men can make as good
laws for women as women would make for themselves.

MRS. JUDITH ELLEN FOSTER, LADY LAWYER.

Miss Frances E. Willard writes an interesting sketch
of this lady, from which the following is condensed.
Mrs. Foster is the wife of Hon. E. C. Foster, lawyer and
politician of Washington, D. C., and her biographer says:

"She read law first for his entertainment, and afterwards by
his suggestion and under his supervision. She pursued a systematic course of legal study, with, however, no thought of
admission to the bar. She read with her babies about her such
learned tomes as Blackstone and Kent, Bishop and Strong,
instead of amusing herself with fashion plates or fiction. She
never had an ambition for public speaking or public life.
Although reared in the Methodist church, she had never, until
the time of the temperance crusade, heard a woman preach or
lecture; but when that trumpet blast resounded, she, in common

with her sisters, responded to the call, and lifted up her voice in protest against the iniquity of the drink traffic. Her acceptance with the people just at the time when she had completed her legal studies seemed a providential indication, and her husband said: 'If you can talk before an audience you can talk before a court or jury,' and he insisted on her being examined for admission to the bar. Prior to this time she had prepared pleadings and written arguments for the courts, but without formal admission she could not personally appear. She was examined, admitted, and took the oath to 'support the constitution and the laws.' Mrs. Foster was the first woman admitted to practice in the State Supreme Court. She defended a woman under sentence of death, and after a ten days' trial, in which our lady lawyer made the closing argument, the verdict of the jury was modified to imprisonment for life. Mrs. Foster enjoys the absolute confidence and support of her husband in her legal work. He was her instigator, and more than any other, rejoices in it."

One of the most successful women in law is Miss Lavinia Goodell, a brilliant woman, who, some years ago, was employed in literary work in the office of Harper's Bazar—a shrewd, quick-witted girl, fond of humor, studious and argumentative. In person she was of medium height, but looking tall from her slender, erect figure, blue-eyed, and with light brown curling hair. At the request of her parents she resigned her position and joined them in the West. She had long had a taste for legal reading, and displayed decided talent for transacting business, and in her early girlish days secretly thought she should like to be a lawyer. But at that time such a career seemed impossible for her, and she gave it up as soon as the idea had taken shape, to do the duty that lay nearest to her.

After joining her parents she was undecided what she should do. Then arose the old longing to study law. She had the leisure for it, and her father encouraged her in it. A lawyer in the town was willing to help her, and so she began to study, without, however, seeing her way clear to the practice of the law. She continued her reading, becoming more and more absorbed in it. At the end of three years of study she decided to apply for admission to the Circuit Court, was examined, passed a brilliant examination, and was admitted. She then opened an office and proceeded in a perfectly business-like way to practice her profession. She won her first suit in a justice's court, and, the defendants appealing, she won it again in the Circuit Court. This success gained her considerable reputation, and gave her a good start. Then she had some criminal defenses and collections, resulting in suits, in which she had fair success. But a case which extended her reputation throughout the country was involving considerable money, in which her client was a woman. The case was carried from the County and Circuit Court, and appealed from them to the Supreme Court, where Miss Goodell won. According to the law of the State at that time, her admission to the Circuit Court, at the outset of her legal career, admitted her to all the courts in the State but the Supreme Court. Upon carrying up her case and applying for admission to this, the Chief Justice refused her, on the ground of sex. She afterwards reviewed his opinion on her own case, and unquestionably had the better of him in the argument. She also prepared a bill and sent it to the State Legislature, providing that no person should be refused admission to the bar on account of sex. A petition asking for its passage was signed by the Circuit Judge and every member of the bar in the county, and it passed, although strongly contested by the opposing party.

Miss Goodell records it as a notable fact, that her best paying clients have been women.

⊸❋CHAPTER VI.❋⊸

The ⋆ Profession ⋆ of ⋆ Medicine.

F "you were always thinking, because you had studied a man's profession, that no one would think of
you as a woman, do you think that
could make any difference to a man
that had the soul of a man in him?

"I don't give up because I'm unfit as a
woman. I might be a man, and still be impulsive and timid and nervous.

"Every woman physician has a double dis-
advantage that I hadn't the strength to overcome—her own inexperience and the distrust
of other women."—*Dr. Breen's Practice by
W. D. Howells.*

THE WOMAN DOCTOR.

It is only a few years since the idea of a woman entering the profession of medicine and graduating as a doctor was something so quixotic, if not actually absurd,
that any girl who alluded to such a vocation was rea-
soned with and talked to as if she had contemplated
moral suicide. Less than sixty years ago, when diseases
were usually classed under the heads of colds or fevers,

a patient who was sick enough to need medical attention was waited on by a pompous, elderly sort of person who brought the whole pharmacopœia of medicine with him in his saddle bags. When he had examined the patient's tongue, felt his pulse, and consulted an old silver fob watch, with grave and decorous air; he either bled or blistered—frequently did both—and gave copious doses of salts and senna, tinct. rhubarb, and a calomel pill of colossal size. If the patient grew worse his head was shaved; and if the fever ran high he was forbidden a drop of water to cool the tip of his tongue, nor could he eat anything but arrow root and water gruel. If it was the old typhus fever, which adults generally had in those days, the fight was a long, hard one, for, between the treatment and the fever, there was not much chance of life, except in the remedial art of nature. Medical science has now discovered a number of new diseases, and developed corresponding cures. The old saddle-bag dispensary has passed out of sight, and a fever-stricken patient is no longer depleted by phlebotomy.

Among the new dispensations of the science of medicine the lady doctor takes a prominent part. What would the Dr. Johnsons or the Abernethys, of the old regime, think if they were called upon to consult with Dr. Mary Jacobi of New York, Dr. Nancy Hill of Iowa, Dr. Gertrude Banks or Dr. Helen Warner of Michigan, all ladies of the highest medical standing, with diplomas from the best medical colleges in the land, with an annual practice each of several thousand dollars, representing individually the States of New York, Iowa, and Michigan. The utmost recognition these skillful scientific doctors could have gained from the old-time medical man would have been, "My good woman, you will make an excellent nurse, you shall have my endorsement."

INTERESTING STATISTICS.

Yet it does not belong to this century to bestow on woman the first medical diploma. In 1799 Mara Zega was a doctor of medicine in Europe, and in Padua there were famous doctresses. Laura Bassi was elected professor of experimental physics in 1793. The universities of Europe had rare and exceptional cases of women who excelled as surgeons, and were highly esteemed for their skill. A number of ladies, some of them members of noble families, graduated both in law and medicine at Padua, in the beginning of the last century. The first woman who was ever granted a diploma in the medical profession in America was Elizabeth Blackwell, who, in 1855, was admitted to the hospital of St. Bartholomew, in London, as walking physician. Ten years later she gave medical lectures in that city, which challenged the attention and respect of the whole medical fraternity. Dr. Blackwell founded the New York Infirmary, where 6,000 patients were treated in one year. Mrs. Mary Jacobi, of New York, is another successful and prominent physician who studied abroad and has successfully competed with the best medical talent of both the New and the Old World.

In 1876 the College of Physicians of Dublin opened its doors to women, and has graduated a number since that time.

In 1877 the senate of the London University passed a

resolution in favor of admitting women. A strong debate
ensued. The resolution was opposed by a few medical
men, but it passed, and women are now admitted to lectures and the usual degrees.

In 1873 a ukase was published in Russia, admitting
women to all its medical schools.

In 1873 the Berne University admitted lady students,
and in 1875 there were thirty-two ladies in the medical
department.

In 1876 the fifteen universities of Italy were in like
manner thrown open to ladies, and in 1873 a lady graduate took her degree at Pisa.

In 1870 the Vienna University admitted women to the
medical degree, and in 1873 a lady student took the
prize in operative surgery.

**In Russia twelve female doctors were in 1883 officially
engaged in teaching medicine to women ; thirty were in
the service of the Zemstras, and forty others were serving
in the hospitals.** Twenty-five female doctors who took
part in the military operations of 1877 have been decorated by order of the Emperor, with the order of St. Stan-
islas of the third class. The number of woman students in Russia is steadily increasing.

There is always among the Sisters of Mercy and in the
Catholic hospitals one sister competent to compound and
administer medicines, and prescribe successfully for the
sick.

In 1870 a state decree in Holland opened the department of apothecaries to women, and in 1873 the University of Groningen, Sweden, passed the first lady graduate in medicine.

The great Swedish University at Apral has thrown its doors open, without restriction of sex, except in theology and law.

In 1875 the College of Physicians and Surgeons of Ontario, at Toronto, gave its first degree to a woman.

The first medical school for women was founded in 1848, in Boston, by Elizabeth Blackwell.

In 1870, or thereabouts, Miss Mary Putman applied to the Paris School of Medicine and was admitted, but as early as 1883 there were some twenty-five ladies in that school. Mrs. Garret Anderson followed her, and these ladies afterwards took their degrees from the École de Medicine.

Of 198 students in the Boston University School of Medicine, a few years ago, 79 were women, and the report from the directors was that the influences of the sexes was naturally beneficial. A letter from one of the principals of the Cleveland Homeopathic Hospital College says: "In so far as woman's presence exerts any influence upon man, there can be no question as to its character and degree. It is broad, decided, and most healthful. It is an influence of restraint on rudeness, boorishness, and vulgarity." The University of Michigan Homeopathic College says:

" The experience of twelve winters in the University has incontestibly proved that the practice is fraught with benefit to both teachers and men and women students." The allopathic departments are even more enthusiastic.

The woman physician has the same course of study to take, the same results to show, and the same recommendation to the public that the male physician has, a

diploma from a medical college, and a certificate from
the State Board of Health. In the end the public must
be its own best tribunal, for mistakes are frequently
made in the name of science, not only by women but by
men, and the people, in either case, are the sufferers.
As Carlyle has aptly said: "Against stupidity the gods
are powerless." In London a public hospital advertised
for a medical man. The English people are the most
conservative people in the world, yet, when Dr. Anna
Clark applied for the situation, and submitted her testimonials, she was unanimously elected.

In Chicago there are several lady doctors who fill
chairs at the colleges of medicine belonging to the different schools. Over one hundred and fifty women are
practising in that city, and in several instances both husband and wife are medical practitioners in different
schools. And just here arises a question of medical
ethics which has been put to a severe test by the recent
trial of Dr. Pardee of the State Medical Society of Connecticut. After ten years of happy married life, Mrs.
Pardee studied medicine herself, and became a graduate
of a homeopathic school of medicine in New York. She
set up her sign on one door-post, her husband's remaining on the other, and in a very little while she had a successful practice of her own. The success of Dr. Pardee
and his wife, Dr. Emily Pardee, seems to have led to an
investigation of their professional relation by the doctors
of the regular medical school, and one evening the pair
received a call from one of them, who asked the male
Dr. Pardee if he consulted with his wife. The answer
was more forcible than polite, and the investigating doc-

tor returned no wiser than he came. There was a meeting of the faculty of the State Medical Society, and they discussed all the pros and cons in the matter, but failed to come to a decision, or to substantiate the charges against Dr. Pardee, and the State Society referred it back to the County Society for further action.

Meanwhile the buggies of the two doctors came round to the door as usual, took the doctors on their several rounds, and, when the drive was over, the homeopathic and the allopathic horse ate their hay out of the same rack, and the two Drs. Pardee sat down to dine together.

In Detroit, Michigan, one of the most conservative of old established cities, as well as one of the most wealthy and beautiful, woman doctors have long since ceased to be a novelty. The best surgeons and doctors in the place consult with them, and they have all the business they can attend to, and are remarkably successful in difficult and severe cases. A number of female students in clinics attend the different hospitals, and are in training for nurses and physicians. At the Michigan College of Medicine and Surgery, located there, they are admitted to lectures and classes, and to the practice of the dissecting room. Fair-haired, blue-eyed women, with delicate, nervous organizations, who are represented as too weak for such an arduous course of study, will cheerfully lop off a limb from a subject on the dissecting table when the interests of science demand it.

AMUSING INCIDENTS.

There is a ludicrous side to the work when women are engaged in it, at times, that lightens its severity and shows that the female doctor is not yet universally adopted. A farmer living near a large Western town was sent in hurriedly to the city to bring the first doctor he could find. He reined his horses up at the door of an office bearing a doctor's sign, went in, and looking at the neat little lady in the consulting room, said hurriedly:

"Where's the doctor? I want him right off."

"I am the doctor," said the little lady quietly.

The man turned red, whistled, then looked perplexed.

"Whew!" he said slowly, "I hadn't calculated on a woman doctor!"

"No," said the doctor, smiling brightly, "a good many people had not. Will you take me, or ride a few blocks further for a doctor of your own sex?"

The farmer looked at her and said grimly, "I haven't much time to wait. Jump in. I reckon Polly will be glad to see you, anyhow."

And Polly was glad, and has employed the lady doctor ever since, when she or any of the family are ill.

When Charles Reade the English novelist, wrote his brilliant story of "A Woman Hater," he did more for the advancement of woman, in the paths of medical science, than whole years of legislation had done. He won over to her side the prejudiced of her own sex. In speaking of women in this work he says, in the closing chapter: "They are eternally tempted to folly, yet snubbed the moment they would be wise. A million shops spread their nets and entice them by their direst foible. Their very mothers—for want of medical knowledge in the sex—clasp the fatal idiotic corset on their growing bodies, though thin as a lath, so the girl grows

"WHEW! I HADN'T CALCULATED ON A WOMAN DOCTOR!"

up crippled in the ribs and lungs by her own mother; and her life, too, is in stays—cabined, cribbed, confined. Unless she can paint or act, or write novels, every path of honorable ambition is closed to her."

I say that to open the study and practice of medicine to women-folk, under the infallible safeguard of a stiff public examination, will be to rise in respect for human rights to the level of European nations, who do not brag about just freedom half as loud as we do, and to respect the constitutional rights of many million citizens, who all pay the taxes like men, and by the contract with the State, implied in that payment, buy the clear human right they have yet to go down on their knees for. But it will also impart into medical science a new and less theoretical, but cautious, teachable, observant kind of intellect; it will give the larger half of the nations an honorable ambition and an honorable pursuit, toward which their hearts and instincts are bent by nature herself; it will tend to elevate this whole sex, and its young children, male as well as female, and so will advance the civilization of the world, which in ages past, in our own day, and in all times, hath and doth and will keep step exactly with the progress of women toward mental equality with men.

THE LADY PHYSICIAN.

Oh, who is this, who casts her rose of youth
    Beneath the feet of pain, nor fancieth
The lily of her ladyhood, in sooth,
    Too white to bloom beside the couch of death?

It is the woman-healer here who stands
   With tender touch upon the cruel knife;
With thought-engraven brows and skillful hands,
   And yearning heart to save the house of life.

Bless her, O women, for it was your call,
   It was the myriad cry of your distress
That urged her outward from the cloistered hall
   To make the burden of your anguish less.

Shine on her, stars, while forth she goes alone
   Beneath the night, by angel pity led;
And shed such lustre as your rays have thrown
   On bridal steps that shine with lover's tread;

Her pathway scent, O flowers that deck the field,
   As from her hurrying feet the dews are driven,
With no less fragrance than your clusters yield
   By dimpled hands to happy mothers given.

And ye, O men, who watch her toilsome days
   With doubted lip in half derision curled,
Scant not her meed of courtesies and praise,
   The bloom and starlight of the spirit world.

For with a sense of loss too fine to own,
   The nestward longing of the carrier dove,
She turneth from her first, entitled throne,
   And all the household walks that women love.

The gracious ministers of little deeds
   And service for the few, by love made sweet;
From these she turneth unto wider needs,
   And pours her ointment on the stranger's feet.

Perchance, amid the clash of busy days,
   She may lay by a trick or two of charms,
May miss of those caressing, dainty ways
   That women learn from babies in their arms.

But even while the battle scars her face,
   And makes her voice stern in the combat rude,
She but refines her best, peculiar grace,
   And proves herself forgetful womanhood.

Katherine Lee Bates.

A PHYSIOLOGICAL PROPOSAL.

Miss Mary Flynn was a Boston girl who was studying medicine, and Mr. Budd was her devoted admirer. One evening while they sat together on the sofa, Mr. Budd was wondering how he should manage to propose. Miss Flynn was explaining certain physiological facts for him.

"Do you know," she said, "that thousands of people are actually ignorant that they smell with their olfactory peduncle."

"Millions of them," said Mr. Budd.

"And Aunt Mary wouldn't believe me when I told her she couldn't wink without a sphincter muscle."

"How unreasonable!"

"Why, a person can not kiss without a sphincter."

"Indeed."

"I know it is so."

"May I try if I can?"

"Oh, Mr. Budd, it is too bad for you to make light of such a subject."

Then he tried it, and while he held her hand she explained to him about the muscles of that portion of the human body.

"Willie," whispered Miss Flynn, very faintly.

"What, darling?"

"I can hear your heart beat."

"It beats only for you, my angel."

"And it sounds as if out of order. The ventricular contraction is not uniform."

"Small wonder for that, when it's bursting with joy."

"You must put yourself under treatment for it. I will give you some medicine."

"Its your own property, darling; do what you please with it."

TO A LADY DOCTOR.

Yes, Doctor, your physic I've taken.
  That surely should conquer my ills;
The bottle was solemnly shaken,
  I dote on these dear little pills.
I've followed your rules as to diet,
  I don't know the taste of a tart;
But, though I've kept carefully quiet,
    The pain's at my heart.

Of course you've done good; convalescence
  Seems dawning. And yet it is true,
I fancy the light of your presence
  Does more than your physic can do.
I'm well when you're here, but, believe me,
  Each day when fate dooms us to part
Come strange sensations to grieve me—
    That must be the heart.

Your knowledge is truly stupendous,
  Each dainty prescription I see,
I read "*Haustus statam sumendus,*"
  What wonder you took the M. D.!
I hang on each word that you utter
  With sage Æsculapian art,
But feel in a terrible flutter—
    It comes from the heart.

Have *you* ever felt the emotion
    That stethoscope ne'er could reveal?
If so, you'll perchance have a notion
    Of all that I've felt, and still feel.
Oh, say, could you ever endure me?
    Dear Doctor, you blush and you start.
There's only one thing that can cure me—
    Take me—and my heart!

                                        Punch.

At a meeting of the Social Science Association, Dr.
Emily Pope read a paper on the Practice of Medicine by
Women in the United States. The object was to show
to what extent they were practicing medicine in this
country; whether the majority of women graduates
devote themselves to its practice; how far their pecuniary success shows a demand on the part of the public
for educated women physicians; what effect the strain of
practice has upon their health; and with what results
to their professional career. Dr. Pope's report is as
follows:

" The 470 circulars sent out to woman physicians have brought
statistics showing that 390 are engaged in active practice, 11
never practiced, 29 have retired after practicing, 12 after marriage, 7 retired from ill-health, and 5 have taken up other work.
These women are in 26 States, New York, Massachusetts, and
Pennsylvania having the largest proportion. Of those heard
from, 75 per cent. were single when they began the study, 19
per cent. were married and 6 per cent. widows; average age
when they began the study, 27 years; 144 practiced less than 1
year; 123 between 5 and 10 years; 23 over 20 years; 341 practiced regular medicine; 13 homeopathy; 10 give no answer; 77
report that they supported themselves from the beginning of
their practice; 34 in less than 1 year; 57 after the first year; 34

in 2 years; 14 in 3 years; 10 in various periods over 3 years; 138 say their incomes are still insufficient, or make no reply; 12 never practiced; 22 are in hospital practice; 30 are not dependent on professional income; only 11 are left who can fairly be said to have practiced over two years without supporting themselves; 32 per cent. of these women have one or more partially dependent on them; 269 are in general practice; 45 make a specialty of female diseases; 4 ophthalmology. Of 130 who have practiced less than 5 years, 76 report health good; 51 health improved; 3 health not good. Of 115 who practiced from 5 to 10 years, 58 report health good; 29, improved; 8, not good. Of 38 practicing 10 to 15 years, 25 report health good; 12, improved; 1, not good. Of 14 practicing 15 to 20 years, 13 are in good health; 1, improved. Of 23 who have had over twenty years experience, 15 are in good health; 1, improved; 1, not good. Of the 13 reporting poor health, only 4 ascribe their illness to practice.

" When the large proportion of women who have practiced from five to thirty years, is seen, without breaking down, but with an improvement of their physical condition, it seems as if some unnecessary anxiety had been wasted on this point. We do not think it would be possible to find a better record of health among an equal number of women taken at random from all the country. In fifteen States, women physicians are on an equality with men as to membership in county and State societies. Sixty-five have married since their graduation, of whom nineteen married physicians; fourteen ceased practice after marriage, the others continue in practice; sixty-seven children have been born to them (without inquiry, many report children strong and healthy). In Pennsylvania, Massachusetts, Iowa and Michigan, women physicians have lately received appointments in State institutions. The board of foreign missions have sent out about twenty women physicians, all of whom have been successful, obtaining practice where men could not. In every case their success has been marked. Women would prefer not to receive all their education from women's schools, as they want the best to be had in all schools."

For this, as for all other professions in which the student would compete successfully, there must be a certain aptitude, a love for the work, and a large amount of firmness of will and physicial courage. A year or two spent in the study of medicine, even if the practice is abandoned, would be a much better use of time than spending it in idle accomplishments. It is always best for the student to attend the college of her own State, graduating from that and finishing her course by a year of instruction abroad, or in some desirable institution in another State. As a student her work never will cease. There must always be close, careful study, lectures to attend and experimental work to be done. She must explore every nook of the wide field of science, testing and laboring for humanity's sake. There are many ills and few cures; but the young practitioner must always remember this golden rule—relief is, next to a cure, the best remedial agent.

The incomes of women doctors average one thousand dollars a year. There are a few notables who receive as high as eight or ten thousand, but there are also a numerous class who do not have more than five or six hundred a year.

Dr. Alice Stockham, who has for many years been a practicing physician in Chicago, and whose husband is also a doctor, is the author of the following:

REQUISITES FOR A PHYSICIAN.

"To be a successful physician a woman must be a lady—a womanly woman. No aping of masculine habits, dress or foibles will conduce to success. She must have an affinity for the work, feel at home in the sick room, with a desire and tact to relieve suffering, devoid of any morbid sensibility at sight of pain, offensive deformities and ghastly injuries and operations; she must be born to command, firm in purpose, and quick to execute, at the same time have dignity and self-control. Nothing must escape her observation. She must be able to reason from cause to effect, strong in convictions, but slow to give an opinion. She needs a love for scientific research, and the ability to apply herself to study."

Among the colleges which admit women on the same terms with the male students, are the following:

The Woman's Medical College, Philadelphia, Pa.; Homœopathic Hospital College, Cleveland, Ohio; University of Michigan, Ann Arbor; Michigan College of Medicine and Surgery, Detroit; Toronto University, Toronto, Ontario; Queen's College, Kingston, Ontario.

✦CHAPTER VII.✦

The ✶ Profession ✶ of ✶ Music.

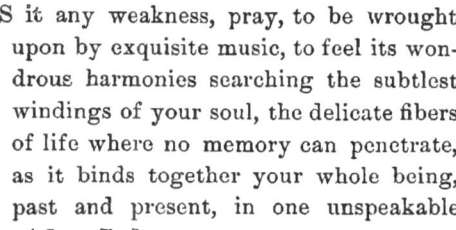

S it any weakness, pray, to be wrought upon by exquisite music, to feel its wondrous harmonies searching the subtlest windings of your soul, the delicate fibers of life where no memory can penetrate, as it binds together your whole being, past and present, in one unspeakable vibration.—*Adam Bede.*

Music resembles poetry; in each
Are numerous graces which no method teach,
And which a master-hand alone can reach.—*Pope.*

" Come, sing to me of heaven,
　Sing to me ere I die;
　Sing songs of holy ecstasy,
　　To waft my soul on high.—*Old Hymn.*

NEGLECTED MUSIC.

It is a well known fact, and one, too, upon which much unfavorable comment has been made, that almost as soon as a maiden becomes a wife and enters upon the duties of a new existence, she ceases to practice the accomplishment with which she was wont to amuse herself and entertain her friends, previous to her marriage. One of the common excuses which a young wife has at her command, when her husband asks her to play, is

this : "I am all out of practice," or, "You know I
have not opened the piano for months." This, too, before
other duties have interfered to occupy her time. It
would seem as if, having married and settled herself in
life, she had no further incentive to exert herself, and
after a year or two she finds that she has forgotten her
music, can no longer execute with ease, and does not
attempt the now arduous task of practicing an hour or
two every day, in order to learn a new piece. Her husband is very fond of music, but soon finds that he is
dependent upon the good nature of visitors who do play.
These are usually young ladies who are quite willing to
entertain him and show off their own accomplishments.
I need not follow the suggestion any further, but human
nature is sometimes very weak, and the serpent too often
enters Eden disguised as an attractive siren. The following story ends happily, and may cause some serious
thinking, followed by a reform in the right direction,
before it is too late. It is an incident from real life,
related by a well-known music teacher of New York
city, and it contains a moral worthy of recognition by
wives:

TWICE IN LOVE.

Two years ago a card was brought into my music-room
bearing the name of a well-known and fashionable married lady. When she was ushered in I was surprised to
see so young looking a woman, though, to be sure, she
is not yet forty, and a fair complexion and clear blue
eyes made her look younger. She seemed a little embarrassed, but asked me to try her voice. I did so, and
found it uncultivated, but it was singularly fresh and

sweet; in quality a light soprano. I told her so, and her face flushed eagerly as she asked :

"Professor, could you teach me to sing ?"

"Yes," I replied, "if you choose to apply yourself earnestly."

"I will; and if you can manage it so that I need not be seen, and that no one knows of it, I will take a lesson every day."

We made the best arrangement we could, and the lady never failed to appear promptly at the hour. She was so anxious and so persevering that she made the most extraordinary progress, and when spring came her voice had so strengthened and developed as to be almost beyond recognition.

During the summer I heard nothing of her beyond mention in the society papers of her being at Saratoga. In the fall she called upon me, and taking both my hands in hers, shook them earnestly as she said :

"Professor, I have come to thank you for making me the happiest woman alive !"

She then told me that her husband, to whom she was deeply attached, was passionately fond of vocal music, and had always regretted that she could not sing to him.

She had never cultivated her voice before marriage, and afterwards the coming of children and the claims of society had prevented her attempting it. But an unlucky day came when Mr. R—— made the acquaintance of a lovely little widow, with a charming voice, who was always ready and willing to sing sweet songs to him, and he gradually fell into the habit of spending many of his evenings with her.

At heart devoted to his wife, he was unconscious of his gradual neglect of her, and would have been astonished had she resented his open enjoyment of these tete-a-tetes. About the widow I am not prepared to speak. Mrs. R——, like a sensible woman, did not resent it, but undermined the enemy, as you will see. Her music lessons she kept a profound secret from her family. In the summer they went, as usual, to Saratoga, and took possession of one of the pretty cottages at the United States Hotel.

The morning after their arrival the local newspapers contained a notice that the leading soprano of the Episcopal church was ill with a throat affection, and the congregation was asked to make due allowance for the disabled choir. The next morning (Sunday), Mr. R——, with two of the children, wended his way to the church of his belief, Mrs. R—— having excused herself from accompanying them.

After the opening service the clergyman announced that a lady from New York had kindly volunteered to sing in place of the sick soprano, and, in consequence, the musical programme would be the same as usual. A few moments later a clear, sweet voice rang through the church, touching the hearts of the people perhaps even more through the exquisite expression and feeling which the music had rendered than the qualities of the voice itself. Mr. R—— was fascinated, delighted, and inwardly made comparisons between it and the bewitching widow, not flattering to the latter. After the services were over he eagerly sought the clergyman to enquire the name of

the charming soprano, whose face he had not been able
to see from his seat.

"Come with me and I will introduce you," said the
clergyman, who knew Mr. R—— by reputation. They
entered the choir together, and the good man began,
"Miss Brown, permit me to introduce ——" when he
was interrupted by Mr. R—— ejaculating, "Great
heavens, it is my wife!" and place and company notwithstanding, he gave her a hearty embrace in his
delight and surprise. To cut the story short, he fell
in love with her all over again, the singing siren was
forgotten, and I don't believe you can find a happier
couple in this great city. Mr. R—— gave his wife a
magnificent set of diamonds, which she wears with a
great deal of pride. All of which really happened.

Music is one of the few accomplishments which can be
turned to account as a means of support. A good player
upon the piano—one who understands the whole theory
of music—can always find a few pupils if she is happy
in her method of imparting instruction. There are, to
be sure, a great many music teachers, but there are also
many pupils, and every year new ones are added to the
list, as children grow old enough to begin with their lessons. Fifty cents a lesson is considered a low price for
a good teacher; seventy cents to two dollars being the
rates employed by ordinary teachers, while professors of
the higher order of music receive from three to five dollars a lesson. Music teachers make a commission upon
every piece of music they supply to their pupils. This
is only fair, as it costs the pupil no more than if purchased from the dealer, who furnishes it to her teacher at

wholesale rates, and saves the pupil the time and trouble of making a selection. It sometimes happens that families expect the music teacher to furnish the pieces at a lower figure, and she deducts her commission rather than lose their custom. This is taking an ungenerous advantage of one who finds it hard enough at all times to eke out a meager support, and is one of the many stumbling blocks which good, unthinking people place in the way of one who seeks to earn an honest living, and which is not to their credit in any way.

If a young teacher finds too much competition at fifty cents a lesson, let her reduce the price until she establishes a name, and has proved that "nothing succeeds like success." Then, with both ability and experience to assist her, she can venture to assert her right to a fair compensation for valuable service.

Teachers of the harp, guitar, violin, organ, zither, and other instruments can be found in every town, who make a living out of teaching, but often a precarious one, owing to the caprices of patrons, who withdraw their custom at the most inopportune time. Of course ladies who find employment in schools, seminaries, or have an established patronage of their own, are to be congratulated, as even the drudgery of music is delightful in comparison to many other methods of support.

Vocal music is also a source of revenue to its possessor. A fine voice has always a commercial value, especially very fine ones, such as that of Christine Nilsson, Adeline Patti, or our own Clara Louise Kellogg, and Annie Louise Cary. Each of the above-named has made a large fortune by her voice, received the notes of commerce for the notes of song in rich profusion, and made fame as well as wealth. In music and in the drama women are paid as well as men for their art.

And in this, as in other and less noble professions, mediocrity can not reach the high vantage ground of success. There may be a great army of singers whose sweetest notes are never developed here,

" —— who die
With all their music in them,"

and the world is unconscious of its loss; but there are also a number found in every community who not only sing execrably themselves, but persist in teaching their execrable methods to others, not for any compensation, but through the force of example. There are others who are not Parepas or Nilssons, but whose home-singing is a source of constant gratification even to the educated ear. There are few mothers who can not croon old nursery songs to their children; but there are some whose melodious numbers are educational in a high degree. In music it is almost impossible, in this age, to make a failure; the critical public taste demands the best, both in instrumental and vocal, and it is well to understand this before lavishing money on a mediocre voice, or capacity to offer it.

PLAYING ON OLD PIANOS.

Sometimes we see an old piano standing in a house, and hear parents say, "We thought it would do well enough for the children to learn to play on." They have imbibed the idea that learning to run the fingers over the keys is learning to play the piano, and no matter how much out of tune the instrument may be, "it will do well enough to learn on." Such people forget that a musical education is more an education of the ear than it is of the fingers, and that every time a child touches one of those old instruments which answers just as well to learn on, "so far as the fingering is concerned," the ear becomes vitiated, the musical sense blunted, and a delicate perception of correct musical sounds is rendered impossible.

MUSIC IN THE GERMAN SCHOOLS.

The Germans are among the most musical people in the world, and while their children were taught music in the public schools, it was found that the hand organs about the streets were out of tune, and tended to vitiate the youthful ear. Accordingly an effort was made to put the vagrant instruments in tune, and keep them so; but, failing to accomplish this, the government prohibited the playing of such instruments on the streets. It was thought necessary to preserve the delicacy of the trained musical sense in the children, and so everything that could vitiate it was discarded.

A lady who possessed a piano which had once been good, and who was really unaware of the effect which Time's effacing fingers had wrought upon its ancient brilliancy, asked a famous German pianist to perform upon it, and after he had obligingly done so, was rash enough to ask him what he thought of the instrument.

"Since you press me for an opinion," replied the eminent artist, "I will tell you first that your piano wants new wires; and, secondly, that the hammers want new leather. And while you are about it," he continued, gradually boiling up, "with your new leather you had better have new wood and when your instrument is thus repaired, the best thing you can do with it will be to make it into firewood and have it burned."

WHAT FOUR LADIES MADE.

There were at one time four ladies in the United States all foreigners, who made large sums of money. They were Patti, Nilsson, Modjeska, and Langtry. Madame Patti received $4,400 a night. Of this she paid $400 a night to M. Franchi, her agent. This gave her $8,000 a week. She sang in New York three times a week, and her pay then was $12,000. She did, during her stay here, sing altogether thirty times under the management of Mapleson, for which she received, net, $120,000. She, therefore, carried away with her about $100,000. What Madame Nilsson got for her services amounted, on the average, to $4,000 a week for two concerts. On a basis of fifty concerts she made, therefore, about $100,000, not much less than Patti, though the latter sang fewer times. Mme. Modjeska received $1,000 daily. But this is a small average, because the receipts often exceeded that. During her engagement at Booth's, at regular prices, she did much better. Her last week came up to $11,000 very nearly. Say $10,000, and her individual share would be $3,000. She played thirty weeks, and on an average of $2,000 a week she made $60,000. Allowing the extra profit for expenses, that is about the net sum she made for the season. Mrs. Langtry's contract with Mr. Henry E. Abbey was that she should receive thirty-three per cent. of the gross receipts each night. Mr. Abbey paid the company and all other expenses. Supposing a business of $1,500 a night—and really the receipts exceeded that, as Mrs. Langtry played to higher prices than other dramatic stars—she received $3,500 a week. It is interesting to note that four ladies carried with them out of the country $350,000 in one season.

PROMINENT daily paper, published in London, Eng.. has this to say of women clerks :

"There are many advantages in women clerks. They are found to be punctual and docile. Their good conduct and decorum after office hours insure a steady attendance not broken down by 'Derby' headaches, or the drowsiness that follows nocturnal dissipation. They have not that genius for getting into debt, which is an indication of superiority displayed by their male colleagues. It is also worthy of note, that the sluggishness of promotion, which is one of the difficulties of all official careers where men are concerned, is got rid of in the case of women. No matter how closely they may restrict themselves to their work from ten to four, the clever, clear-headed, vigorous young girls who are government clerks are ready enough for society in the evenings. They enter it with freshness of feeling, because they have honestly earned relaxation; and the fact that they are pecuniarily independent, enables them to meet men frankly and on equal terms. Their very success in examination and in office life, implies their quickness, brightness, and good health, and these are the qualifications that tell in a sweetheart and wife, as well as in

A POSTOFFICE CLERK.

The result is that they get married off with reasonable celerity, and thus the official field is kept clear by the weeding out of brides, who relinquish red-tape for orange blossoms, new girls coming in to take their places. For those, however, who can not or will not marry, the office duties provide a quiet, steady and decorous career. Most of them live at home; many help to support a relative; all have shown, by their docility and steadiness, that a young woman is ready to work hard for half the pay that will content a young man."

There does not seem to be that fine and distinctive sense of justice in the last statement that all liberal-minded people would like to see exemplified, in equal pay for equal work; but it is to be hoped that the young man either did better work or supported more relatives on his double amount of pay. In regard to government lady clerks in this country we have even a more flattering picture. They are represented as more industrious, more punctual, more painstaking, more obedient, more patient than the men, in similar situations. It is doubtful if anywhere in the world is assembled so large a body of women as these employes, possessed of such social virtues, such fine breeding, and such social accomplishments. Of course there are a few among them with giddy heads or false hearts. Although there have been some pretty faces that have married their owners to a senator, a judge, a governor—in one instance to a foreign nobleman—no expectations of that romantic sort are cherished by the rest. There is a certain proportion who go into the best society and shine there; in fact, they have never left the society in which they were reared. They change their office dress after the hours of work are over for a calling suit, and then proceed to make visits, and they attend such of the evening entertainments as they please; being the daughters or widows of admirals, senators, and other dignitaries of the past; the daughters and wives of similar dignitaries of the present; being perfect ladies, they command the treatment of ladies, and enjoy their social life. Among the ladies of distinguished lineage who have been in the Treasury Department at Washington, are Mary E. Wilcox, adopted daughter of General Jackson, and daughter of Donelson, who ran with Fillmore for vice-president, and god-daughter of Van Buren; Charlotte L. Livingston, whose husband was a grandson of the distinguished chancellor; C. E. Morris, a granddaughter of Robert Morris; Sophia Walker, a daughter of Robert J. Walker, Polk's secretary of the treasury; Miss Dade, a descendant of John Randolph, and niece of Winfield Scott; Helen McClean Kimball, widow of General Kimball, killed in the Mexican War; Sallie Upton, daughter of Francis Upton, of Brooklyn; Mrs. Granger, the widow of General Gordon Granger; Mrs. Tyndale, widow of the Hon. Sharon Tyndale, of Springfield, Ill., and others.

Of course the opportunity to secure such positions was a great blessing to many widows and orphans of gentlemen who had died in one branch or another of the government service—women who had either starvation or intolerable dependency before them. The salary of a majority of the clerks is nine hundred dollars a year, paid monthly; a very few have one thousand dollars, and a still smaller number enjoy a remuneration of twelve hundred dollars. They go to the rooms which the government provides at nine o'clock in the morning, remaining until four in the afternoon, and they work constantly nearly all that time. It is not a position of emolument without labor, by any means, and any who have imagined the office a sinecure, will please read the following detailed account of their duties:

They bend all day over their desks.

They copy letters from hour to hour, in round hand, without erasure.

They compute.

They keep books.

They make clean records in big ledgers.

They register bonds.

They print and cut, and file and sort.

They count with the accuracy and dexterity of machines, and in a manner that it is perfectly wonderful to observe, seeing and reckoning at a. single glance, not only the figures telling the denomination of a bill, be they one or five, or twenty or a hundred, but those also at the same time telling the date of the series, and those which are to be found in a red-line, both under the treasury seal and near the upper right hand corner, thus keeping at once a double tally. They have great skill, too, in making out the face of money that has been injured by fire or water, masses of charred rubbish that one would never dream to be anything but embers, and that which has been water-soaked to a ball of pulp, are restored by their patient research so that a good part of the original worth is made out and redeemed. Having so little of their own, there is something pathetic in the way in which they handle money by the million, none of which has ever been known to stick to their fingers.

For many years all the writing and copying work was given out at the department for ladies to take to their homes, and it was paid for under a tariff of ten cents for every hundred words. This was before the era of female clerkships, when a lady was supposed to lose caste by doing anything in the shape of public work. For the past thirty odd years, however, the ladies engaged in department work have been admitted to formal clerkships, with stated salaries.

The Treasury, Postoffice, Patent offices, the Smithsonian Institute, and Pension Office all employ a number of ladies, but it is next to impossible ever to find a vacancy, owing to the fact that a lady in office who intends to resign—and this is equal to the oft-quoted remark, that few die and none resign—knows immediately of an acquaintance or friend who has capabilities for the work, and who steps in as she steps out. Women without influence, political or other, can not expect to gain the position simply because they can perform the duties. Five hundred women could do that. We hear sad stories of delicate, high-bred girls who have lingered year after year at the capital, filling inferior positions, while waiting—waiting for a seat in congressional halls. One bright girl did get in by perseverance and pluck, if her story is true. Here it is:

HOW ONE WOMAN GOT INTO THE DEPARTMENT.

One bright morning the Hon. John Sherman was sitting in his office when suddenly a bright-haired, pretty girl dashed into his presence. She was apparently sixteen, and had about her an air of business which even the cold gaze of the Ohio statesman could not transform into maiden fright or flurry. Deliberately taking a seat the girl said:

"Mr. Sherman, I have come here to get a place."

"There are none vacant," was the frigid reply.

"I know you can give me a place if you want to," persisted the girl," and I think I am as much entitled to it as anybody. My father spent his life in the United States army, and when he died he left nothing. The responsibility of the family rests on me, and I think I have as good a claim as anyone on the government."

"What kind of place do you want?" asked Mr Sherman, compelled to say something.

"I don't care what it is, but I must have work at once."

Mr. Sherman assured her that there were dozens of applicants for every one place, and there was very little chance.

She very deliberately told him that such an answer would not do, and declared if he would allow her she would come up every day and black his shoes for him if he couldn't do better for her.

The secretary was struck with her determination and charmed by her bright face and her sprightly manner. He told her to come back. In less than a week she had a good place in the treasury.

Every morning she walked to the department with

"MR. SHERMAN, I HAVE COME TO GET A PLACE."

the step of a business woman, who was proud that her
delicate hands could be the support of others. She received one hundred dollars a month, and supported in
comfort her mother and sister. This brave and successful
young woman was Miss Mary Macaulay formerly of
Atlanta, Georgia. Her father was a lieutenant in the 18th
infantry.

Another account of the treasury girl may not be amiss
here. It is from the pen of a well-known Washington
lady, who said:

"I am boarding in the same house with a young girl who is a
clerk in one of the departments, and as it is new to me to see women
thus occupied, I willingly accepted her invitation to accompany
her to the Bureau, where she is employed. It looks strange,
because I am unaccustomed to it, to see a young lady take her
hat and walk off to her office at nine o'clock. This young girl
is a Virginian, an orphan, very nice and lady-like, and very
poor. She has quite an air of business about her, is perfectly
self-reliant and independent, and likes her occupation well.
Her office, where she writes at a separate desk, is in a large,
quiet room, where only two other clerks are employed, and
everything is comfortable and orderly. When we reached the
door my companion walked in and hung up her hat composedly,
and then sat down to the work of the day."

· Compared with the sewing or teaching, which usually
seems the only resource for Southern girls who are
forced to support themselves, office work or professional,
duties present many attractions. This young lady's
employment, with its comfortable salary, is far preferable to the drudgery of teaching and the small pay,
which is the lot of young girls who are trying to earn a

7

living. There is nothing injurious in the occupation or the companionship it brings to the woman who is pure and high-toned in character, seeking from preference a home with refined people who live plainly. She seems like a daughter of the house. This little description of her room gives an insight into her character and tastes :

" Her little room, which adjoins mine, is full of knick-knacks, the gifts of loved ones in better days, or the work of leisure hours. Here are the tiny clock and sewing machine which, with her neat and simple wardrobe, represents her all of worldly goods. After her office work is over she comes home cheerful and bright, brings her sewing into the sitting-room where the family assemble, and whence I can hear merry laughter, as the little circle talk over the incidents and adventures of the day."

The dark side to this is the yellow envelope of dismissal. What it means to the one dismissed may be inferred from the fact that the notice is no longer delivered to the department clerk at the office, the fainting and hysterics which ensue upon the receipt of the missive, causing much excitement and sympathy, and seriously interfering with the routine of business. The letter is left at the home of the employe, and it gives no reason for the dismissal, and there is never the slightest hopes of re-instatement. It often causes a serious illness, which is as nothing to the more lasting sickness of the heart, at the long prospect of enforced idleness. Some have been fortunate enough, or provident enough, to be able to lay up a little for this rainy day; others have friends to depend on. It is hoped that in all cases the dark day ends with the night, and "joy cometh in the morning."

~❧CHAPTER IX.❧~

A * Lady * Government * Official.

ISS Ada Sweet, U. S. Pension Agent, whose portrait will be found elsewhere, is one of our highest representative women who have solved the problematical question of what can a woman do. Since she was fifteen years old, Miss Sweet has been self-supporting, and for over eleven years she filled one of the most responsible positions under our government, and the only one solely managed by a woman. She is an admirable example of a business woman, since she is, at the same time, a member of the highest social circles, has the manner and appearance of a lady who has never stepped outside of society circles, and finds time to be always well and fashionably dressed. Our readers will, no doubt, prefer to read Miss Sweet's own kindly response to a request for some particulars of her life, which we append, although it was not intended for publication in this shape. Following the sketch is a poem by this accomplished lady, which I have copied from a magazine, without her knowledge, but which gives the domestic side of her character. To her many personal friends who know the peculiarly sad closing of that precious home life, it will have an exceptional interest, while all must admire its true poetic inspiration. There are still precious flowers left in the home garden, which owed much of its sunlight and bloom to this young gardener.

DEAR MRS. RAYNE:

I give you, below, a sketch of my life, as a basis for what you may desire to say.

I am the daughter of General B. J. Sweet, and was born at Stockbridge, Wisconsin, Feb. 23d, 1852. My childhood was passed in Wisconsin until 1863, when, my father being in command of the U. S. Post at Camp Douglas, Chicago, the family moved to Chicago, remaining there until the close of the war, and then taking up a permanent residence near that city.

My father lost the use of his right arm by a wound received at the battle of Perryville, Ky. I commenced to assist him in his office work—he was a lawyer—when I was fifteen years of age.

In 1868 father was appointed U. S. Agent for paying pensions at Chicago, and I entered the office. Father was anxious to have me learn the business thoroughly in all its branches, and I commenced as a copyist, gradually rising as I learned the different duties and occupations incident to the disbursing of money. After two years I took entire charge, under my father's eye, of course, and when he left to take the place of Supervisor of Internal Revenue, in April, 1871, I remained with his successor, as chief clerk, until January 1st, 1872, when I joined father at Washington, where he had just taken the place of Deputy Commissioner of Internal Revenue. I acted as his

MISS ADA SWEET

secretary until his death, which took place when he was but forty-two years of age, January 1st, 1874.

I was the eldest of four children, and the effect of the panic, and the general depreciation of property upon father's estate, soon made it apparent that to me, mother and the children must look for support and care.

In Washington we had many most kind and influential friends, among them President Grant, and he, knowing that I had proved myself fully competent to perform the duties of Pension Agent, during the incumbency of my father and his successor, promptly acted upon the proposition that I should be appointed U. S. Agent for paying pensions at Chicago. The nomination was made March 19, 1874, and confirmed by the Senate, without reference to a committee.

Pensions were paid from the Chicago office, at that time, only to persons residing in a district known as Northern Illinois, the State being divided into four districts, with one disbursing office in each. In May, 1877, all these offices were consolidated at Chicago, and July 1st I commenced paying pensions for the whole State.

In March, 1878, my four years commission expired, and President Hayes re-appointed me.

Again in March, 1882, my commission was renewed by President Arthur, upon the advent of the Democratic party in 1885, I was asked to resign, but knowing that the Commission of Pensions had no right to dismiss pension agents, I appealed to President Cleveland, who sustained my position. Later in the year I did resign to go into other business.

This is the first case in which a woman has been appointed as disbursing officer for the United States.

I managed the office on a strictly business basis, in no case appointing clerks for political reasons, or because they were recommended by influential politicians. I studied the methods of our best business men, and modeled my office on the plan of the best business houses of Chicago, more than after the idea of an ordinary government office. Many of the best places were held by women clerks, and never did one fail to meet all the duties entrusted to her, to my entire satisfaction. One of the most pleasant features of my business career, to me, is the help and training I have been enabled to extend to women who are honest and industrious bread winners for themselves and others dependent upon them.

Very truly yours,
ADA C. SWEET.

THE GARDEN.

I lean against the shaking fence,
And look upon the dwelling whence
   Have gone the hearts that made it home.
No well-beloved face looks out;
The vines no longer climb about
   The doors, and blossom into foam.

Around the house there is no sign
Of aught that made it home of mine,
   Well-known, familiar, yet 'tis strange.
But in the garden I can see
The trace of loving care—to me
   The flowers smile, "We do not change."

Three summers now the sun and rain
Above those patient hands have lain
   That worked and planted flowers here.
And yet the red petunias stand,
Unchecked by weeds on every hand,
   And tall blue larkspur shows no fear

One tiger lily rears her stalk
Close to the ruined gravel walk,
   And nods across the grass to me.

White feverfew shines brave and fair,
Lifting its face to sun and air,
  And mignonette grows rank and free.

Yet Mother, Mother, all of those
You loved the best, your favorite rose—
  Your pets and darlings are no more.
They could not live but by your side;
They flourished in your simple pride;
  For you their buds and blossoms bore!

But in a garden that you know,
Even yet, some flowers you planted grow,
  And those you cherished, loved the best.
They do not fade with passing years;
No winter blights, no summer sears
  The leaves your tears and prayers have blessed!

Ada C. Sweet.

⚛CHAPTER X.⚛

Women of Enterprise.

"Art thou poor, yet has thou golden slumbers,
O sweet content?
Work apace, apace, apace, apace,
Honest labor bears a lovely face."

PLEASANT story comes from over the seas of how one Madame Charlotte Erasmi, a German widow with six children, earned a competency for herself and built up a great business house in the quaint town of Lubeck, more than twenty years ago. She started a tiny shop for the sale of canned fruits and preserved meats. She canned the fruits, meats and vegetables herself, and they were all of superior quality, and presently came into good demand. Madame Erasmi was a woman of energy and intelligence, with business tact enough to see upon which side her bread was buttered. Step by step she enlarged her factory and her sales, shrewdly and carefully, until the tiny closet, which at first held all her earthly possessions, grew to fifty times its original size. She educated her

children, meanwhile, in the best schools in Europe, and
brought them up to be a credit to themselves and society.
Her business now included the preparation of ship's provisions, potted meats, and fish of all kinds, canned aspar-
agus and other vegetables, canned fruits, jellies, fruit
syrups, extract of meat, and nearly a dozen different
canned soups.   She has a branch house in London, a
large trade in New York, and sends her goods all over
the world.   Her business card reads as follows:

CHARLOTTE ERASMI,

COURT PURVEYOR TO HIS MAJESTY

EMPEROR WILLIAM I.

FACTORY FOR CANNED PROVISIONS.

Kaiser Wilhelm himself wrote her a letter of commendation, and she has received prize medals and certificates
from Lubeck, Hamburgh, Copenhagen, Rheims, Berlin,
and from the World's Exposition at Vienna.   The policy
of Madame Erasmi has been to take her sons into
partnership as fast as they became of age, and she has
thus established a business which will no doubt run
down through several generations.   All honor to such a
woman !

What can a woman do?   So much has one woman
done, at any rate.

A PIONEER.

The first respectable woman who dared to set foot in
the streets of Leadville was Mrs. Sarah Ray, who took
in washing and made a fortune of $1,000,000.   She dug
in the mines, scoured the plains as a scout, and last, but

not least, took in washing from the Leadville miners,
and to-day has a snug little fortune that gives her an
income of $30,000 a year. She is now fifty years old,
weighing some one hundred and fifty pounds, and is
rugged and well. She educated her handsome daughter
in an Eastern school, and although deprived of it herself,
she is a firm believer in the advantages of higher education.

HONOR TO WHOM HONOR IS DUE.

Mrs. Margaret Haighey, of New Orleans, made a business of cheap restaurants, where a man could get a cup
of coffee and a roll for five cents, founded and supported
three orphan asylums, and did other good work with the
means she accumulated.   When she died two governors,
the mayor of the city, and the leading editors were her
pall-bearers, and the archbishop of the diocese conducted the funeral services, and when the procession
passed the Stock Exchange the members stood with
uncovered heads, and all classes united to do honor to a
noble woman. Mrs. Haighey never wore a silk gown or
a pair of kid gloves in her life. She lived in the utmost
simplicity, and did good with her money.

A SUCCESSFUL BUSINESS.

Among women who have achieved success may be mentioned Mrs. E. S. Chapman of New York City, who created
a new and special industry for women, on a large scale,
but with a very small beginning. Mrs. Chapman's first
venture in the line of earning a livelihood was that of
making large collars for children, out of rick-rack, which
is a lace made of rows of white serpentine or feather-edge

braid, crocheted together and shaped into collars, and also in lace stitches and crochet stitches, executed with crochet needles and knitting cotton.

The demand became so great that her own hands were unable to supply it, and she began to employ women and give instruction in the art, which was simple and easily learned. Within five years Mrs. Chapman had eight hundred women on her books, living in different parts of the State, and in New Jersey and Long Island. They were mostly married women, and did the work at their homes, and as a help toward a little pin money, some of the ladies going in their own carriages to get the work, doing it as a pastime for leisure hours. It is not, of course, very remunerative, but is easily taken up at odd times. The pecuniary result of ten hours' steady labor is about one dollar. The articles include lace covers for the toilet, collars, cuffs, dresses, caps, shams, curtains, coverlets, and other things indefinitely. Seventy-five thousand collars were supplied in one year to a single wholesale house that takes all of Mrs. Chapman's work.

WOMEN AS DENTISTS.

There are a number of ladies who have learned the profession of dentistry, and a few who are engaged in a successful practice. Among successful dentists may be mentioned Mrs. Elizabeth Morey, of New York City, who acquired a knowledge of dentistry from her husband. Mrs. Morey practiced in connection with him for several years, and was the inventor of the skeleton tooth, which she devised for a lady patient who had what is ·

called a pin tooth—a tooth much smaller in size than the others, and detracting from their uniformity of appearance. Mrs. Morey left the tooth without pulling, as it was sound, and originated a hollow artificial one, which she fitted over this tooth, making it uniform with the others, on the same principle that crown teeth are now inserted. She believes that the first principle of dentistry is to save, and not destroy, teeth, and thus worked out her idea. Mrs. Morey was master of the three distinct branches of dentistry—the surgical, operative, and mechanical. When asked if she thought women fitted for the profession she replied:

"In my opinion they are better fitted than men to make good dentists. The latter use too much force, and often crush a tooth or injure the jaw, in taking one out. When I am obliged to pull a tooth I take it out whole. Men are, perhaps, better adapted for the inventive and mechanical parts than women. It is very injurious to delicate eyes to work with a blow-pipe before them, for fine gold requires a high degree of heat.

"Dentistry is an art that demands not only constant practice but constant study, for things are daily occurring that require some new invention. Out of five hundred cavities not more than two will be alike. Therefore, women who want to become dentists should possess inventive faculty.

"There is a wide field in dentistry for women, and I should like to see some philanthropist found a school in which women could study by themselves, though I can not see why they should not study in classes with the other sex, just as lady students of medicine and other sciences do, for dentistry is a science, and one as old as the pyramids."

In answer to a question as to what particular class her practice was confined, Mrs. Morey further said:

"I have a large practice among ladies, but my husband has still larger, for the reason that many women object to being treated by one of their own sex, saying that they have no confidence in women; but I think their prejudices would be easily overcome, as it has been in the case of female physicians, if ladies knew that practitioners of their own sex had graduated at a regular dental college. My husband prefers ladies as patients, while I prefer gentlemen. I find the former nervous, frightened and distrustful of my ability, while gentlemen seat themselves in the operating chair with an appearance of the greatest confidence, undergo the operation without a groan or a quiver, and when it is over they get up, pay their money without a murmur, and go away contented and pleased."

The work which entitles a woman to be called a dentist is that of filling teeth with gold. The merest tyro can fill them with amalgam. Every dentist's office has a lady attendant, whose duty it is to hand water for rinsing the mouth, hold napkins, replace instruments, and steady a nervous lady's head or soothe a frightened child in the operating chair. These can not be even called assistant operators, as in order to be such they would have to assist the principal in filling teeth and in various other operations of the profession. There are between four and five hundred practicing lady dentists in the Union at the present time. There is no reason why women should not choose such a profession, and it would be especially valuable in the department of children's teeth, a branch of the business that is much neglected. The science is by no means as difficult to learn as that of medicine.

An interesting letter writer adds this :

"There are now several skillful lady dentists in Chicago, among whom is Dr. Harriett E. Lawrence, who is kept busy with a practice which is credited with being the largest and most lucrative enjoyed by any woman dentist in the world. Those to whom the idea of a lady dentist is new, often express surprise and doubts of its being a suitable feminine profession. To such, we can say that these ladies and others have proved their fitness by their work and their right to the tools, by showing how well they can use them. Several hours spent in the dental chair of a lady operator afford a fine opportunity for reflection and observation on this new departure in woman's work. There were sympathetic, kindly words and looks, but, none the less, vigorous blows on the wicked little wooden wedge that sets one's nerves all quivering.

"'Don't be afraid,' said Mrs. L.; 'my hand is perfectly steady. I will not break the tooth.'

"Rubber choked my utterance, but faith never failed, and she worked on, filling the frail shell, building it up to its original proportions, and finishing it off so carefully, that if I could spare it, I would like to send it to the next exposition as a specimen of dental skill. Prejudice discarded, the nice, delicate, patient, careful work required in modern dentistry seems especially adapted to the deft fingers of women, and one advantage that occurs to me as likely to be gained by the increase of women in the profession, is that children's teeth will be better cared for, thus preventing much suffering, and promoting health and beauty."

THE FIRST LADY DENTIST.

The twenty-ninth annual commencement of the

Pennsylvania College of Dental Surgery was held at the Academy of Music, Philadelphia. The report is as follows :

"Of the one hundred and three graduates, nine were ladies, all of whom ranked among the twenty highest students of the class. There are four ladies already in the senior class for next year, besides other applicants for admission. It is considered that the presence of these ladies has been of great advantage to the character of the class, as the uncouth element formerly obtaining in medical schools has been entirely subdued by their presence. It is to be noticed that two of the graduating ladies are German.

"The first lady dentist ever graduated in this country was sent out from a Cincinnati dental college, and during the war this lady returned the largest income of any dentist west of the Mississippi. In 1867, two ladies were graduated at the Pennsylvania College of Dental Surgery, both of whom returned to Germany for practice. In 1874 Miss Ramborger, of this city, a most successful practitioner, graduated. After her graduation, the college shut its doors upon women students for four or five years. Since then it has again received them, and forty-eight have been graduated in the fifteen intervening years."

Here is a new business for women, and one which is in constant demand. The results should encourage women who need occupation and income, and who have mechanical tastes, to acquire a knowledge of dentistry.

COMMERCIAL TRAVELERS.

Perhaps this business, to a modest, retiring woman, is the hardest in which she can be called to engage, but if she has dear ones dependent on her, she will not hesitate at a good offer. The best houses in business send out lady agents to canvass the different cities and appoint local agents to sell goods. It may be tea or coffee, spices, gloves, corsets, millinery, yeast powder, boots and shoes, any line of dry goods, or a patent boiler; but the lady commercial traveler will find that she can not only travel and sell goods successfully, but retain the respect of all with whom she comes in contact, if she conducts herself as a lady and attends strictly to the business interests of the house she represents. At least a dozen of large New York houses have sent out respectable, well-tried female clerks to sell sample goods and work up a new line of trade. The success of the ladies has been something phenomenal. They hardly, in a single instance, failed to secure large orders, and they did not, in a single case, meet with any discourteous treatment or rebuffs, either from the merchants from whom they solicited orders, or their brothers of the road. In the interests of sewing machines, pianos, crockery-ware, ready-made underwear, and other lines, women make the best solicitors.

TYPE-SETTING.

This rather fascinating occupation for women must be learned by a regular apprenticeship in a printing office, and will command pay just as soon as the compositor can set from copy with no more than the ordinary mistakes of type. The typo begins on reprint. the first thing is to learn the boxes in which the type is kept, and the names of the different fonts of type will be acquired as the apprentice advances. Ladies are found as type-setters, and occasionally as fore-women, in the composing rooms, but there is some difficulty in accustoming the men employed to this innovation, and Printers' Unions will not, as a general thing, allow their members to work in the offices controlled by them; however, in some of the larger cities there are ladies who belong to the Union. Women are not adapted to the work on a daily paper, which must all be done at night; but in the offices of weekly papers they do good service, and they have been employed on the dailies, the Chicago Times being one of the papers which for some time employed lady compositors. They can earn, on an average, ten dollars a week, or, in technical language, can set eight thousand ems per day. Many women have set up the articles in their own papers, read the proof, made up the forms, and worked the hand-press on which they were printed. It is not at all uncommon to find in the office of a local country paper that all the work is done by the wife of the editor and publisher, with a small boy for assistant, while the husband is off electioneering, collecting bills, and doing outside business. It is a profession that is easily acquired, and no more injurious than any other species of close confining work.

And right here I would like to call the attention of women to the fact that they do not unbend from the burden of their duties as men do. A man locks up his printing-house or counting-house and goes home to rest and read the papers or enjoy social recreation in any form that presents itself. A woman goes home to encumber herself with petty cares—sew a dress waist together, mend old garments, baste ruffles into a cos-

8

tume for the morrow, or take up some new form of work and worry. She is not satisfied with doing a man's work all day, but she will employ herself with a woman's work all the evening, vainly imagining that she finds rest in a change of labor. It is all a mistake. She wants a brisk walk in the open air—a pleasant chat with lively company—something that will divert her mind from work and weariness, as a ride or a stroll does her stronger brother; but she can not sew, knit, or embroider, or do other work until a late hour every night, when she has worked nine hours of the day; she will break down in health, and the fault will be laid ignorantly at the door of her trade or profession.

PROOF READING.

There are very few good proof-readers even among men, and those who are experts command a good salary. Proof-reading is taught in some schools as a branch of education, but is seldom imparted with any accuracy, the average scholar preferring some other study. A good proof-reader needs to be well educated, a person of careful observation and fine intelligence, with a quick eye for disarranged letters and wrong type, as well as a perceptive faculty that will enable him or her to substitute the proper word in the place of one that is obscure or unintelligible. The alphabet of proof-reading must be learned carefully, each office differing slightly in its method of using the signs, and the proof-reader must be an accurate speller.

WOMEN AS INVENTORS.

It is said that women are not successful in inventing. Perhaps history records their failures rather than their successes. The spherical shape of the bullet is the result of a woman's experimenting. Two young ladies, cousins, one living in Cincinnati, the other in Louisville, put their heads together and invented an ironing pan, on which they have taken out a patent, and from which they expect to realize a fortune. From the time of Adam and Eve women have used an old saucer turned bottom side up, an old horseshoe, an oyster can, and a hundred and one other contrivances to place the hot iron upon while turning a garment or when wishing to lay down the iron for a moment. But, as many a housewife knows to her sorrow, ironing-boards can not be disturbed without upsetting the iron, thereby endangering the toes of the ironer. These young ladies hit upon the idea of making an ironing pan, to be sunk into the board, and thus kept stationary, being of such a depth as to hold the iron in safety while the ironer twists the board in whatever direction desired. They received an offer of five thousand dollars for their invention as soon as it was perfected and the patent obtained, but they refused to sell, and concluded an arrangement which gives them a liberal profit.

Mrs. Loretta Brownlow, of Illinois, patented a simple and convenient invention for crushing and straining fruit required in making jellies.

Catharine Littlefield Greene, widow of Gen. Greene of revolutionary memory, invented the cotton gin. She lived in Georgia, and saw that it took a negro a full day to separate the seed from a pound of cotton. Eli Whitney, of Connecticut, was then boarding with Mrs. Greene, and his ingenuity was called into play for the construction of a machine to do the work. "The wooden teeth at first tried not doing their work well, Mr. Whitney wished to abandon the machine altogether; but Mrs. Greene, whose faith in ultimate success never wavered, would not consent; she suggested the substitution of wire. Within ten days from the first conception of Mrs. Greene's idea, a small model was completed, so perfect in its construction, that all succeeding gins have been based upon it." The invention enabled a single laborer to clean 300 pounds of cotton in a day, instead of a single pound, and soon made cotton the leading staple of the South.

Miss Louise McLaughlin, of Cincinnati, invented a method of under-glaze painting upon pottery, and desiring that all artists should share in its benefits, explained her process to every one who asked her, and even wrote a book giving this information.

The Burden horseshoe machine, turning out a complete shoe every three seconds, was a woman's invention, and, at a renewal of the patent in 1871, it was claimed that $32,000,000 had been saved to the public during the fourteen years of its use.

We should hardly expect to find a woman's work upon a reaping and mowing machine, but Mrs. Ann Harned Manning, of Plainfield, New Jersey, in 1817–18 perfected a system for the combined action of teeth and cutters, which was patented by her husband, William Henry Manning. She also made other improvements, of the benefit of which, not having taken out a patent for the same, she was robbed after her husband's death by a neighbor, who procured a patent in his own name. Mrs. Manning also invented a clover cleaner which proved very profitable to her husband, who held the patent. The name of Mrs. Elizabeth Smith, also of New Jersey, appears as patentee of a device whereby knives can be adjusted upon a reaper or mower while the machine is in motion.

Among other inventions by women is that of a baby carriage, the patent for which a San Francisco lady sold for $14,000; the paper pail, invented by a Chicago lady; the gimlet-pointed screw, which was the idea of a little girl; an improved spinning machine and loom; a furnace for smelting ore; an improved wood-sawing machine; a space-saving clothes mangle; a chain elevator; a screw-crank for steamships; a fire escape; a device for correct pen holding, for use in schools; a wool feeder and weigher; a self-fastening button; a process for burning petroleum to generate steam; a spark-arrester for locomotives; a danger-signal for street crossings on railways; a plan for heating cars; a rapid change box, convenient for use at railway stations and ferries; syllable type, with the necessary apparatus for their use; machine for trimming pamphlets; writing machine; signal-rocket, used in the navy; deep-sea telescope, invented by Mrs. Mather and improved by her daughter, for bringing the bottoms of ships into view without raising them into dry-dock, and for inspecting wrecks, removing obstructions to navigation and making examinations for torpedoes;

improvements in sewing machines, and many other devices which are in common use.

The machine for making satchel-bottom paper bags, which has attracted much attention for its complicated mechanism and extraordinary ingenuity, is the invention of Miss Maggie Knight, who has since invented a machine for folding bags, and herself superintended the erection of the machinery at Amherst, Mass. A Hoboken lady, having had her dress spattered with mud by a clumsy street sweeping machine, invented the Eureka street sweeper.

The Metropolitan Elevated Railroad Co., of New York City, paid Mrs. Mary Walton ten thousand dollars for an invention which deadened the noise on their lines, and a royalty forever. She was fifty years old when she made the discovery of her inventive faculties.

MRS. POTTER PALMER.

The United States Government was the first to recognize woman and place her on an equality with man in any great national enterprise, and probably no equal opportunity was ever given to woman to display her ability, as when Congress by special Act, created a board of Lady Managers for the World's Columbian Exposition.

This Board consists of 117 members gathered from every state and territory in the Union, and Mrs. Potter Palmer was, by them, chosen President. Mrs. Palmer was without previous experience as presiding officer, but that she was capable of assuming such a position is demonstrated by the wonderful success of this company of women, and the work they have performed under her leadership. Her keen intellect and appreciation of her great responsibilities are well illustrated in the few remarks she made on accepting the office of President.

Among other things, she said: "We must seriously realize the greatness of the opportunity which has been given us. I felt yesterday, as the ladies met in this room, and the North shook hands with the South, the East with the West, that this first meeting in sympathetic intercourse, of women from all parts of the country, and their learning to work with and understand each other, must result in a great broadening of the horizon of all concerned."

No woman has greater responsibilities or is more widely known, and the success of Mrs. Palmer and her co-workers only demonstrate "What a Woman Can Do."

A WOMAN ARCHITECT.

When the Board of Lady Managers for the World's Fair was created, and $200,000 voted them with which to erect a building, they desired that all the work, except the manual labor, should be performed by women. They at once advertised to give $1,000 for a design made by a woman, that should be acceptable. Some thirty designs were received and all possessed of merit, but it was decided that the design made by Miss Sophia Hayden, of Boston, was the most perfect and displayed the greatest mechanical skill and study. Miss Hayden received the reward, and was called to Chicago to take charge of erecting the great building. She thus not only made the general design, but has furnished the working plans in all their details. This is still more remarkable when it is known that Miss Hayden was but twenty one years of age.

CHAPTER XI

Stenography and Type-writing.

S an admirable example of the adaptability of womankind to the twin arts of stenography and type-writing we present Miss Bertha Louise Parker. She is a native of Pennelville, Oswego county, New York; her early education was had in the public schools there and at the academy at Phœnix.

In 1887 she began to study shorthand and tpye-writing at Lavere's College, Oswego, there learning to use the Remington type-writer, in which work she displayed remarkable deftness and ability. In the following year she entered The American Writing Machine Co.'s branch office at Cincinnati in the capacity of a stenographic amanuensis. Upon taking this position it became neces-sary for Miss Parker to learn to use the "Caligraph," to which she at once devoted all her energies, and to so good purpose that in the space of a few months it became evident to her employers that she was destined to take a prominent rank among the fastest type-writers of the country. Her machine speed soon became such that

120

Miss BERTHA LOUISE PARKER.

shorthand was unnecessary except in times of emergency, her dictations being usually taken direct on the machine at a rate that more than equalled the average speed of ordinary stenographers. Despite her phenomenal ability with the Caligraph, Miss Parker has been too wise to allow her shorthand to fall into disuse, and carefully keeps in practice with her pencil and note-book, finding frequent occasion for its use when her Caligraph is not available.

Miss Parker's present speed with the Caligraph, on a memorized sentence, is 194 words in one minute ; on dictated matter, 111 words in one minute. Aside from the wonderful speed displayed, the perfect ease and grace with which her rapid writing is done, the entire absence of contortion or effort so common to fast writers, adds a charm to the performance that makes it especially enjoyable.

Miss Parker exemplifies thoroughly the adaptability of her sex to business and its requirements, and especially to that branch of business in which so many women have found independence of support, and emancipation from drudgery, viz., stenography and its handmaid, caligraphy.

Miss Eliza Boardman, now Mrs. Burnz, enjoys the distinction of being the first woman in America to learn and adopt shorthand-writing as a means of earning a living. She learned the Isaac Pitman system in 1872 ; but has since invented a system of her own. It is called the Burnz system of shorthand. She derives a nice income from the sale of her books on "Phonetic Shorthand."

It was Mrs. Burnz who, in 1872, first suggested to philanthropical Peter Cooper the idea of establishing a free school of shorthand writing for women at Cooper Union. The idea was rejected by the trustees, for three specified reasons. First. The art was difficult and complicated, requiring a long period of study and practice to use it successfully. Second. The places where shorthand was practised were not suitable for the presence of women. Third. The business was a very limited one, and already occupied by competent practitioners.

She obtained the opinions of the famous stenographers on these objections; and Ned Underhill, the "Grandfather of Stenography," Thomas D. Stetson, Bob Bonynge, C. C. Hine, and other shorthand reporters, whose names are known to the profession, wrote a unanimous opinion that the blue-eyed Mrs. Burnz was right, and the honorable trustees were wrong.

Then Peter Cooper said he would set aside a room for a class if Mrs. Burnz would teach it free, and the strong-hearted little woman began this work of love, which she continued for many years.

Some of the graduates of this department at Cooper Union have become famous ; among them Mrs. Clara E. Brockaway, who is a court reporter, and Alice B. Carnack, a lecture reporter.

There were not more than six women shorthand writers in New York in 1872. Among the first ones were Marion Dowd, Harriet Stafford, and Jennie Turner.

There are now more than five thousand women, young and old, who are earning wages in New York and Brooklyn as stenographers, a host of them combining the manipulation of the type-writer with their shorthand work.

Another example of woman's success in shorthand work is Miss Madge Eiler, whose home is in Mellenville, Columbia county, N. Y. She began the study of shorthand a little over five years ago at the Troy Business

College.   She had a good English education, with some
knowledge of German.   She secured a position with a
well-known firm in Philadelphia, Pa.   Here her knowledge of German was a help to her in her work, as among
the correspondents of the company for whom she worked
were those who wrote and read nothing but German.
She was able to transcribe the letters taken at dictation
into German on the type-writer.

The general secretary of the company speaks very
highly of her work.   He says that when, in 1890, he required the services of a stenographer, he was so fortunate
as to meet Miss Eiler and employ her.   He states that
she has shown herself in every respect equal to the duties
of her position.   He also referred to an exceptional case
in which she acted during several days as stenographer
in court during the trial of an issue of considerable importance, and said that there she discharged the duties
she had assumed to the entire satisfaction of the court
and counsel.   Not the least exception was taken to the
accuracy of her stenographic report or to her type-written
transcript.   She gets a salary of eighteen dollars per week,
but she has often made as high as thirty dollars per
week by reporting speeches and copying manuscript in
addition to her office work.

Shorthand writing is a very artistic work, and is well
suited to the finer nature and more delicate organization
of womankind.   No profession affords a better opening
for young ladies who desire to earn their own living than
does shorthand and type-writing, and we know of no
more agreeable and profitable employment in which they
can be engaged.   The prejudice against employing young
ladies in office-work is rapidly dying out.

The stenographer must not be a mere machine. Some one has said of them that you drop the words into the ear and they come out at the ends of the fingers. It was an insult to all active, thoughtful workers in this employment. An error on the part of the dictator is not corrected by this sort of amanuensis.

Many questions have been asked in regard to the requirements for amanuensis work. In many cases, the reason of failure was that there was not an adequate preliminary education. Before taking up the study of shorthand, one must be a good English scholar. Especially must one be a correct speller and a good grammarian, and understand punctuation, capitalization, paragraphing, and the subject of correspondence, and have a knowledge of the forms and terms used in business.

To learn shorthand one must have an abundance of patience, a good memory, a willingness to work, and besides, plenty of perseverance. Not every one can boast of this last possession, which is so essential to continued practice, upon which success depends. After learning the principles of shorthand, one should acquire a speed of from 80 to 125 words per minute, and be able to transcribe the same on the type-writer at the rate of from 30 to 50 words per minute.

The requirements I have mentioned thus far refer principally to ability. There are other things besides ability that go to make a first-class amanuensis. Loyalty to your employer is one. Good temper, common sense, a general acceptableness in personal appearance, and the faculty of seeing things to be done with the disposition to do them, are others.

The Mail and Express recently had an article on fast

phonography and type-writing in which was said: "The highest authentic speed in shorthand that I know of was the feat of a lady, Mrs. Mollie Berney, a Munson writer, who wrote 307 words in one minute." There are gentlemen, however, who claim to write over 300 words per minute.

The wages paid are good, and range from $7 to $25 per week according to ability and the amount of work done. Some who are paid a salary by the year receive even more than this.

The lawyer now sits down and dictates to his lady stenographer his brief (though it may be anything but brief), which she writes down in shorthand as fast as he rattles it off, and then her nimble fingers transcribe it on the type-writer at the rate of twelve to thirty folios an hour, as legibly as it could be done by the printing press.

The editor finds in her a valuable assistant, and not many editorial sanctums, except in country towns, even if only a weekly paper is published, are without a stenographer.

Besides being employed in professional offices of all kinds, the stenographer is employed in insurance offices, railroad offices, publishing houses, banking houses, manufactories, and in all large business houses. Many private secretaries are also stenographers.

The demand for skillful operators is daily increasing, and many firms are just beginning to awaken to the great advantage gained by employing them.

Shorthand is an accomplishment, and may be made use of in many ways besides using it to make money.

Some years ago Bishop Simpson delivered an eloquent address in the Metropolitan M. E. Church of Washington, D. C., on the occasion of an anniversary of the Colonization Society.

In the audience was a lady with a tablet and pencil, who wrote the glowing language of the speaker, which fell like a string of diamonds and pearls from his lips. Leaf by leaf she tore rapidly from the tablet and handed to the gentleman by her side, who read them with avidity. Those seated back of her surmised that she was a pupil of stenography, and was submitting her notes for criticism. But it was found out afterwards that the gentleman was her husband, and was entirely deaf, and she had acquired the art of taking notes in this way that she might thus afford him the pleasure of enjoying such lectures.

Among the schools that are successfully teaching shorthand and type-writing are the following :

Lavere's College, Oswego, N. Y.; Troy Business College, Troy, N. Y.; Albany Business College and School of Shorthand and Typewriting, Albany, N. Y.

WOMEN AS PHOTOGRAPHERS.

There are nearly twelve hundred lady photographers in the United States. The requisites for this business are patience to continue steadily in one line, improving one formula, a preliminary education in the science of photography, a knowledge of the chemicals used, and a few hundred dollars. It costs from forty to seventy-five dollars to build a good skylight. The instruments and chemicals must then be purchased, and these will range in price from one hundred to one thousand dollars, the latter being the cost of an outfit for a handsome gallery, with furnishings, scenery, and all modern equipments.

Once started, the expense is in the salaries paid to assistants, and rent. The business pays at the rate of one hundred to three hundred per cent. on the cost of the material used. Many ladies are their own operators; do their printing, mounting and finishing entirely themselves. Others employ a man who can do the work, while they take care of the rooms and attend to orders. Women naturally understand posing effects, colors in dress, and all the peculiar phases of the children's picture business better than men. The criticism of a well-known photographer is that they finish up in too light and sketchy a manner, are not deep and bold in shading, and do not give the same care and study to the work that a man does. It is a fact, however, that many women are engaged in the business, and make good pictures, though no particular one has acquired fame for specimen work. The following extracts from a letter written by Mrs. J. H. Parsons, of Ypsilanti, Mich., who was for many years established there as a photographer, are of interest in this connection. Mrs. Parsons writes:

"For the benefit of any sister seeking a place among the limited situations for our sex, I would say that women can succeed in any department of the photograph business, though I should not have chosen it as a life-work had not circumstances pressed me into service.

"My husband and myself were both teachers when we were married. He was a teacher of a commercial school when the war broke out and took so many of the class of young men that were beginning a business education that he dropped his professorship and took up photography. I learned printing of him,

and afterwards, as his health failed, I assisted in different departments, and when he finally died, leaving me with a family of five
little ones, I took his advice, and carried on the work very successfully for twelve years, when I married again.   I hope you
will make it a successful medium in giving encouragement to
our sex, compelled by adverse circumstances to support themselves, for all cannot be teachers, clerks, or seamstresses."

It is a common circumstance to find the wife or sister
of a male photographer employed in the office, which
needs, if at all successful, a working force of at least
three persons—the operator, office clerk, and general
manager.   It often happens, however, that one enterprising individual fills all the departments, taking the
order, posing the sitter, making the negative, and printing the pictures.   Babies are a good deal of trouble, but
they are also a source of emolument to the office.   Some
photographers make a specialty of small children, and
do very attractive work.   If the parents are pleased with
the first picture, they are apt to have the little one taken
frequently.

HOW THE BABY'S PICTURE WAS TAKEN.

We must carry our beautiful baby to town
  Some day when the weather is fair, we said;
We must dress him up in his prettiest gown,
  And wave his hair on the top of his head.

For all his cousins, and all his aunts,
  And both his grandmothers, proud and dear,
Declare it is shameful, and every way blameful,
  To have no picture of him this year.

We carried our child to the town one day,
  The skies were soft and the air was cool;

We robed him richly in fine array,
  Ribbons and lace, and Swiss and tulle.

He looked like a prince in the artist's chair,
  Sitting erect, and brave and grand,
With a big red apple he scarce could grapple,
  Held close in the palm of one dimpled hand.

" He is taking it now." We held our breath.
  We quietly peeped from behind the screen.
' What a pose," we whispered; then, still as death
  Waited, and baby was all serene.

Till the critical moment when, behold!
  The sun was catching that lovely look,
Such a terrible roar, it shook the floor,
  And *that* was the picture the swift sun took.

✵CHAPTER XII.✵

Women ✳ as ✳ Wood ✳ Engravers.

OMEN who engrave on wood, says a writer in Harper's Bazar, will tell you that this exacting occupation tries them less than sewing does; and if, after seeing them bent over the magnifying glass through which they follow the movement of their tools along the surface of the boxwood, you ask if their eyes do not trouble them; they will smile and say that the exercise strengthens the optic nerve. Seven or eight hours a day they will work without excessive fatigue, and then some of the most sensible among them will put themselves through a course of calisthenics and resume business in the morning fresh as daisies. It is only a popular fallacy, they say, that the practice of the art of wood engraving is particularly trying to body and mind.

Those women, like their brothers of the same profession, belong to two classes—those to whom wood engraving is an industrial art, and those to whom it is a fine art The lowest order of engraving done by the former is transfer work, in which their duty is to make a *fac-*

simile of an engraving. Take a picture, for example, from a newspaper, soak it in an alkali solution, lay a block of boxwood upon it, put the whole under a press, and when it comes out there is stamped upon the block a copy of the picture. All that the engraver has to do is to cut out the lines one by one as they lie before her. A few weeks practice is sufficient to qualify her for such a task as this, and many women and men are so occupied to-day.

But the function of the art engraver is different, and the highest exercise of that function consists in reproducing upon a block of wood the effects of a masterly oil painting. Here it is not a *fac-simile* reproduction that is possible. Every line that she cuts must be an invention of her own to express the desired result. In the former case the lines are ready made, traced out for her in advance; in the latter case she begins with no lines at all, the surface of the block containing only a photograph of the oil painting, and requiring her to choose the kind of line and the number of lines requisite to the proposed reproduction. Moreover, so far-reaching, varied, and remorseless are the demands made upon the artistic wood engraver of the present day, that she finds it indispensable to become possessed of the art of drawing and painting; or, at least, a fair knowledge of such, if she is to do the best work and win the best prices. She can not cut the necessary outlines unless she is a draughtsman. She can not cut the necessary tones or tints unless she is a painter. She must possess a practical acquaintance with the whole business of laying on paint, if she is to give to her wood-cut the feel-

ing of an oil painting. The best men engravers in the
United States—that is to say, the best in the world—
have recognized this fact, and are acting upon it. And
the same is true of the few women engravers who
alone deserve to rank with them. And the fact that
there are but few of them shows, not that women engravers are not the peer of men engravers, but that they
are not so many, nor had so long an experience. The
profession of artistic wood engraving itself, as the
term is now understood, is a little over fifteen years
old; and it is about twelve years since the foremost of
the wood engravers have acted up to their conviction,
that a knowledge of drawing and painting is a prerequi-
site to the successful reproduction of an oil painting.

It is the acquisition of this preliminary knowledge,
very much more than the acquisition of the technique of
her profession, that demands of a woman who aspires to
become an artist engraver a long apprenticeship.

The most successful of the few women engravers who
have fought their way into the front ranks of the men
engravers took eight years in accomplishing this feat,
and she was still on the march forward. Before this
she was offered more orders than she could execute, and
some of her best work paid her at the rate of sixty
dollars a week. It is very beautiful work, indeed, with
no trace of the so-called feminine weakness and indecision. The execution is as steady and self-contained as
was the intelligent purpose that inspired it.

TERM OF APPRENTICESHIP.

But eight years is a long time you will say—disheartening long. Let us consider the matter. Here is a boy who, at sixteen, leaves school to become a doctor or a lawyer. At twenty he is just out of college, three years later he has just taken his degree, and one year later still, how often do we find him in a position to earn two, three, or four thousand dollars per annum ? Yet he has spent eight years, and we will not say how many thousand dollars. Look now at his sister, desirous of acquiring a not less honorable profession. It is entirely practicable for her to leave school in her twelfth year, begin the study of wood engraving, and at twenty years of age become the possessor of a profession which will handsomely remunerate her as long as she chooses to practice it.

In one of the classes of the Cooper Institute, New York City, were two clever girls who, in the second year of their training, made six hundred dollars each by executing orders for publishers. One summer, in the same place, twelve pupils earned twelve hundred dollars in the same way—a sum more than sufficient to meet their necessary expenses, amounting, as it did, to an average income of eight dollars and fifty cents a week apiece, when the price of comfortable board and lodging need not have been more than five dollars a week.

A teacher of a class of woman engravers is asked what he thinks of engraving as a field for woman's genius, and in his answer says : " A woman's sense of touch is equal to a man's, her sight is equal to a man's, her capacity for adapting means to ends is equal to a man's, and her fortitude is greater. As for her physique, it is fully equal to the demands made upon it, and a clever woman is a born artist. Her only inferiority to her masculine rivals lies in her less degree of smartness in sharpening her wood-cutting tools; but she can get her brothers and bachelor cousins to do that for her; and when she has fitted herself for the work of an artist engraver, she will make more money in a week than some of her sisters who practice 'high art' are making in a year."

The teacher might have said that a woman's sense of touch is superior to a man's. In the Elgin watch factories the most delicate and difficult parts of the fine work is done by young women whose perception of touch is so exquisitely nice that the finest hair held in their sensitive finger ends seems to be of the dimensions of a whip cord.

MRS. GENERAL SHERIDAN.

Before Irene Rucker, the daughter of Col. Rucker of the U. S. A., was married to General Sheridan, she was accustomed to engrave blocks of wood for a wood engraving firm of the City of Chicago, and many a piece of work was sent out from that establishment, which was supposed to be the work of apprentices or workmen, which was really done by the lady who became Mrs. Sheridan, who worked industriously and was paid a handsome sum weekly by the engraver, who, upon hearing of her intended marriage, exclaimed: "There! its just like a woman to go and ruin her prospects, just when I really needed her work, too!"

A celebrated artist engraver of New York City, says that he has had many women pupils, and they are all doing splendidly.

MUSICAL WOOD ENGRAVING.

It is related of the best lady engravers, that they not only call on painting and sculpture to assist them in their career of wood engraving, but they demand the help of music, and attend concerts and oratorios, at which the divine strains inspire them with melodious tones which they cut into the wood the next day.

WOMEN IN ART.

Moncure D. Conway wrote from London that Mr. Ruskin had been praising the work of Mrs. Lakey, of Chicago. This lady had exhibited a half-dozen pictures in London, which might well inspire any one who had eyes with high hope for the future of American art. The largest of these pictures represents the lord of a small herd, a superb bull, haughty and dignified, with cows of various color around him. They are wading in a placid pond, with a fine landscape beyond them and a warm sky over them. The same writer said: There is an American lady here, Mrs. Merritt (formerly Miss Lea, of Philadelphia), who recently painted a superb Artemis, which I believe to be the best flesh any American has painted over here.

Except Anglica Kauffmann, Mary Moser was the only lady who has ever been a member of the Royal Academy. Her father, George Moser, was one of the original founders, and during his life its keeper. She was greatly admired by Queen Charlotte, and decorated a room at Frogmore for $4,500. She was married to Hugh Lloyd, lived in Fitzroy Square, and was buried at Kensington. She was celebrated as a flower and historical painter.

CHAPTER XIII

The ⊛ Profession ⊛ of ⊛ Telegraphy.

HOW SKILLED LABOR REMUNERATES WOMEN.

T the headquarters of the Western Union Telegraph Company, on the northwest corner of Dey street and Broadway, New York City, more than four hundred young women are employed as operators, and in the branch offices of the company throughout the country hundreds of others find an opportunity to earn a living. Many private offices, too, are served in similar fashion.

The supply of such operators at present is much in excess of the demand. Of the fifty pupils who last year graduated from the Cooper Union Free School of Telegraphy for Women, only about twelve have thus far obtained situations. The central office of the Western Union Telegraph Company is constantly educating young women for such work, although conducting no regular school, and more girls are prepared for the work there than can find positions. The girls who act as messengers in the vast operating rooms on the upper floors are continually picking up professional information, and it is a favorite practice for any one of them to do a companion's work as well as her own a part of the day, thus leaving her comrade free to practice herself in the use of the telegraphic instruments. These messengers receive from fifteen to twenty-five dollars a month, and when they have become skilled operators, from thirty to sixty-five dollars a month, the average salary of the skilled feminine operator being about five hundred per year. The highest salary of the male operators is one hundred and ten dollars a month, and their average salary about seventy dollars.

Why this difference? Chiefly because a man's endurance is greater than a woman's, and because the men are liable to be called upon by night as well as by day. The best of the male operators will receive and transcribe a telegraphic message of fifteen hundred words in an hour; will transcribe it so legibly and carefully that it may be handed to the compositors of a newspaper in the shape in which it has left his hands. When the annual President's Message is in progress of being telegraphed from Washington to New York City, this dexterous feat of receiving and transcribing is by no means a rare one. But telegraph superintendents say that they do not call upon women to perform it, and do not expect such a service of them. "Considerable nerve" is required to execute this task—more "nerve" than a woman is supposed to have in reserve at any hour of the day or night. Comparatively few men, indeed, can do it.

In another respect also, the women operators have been found inferior to those of the other sex—they are oftener absent from their duties. When speaking of book-keepers I had occasion to quote some testimony of another sort: "Our women book-keepers," said a publisher, "are detained from their duties by sickness or other cause no oftener than our men book-keepers." But of the more than four hundred women operators at the central office of the Western Union Telegraph Company about one-twelfth are expected to be absent daily, and arrangements are made for supplying their places. So large a proportion may not fail to put in an appearance to-morrow, but if it does fail, the vacant chairs will be filled without inconvenience to the company. Experience has shown that the deficit is liable to occur, and that the supply for it must be in readiness. It is not entirely clear why this discrepancy between the book-keepers and the telegraph operators should exist, but the labors of the latter are probably more exhaustive, and their surroundings less favorable from a sanitary point of view.

In one particular, however, the women operators are more satisfactory than their male rivals: they are more punctual, less frequently late in the morning, for the reason, it is said, that their method of spending their evenings is usually more wholesome than that of their brothers. They work about nine hours a day, and when intending to begin a day's work are promptly on hand at the hour appointed. Furthermore, their employers (I am speaking particularly of the officers of the Western Union Company) are favorably disposed to the practice of using women's services in telegraphy, referring in respectful terms to the results of experience in this

direction, and frankly expressing the opinion that
women make good operators. From business motives
these business men are ready to avail themselves of
woman's skilled work in telegraphy. Sentimental con-
siderations, philanthropic or otherwise, do not enter into
their summing up of the case. Speaking for themselves,
and in the light of an extended observation, they approve
of the employment of women operators; and I desire to
invite especial attention to this fact, because in the series
of articles now in hand I propose to treat of the subject
of the remunerative aspect of skilled work for women
entirely from the point of view of the business man, and
never from the point of view of the theorist.

For the women themselves the practice of telegraphy
has certain simple and definite attractions. It does not
soil their dresses; it does not keep them in a standing
posture; it does not, they say, compromise them socially.
A telegraph operator, they declare, has a social position
not inferior to that of a teacher or governess. Some
kinds of skilled work, they insist, are positively objectionable: "In a factory one's clothes are misused; in a
store one can never sit down; in the kitchen of a private
house one is only a servant, even though a *chef*," and
to regard these objections as merely sentimental and
unworthy. of serious consideration would, they claim,
be a mistake. At any rate, the pursuit of telegraphy is
free from these inconveniences. Moreover, the young
women operators at the Western Union Company's headquarters are treated by their superintendent—a young
woman very proficient in her profession—with sedulous
courtesy. She addresses them, not familiarly by their

Christian names, but by their surnames, with the prefix "Miss," and she insists upon their addressing one another in the same considerate fashion, except, of course, when one of them is speaking to an intimate friend. She does not scold them, and as for cases of insubordination on their part, these are of the rarest occurrence—say only two or three in half a dozen years. Still further, the work is not continuous; during working hours there are many resting times. When a message has been dispatched or received, the operator may, and often does, take up her knitting, crocheting, or sewing, passing pleasantly the interval until the arrival of the next message. Reading is forbidden, because it is supposed to absorb the attention to a greater extent than either of the other diversions; but conversation in a low tone is encouraged. Among the more than four hundred faces the sunny and healthful ones have an immense majority.

To offset this credit column several entries are to be made on the debit side of the account. In the first place, there is the disease known as telegraph cramp, the diagnosis of which has not yet been thoroughly ascertained by the physicians. An operator stretches out her hand to press her finger upon the button of the instrument, and suddenly her arm refuses to obey her will, and lies numb on the desk beside her. If the tendons of her wrist had been cut through, her manual helplessness would not be greater. The strongest voluntary force is too feeble to make itself felt at the ends of the fingers. The operator simply can not do her work. Twenty-five or thirty of these four hundred young women are subject to periodic attacks of this disease, and not one of the others knows how soon she herself may be seized with it. There is no remedy but rest from telegraphing, and exercise in the open air. In the next place, in order to become a first-class operator, four or five years of resolute practice are necessary, even when one has what is known as "a good ear." The course of seven or eight months' training in the Cooper Institute, or any other school, is only preliminary; every graduate, no matter how fervidly expressed in her diploma is the story of her accomplishments, must pursue the practice of her profession for at least four years before attaining the rank and emoluments of a first-class operator. Here is a young woman, say eighteen years old, in the second year of her course. Her pay, we will say, is as yet only thirty-five dollars a month, and if she depends entirely upon her earnings for support, she is likely neither to save a cent nor to waste a cent. Her board and room will cost her probably at least six dollars a week, or, if she has a room-mate, possibly five dollars; her luncheons, her car fares, her washing, half as much more, without any extravagance on her part; her office dress, even if she make it herself, will take eight dollars out of her pocket-book; her bills for other clothes, for shoes, for hats—well, it is easy enough for her to expend ten dollars every week in the year, and her salary is not nine dollars. Next year, perhaps, her salary will be raised to ten; but no matter how proficient she may become, it is not likely to be more than fifteen dollars a week. Several years ago the earnings of both men and women operators of the first class were greater than they are now, the former receiving fif-

teen hundred dollars a year instead of the present thirteen hundred and twenty dollars, and the latter nine
hundred dollars instead of the present seven hundred
and eighty, although at that time the cost of living was
higher, and the number of working-hours (for the men)
greater.

Another drawback to the practice of telegraphy as a
profession is the constant liability of the operator at the
other end of the line to quarrel with you when you can
not understand his or her message; and when he or she
is surly of disposition, and captious of soul, the patience
of the operator at this end of the line is sorely tried, and
often wrought into an inexplicable tangle.   Furthermore, unless one keeps in continuous practice, her facil-
ity in sending or receiving messages becomes less very
rapidly.   It is practice that not only makes perfect, but
keeps perfect.   The most enthusiastic learner tries to
procure a small telegraphic instrument with a short circuit of wire—no matter how short if only continuous—
and set it up in her room at home.   The entire appar-
atus need cost only three dollars and seventy cents; and
if, while waiting for a situation, or while temporarily
engaged in other pursuits, she sets apart some time daily
for exercising her fingers upon it, the best telegraph
operators in the world would be the last to dispute the
wisdom of her course.

In the brokers' offices on Wall street, and thereabouts,
the hours of service are shorter, and the remuneration
often greater, than in the Western Union offices.   Most
of the work is done from ten to half-past three o'clock,
and very often free luncheon is provided, which the

young women operators estimate as equivalent to a bonus of ten dollars a month. The requirements of the situation are, to be sure, more exacting than those of general business, and mistakes are usually of more serious import. In branch offices in New York City and the country the average pay is thirty-five dollars a month, and the services of the women who receive it are much more highly valued by the Western Union Telegraph Company than are the services of the men whose salary is the same. One young woman who acts as manager and operator in one of the city offices receives sixty dollars a month, and is considered to exhibit business qualities which few men possess.

⊹CHAPTER XIV.⊹

Lady ⋆ Book ⋆ Canvassers.

I T is doubtful if there is any work more especially suited to the taste and capacity of a bright, energetic woman, with a good fund of common sense about her, than the sale of subscription books throughout the country. There is just enough variety about the business to prevent it from becoming monotonous, and it pays well if the book for which the agent is canvassing has sufficient merit to recommend it to the public, and I would advise ladies to be sure they are right in this particular before they go ahead. The best books published now—that is, the most valuable to have in the family — are sold entirely by subscription, and much pains is taken in selecting good canvassers who will confer honor on the business, as well as solicit numerous orders. It is by no means necessary that the lady book agent should go out on a canvassing tour—as suggested in a recent work on the subject—armed with a revolver, and bearing a fictitious name. There is nothing in the work to be ashamed of. On the contrary, the lady agent will find in the same

144

field of labor the wives and widows of lawyers, doctors, statesmen, and army officers—women who have been well educated and reared in a position of luxury, and whose health would not permit them to fill indoor situations, even if they could obtain them. Some of these agents make as much as two thousand dollars a year; others easily realize a profit of one thousand dollars over and above all expenses. The necessary qualifications are so varied that it would be impossible to enumerate them here. Much depends on personal magnetism and a quiet, lady-like persistence in representing the merits of the book, and in adhering strictly to business in such a manner as to win the respect of the parties who are solicited to subscribe. The true lady will compel every man into whose office or store she enters, to treat her as he would wish his own mother or sister to be treated at the hands of other men. She has a right to be heard; has just as good a right to demand a market for her goods as he has for his, and both parties must approach each other on the basis of mutual respect and tolerance.

Ladies who go into strange towns to canvass should endeavor to obtain board in a respectable private family, if they expect to remain some time in the place, and then begin systematically a course of regular canvassing, allowing no temporary worries and disappointments to dis· courage them. The agent must not be too sensitive, or forget for a moment the object she has in view, that of making an honorable living. She will, if she is wise, always leave a good impression upon those whom she meets, whether she makes a sale or not; the way will be smoother then for a second visit. She will clearly define

10

the scope and value of the work she is endeavoring to sell, but will make no statements which she can not substantiate. To be able to do this, she must make herself thoroughly acquainted with the work, and also have confidence in the publisher who employs her; and a good publisher will never send out a rubbishy book. She must be in entire sympathy with her work, and know what she is talking about. Such an agent can not help being successful.

Lady agents will do well to dress in a quiet manner, wearing but little jewelry, but presenting a neat, lady-like appearance, winning rather than demanding attention, and putting aside any attempt at compliment or raillery from strangers with a quiet dignity of manner, but at the same time continuing pleasantly in the safe and straightforward path of business. They will find that it depends much on themselves whether they are successful or not. Even if they do not succeed at once, there is a possibility that they may do well the next time, or, at any rate, they will leave that good impression which will smooth the way for a later venture.

The agent who regards her business as a permanent one, will see that her books are all delivered to customers as per agreement, and in as agreeable a manner as the order was taken. One of the most successful lady agents in the State of Illinois, who has by means of her book sales purchased a charming home, says that she truly believes that her customers are always glad to see her, no matter what she brings them, sometimes a book, often a paper or magazine. She is neither young nor pretty, but she has that method of attracting and com-

manding respectful attention which is so necessary to
her business. She boards always among the best people,
and is in the true sense of the word a lady.

OTHER AGENCIES.

Sewing machines have been a very popular method by
which women make money, both in selling the machines
and in operating upon them. They offer very suitable
employment, and although there is less demand for them
than formerly, and the profits are cut down, there is still
money to be made in that special department.

Organs and pianos can be bought and sold by one who
understands the business and is disposed to turn an
honest penny. Music teachers make considerable money
by taking an order for a piano and turning it over to a
dealer, who, on a fine instrument, will pay a commission
of from $50 to $100, the parties who are purchasing paying for the instrument its regular retail rates.

Cooking stoves, which are always in demand, and
which any woman can talk about intelligently, can be
sold from circulars and photographs, and the old ones
taken at a fair estimate in part payment, the dealers who
send out the agent managing the moving and freight of
the goods.

Corsets offer another good and useful article for which
ladies can canvass, and need meet only their own sex in
making sales. Some women make $20 a week selling
corsets. It may not be the most agreeable method of
making a living, but half a loaf is better than no bread.

Insurance companies employ a number of lady agents,
who solicit orders, fill out the policies, and make a cer-

tain percentage upon each new member.   This business
ranks about the same as the book agency.

Charts for cutting dresses, boots and shoes, small
patent articles such as pillow-sham holders, and a great
variety of household articles, are sold by ladies, but
these belong more particularly to the commercial
travelers.

CHAPTER XV

N the past few years there has grown out of the æsthetic atmosphere a new and important industry for women in the organization of so- cieties for promoting the use and sale of fancy and decorative work, hand-paintings on panels and screens, and every sort of hand decorated articles for use or adornment in the home. These are sent in to what is known as an "Exchange for Women's Work," numbers of which have grown up through the country, and sold for the benefit of the manufacturer or artist, with a small commission, which goes to the Ex- change. Everything that can be used in the household is for sale or on order at these places. Bread and cake are supplied to families daily, and the makers remain unknown, some of the best society ladies thus employing their surplus time to increase their skill in cooking, at the same time adding not a little to their pin money. The judicious way of carrying on the business largely by orders prevents loss to either party. The ready sale of preserved and spiced fruits, pickles, jellies

and cakes, has offered to many ladies a satisfactory
return for their work, the receipts from this department alone, in the New York Exchange, amounting
the first half year to $6,000. The consigners of goods
pay for yearly membership a sum of $2 or a trifle more,
and from ten to fifteen per cent. on the goods, according
to the class, ten per cent. being, however, the regular
price. As the work is nearly all the result of private
enterprise, it is much better than the same class of goods
found in stores; and there is such a general assortment
that almost everything in manufactured goods can be
found there. There is also the modern supply of bric-a-
brac, old china, fine needle work, rare vases, and often
the articles of ancient value that used to find their way
into the pawnbrokers hands to raise money for immediate
necessity, are disposed of in these places at something
like an approximate value, the class of people who
patronize them being connoisseurs in art. It will be
remembered that this is a woman's institution, organ-
ized and conducted solely by women, and patronized by
them. It is an auxiliary to the Decorative Art Society,
many of the ladies engaged in this work being sub-
scribers to that, and, consequently, friendly to its aims
and purposes. They appreciate the work as a school,
recognize in many of their own best things the teachings
of that society, and claim that in furnishing a salesroom
for the articles rejected, because not up to the artistic
standard, yet in many cases beautiful and saleable,
they are helping those who, thoroughly imbued with a
proper ambition, can not afford to improve unless their

unfortunate efforts can give them the means for another trial.

Of course the work offered to the Exchange must pass a careful examination or it will not be admitted. The rules which govern the organization are about the same wherever the Exchange exists, and inferior work would soon injure the reputation of the institution. The managers have made a wide detour from the first straight line they laid down, and now have the articles of use in the majority; and the report of the New York Woman's Exchange states that "the managers of the Exchange also extend a helping hand to the many intelligent and cultivated women who are not and never can be artists, and who, when changed circumstances and common sense demand that they shall help themselves, have the wisdom to do what they can find a market for; and we hope in time to be able to induce many with no talent to throw away their paint brushes and follow the example of those who contribute to our department of useful things." The census estimates that in the United States there are twenty thousand women who make their living canning fruit and vegetables.

In order to reach any of these institutions it is only necessary to send a stamp for return postage and address the Exchange for Woman's Work, New York, Chicago, Cincinnati, Boston, Detroit, Mich., Cleveland, Ohio, Milwaukee, Wis., or any of the cities in which they are located, writing the full address, town, county and State, with postoffice number, and requesting a circular which will fully explain their manner of doing business. The New York Exchange announces that in the time during which it accepted for sale sixteen thousand articles, it rejected only twenty-five. The membership to this institution is now $5 yearly. Among the articles sold at these places may be enumerated all kinds of Christmas and birthday gifts, banners, lambrequins for mantle shelves, embroidered pillow-shams, napkin bands, suspenders, slippers, toilet articles, shoe bags, whisk holders, toilet bags, Macramé lace fringes and shopping satchels, silk mittens, crazy silk work, and whatever is new and popular at the moment. In the cookery department loaves of good home-made bread, tea biscuits, cakes of all kinds, large and small, Charlotte Russe, and any delicacies for the table that can be safely moved in transportation.

SOMETHING FOR WOMAN TO DO—A LADY WHO EARNED $10,000 A YEAR FROM PRESERVES AND PICKLES.

A lady wrote from Boston: " I have often heard complaints that there was nothing for women to do by which they could earn as much money as men. Perhaps there is nothing in the same line of business as that followed by men; but taking all the professions followed by women, it seems to me that there is a great deal of money made by them. The enormous sums paid singers and actresses are too well known to need mentioning. But there are other lines of business that women may follow, who have no natural gifts such as these. I heard the other day of a lady who made a handsome income for herself, and all in the most quiet way. This lady was a Miss Martin, and she was the daughter of a gentleman living near Auburn, in New York State, who at one time was very wealthy; but although the family

still lived in the old homestead, which was a noble mansion, they were very much reduced in circumstances. Miss
Martin, when she became old enough to want money,
and to know that it did not always come for the wanting, cast about for something to do by which she could
earn her living and not be dependent on her father. It
seemed as though all the avenues were closed. She was
not gifted in any particular way, though she was a
woman of excellent education, and had all the advantages that came from a high social position. But she
neither sang well enough for the stage, nor had she any
histrionic talent. In giving the subject serious consideration, she remembered that there was one thing she
could do very well, and that was preserving. She told
her friends that she was going to make a large quantity
of pickles and preserves of different kinds, and she
wanted to sell them. Knowing what an excellent housekeeper she was, they knew that anything that was made
under her supervision would be sure to be good, so she
had no trouble in selling all she had the first year. The
second year she made more yet, and was unable to supply the demand. The third year she increased her facilities, and her reputation had by this time spread so far
that she did a very large business, and even sold to some
of the larger stores of New York. And so she went on
in this way until her profits from pickles and preserves
reached the very comfortable sum of $6,000 to $10,000
a year, and she only worked from May to November.
Auburn being a little far from the New York markets,
where fruit could be bought best and cheapest, Miss
Martin went down and took a place at Glen Cove, to

gain the advantages of a nearer residence to New York. One of the secrets of Miss Martin's success is that everything she made was the very best of its kind. All the ingredients she used in her pickles and preserves were the best in the market, and though she employed a number of men and women, she superintended everything herself, and while her articles were all in the shops, they had a home-like taste that was unmistakable. All the jars bore her initials, written in *fac-simile* of her autograph, on a neat label on the side. A sister of Miss Martin, seeing her success, cast about for something to do. Of course she did not want to go into the same line of business, and finally she struck upon cake-making as a means of livelihood, and her cakes became almost as celebrated as her sister's pickles and preserves. She lived at Auburn, but she received orders from New York, and even Newport. Miss Martin's cakes were considered an essential part of a well regulated family in New York.

PURCHASING AGENCIES.

In many large cities there are ladies who make a livelihood by purchasing goods on commission, their customers being persons who live at a distance from the metropolis, and who send to them for dress goods, millinery or house furnishings; anything, in fact, from a bridal trousseau to a paper of pins. These shopping agents charge a small commission to the customer, while the merchant sells to them at wholesale rates, so that they average a profit of twenty-five per cent. on all money expended. It is a safe and pleasant business, the parties transacting it being mutually endorsed by responsible people.

Among the trades which are specially adapted to deft feminine fingers are the fine arts of repairing and riveting broken glass and China, mending delicate fans, and restoring chipped pottery. There is no known reason why a woman with a fair musical ear should not practice tuning pianos: this is an occupation which requires little outlay in the way of implements. Another profession in which a woman of artistic tendencies could turn with profit in this æsthetic age is adviser in relation to artistic furnishing of houses, selecting hangings, stained glass, oriental rugs and fine furniture on commission. This profession is not necessarily attached to, though supplemental to a knowledge of, architecture, and the Garrets have made this business very profitable. It must be borne in mind that most of these suggestions are applicable to dwellers in large cities, where there is sufficient demand to create the supply.

Correcting proof, not for printers so much as for authors, preparing manuscripts for the press, and furnishing indices to works of importance, demand an eye well trained to the latest English exploits in preferred spellings, a fair knowledge of modern and classic languages, or, at any rate, an enterprising intimacy with their dictionaries, besides a good knowledge of the subject of any work.

Already we hear of a few women who have made notable success at indexing libraries, both in Boston and in Philadelphia. This is an occupation that all assistant librarians should expect to grow up into, as the catalogue maker stands next in importance to the book maker. It is, besides, valuable as educational aid, and there is no trained teacher or professor but might be proud to succeed in it.

MENDING AND DARNING.

Some old ladies who are neat and handy with the needle make quite a little money by darning and mending, filling up their otherwise spare time profitably and pleasantly. But even to succeed in this they must be artists. Is there anything more uncomfortable than a rough, unseemly darn? Many a man will wear hose that are as perforated as a sieve rather than encounter a hasty darn. As a general thing, young men away from home have no one to call upon to perform this kindly office for them excepting their washerwomen, and these are by no means adepts in the art of darning or mending, and the youth who has been accustomed at home to having his hose mended and ready for him to draw on, the missing button replaced, the torn or fringed garment neatly repaired, devotes his Sundays to a renovation of his wardrobe, or goes ragged.

Now, suppose he paid 5 cents a pair to have his socks darned, 2 cents each for buttons sewed on, 3 cents for a patch, or 25 cents a week to have his clothes kept in good repair, how small a sum for comfort, and easily saved out of a small salary, by abolishing some trifling expense of cigars or car fare. A class of these young men could be easily obtained, and to this industry could be added family mending, carpet repairing, lace darning, linen marking, etc. A skillful woman could make a living easily out of these fragmentary industries. But here, as in all other branches, comes in the question of fitness, adaptability, system. Good menders, who are willing to serve the public, are just as hard to find as trained help in other and more important departments.

READY WRITERS.

In large cities like New York there are women who make a living by writing letters, principally for servants or people of neglected education. They write a beautiful chirography, and are happy in expressing the sentiments of their different employers; the service rates from 10 cents to 25 cents a letter. These writers are gifted with vivid imaginations, and they can indite a love-letter, a message to distant friends, a business mis-sive, or a lecture or political address with the utmost ease. There is one woman in New York who makes considerable money out of the work. She has a suite of rooms plainly but comfortably furnished, and her customers have regular hours to see her, when she writes to their dictation, charging by the hour, which she divides in sections, not engaging her pen for less service than that of a quarter hour. Her terms are one dollar an hour, and the people who employ her are of the better sort of uneducated trades people, who are ashamed of their ignorance. She writes fluently in French, German, Italian, and English, and shrewdly insists upon furnishing her own paper, envelopes, and stamps, upon which she realizes a small per centage.

There are also women who write verses for valentines,

mottoes for candy, obituary notices, advertisements, circulars, visiting cards, cards of condolence, etc. The
type-writer and copying press have taken a great share
of the copyist's work from her, but many girls and
women are yet employed on law work, copying the
voluminous legal writings, which result in every important case.

MRS. EDNA C. NOBLE.

⇥CHAPTER XVI.⇤

The ⋆ Profession ⋆ of ⋆ Elocution.

O the student, reading and declaiming poems and prose selections now offers a really important field of labor in the smaller towns and cities where there are no theatres, giving a very fair remuneration to the public reader. In larger towns it is the custom for wealthy society ladies to invite them to furnish an evening's amusement and entertainment to friends, and the young debutante in this particular branch need have no false ideas of pride in regard to a paid invitation, where she can do honor to her profession, charm a circle of interested listeners, and add ten, fifteen or twenty-five dollars to her income. It is understood that she is a professional reader, and not an amateur or volunteer. She makes her entrance at the hour designated by the hostess, reads her selections, with brief interludes of music, and when she has finished quietly withdraws, regarding the guests simply as an audience. There is nothing derogatory to the dignity of any lady in giving these readings or recitations. She takes the same stand that the pianist or other musical artist does, who, if he be an artist, rises superior to any mere pretention to the claims of society, and distinguishes himself as an exponent of his art. To insist on being a guest is lowering the standard of professional dignity. That matter will adjust itself in small social circles, but in the severe ethics of metropolitan society rules are arbitrary, and an attempt to break them would result in disagreeable failure.

Schools for elocution are now established in Boston, New York, and many smaller towns, and they offer great advantages to the student, as in developing the voice the lungs are strengthened, the general health improved, and an easy, graceful manner acquired, together with a culture which comes of the combined forces of æsthetic development included in the studies of this course of education. In Detroit, Michigan, there is a training school in elocution and English literature, managed and sustained by Mrs. Edna Chaffee Noble, whose portrait will be found in this work. Mrs. Noble is assisted by a large corps of teachers and professors, many of whom are graduates of her school, and are now reimbursing themselves in this manner. English literature, classes in Shakespeare, in mythology, in many ancient and abstruse studies are included in the course, but the aim of the school is to teach a high standard of elocution. It is, perhaps, a sufficient diploma for Mrs. Noble, that her scholars are many of them successful teachers, and earning a good living, while ladies who studied with her for the advantage of the culture elocution gives, have the power to gratify themselves and their friends by the accomplishment. The Detroit School of Elocution has sent its pupils out as readers north and south, east and west, and they have the capacity of filling halls wherever they go with a paying audience. The labor of the course is severe, but it is thorough and beneficial.

There is now a literature of elocution, so that the reader can, without difficulty, find grave or gay selections, new methods to please, and so fill out an evening with a variety that gives the vocal organs full scope for all their powers. The elocutionist can imitate a bird singing, a chicken piping, machinery creaking, a child laughing, or a piano playing. She can make her listener cry or laugh at will. She can read tragedy or comedy with a stage effect that gives it all the attractions of a theatre, without its associations, and she can whistle like a boy, or like a steam engine—things that seem of little account, but which require months of careful study to accomplish. Mrs. Noble has made her school a financial as well as an educational success. The course includes the whole science of elocution, voice-building, vocal physiology, and other calisthenics of the organs of speech. Mrs. Noble is the director of the school; the faculty consists of an equal number of male and female professors.

"A great deal," says N. H. Gillespie, "has been said and written upon the subject of elocution. Authors and teachers have furnished excellent rules for pronunciation and the correct modulation of the voice; they have explained the nature and use of stress, volume, pitch,

11

slides, inflections, and all the other elements which enter into correct reading and speaking.

This drill, however, though very useful and even necessary to a successful cultivation of the art of speaking, will never make an elocutionist. It may render a person a good mimic or imitator, but that is all.

To become an elocutionist in the true sense of the word, one must learn to do what Dr. Johnson declared was done by Garrick, the celebrated actor. When asked his opinion of the reputation attained by that wonderful interpreter of Shakespeare, he replied: 'Oh, sir, he deserves everything he has acquired for having seized the soul of Shakespeare, for having embodied it in himself, and for having expanded its glory over the world. ' Yes, herein, lies the secret of elocution—one must seize the soul of the author whose thoughts he would reproduce; he must embody that soul in himself, making it a part of his own being, and then he will speak with that forcible eloquence which alone deserves the name of elocution.

Having ascertained the meaning of the author, the next and most important step is, as Dr. Johnson has it, to seize and embody in one's self the soul of the author. This is accomplished by studying carefully the character of the man, ascertaining his peculiarities, his habits of thought, his natural disposition and temper—in a word, the tone of his mind.

Then comes the last step, which consists in putting one's self, for the time at least, in that man's place, creating in one's self a tone and habit of thought similar to his, and striving to feel as he most likely felt while writing, or as he would probably feel were he to deliver orally what he had written. Thus prepared and worked up into the spirit of the author, the speaker may fearlessly come forward and feel perfectly confident that with ordinary speaking ability he will express forcibly the thoughts of the author. And this is true elocution."

The following address, delivered to the graduating class of the Detroit Training School, by Mrs. Edna Chaffee Noble, is worthy of careful reading.

THE STUDY OF ELOCUTION.

In coming before you in the past, I have avoided everything that seemed explanatory of the use or abuse of the art I taught, thinking the time of my pupils so precious that it would be a waste to talk of that with which I hoped and thought they were already familiar. I think I should have used a part of the time at least more fitly and wisely, had I striven to impress upon them the true value of the study of elocution. I find that many persons of broad culture and education have given little thought or care to the art of delivery, and the greater number of my pupils have studied with me because the study was novel or pleasing, or to pass away time, or because a friend studied, or to make a little show with a few select recitations, and I now believe that very few understood the value of close application, of regular, thorough drill, of well-seasoned and well-timed practice in this work. A little thought upon this shows me that there have been few subjects that are of the least importance as educators in our land, where none need be ignorant, that have been so little written upon or talked about, or held up as worthy working for, as this study of training the natural voice to its highest powers in speaking, this study of modulating voice and breath into distinct and separate forms, this study at its best, of rendering thought and feeling tangible, that others may grasp it and look at it as we do, this study so neglected of bringing to the highest development articulate sounds, is the great gift from God which distinguishes us from the brute.

The art of speaking well is a characteristic mark between the educated and the unlearned, and is closely connected with labors in the highest walks of ambition and taste; yet, with many, elocution is a term representing something that is considered entirely artificial, worse than unnecessary, and the results of its study altogether to be deplored, and they even go so far as to speak lightly, and even contemptuously, of it. A few sentences expressing doubts in the mind of some candid person, in regard to the beneficial results of elocution in the community, came to my notice a few weeks ago, and, I remember, elicited much comment from members of this class, and much surprise. Your own fresh interest could not allow that another's thought upon this subject should differ from your own. Criticism and doubt are good if founded upon thorough knowledge, but many to-day find it easy to pass judgment upon a subject of which they are totally ignorant, and criticise in proportion, as they have not studied.

Dr. Holmes says a man behind the times is apt to speak ill of them, on the principle that nothing looks well from behind. Let us hope that this doubter is viewing the art of elocution from behind, for whoever is ignorant of a subject can not seriously appreciate it, or criticise its merits or demerits, much less define the harm or good of its being. There are reasons why the common observer should criticise a subject he has not investigated. The efforts to which his attention is usually called are the results, not of finished, careful training, but are the crude attempts of a person who has mastered the beginning of an art,

and mistaken it for the end. How many years are spent in
incessant toil, in close discipline, in orderly tasks, to produce
accomplishment of voice for singing? How many weary hours
of practice upon the piano, the careful lessons in touch and
style, the earnest application of ear and eye—the giving of
one's life and fortune to the acquirement of an art which not
one out of one hundred ever uses for one's own pleasure or profit,
or for the delight of others? Compare these *worthy* efforts with
the feeble attempts to master the art of elocution, and no longer
be surprised that mere lookers on should "consider it a serious
question whether elocution does not do more harm than good in
the community." It is not easy to impress upon people the
value of elocutionary study, or the necessity to spend time and
money in the acquirement of this art, because the belief has,
through some means, gained a strong hold that reading is not a
subject that can be taught; that it has no rules, no principles,
except those of nature, and that in this work nature must exercise her own powers. The opinion is common that the ability
to read well is a talent, an unstudied and unsought power, given
to one and denied another. "In this world all things bear two
meanings—one for the common observer, and one for the mind
of him who, with an earnest purpose and steadfast, loving heart,
penetrates into those mines of hidden riches, the treasures of
science and imagination." These two interpretations are given
to all arts, and especially to that science and art of all that is
embodied in the word elocution. Undoubtedly something
depends, in reading, upon natural talent, but hard work is necessary to liberate the wondrous manifestations of human thought
and life which are prisoned behind those bars, the closed lips.

Reading is not like many other arts, absolutely forbidden to
those who have not served an apprenticeship. Painting and
sculpture are unnoted by comment, unless the skilled hand has

wrought. But the rudest and most uneducated handle these tools of speech every day; and it is only the skilled tongue that can lift them out of their ordinary life, through this art of arts, and place the result beside the masterpieces in marble and color, and beyond the reach of vulgar criticism.

THE THOUSAND-FOLD HABIT OF SPEECH

has made its processes so unconscious that when they at first become conscious they are almost sure to become unnatural. Legouvé gives an account of a character written for a child in one of his plays which was given to a girl of ten, full of grace and intelligence. He says: "At the general rehearsal my little actress did wonders, and a spectator sitting in front of me applauded very loudly, exclaiming, 'What truth, what simplicity! It is very evident that she has never been taught to do that.' Now, for a whole month," Legouvé says, "I had done nothing but teach her that part, intonation by intonation. Not that in any way it was beyond her childish capacity, for many of the expressions were borrowed from my little actress herself. But so soon as these expressions were embodied in her part, so soon as she had to recite them, every trace of naturalness vanished. What she said to perfection when she spoke for herself, she uttered coldly and unmeaningly when she spoke for another; and it cost me much time and labor to bring her back to herself; to reteach her. It thus appears that reading is so deep an art that it must be taught to those who reveal it to us." Art and nature will never perfectly blend until those who attempt to become artists in this direction are willing to serve as faithfully for this acquisition, work as devotedly, with as much consecration, and give as much time to its study and practice as they would in the cultivation of any of the higher arts.

Popular prejudice often deters people from even an investigation of very important subjects. Six years ago fully one-half of my pupils came secretly to take their lessons in elocution. Clergymen and married ladies were among the timid; they feared people would know they were making an effort to over-come harshness of voice or awkwardness of manner. "God's highest gift to man is speech, and it is too solemn a thing to treat so lightly. It grows out from our life, out of its agonies and ecstasies, its wants and its weariness. Speech is the temple in which the soul is enshrined." Why should we not be proud to keep such a temple in repair? Our commonest words, if prop-erly uttered, hang pictures before our eyes more wonderful than the paintings of the greatest masters, for nowhere does man as artist come so near the Divine Creator as in the words he uses, —out of our mouths are we condemned or exalted. *Legere est illuminare.*

We are now at the end of our short journey together. Columbus took note of his passage on his voyage of discovery, and could make it again unaided, but many of the men who were with him knew only of the fathomless, stormy sea. May I not hope that a way has been noted by you so that you may make subsequent passages alone. Mark that I say *a* way, not *the* way. Let me entreat you not to make your method your idol. "Iron is essentially the same everywhere and always, and because the sulphate of iron differs from the carbonate of iron, do not forget that it is iron all the same." Elocution is elocution, and because the Smithate elocution differs from the Brownate, do not let that render you intolerant of all that does not bear the seal of the Detroit Training School. Do not label your wares like vendors of patent medicines, saying all are base counterfeits unless bearing this seal. In fact, do not talk too much about yourselves or your work. "A little knowledge is a dangerous thing"—dangerous, because it is apt to make us conceited, and conceit hedges up the path to newer knowledge, and although I would most heartily urge you to faith in your work and enthusiasm for it, yet do not let your ardor be one that will lower your art in the minds of the disinterested. There was once a simpleton who had a house to sell, and had constantly on exhibition a brick as a sample of his great possession. A consciousness of knowledge is best made known by doing something so well that the deed will speak for itself, and will require no puffing or labeling. Do not be too sure that the value your friends set upon your accomplishments will at all coincide with your market value; and do not be discouraged if the public estimate your worth below your own fixed ideas. "Do the prettiest thing you can and wait your time," for if you have powers beyond the ordinary, be sure there will be a time and place for the exercise of those powers.

The world, in its need, is keen to detect the best, and requires no sign to designate its abode. You must not rest upon the laurels you have already won, but remember that "It never rains roses; if we want more roses we must plant more trees." Work is the only key to success. Burns plowed the daisy under before he lifted it up to bloom in immortal verse.

No clock ever yet struck twelve without giving all the strokes from one, and I hope you have learned this most valuable lesson, that you can not hope to compute the highest numbers in the problems of life or fame without counting patiently the units.

CHAPTER XVII

The * Profession * of * Nursing.

HE stranger in New York who may chance to visit the east side of the city, in the neighborhood of Twenty-sixth street, will have his attention called to a long, grayish, four-story prison-like structure, with a wing, situated in a block which extends to the East River, and inclosed by a high, forbidding stone wall. This is the Bellevue Hospital, the chief free public institution of the kind in America. For many years it has been famous for the high medical and surgical skill of which it is the theater, its faculty embracing many leading members of the profession in the city. For many years to come it is likely to be popularly associated with another high development of the curative arts,—the results of the founding, in 1873, of the Bellevue Training School for Nurses, and of a new profession for women in America.

Not long ago a lady living in the suburbs of one of our eastern cities, whose daughter was ill with fever, was urged by her physician to employ a professional nurse. She was loth to do this, but, as the malady increased in virulence, she finally yielded. The following morning the servant announced "the nurse." To the mother's imagination—overwrought as it was by lack of rest and by unremitting watching—the words called up the most disagreeable anticipations of a careless and disorderly person, and perhaps even a dark reminiscence of Sairey Gamp scolding, trembling invalids, removing their pillows, or drinking copiously from black bottles, while grim-visaged Betsey Prig looked on with unconcern. With these pictures of the professional nurse before her, she descended to the hall. There, to her surprise, she found a young woman of intelligent face, neat apparel, and quiet demeanor.

"You are —— "

"The nurse, madam."

Saying which, the stranger exhibited a badge inscribed with the words, "Bellevue Hospital Training School for Nurses," and decorated with a stork, the emblem of watchfulness.

The physician now appearing, the nurse listened attentively to his instructions. Her movements, while preparing for duty, inspired with confidence both mother and patient. Her skillful hand prepared the food, her watchful eye anticipated every want. She was calm, patient, and sympathizing; but, though eager to please and cheer the invalid, she did not stoop to simulate an affection she did not feel, nor to express hopes of recovery that could not be realized. The exaction, the impatience incident to illness, seemed but to incite her to renewed effort in behalf of her charge. She met every emergency with knowledge and unruffled spirit. To the physician she proved an invaluable assistant, executing his orders intelligently, and recording accurately the various symptoms as they were developed. She watched the temperature of the room as closely as she did that of the patient, and, while always polite and obliging, was never obsequious. The mother had doubtless heard indirectly of the school of which her efficient nurse was a graduate, but she was, as many others are, unfamiliar with its work and aims.

When the managers of the training school announced, some years since, that they would send nurses to private families in cases of illness, the applications were so few that they were led to fear that this branch of the school would be unsupported, and that the nurses would find themselves deceived regarding their future prospects. But the value of the trained nurse, little known at that time in America, soon began to be recognized, and the demand for such services increased, until, at the present time, there is a greater call for nurses than can be supplied. Many who formerly refused to consider a suggestion to call in a nurse, now eagerly apply for them; and surgeons, in certain instances, have refused to perform operations without the subsequent assistance of a trained nurse.

Before going to a private house, the nurse is carefully instructed by the superintendent. She must not leave it without communicating with her, nor return from her duties without a certificate of conduct and efficiency from the family of the patient or the physician attending. She is expected and urged to bear in mind the importance of the situation, and to show, at all times, self-denial and forbearance. She must take upon herself the entire charge of the sick room. Above all, she is charged to hold sacred any knowledge of its private affairs which she may acquire through her temporary connection with the household. She receives a stipulated sum for her services, but this will not always compensate her for the annoyances with which the position is occasionally beset.

The nurses at the Bellevue school may be divided into two classes: those who study the art of nursing with a view to gaining a livelihood or supporting their families, and those who look forward to a life of usefulness among the poor sick. All are lodged and boarded free of charge during the two years course, and are paid a small sum monthly, while in the school, to defray their actual necessary expenses, and, in order to avoid all distinction between rich and poor, every nurse is expected to receive this pay. The scheme adopted—that developed by Miss Nightingale—demanded in the applicant a combination of requisites the mere enumeration of which appalled many who had been encouraged to seek admission to the school. These are : Good education, strong constitution, freedom from physical defects, including those of sight and hearing, and unexceptionable references. The course of training consists in dressing wounds, applying fomentations, bathing and care of helpless patients, making beds, and managing positions. Then follow the preparation and application of bandages, making rollers and linings of splints. The nurse must also learn how to prepare, cook, and serve delicacies for the invalid. Instruction is given in the best practical methods of supplying fresh air, and of warming and ventilating the sick room. In order to remain through the two years' course and obtain a diploma, still more is required, viz: Exemplary deportment, patience, industry, and obedience. The first year's experience was far from satisfactory. Among seventy-three applicants, hailing from the various States, only twenty-nine were found that gave promise of ability to fill the conditions. Of these, ten were dismissed for various causes before the expiration of the first nine months.

The "Nurses' Home," the headquarters of the school, is No. 426 East Twenty-sixth street, a large and handsome building, erected for the purpose and given to the school by Mrs. W. H. Osborn. From the outside of this building the tastefully arranged curtains and polished panes of its several chambers present a striking contrast to the somber, frowning walls of the great charity hospital opposite. Besides studying from text-books, and attending a systematic course of lectures, the pupils are occupied by the care of the patients in the hospital, and in the general management of the wards. The nurses are taught how to make accurate observations and reports of symptoms for the physicians' use, such as state of pulse, temperature, appetite, intelligence, delirium or stupor, breathing, sleep, condition of wounds, effect of diet, medicine, or stimulant. The nurses are furnished with diplomas, signed by the managers and the examining board of the hospital, when they begin their several careers. Some are called to superintend State and city hospitals, a continually increasing num-her seek private practice, or rather are sought by it, while not a few devote themselves to the sick among the poor.

The value of the service performed by these noble women can not be adequately estimated without visiting the tenement-house district wherein it is performed. They lodge in a house provided for the purpose by the Woman's Branch of the City Missions, by which tney are supported, and are to New York what the " District Nurses" are to London. From early morning until evening they endure fatigue, heat, cold, and storm, in their efforts to relieve the distressed. Neither the gruff responses, nor the ingratitude of those for whom they toil, have, in a single known instance, forced them to cease their work. An equally zealous person, without the advantages of a nurse's training, would fail signally where she would succeed. For the mere attendance on the invalid is not the whole of the service performed by the visiting nurse. She sweeps and cleans the rooms, cooks the food, does the washing, if necessary, goes upon errands—in short, takes the place of the mother, if she be ill. All this has been learned at the training school. Neither illness nor death itself can appall her: she has served a long novitiate in nursing the one, and the other has long since lost its terrors.

In addition to this field in New York City and vicinity, there is an increasing demand throughout the country for experienced nurses to take charge of hospitals and schools. Graduates of the Bellevue school have been called to be superintendents of the nursing departments of the following institutions: Massachusetts General Hospital; Boston City Hospital; New Haven City Hospital; New York Hospital; Mt. Sinai Hospital, New York City; Brooklyn City Hospital; Cook County Hospital, Chicago; St. Luke's Hospital, Denver; Charity Hospital, New Orleans, and the Minneapolis (Minn.) Hospital.

During the twenty years of the Bellevue Training School for Nurses existence, four hundred and twenty-four pupils have received diplomas, more than half of whom are now practicing in New York City.

While Miss Nightingale's theories are the basis of the Training School, its managers have found it necessary to depart from the English system in some important particulars. For instance, Miss Nightingale regards it as indispensable that the superintendent and the nurses should live within the hospital. "Our experience is the reverse of this," say the committee. "American women, being of a sensitive, nervous organization, are at first depressed by the painful aspects of hospital life, and, when they become interested in the work, take it greatly to heart. Hence it is of importance to have a cheerful, comfortable home where they can each day throw off the cares of their profession." To the restfulness of the Home is attributed the exceptional health of the nurses, among whom but few deaths and very few dangerous illnesses have occurred since the opening of the school, almost twenty years ago. Another necessity in an American training school is the abolition of caste. In England the "ward sister" (who has received thorough training) is expected to be a lady, superior in social position and intelligence to the nurses, who are drawn from the class of domestic servants. At

Bellevue, the preliminary examination, and the high standard subsequently exacted, exclude, and are meant to exclude them. But among those who enter there is no distinction. All submit to the same discipline and perform the same duties, none of which, being connected with the sick, is considered menial.

The above article has been carefully condensed from an exhaustive account of the system as practiced at Bellevue, which was published by the Century Magazine. Any one who has had experience with the despotic nurse of the past, the stupid, ignorant and opinionated woman who, in her superannuated days, goes out nursing, will bless the present innovation whereby a young, strong, educated woman is placed in charge of the sick patient. The new professional nurse is the doctor's second, and can determine in his absence what to do to save the life of a patient, and will not predict the death of a sick person if a dog chances to howl in the neighborhood. There could be no better profession for the development of all the finest and most womanly qualities, or one in which the laborer is more worthy of her hire.

—❖CHAPTER XVIII.❖—

Gardening.

T is a matter of surprise that so few American women attempt to earn a living in this way, and that a work that is both pleasant and profitable should be left almost entirely to the foreign born population. Every housewife requires the change of occupation which a few hours of gardening every day in the summer would give her, and if she has no desire to make her work remunerative, she can add a greater beauty and sweetness to her own life and that of her family, by furnishing them with flowers which she raised with her own hands, or increase the attractions of her table by a variety of good, seasonable vegetables during the year. She will also improve her health by the amount of out-door air and exercise the work will require. Gardening is a delightful womanly occupation, cleanly and health-giving. In this country the soil is easily tilled, especially in prairie sections, where stones are so rare that a traveler, in recording their scarcity, said that when his dog saw one he stopped and barked at it. There are many

women to whom a garden would be of great assistance,
for if they possess a plat of land on which they can raise
flowers and vegetables, these may be made to yield them
a good harvest. For instance, if they live within easy
reach of the railway depot or junction where passengers
stop to partake of meals, or to change cars, they can
find a ready sale for small boquets, bunches of flowers
tastefully arranged, or button-hole favors at five or ten
cents each. The tired and depressed traveler would feel
refreshed and cheered by the bright greeting of the
lovely apostles of Flora, and the gardener would realize
a capital for her labor. There are numerous stations in
New England where little bare-footed boys sell small
bunches of arbutus and fragrant clusters of pond
lilies, and often realize enough money to clothe themselves in winter.

Gardening is an occupation particularly well adapted
to women, as it offers a healthy employment in which
delicacy of touch, judgment, calculation and expectation
are all realized without an undue amount of bodily labor.
Nature must be waited upon, encouraged, directed and
watched, to produce a full development of her powers;
and there is a growing tendency to elevate the work of
the gardener, and to present an attractive and interesting field for woman's skill and enterprise in this direction. There are many ladies who devote their time in
spring and summer to the cultivation of flowers and fruit
in the garden, and in winter take a great deal of interest
in their conservatories and greenhouses, in directing and
overseeing their gardens, or take the charge themselves,
and find great enjoyment, as well as health, in the occu-

pation. This pursuit surely presents many attractions to those who are forced to depend upon the work of their own hands for subsisteuce, and it would be far more desirable than constant, sedentary employment such as sewing. With the flowers early vegetables could also be raised and sold to advantage. In the vicinity of cities and towns a market for such commodities can always be found; the supply rarely exceeds the demand. It has been said that flowers will grow better under the kindly care of women, and a widow or single lady, living alone, could invest a very small sum of money in bedding out plants, annuals, vegetables, and fruits, and, with the assistance of a boy of all-work, make quite a tolerable support. Most women to whom such a life would be agreeable and desirable, possess enough strength to attend to the work of superintending and directing matters, and a boy could do the digging, weeding, and watering. In England there are already hundreds of women at work in nurseries and greenhouses, and they do all the grafting, budding, and repotting of plants, with quite as much skill in the handling of them as the male operatives possess.

At the present time flowers are more sought after than ever before, and if women would become more skilled in floriculture they would soon find a large field for their labors. The gains of women gardeners would be of more account than those of seamstresses and shop-girls. Of course there is work in it. I have yet to see the occupation that pays which does not demand head or hand labor. But the work can be so arranged as to leave the hottest hours of the day for rest and leisure. It is really surprising that this branch of labor has not been adopted by woman for profit long ago, as so many ladies devote so much of their time to it for their own gratification. In Germany and Switzerland women are now taught the culture of flowers as a profession, and many women are earning their living as gardeners, not only at their own homes, but in the employment of others. Doubtless there are many young women who would find in the garden not only the natural roses which bloom there, but the roses of health with which to adorn their cheeks. Such an instance recurs to the memory of the writer. A few years ago a young girl who appeared to be fatally ill with consumption went to live with some friends in the country, and amused herself in her moments of temporary strength by playing with the children at making garden. In a little while she found the health-giving properties of air and exercise, and gradually her lungs recovered. She gained flesh, and to-day she is a robust woman, and she declares that a spade was her doctor. She is one of the most successful gardeners in Ohio at the present time.

A STRAWBERRY FARM.

Strawberries offer another excellent avenue to money-making for women. An acre of strawberries will yield from 1,200 to 2,000 quarts. The yield will never be less, and it is often much more. In a fair season an acre of strawberry farm will pay a net profit of from $150 to $175 per acre. The first berries command a ready market at $1 a quart; but at an average of ten cents a quart from first to last, the farm will pay its owner handsomely. Twenty acres of strawberries in the State of Georgia brought in $1,300 in cash to its owner, by the middle of April, and at that date the season had only begun, as the North is still in the embrace of winter at that time. The price then was thirty cents a quart. Speculators visit strawberry farms both North and South, and offer a certain sum per quart for the berries on the vines, which pays the owner a handsome sum without the lifting of a hand. A lady who lived in a home of luxury in Freeport, Ill., made a handsome fortune out of strawberries. She kept a man to work the farm, hired children to pick the berries, and took orders from commission houses and families herself, not disdaining to deliver the berries from her own carriage or wagon, both of which she handled herself. In the South, strawberries pay better than cotton for women to handle, and in the North the home berry is in excellent demand when the Southern season is over. The business is both a pleasant and remunerative one, and essentially a feminine occupation.

In regard to the labor of gardening, a forcible writer, in speaking of the Dutch, Flemish, and German women, who help the husbands and fathers in the field, says:

"The women positively delight in this free, active and nomadic life, and one of the chief charms was the astonishing health and strength they attained. Their limbs became muscular, they had the digestion of ostriches, and aches and pains were unknown to them; they, in fact, enjoyed the most exquisite of all human sensations, perfect health. How many American women enjoy that for even five years after they are sixteen. If the labor is not excessive it is desirable. It produces the strong, hardy women who rear a stalwart race. Half the fine ladies who now find a few turns on the piazza almost too much for them, would be all the better for a graduated scale of garden work. Beginning with a quarter of an hour a day, they would find at the close of a month that they could easily do their two hours, and that they ate and slept as they had never done before, while they forgot that any such evils as nerves had an existence."

WHAT ONE WOMAN DID.

Some years ago Miss Belle Clinton, of Nevada, Story county, Northwestern Iowa, was a school teacher full of life, health, fun, and enterprise, rosy of cheek and sturdy of limb, quite too full of health and vigor to sit down contentedly and day by day teach the young idea how to shoot, at so much a head, so she concluded to do something that would bring in more money, and at the same time furnish more scope for her powers, and what she did do can not be better told than in her own straightforward way:

"I saved $160 from the money I earned teaching school, borrowed a span of horses from my father, rigged up a prairie schooner, and started with my little brother for Dakota. I never had such a good time in my life, or such an appetite, and everybody was polite and pleasant to me. I received the utmost courtesy everywhere. Rough, rude men would come to our camp, and after I had talked to them awhile offer to build my fire, and actually bring water to me. We went up through the wheat country, which they call the Jim River country. It is about one hundred miles east from the Missouri Fort Sully. I homesteaded one hundred and sixty acres of land. Then I took up a timber claim of one hundred and sixty acres more, and with the help of a hired man set out ten acres of trees. This gave me one hundred and sixty acres more, so I then had three hundred and twenty acres. The trees were young locust and apple and black walnut sprouts. I sowed a peck of locust beans, a pint of apple seed, and two bushels of black walnuts in our garden, in Iowa, one year before. These sprouts were little fellows, and we could set them out just as fast as we could get them into the ground. I believe my three thousand little black walnut sprouts will be worth twenty dollars apiece by the time they are fifteen years old. My locust trees will some time fence the whole country.

"Next we built a shanty and broke up five acres of land, and in the fall we returned to Iowa to spend the winter. In the spring went back with more black walnut and locust sprouts, and took up another claim of one hundred and sixty acres. The trees are just what I wanted to plant anyway, and they will pay better than any wheat crops that could be raised, only I must wait for them several years; but I can wait."

Is not this a splendid example of what pluck, determination and energy will accomplish ?

Here is the story of a young woman who, at twenty years of age, was the owner of four hundred and eighty acres of as fine black prairie soil as can be found in the United States, and all of it gained by her own indomitable pluck and energy. It pays to be enterprising. What woman has done woman can do, and Miss Clinton has positively illustrated the saying that "Where there's a will there's a way." No young woman with the true American spirit can read the story of Belle Clinton without being stimulated to the greatest effort; she will ask herself "What can I do to become independent," and suiting the action to the word will go onward to success.

YOUNG WOMEN INVESTING IN LAND IN DAKOTA.

A young widow who came to Lisbon, Dakota, took a pre-emption claim to 160 acres, proved up and got a title to her land, then took another claim under the homestead law of 160 acres more, on which she resided, and as the possessor of 320 acres of the richest soil in this country, she was, of course, considered worth a handsome fortune in her own right.

Here is another example of this same enterprising spirit that is the secret of success in every case. The author will feel herself amply repaid for writing this book, if through its influence young women will realize the abundant opportunities which lie open before them, and encouraged by the examples of these noble women who have succeeded in life, will put forth their own best efforts to reap as great a reward.

❖CHAPTER XIX.❖

Raising ❖ Poultry.

DOES POULTRY PAY?

F proper care is taken of poultry there is no doubt that it pays. No business can be made profitable without careful attention. A great many people feed their poultry regularly, but neglect to give them drink, and then say that it does not pay to keep poultry.

"The best drink," says an author on the subject, "that can be furnished for hens, is sour milk, and, if possible, it should always be by them. Scraps of meat, fish skins, etc., are excellent for fowls. Do not feed on clear corn or meal, but vary their food as much as possible. In the summer feed once a day, but in the winter give them a second feed just before they go to roost. Always give just what they will eat up clean. Hens fed this way will lay all winter if they are of the right breed. The Brown Leghorn hens will lay all the year round. Brahmas are also excellent.

Mrs. Eliza Twynham had a flock of fourteen hens, and

during one summer sold twenty-five dollars worth of eggs and raised a flock of chickens. Her hens had proper care, and they well repaid it. This was keeping poultry on a small scale, but had the lady gone into the business she would have made it pay handsomely. The eggs of fancy fowls sell at $3 a dozen for breeding purposes, so that more money is realized in keeping a small number of a choice breed. They will require a little more care, but will amply repay the trouble. The owners of fancy hens often sell their eggs to neighbors at an ordinary price—25 cents a dozen—but they first dip them in boiling water to prevent incubation, should there be any deception in the matter.

It is quite a curiosity to visit one of those fancy hen farms, which are frequent in all the States, and often kept up with great care, and even elegance. Their houses are heated, ventilated, provided with all patent appliances for their comfort, and kept in apple pie order. They have stairs by which they ascend to their roost, and they are provided with a court yard, in which they can enjoy the air and sun light. These three things fowls must have, if they would thrive—air, light, and exercise. They must not only be kept free from chicken lice, but their flesh, if they are to be sold, must be of fine quality. While the eggs of fancy fowls pay the largest profit, the flesh of the ordinary yellow-legged barnyard fowl can not be improved upon. Much judgment must be used by people who sell fowls for market, if they wish to gain a reputation for their poultry. Cockerels, pullets, and fat laying hens are good marketable wares, but a hen that has just thrown off a brood, or is ready to go on a nest of eggs, is not in condition for the table. Any one living near a large city can get high prices for early spring chickens, a pair of them being worth $1.50 in February or March, and commanding a high price all the season.

MONEY IN EGGS.

The time has come when the business of egg-production will take a fixed place among the food industries of the country. Eggs are a healthy and nourishing substitute for meat, and are generally cheaper in proportion to their nutritive qualities. It is estimated that the annual production in the United States amounts to 12,000,000,000, of which 3,500,000,000 are sent to New York. Great Britain imports 900,000,000 eggs from the continent. They represent the value of 15,000,000 more, while Ireland furnishes 500,000,000 in addition, and the home production is nearly equal to the importation from the continent. The business of poultry raising is a safe and pleasant one—safe in a pecuniary way, because there is a very small amount of capital invested, and pleasant, because it gives woman what she needs, a healthy out-door exercise. Three dozen good common fowls will furnish the stock in trade to start with, and a clean, dry, comfortable shed, with nooks and corners for them to lay in, will answer as well, if not better, than a patent hen house with sanded floor, where the hens go up a flight of stairs to bed, and lay their eggs in nests as fine as jewel boxes. Get both hens and advice from a successful poultry raiser, and be careful of having too fine poultry for the purpose of selling eggs as an article of diet.

No eater can discriminate between boiled eggs at three
dollars a dozen and boiled eggs at twenty-five cents a
dozen, if both are fresh; the money lies in the breed,
which is a matter of fancy rather than of fact, and the
three dollar a dozen eggs cost fifty cents apiece to raise
them often, high-bred fowls being so delicate they are
apt to catch cold if they get their feet wet. With the
barnyard fowl it is a different affair; it keeps itself in
fine flesh by running after its grub; it has settled
domestic habits, and is not inclined to be sick and ail-
ing, and it lays a large, good looking egg that is both
sweet and rich. During the fall season hens that run at
large have the grain fields to glean from, and the flesh of
such fowls is superior to any cake-fed birds. There is
money made from the incubator, but machine raised
birds are inferior to the mother-hatched, and weaken as
they grow to maturity, and the whole business is a
trouble and often a serious loss, although some few are
successful in producing a delicate article of spring
chicken. It is easy to experiment in this business,
which can be carried on without interfering in domestic duties or other work. The following brief sketch
may be of interest to those who contemplate going into
that branch of speculation.

TWO WOMEN IN BUSINESS.

"In the spring of 1876," writes Miss Helen Wilmane,
"finding myself in a position where it was necessary to
make some exertion for my own living, and being also
averse to the kind of work usually delegated to my sex,
I formed a partnership with another woman whose situ-

ation was similar to my own, and we went into the poultry business together.

"After we had decided what we wished to do, it required
a vigorous looking about to find the place we wanted.
But we did find it on the banks of Clear Lake, well up
towards the northern boundary. A farmer who occupied a large tract of land, and had built a fine house
near the center of it, left his old one standing in an isolated corner, the picture of loneliness and despair, as
seen through the eyes of the rich, but a very haven of
rest for two tempest-tossed and homeless women such as
we were. And then, too, it was on the banks of the
lake, a fact that made amends for many disadvantages.
Oh! that lake, thirty miles long and ten miles wide, dotted with evergreen islands! It comes back to me now
like the memory of a lost Paradise!

Behold us, then, settled with one hundred hens, fifteen ducks, and a dozen turkeys, Mr. Worth trusted
us with a ton of wheat, and we were equipped. The
ducks took to the water, where they seemed to earn
their own living, as they treated our store of provisions
with contempt. They waddled home every night to be
shut up, and we found their eggs in the pen every morning. We sold our hens eggs and set our hens on duck
eggs. As we kept an account of all our transactions, I
will now refer to my book, which I still keep in remembrance of some of the happiest days of my life.

" I find that on March twentieth we had forty hens
sitting on ten eggs each—four hundred eggs in all—with
seventeen young ducks hatched out. On April twentieth we had thirty-six hens sitting on ten eggs each,

three hundred and twenty-seven nice, healthy young ducks. A month later we closed out the duck factory, with five hundred and thirty small fry on hand.

"Nothing gives me more pleasure than to see things grow—living animals more especially. Our little ducks were a perpetual study to us. Many of them were individualized by special characteristics, so much so that we named them accordingly. I am sure we brought little science to bear on our poultry raising, but we made a very fair success of it. We lived comfortably and happily, and realized nearly three hundred dollars when we sold off our surplus stock in the fall. We thought it much better than taking positions in establishments not our own. We were free, and we appreciated the situation. And then the occupation itself was full of interest. Never a day passed that we did not find something to laugh at amongst our numerous family.

"We carried our poultry through another year, and with still greater success. We would probably be engaged in it yet but for a male biped, who, perceiving how well my partner could live without him, made the discovery that he could not live without her. This dissolved our partnership, and terminated a never-to-be-forgotten period of my life."

Geese are abundantly raised in the suburbs of cities by the foreign population. They are noisy birds, and must be within easy reach of water. Their feathers are more valuable than their flesh in this country, where the turkey is the favorite of the table. The last is a very profitable fowl, but difficult to raise. Eternal vigilance is the price of turkeys. The young die on the slightest provocation, and the mother-bird is a very poor protector of her young. The larger the flock the safer the birds, and the more probability that the young will grow to maturity. They require a good deal of food, carefully prepared. Tender greens and Indian meal, wet up in a mass and crumbled to them, are fattening. They should be June birds to be in good order at Thanksgiving. They like a hot, dry season.

Pigeons, if kept in large quantities, are profitable, as they are always in demand in the markets. They will range with the fowls at feeding time, and cost little or nothing to keep. Ducks are troublesome, but they pay very well for their keep. They must be raised near a large pond, or they will stray off in search of water. It is just as well to keep all the different varieties of poultry, as one will create a market for another. But hens are in demand all the year round; ducks, geese, and turkeys only at the holidays and during the winter season. A woman who will make a specialty of sending choice, well-dressed, dry-picked poultry to market, can not fail to make a handsome profit out of her work, which is a sphere of labor pre-eminently suited to her domestic tastes.

A compiler of industrial statistics has this to say concerning poultry:

VALUE OF THE POULTRY BUSINESS.

"Every business that increases national wealth and promotes individual comfort and prosperity possesses an interest to the philanthropic commensurate to its importance. It is impracticable for census reports to fairly represent every industry. Should it be done in the simple matter of poultry and eggs, the figures would astonish those who have given the subject only a mere passing thought. I am certain that the value and importance of the poultry business, as a source of national wealth, has not been fully appreciated. Judging from the census reports of the State of New York, I am led to believe that the actual value of poultry in the United States is scarcely realized.

"There can be but little if any less than 4,000,000 farmers' families in the United States that keep poultry—hens simply. It is reasonable to suppose that on an average each family keeps at least 12 hens, and that each hen lays 100 eggs annually. This would give an aggregate of 400,000,000 dozen eggs, which, at a net valuation of 10 cents a dozen to the producer, would make the net proceeds to the farmers $40,000,000 ! Does this startle the reader ?

"In New York alone, twenty years ago, the census report set down the actual value of poultry at $3,000,000. The city of Boston, according to statistics, expended for eggs in 1869 $2,000,000, and for poultry the same year $3,000,000, making the enormous sum of $5,000,000 expended in a third-class city for poultry and eggs. I have no doubt but the estimate of $25,-000,000 for eggs is a low one, while that of poultry sold would swell the amount of the poultry interest to more than $250,-000,000. And this refers to hens alone. The additional amount in geese, turkeys, ducks, guinea fowls and pigeons I will not attempt to consider."

⊸⟊CHAPTER XX.⟊⊸

Bee-Keeping.

SUITABLE EMPLOYMENT FOR WOMEN.

" Oh! the transporting, rapturous scene,
    That rises to our sight!
Sweet fields arrayed in living green,
    And rivers of delight!
There generous *bloom* in all the dales
    And mountain sides will grow,
       There rocks and hills, and brooks and vales
        With milk and *honey* flow."

If I follow the wild bee home,
    And fell with a ringing stroke
The popular shaft of the oak,
    What shall I taste in the comb
And the honey that fills the comb?

BEE-KEEPING, although a laborious employment, demands no great outlay of strength at one time. It embraces the performance of many little items, which require skill and gentleness, more than muscle. The hand of woman, from nature, habit, and education, has acquired an ease of motion which is agreeable to the sensibilities of bees, and her breath is seldom obnoxious to their olfactories, by reason of tobacco or beer.

Women have demonstrated that the making of hives and surplus boxes is no objection, as they have purchased them in the flat, nailed and painted them. The hiving of swarms is neither more difficult nor dangerous than the washing of windows or milking. The right time to extract honey, or to put on, or take off surplus boxes, requires no more tact or skill to determine than the proper fermentation of bread, or the right temperature of the oven required for baking. Woman is in her allotted sphere while raising queens and nursing weak colonies, or caring for the honey when off the hive.

The most powerful argument in view of the suitableness of bee-keeping for woman is this: That it is something she can do at home, and not interfere with her domestic duties. Many women of small means have young children depending upon their exertions for support, and remunerative work to be performed at home brings very little in the market of to-day. For instance, the making of overalls at five cents a pair, and shirts at fifty cents per dozen. She is compelled to accept less pay than men for the same service performed. We had a friend, chosen as principal of a school on account of her efficiency, but who was compelled to accept lower wages than her predecessor, who was a man, and dismissed for his incompetency. But we have never found a dealer unscrupulous enough to offer less for a pound of honey, because it was produced by a woman.

To engage in bee-keeping as a business, it is necessary to understand the nature and wants of the honey-bee, and a knowledge of its management. This may be obtained in theory, by a study (not merely a reading) of all the standard works extant, and journals devoted to the science of bee culture. Add to this the practical use of the knowledge obtained in some large apiary for a year or two, if possible, and then you will be prepared to look for a location (as the young M. D. would say). "Do not try to build up by crowding out some one already established; there is room enough for all the bee-keepers of the United States for some time to come."

If surplus honey be the object sought, get the very best unoccupied field, if possible, where soft maple, red raspberry, white clover and basswood abound, without special reference to railroad facilities. If the rearing and sale of superior colonies and queens be the object in view, mail and railroad facilities are very important.

Thus armed and equipped as the law directs, a few hundred dollars may be invested in bees, with better prospect of satisfactory returns, than an equal amount in almost any other direction.

There are many successful apiarists in this country who are women, and their number is yearly increasing. It is a healthful and delightful pursuit, and every woman who engages in it, with some knowledge of the habits of bees, and the method of taking care of them, will be fully rewarded for her trouble by a fair measure of pecuniary success. There is no prettier sight than the long rows of bee hives back of the farm house, flanked by a shady orchard, and occupied by a busy community of these little artistic workers, whose industry is a watchword in the ranks of humanity, and who do their work by instinct so much better than many human workers do theirs by the higher gift of intellect. There is so much to observe about these little people that she would be a dull scholar who did not find many a lesson to study and remember in watching their wonderful system, their strict discipline, industry, and the exquisite delicacy of their work, their allegiance to their queen, and the remarkable instincts which govern them in their busy hives. Bees are no longer a primitive people. They are educated now and surrounded with the energetic contrivances of civilization.

PROGRESSIVE BEE CULTURE—PAST, PRESENT, AND PROSPECTIVE.

Scientific bee-culture may properly be said in this country to be confined to the last forty years. The first bees in America were imported into Pennsylvania about the year 1627. We also have accounts of bees being brought from England to New York and Virginia about the year 1685. From that time forward they have been disseminated to every part of the United States and Canada. Until the last thirty years all these were of the German or black variety. Until 1851 they were kept in the loggum, box-hive, or straw-skep. The hives were generally set in some out-of-the-way place, and but little attention given them, except at swarming or robbing time. The weak ones were often brimstoned in the fall, and the little honey they had was about the only surplus the owner obtained. Sometimes a cap of twenty or thirty pounds of white honey taken from the strongest colonies was considered quite an acquisition. The man who could protect himself in veil and gauntlets, envelop himself in smoke, and then approach a hive in early morning, burst off the top, and cut out thirty or forty pounds of honey, was considered quite a bee man.

In the year 1851, the Rev. L. L. Langstroth invented

the movable comb hive, which bears his name. About the same time the Rev. Dr. Dzierzon, of Germany, also made a similar invention in Europe. From that time forward an entirely new era in bee-culture was inaugurated, both in the Old World and the New. Discovery after discovery in the natural history of the honey bee was made, and as truth gradually came to the light, superstition was dissipated, and instead of a "venom-tipped warrior," always ready for fight, bees were found susceptible of education and control, the same as other farm stock. Colonies were not only increased at pleasure by this system, but the bees were effectually guarded against many of their enemies, and vast stores of white honey obtained where almost none had been secured. Literature upon subjects pertaining to bee-culture, for the first time began to assume a respectable place. The able work of Langstroth, and numerous articles from his pen, as well as from Samuel Wagner, Quinby, and many others, soon developed a desire for reading upon this subject, which resulted in establishing the American Bee Journal, and a special department devoted to bee-culture in nearly all the leading agricultural papers in the United States. The number of bee papers has been increased in this country in the last few years, until at present we have many, both weekly and monthly. Also, such able works as the "Manual of the Apiary," by Prof. A. J. Cook; "Quinby's New Bee-Keeping," by L. C. Root; "A. B. C. of Bee-Culture," by A. I. Root, and a host of smaller works by able authors.

Many other movable comb hives, besides that of Langs-troth's, have been invented, each claiming some excel

lence over others, but the original invention still holds
its own, and is adopted by a majority of the leading
apiarists of America, and remains substantially as it left
the hands of the great inventor forty years ago. Most
other hives are complicated, and have many useless
appendages, defeating the very object for which they
were invented. They look very attractive, and work
nicely at a fair, or on a show table, but, with a swarm of
bees in them, all their movable and adjustable parts are
waxed firmly together, and to loosen them jars them and
makes the bees hard to control.

Improvements in receptacles for nice comb honey have
been nearly as great as those of the hive. In place of
the old box cap, we now have the neat and convenient
prize section box with snow-white combs of honey, which
may be kept in virgin beauty, and free from waste almost
indefinitely. The honey extractor is a long stride in progress, which can scarcely be realized. Its numerous benefits, only those who have used can estimate. By it the
amount of honey obtained can be more than doubled,
and many difficulties in successful bee-keeping obviated,
while the delicious sweet, free from wax and all foreign
substances, presents to the eye and palate a treat not to
be despised.

There are in America about 3,000,000 colonies of bees,
but our reports are from less than a quarter of a million,
or one-twelfth of the whole. If the one-twelfth that are
reported are a fair average of the whole, then the crop of
American honey for one season amounts to 120,000,000
pounds. If we call it only one hundred millions, it is
worth $15,000,000.00. Surely the industry is of suffi-

cient magnitude to satisfy the most enthusiastic of its devotees.

There is a charming little work called "The Blessed Bees," written by a minister, but wholly wanting in a most important quality, veracity. At least bee men so regard it. I give an extract from its pages as a specimen of enthusiasm on paper, and which under favorable circumstances, might have been true. The writer says :

"Bee-keepers will always be of two classes. First there will be those who will keep a few swarms for pleasure and profit, but whose main business is something else. There are very large numbers of men and women in country, village, or city, who could keep a few swarms of bees, and who could derive from the care of them health, recreation, and a small profit. Let such get a book on bee-culture that is up with the times, subscribe for a good journal devoted to bee-culture, get a swarm of bees, and go to work. They will find the health and pleasure that always come from an avocation that takes the mind from the regular work, and they will get enough profit to pay them for their time.

"The second class of bee-keepers will be those who make it their principal or only business, who follow it for a livelihood. There are not a few who already do this, and the number is increasing every year. There is at present no branch of rural industry that offers better chances for success to the intelligent, energetic man or woman. Begin slowly, learn the business, advance surely, and soon a healthful and delightful business can be built up which will give a fair income. There are now in different parts of the country many who number their hives by the hundred—a few who number them by the thousand.

"In the course of one year devoted to a careful practical

study of bees and bee-culture, the whole business can be thoroughly learned in a general way, but there will be constant experiments to make, and it is only by experience that the best knowledge of the industry can be gained. To follow the business with success will demand the same business qualities that command success in other callings. There will be much in location and in favorable conditions. Eternal vigilance is the price of honey as truly as it is of liberty."

"The investment in the business was $830.81. I had a clear cash gain of 360 per cent." This was for seven months work among the bees. His gain in stock was $780. Adding the cash gain to this makes a total gain of $3,776.72. There was to show for this either cash on hand or bees worth more than their estimated value. Bee culturists are apt to consider the story in this little book romantic and not of practical worth, but it is delightful reading, and there are some truths in it. Professor Cook gives the gain as frequently reaching 500 per cent. But these are exceptional cases. The "Blessed Bees" is so full of enthusiasm that it helps one to make an effort in that direction, and it gives the bright side in the most delightful manner, as when the writer says, in speaking of the product:

"I classified the honey into four grades, and named the grades Apple Blossoms, White Clover, Linn, and Fall Flowers. These names designated as accurately as any I could think of the exact sources whence the honey was gathered, and they were attractive names that would call up in minds of all, visions of the beautiful country in the time of apple-bloom;

'One boundless blush, one white-empurpled shower
Of mingled blossoms.'

Of the starry carpet of green and white which in June the clover spreads over hills and valleys; of the honey-dripping lindens from among whose blooming branches the eager bees send down a soothing murmur that lulls one like the perfume of the Lotus; and of the wild forest nooks and lonely swamps, and brambly hill-sides that assume such gorgeous hues when golden-rod and asters and coreopsis fling out their brilliant banners in August and September."

All this might be practically true, but authorities on bees say that the whole story existed only in the prolific brain of the writer. The Bee-keeper's Guide; or, the Manual of the Apiary, by A. J. Cook, Professor of Entomology at the State Agricultural College, Lansing, Michigan, is a reliable and scientific work on the subject. It costs, bound in cloth, $1.25. There are many valuable text-books, any of which can be obtained from Baker & Taylor, 742 Broadway, New York City. I give this gratuitous information for the benefit of women who, living remote from cities, may be uncertain where to send or whom to address.

TRAVELING BEES—A CAR LOAD OF BEES.

On Saturday a car was switched on the East Tennessee & Virginia Railroad, and moved south.

It was filled with bee-hives. One hundred and forty of the latest styles of bee-hives, piled systematically on top of each other, and, to the foreground, a philosopher with his bed and board.

"Where are you going to take your bees?"

"To Florida for the winter. My name is Thomas McFarland Jackson, and I live in Northern Missouri.]

have large apiaries that are forced to lie idle in the winter. I am going to take this car load of hives to Florida, where they can get honey every day in the year. As soon as the clover is out again in Northern Missouri I will take them back there."

" Will it pay you to move them ?"

"I think so. It costs me less than a dollar a hive for transportation, and each hive will have from $6 to $7 worth of honey in it when I bring them back. That is what Italian bees, I sent to Florida last year, did last winter. Only Italian bees will thrive in Florida, as the moths eat up the common bees."

" Will you live in the open air there?"

"I am going to camp around with my bees. I believe I will bring back about $1,000 worth of honey in hives that would otherwise lie idle all the winter and be empty in the spring."

This migratory bee-keeping has been practiced from the earliest ages. In Egypt it has been kept up for thousands of years. Mr. T. F. Bingham, of Michigan, and others have practiced it; but nearly all have abandoned it, because it did not pay them.

Mr. Perrine, of Chicago, Ill., some years ago, lost several thousand dollars in a similar manner. He had a floating apiary, arranged to run up the Mississippi river from New Orleans, following the bloom till he was to reach Minnesota; but it did not work. Too many bees were lost, and the projector is now wiser, and $10,000 poorer.

FIVE HUNDRED POUNDS FROM ONE COLONY.

I commenced the season, about June 1, with 30 colonies, almost destitute of honey; increased to 65, in fine
condition for winter, and obtained 4,538 lbs. of honey
(807 of comb, in 2-lb. boxes, and 3,731 of extracted); I
have about 300 lbs. besides, stored away, and not counted
in my report. My best yield from one colony was 486
lbs. of extracted. I think that I took enough comb
honey from it, not included in count, to make over 500
lbs. I fed about 3 lbs. of sugar in spring, but the bees
received no other help; got no increase. Time of extracting: July 5, 42 lbs.; 15, 26 lbs.; 21, 68 lbs.; 28, 75 lbs.;
Aug. 24, 90 lbs.; Sept. 7, 105 lbs.; 19 and 20, 80 lbs.
Had I used three instead of two stories for surplus, I
think I could have obtained at least 600 lbs. I was
crowded too much with other work to attend to it as I
should, or I could have made a much better showing for
my bees. The cell producing this queen was obtained
from a strong colony of bees which started only this one
cell, during the basswood harvest. Could I have another
such season (which was very poor at the commencement), and such a queen, I think that I could get 800 or
1,000 lbs. of honey. If cold weather kills bees (which I
think it often does), we may look for considerable mor-
tality among our pets next spring. The lowest temperature noticed here, so far, is 35° below zero; it was 29°
below on Feb. 2, at sun rising; and away below every
morning since. My bees all answered to the roll call a
few days ago, and seemed in good condition. I have

them in a good dry cellar, with about 5 inches of leaves packed above most of them.

W. C. NUTT.

Mrs. L. B. Baker reports, in the Bee-Keepers' Magazine, that in the first year she had two swarms of bees which gave her a profit of $103.15, or $51.56 per swarm. The second year she made a profit of $59.85 per hive. Mrs. John Baker, of Wyandotte, Michigan, has a few hives in her beautiful, well-kept garden, which yield her an annual supply of about five hundred pounds of delightful honey, about half of which she sells or exchanges for groceries. This lady keeps summer boarders, does her own cooking, takes care of a large flower garden, and finds time to devote to intellectual pursuits.

Mrs. L. Harrison, of Peoria, Ill., is another bee-keeper, and one who is considered an authority upon all matters pertaining to the apiary.

SUPERSTITIONS ABOUT BEES.

Curious superstitions prevail in England as to the relation between bees and their owners. A magazine contributor mentions several of these fancies as follows:

"All of 'em dead, sir—all the thirteen. What a pity it is!"

"What's a pity, Mrs. —— ? Who's dead ?"

"The bees, to be sure, sir. Mrs. Blank, when she buried her husband, forgot to give the bees a bit of mourning, and now, sir, all the bees be dead, though the hives be pretty nigh full of honey. What a pity 'tis folks will be so forgetful!"

The good woman continued to explain that whenever the owner or part owner of a hive died, it was requisite to place little bits of black stuff on the hive, otherwise the bees would follow the example of their owner. Her husband, who listened while this scrap of folk-lore was being communicated by his wife, now added:

"My wife, sir, be always talking a lot of nonsense, sir; but this about the bees is true, for I've seen it myself."

This custom of putting the bees in mourning is very common, and is strictly adhered to, from an apprehension of its omission being attended with fatal consequences.

At Cherry-Burton, on a death in the family, a scrap of black crape is applied to each hive, on the occasion of the funeral, and pounded funeral biscuit, soaked in wine, is placed at the entrance to the hive.

"A neighbor of mine," says another writer on this subject, "bought a hive of bees at the auction of the goods of a farmer who had recently died. The bees seemed very sickly and not likely to thrive, when my neighbor's servant bethought him that they had never been put in mourning for their late master. On this he got a piece of crape and tied it to a stick, which he fastened to the hive. After this the bees recovered, and when I saw them they were in a very flourishing condition—a result which was unhesitatingly attributed to their having been put in mourning.

A singular superstition prevailed formerly in Devonshire—the custom of turning round the bee hives that belonged to the deceased, if he owned any, at the moment the corpse was carried out of the house. The following painful circumstance occurred at the funeral of a rich old farmer. Just as the corpse was placed in the hearse, and the visitors were arranged in order for the procession of the funeral, some one called out, "Turn the bees." A servant, who had no knowledge of such a custom, instead of turning the hives round, lifted them up and then laid them down on their side. The bees, thus suddenly invaded, instantly attacked and fastened on the visitors. It was in vain they tried to escape, for the bees precipitately followed, and left their stings as marks of their indignation. A general confusion took place, and it was some time before the friends of the deceased could be rallied together to proceed to the interment.

Another old superstition was that of ringing a bell when the bees swarmed, or beating on pans, ringing gongs, or making a great noise, which was supposed to induce them to settle. This is done in parts of Michigan and the prairies of Illinois to-day, and, unlike many other old customs that seem to have no meaning, it originated in a known law. It was a rule in Germany, that when bees swarmed, if a hive left home and settled upon some other place, that whoever owned the place on which they alighted should become their rightful possessor. This law was not available, however, if the owner of the bees followed and kept them in sight all the way; but in order to prove that he had done this, he was compelled, as he ran, to ring a large bell, and thus make his presence and his rightful ownership known.

People, in old times, were very ignorant of the habits or workings of the bees. They were afraid of them. Bee-stings were not then considered good for neuralgia, nor was there any neuralgia. The colony was said to be ruled by a king, whom all obeyed. The drones were females which laid all the eggs, and the workers were— well, only stingers. In short, scarcely anything was known about bees, and success was attributed almost entirely to luck.

Our own poet, John Greenleaf Whittier, has embodied the funeral superstition in a poem, which is so characteristically beautiful that I give it entire.

TELLING THE BEES.

Here is the place; right over the hill
　Runs the path I took.
You can see the gap in the old wall still,
　And the stepping stones in the shallow brook.

There is the house, with the gate red-barred,
　And the poplars tall;
And the barn's brown length and the cattle-yards,
　And the white horns tossing above the wall.

There are the bee-hives ranged in the sun;
　And down by the brink
Of the brook are her poor flowers, weed o'errun;
　Pansy and daffodil, rose and pink.

A year has gone, as the tortoise goes,
　Heavy and slow;
And the same rose blows, and the same sun glows,
　And the same brook sings of a year ago.

There 's the same sweet clover smell in the breeze.
   And the June sun warm
Tangles his wings of fire in the trees,
   Setting as then over Fernside farm.

I mind me how, with a lover's care,
   From my Sunday coat
I brushed off the burs and smoothed my hair,
   And cooled at the brook side my brow and throat.

Since we parted a month had passed,
   To love, a year;
Down through the beeches I looked at last,
   On the little red gate and the well sweep near.

I can see it all now, the slantwise rain
   Of light through the leaves;
The sun-downs blaze on her window pane—
   The blooms of her roses under the eaves.

Just the same as a month before—
   The house and the trees,
The barn's brown gable, the vine by the door;
   Nothing changed but the hives of bees.

Before them, under the garden wall,
   Forward and back,
Went drearily singing the chore-girl small,
   Draping each hive with a shred of black.

Trembling I listened; the summer sun
   Had the chill of snow,
For I knew she was telling the bees of one
   Gone on the journey we all must go.

Then I said to myself, " My Mary weeps,
   For the dead to-day;
Haply her blind old grandsire sleeps
   The fret and pain of his age away.'

But her dog whined low; on the door-way sill
  With his cane to his chin,
The old man sat, and the chore-girl still
  Sung to the bees stealing out and in.

And the song she was singing ever since
  In my ear sounds on—
' Stay at home pretty bees, fly not hence,
  Mistress Mary is dead and gone."

N.

CHAPTER XXI

Dressmakers and Dressmaking.

FLUENT and sensible writer in the Bazar Dressmaker says that the highest ambition of a young dressmaker is to stand at the head of her profession as a cutter and fitter. Reader, if you have that ambition, and have patience to go forth, step by step, learning each lesson as you go, you will be rewarded with success. Bear in mind that Pingat and Worth, now the two greatest dressmakers in the world, were once as ignorant of dressmaking as you are. It was by gathering up the little things and binding them together that they became great.

In the United States there are many who excel in trimming, draping, and in giving an air of style, but who are poor fitters. A want of this knowledge precludes the possibility of their reaching the highest position in their profession. The difficulty in gaining the higher art is the want of a knowledge of the lower art. A young woman who wants to become an expert in the art must begin at the beginning. All knowledge outside of this is superficial, uncertain, and unsatisfactory.

The question which every young woman is likely to ask herself is this: "How shall I excel as a cutter and fitter?" To the mass of dressmakers, and especially to those who are about to start in the business, no theme can be of deeper interest than this. Hundreds of young women long, with an intense anxiety, to learn the art of cutting and fitting thoroughly.

Now, it is an actual fact, that, as a rule, dressmakers are deplorably ignorant of even the first principles of their profession. The people are beginning to open their eyes to this fact, and schools for dressmaking are now established in various parts of the country. But it is not convenient to take long journeys, or spend a season, at great expense, away from home, in order to learn the art, if it can as readily be learned from textbooks at home. It has been a favorite boast with the average dressmaker that she never served an apprenticeship at the business, but "picked it up," a fact patent to all of her customers. Ladies are tired of this slipshod way of having their dresses made, and now that every second family in a village goes abroad, something after the French style of fitting and making is demanded. American ladies use rich goods. The wife and daughters of a tradesman dress in silks and satins every day, and the American woman has a good figure when it is not distorted by a wretchedly fitting dress. So the village seamstress may as well awaken to the fact that she must take a preparatory course of instruction before putting her shears into the rich materials now used in even plain outfits.

If she is not obstinately and blindly wedded to her native ignorance, and prejudiced, she will soon learn the few simple but also perfect and absolute rules which govern the whole business, and find that when she has once mastered them it will be absolutely impossible to make a mistake. In these days of progress, when a new creed is formulated, there is room left for amendments. So in the simplest designs of use in our everyday work we need to leave a margin for improvements. Each year will change the cut of a sleeve, the length of a waist, the slope of a shoulder—it may be only an inch—but as some one has wittily said, an inch taken from or added to the length of a nose would make a vast difference to the other features. The old-time seamstress who went round spring and fall into country homes, carried her patterns with her, and they served for years in the same families, the difference being a seam folded in or let out. It is estimated that there are eight thousand dressmakers in the City of New York, exclusively engaged in making ladies' and children's dresses. This includes more than three hundred men dressmakers. The wages rate from four dollars to sixty dollars per week. The price is graded according to ability. In one establishment in New York there are sixty men dressmakers employed. The average wages are thirty-one dollars a week. Some make as high as fifty dollars per week. In all large cities, and especially in the City of New York, there is a constant demand for good fitters, at salaries ranging from fifteen to forty dollars per week.

There are hundreds of young women throughout the country who have the taste and the talent to fill such a situation. All they want is opportunity and a knowledge of the laws which govern the art of dressmaking. Every dressmaker should be able to conscientiously answer yes to the following questions before she applies for a responsible position :

THE DRESSMAKERS' QUESTION CHART.

1. Do I understand the art of cutting and fitting, and am I able, without delay or fault, to make a dress and send it home complete, without refitting or trying on ?

2. Do I understand the English system of drafting or cutting by rule—that is, am I able to take the measure, and with the same inch tape cut the garment just as the tailor would cut a coat ?

3. Am I able to fit as the French fit—that is, can I take the measure or impression, as the French call it, just the same as the glovemaker takes the measure or impression of the hand, and from this cut and make a dress, without refitting, and feel assured that the customer will be pleased with the fit of the dress ?

4. Can I make my own models and cut my own patterns without the aid of charts or machine of any kind ? Can I reproduce patterns or styles from any book ?

5. Do I understand the art of basting ? Do I know that without this knowledge it is impossible to make a perfect fitting dress; that each seam requires different treatment; that some have to be stretched, while others are held full; that the lining, too, should be basted so as to yield to the pressure of the body; that some parts

must be quite loose on the material, while other parts must be tight? Do I know that without this knowledge I can not excel as a fitter?

These are the qualifications necessary to ensure success. It is evident from the badly fitting dresses everywhere to be seen, that all dressmakers have not these accomplishments. The first essential in the education of a dressmaker is basting; the next of importance is cutting and fitting. The majority of dressmakers are poor basters, consequently poor fitters. In order to get this knowledge it is necessary to begin at the beginning, and this is the reason there are so many poor fitters and unsuccessful dressmakers. They do not begin aright; their knowledge is superficial, uncertain, and unsatisfactory. Any young woman with taste, no matter what her station in life may be, if she is a good plain sewer and baster, with an honest pride in taking care of herself, can learn the *French system* at her own home in less than three months. An experienced dressmaker can learn the system in a few hours.

We are not in the least interested, financially or otherwise, in the introduction of this system, but believe it to be the best now in use. It was introduced in Paris in the year 1868, and there confined to a few first-class dressmakers. It is now in general use by the best dressmakers in Europe and America. The question is frequently asked, "Can the work be done?" If those who ask the question have never seen Paris-made dresses, they can form but little idea of the art of dressmaking, or to what perfection the business has been brought by the use of this system. A few years ago it was considered a good day's work to fit six dresses, and then they had all to be refitted. With the French system four times the amount of work can be done, as compared with other systems. It is no uncommon thing for the head fitter in one of the large establishments in New York to fit thirty ladies in a day. The French system can be learned in a very short time from the printed book of directions.*

PLAIN SEWING.

How many women are there who can make a beautiful button-hole ? How many who can do fine and elegant needle work, as it used to be done before the era of sewing machines ? It is next to impossible to find such an one who takes in sewing. There are a few, and their work is monopolized by the happy families who discovered them. They are never idle. The average seamstress makes everything on a crazy machine that runs off the track persistently, and what she finishes with the needle is an awful alternative. There are but very few women who are so proficient that they can begin and finish a garment without making a single mistake. To accomplish fine needlework is not only an art, but one which may at any time be turned to account in a pecuniary way, as expert needlewomen are constantly in demand. Hand sewing is still considered superior to machine work, and the goods sold in the Ladies'

---

*The complete book, "The French System of Cutting and Fitting," is $7. The abridged edition, which contains all the most important rules for, a beginner, is $1.50. B. S. Elms, Springfield, Mass., is the inventor of the "Tailor System" which is quite popular. For information address as above.

Exchange, and in some of the best stores in the large cities, are of fine needle work. There are several stores in New York devoted to the sale of ready-made underwear, all of which is done by hand, and the prices are proportionately high. So difficult has it been to obtain these goods that large orders have been sent to convents to be filled by the sisters and their pupils. The old style of hemming, over-seaming, felling and gathering can not be improved upon, and many old ladies are doing this rare work, and keeping themselves comfortable in their old age. Girls are not as healthy to-day, with their idle hours out of school, their music and other accomplishments, as they were in the old times, when they were obliged to do a stint every day.

In regard to sewing as a method of earning a livelihood, she who excels in producing a finished garment will find a steady market for her labor. Some ladies who live quietly at home spend much of their spare time in filling orders for bridal outfits, infants' wardrobes, and children's clothes, making a specialty of white goods. Others make shirts only, and are besieged with orders, one customer recommending another. It is often remarked of some woman who is engaged in dressmaking or plain sewing, that she has no sign over her door or in the window. The secret of this is that the successful modiste has no need to advertise, her work speaks for her, and people are only too glad to employ skilled labor.

A little boy who had heard his mother wish a great many times that her sewing was done, was walking out with her one day and suddenly exclaimed: "Look,

look, mamma ! there is one woman who has all her sewing done."

He had discovered a sign which said, "Sewing done here."

A French authority takes a lofty view of the dressmakers' vocation. She must have the artist's eye to judge of the effects of color, the sculptor's faculty for form, that she may soften the outlines, turn the figure to the best advantage, and arrange the drapery in harmonious folds. She must know history in order to take from different epochs particular details suitable to various styles of beauty, and to be sure of making no mistake in the matter of accessories; and she must be a poet, to give grace and expression and character to the costumes.

THE ETIQUETTE OF DRESSMAKING.

I presume there are three dressmakers out of every twenty-five who present the appearance and manners of ladies to their customers. The dressmaker we most frequently meet with, even in the highest grades of the profession, is a dilapidated looking woman, dressed haphazard in a cheap, ill-fitting costume, who has nothing in her own appearance to suggest a single idea of what her work is. Instead of being interested in her customers' wants, she begins a doleful story of how one girl is sick and another has left her in the middle of the season, without giving warning, or relate her own domestic troubles, or the remissness of some of her customers. When she finally gives her attention she brings in an armful of French fashion papers, and asks the customer to select something, instead of selecting and suggesting the styles herself, and the lady, who wants her new dress stylishly and fashionably made, goes away with no idea of what it is to be, and with no confidence that the dressmaker knows any more about it than she does.

Whatever is worth doing is worth doing well. The dressmaker demands a compensation for her work that is not always commensurate with its value. The making of even an ordinary dress is equal in expense to the cost of the material, and should add correspondingly to its value. It is not the mere cutting and stitching of the cloth into a garment that is required—the family seam-stress could do that, or a woman hired to sew by the day —but it is expected to result in an artistic and becoming costume—the effect of taste, skill, and experience combined. Anything else is a fraudulent imposition on the confidence of employers.

The woman, then, who would succeed, must work conscientiously, be just in small as well as large dealings, and endeavor to inspire confidence in those who would employ her, by wearing the attractive products of her own skill, and surrounding herself with the tokens of her success. And, above all, let her keep her domestic troubles and the wrangles of her workroom out of sight, and as separate from her business life, as she would the bread and butter of the nursery from her customers' silks and satins.

BROIDERY-WORK

By Margaret J. Preston

Beneath the desert's rim went down the sun
And from their tent-doors, all their service done,
Came forth the Hebrew women, one by one.

For Bezaleel, the master,—who had rare
And curious skill, and gifts beyond compare,
Greater than old Misraim's greatest were,—

Had bidden them approach at his command,
As on a goat-skin, spread upon the sand,
He sate, and saw them grouped on every hand.

And soon, as came to pass, a silence fell;
He spake, and said: " Daughters of Israel,
I bring a word; I pray ye hearken well.

" God's tabernacle, by His pattern made,
Shall fail of finish, though in order laid,
Unless ye women lift your hands to aid!"

A murmur ran the crouched assembly through.
As each her veil about her closely drew—
" *We are but women! What can women do?*"

And Bezaleel made answer: " Not a man
Of all our tribes, from Judah unto Dan,
Can do the thing that just ye women can!

" The gold and broidered work about the hem
Of the priest's robes,—pomegranate knop and stem,—
Man's clumsy fingers can not compass them.

" The sanctuary curtains, that must wreathen be
And bossed with cherubim,—the colors three,
Blue, purple, scarlet,—who can twine but ye ?

" Yours is the very skill for which I call;
So bring your cunning needlework, though small
Your gifts may seem: the Lord hath need of all!"

O Christian women! for the temples set
Throughout earth's desert lands,—do you forget
The sanctuary curtains need your broidery yet?

⚬CHAPTER XXII.⚬

The ⚬ Housekeeper.

N O high or noble position was ever attained without taking up and bravely bearing some cross. No path ever led to that which was worth honest labor without some thorns. No woman can build a most precious home who does not well understand that she must, for the crown that is set before her, cheerfully accept much labor, suffering and self-sacrifice.—*Mrs. Henry Ward Beecher.*

It is in the natural condition of things that all women should be housekeepers, whether they ever keep house or not, and in order to be successful in administering the affairs of the kingdom of home, every young girl should, if possible, learn the practical routine of housework, performing with her own hands the various duties which pertain to it. This need not interrupt her studies or her attendance at day school, or interfere with the acquirement of some trade or profession, but can be taken up as a means of exercise, or at times when she is not studying or employed at other work. There are in all girls' lives some years of waiting, which can be profitably employed in learning to make home comfortable. That is the great incentive; it is not the mere handling of a lot of senseless pots and pans, the washing of greasy dishes, the sweeping of dusty rooms. It is a labor of love for dear ones dependent upon us; it is even more a form of religion, for labor is worship.

> " Labor is rest from the sorrows that greet us;
> Rest from all petty vexations that meet us;
> Rest from sin-promptings that ever entreat us;
> Rest from world-sirens that lure us to ill."

No woman need ask for a happier task than that of administering to the wants of those she loves; but it requires education, adaptation, and natural tact to fil' the position with satisfaction to herself and others Housekeeping can be raised to a science, or reduced to a mere menial occupation. A poor housekeeper will take a great many unnecessary steps, which do not accomplish anything; she does not understand the art of labor-saving. We are all acquainted with families where the work is never done; the members do not seem to be idle, but, instead of driving the work, it is forever driving them. On the other side, we can recall households where there never seems to be any work to do. With an equal number of members, and as many duties to be attended to, there is no hurry or worry going on. The rooms are always swept and dusted, the dishes washed, the pots and pans scoured bright, and the ladies of the family seem to have plenty of leisure, and this, too, where no domestic is kept, or, at the most, a small assistant, to fetch and carry. The secret of it is—system. There is no machinery in the world that does such perfect and valuable work as human hands, and these are regulated by the head and heart. When a painter was once commended for his fine sunsets, he was asked what he mixed his colors with, and his answer was, "With brains, sir."

A writer upon this subject has lately shown that many of the ills and diseases prevalent among women in our day are no doubt traceable to the sedentary mode of life so common among them. The progress of modern industrial art has done away with much of the household drudgery to which women were formerly subjected, and the result is, in too many cases, want of sufficient occupation for needed bodily exercise. The fruits of this state of things are strikingly exhibited in certain observations made by the late Mr. Robertson, a Manchester surgeon, who found that in women who themselves performed all their household work, there was no trace of certain complaints; that these complaints begin to make their appearance in women with one servant, become more pronounced in women with two servants, or worse still with those who have three servants, and so on. He showed statistically that the deaths from child-birth were four times greater in the case of women with four servants than those with none.

There must be many things taken into consideration, however, by the woman who does her own housework. and wishes to preserve her health. There is no economy in doing without a servant at the expense of doctors' bills and nurses' charges. It is better to do without silk dresses and other luxuries which are obtained at that sacrifice. There should always be some help in the family, if possible—a pair of strong arms to do the rough work and save steps, and to be in the kitchen when the mistress of the house is attending to her duties elsewhere. In describing a household, where there is no servant kept, we are presuming that there are several ladies in the family to assist each other. A wife who keeps up her position as mistress of her home, does the kitchen work, presides at table, and entertains as hostess, receives and returns calls, and possibly takes care of her children, is doing too much, and must eventually break down under the strain, and become a peevish, dissatisfied, faded woman, whom it is a trial to live with. In such a case it would be infinitely preferable for the wife to earn the money to pay a girl with, in some profession adapted to her strength and tastes. It must be remembered, too, that this accumulation of service is a labor of love. As a general thing the wife does not receive any pecuniary compensation which she can call her own.

UNPAID WORKERS.

A little boy on his way to build fires in an office, while the stars were still in the sky, told the writer: "My mother gets up, builds the fire, gets my breakfast and sends me off. Then she gets my father up and gives him his breakfast, and sends him off. Then she gives the other children their breakfast, and sends them off to school; and then she and the baby have their breakfast."

"How old is the baby," I asked?

"Oh, she is most two; but she can talk and walk as well as any of us."

"Are you well paid for your work?"

"I get $2 a week, and father gets $2 a day."

"How much does your mother get?"

With a bewildered look he answered:

"Mother? Why, she don't work for anybody."

"I thought you said she worked for all of you?"

"Oh, yes; she works for us, but there aint any money in it."

This wife of a day laborer represents a large class of women who work hard. The compensations of affection, the love of husband and children, and the nameless and numberless blessings that come with and belong to the family life, can no more make up to a wife the loss of all money value for her services than they would to her husband, if the same poverty of position were thrust upon him.

The same picture is represented by another child. This time a little girl was asked if her mother's hair wasn't beginning to turn gray on the top of her head; the child answered innocently that she did not know, her mother was too tall for her to see the top of her head, and she never got time to sit down! It is to be hoped that at the end of every year she found herself in possession of a sum of money for which she was not obliged to render any account—money, the use of which would be sweetened by the honorable toil that won it. And just here I would say that while I would advocate no sordid service in the family, I do think that toil, without recompense, is as husks to the soul. The children may have enough to eat and drink and wear, but let them have a little spending money, to earn which they may run errands, sew on patches, or do any little service that has not the interest of a great deed. It will encourage them to do their work well, and teach them the value of labor.

KEEP AN ACCOUNT.

The faithful mistress of a household will soon learn the necessity of keeping strict account, year by year, of the expenses involved in housekeeping, even to the soap, matches, tacks, brooms, pails, etc., which a reckless or incompetent girl will waste and destroy; also the current expenses of food.

> " The butcher, the baker,
> The candlestick maker,"

will charge exorbitantly if left to themselves; at least their patrons always think so, when their bills are presented at the end of a month. "What!" says the astonished housekeeper, "ninety cents for beefsteak; I never had any such amount at one time."

Now she refers to her itemized account book, and finds out that on that day she had baked fish, and no beefsteak; it is an error of the butcher, and she does not pay for his mistakes. So with all other expenditures. She has heard that a thriftless wife can throw out of the back door, with a spoon, all that her husband can bring in the front door on a shovel, and she is determined to be prudent and vigilant. She has a list of all articles in use down in her book—bed linen, table linen, towels, rollers, dusters, dish cloths, lamp cloths, and all culinary utensils. Her damask towels do not masquerade in

15

the kitchen as dish wipers. The cat does not break her dishes or eat cold joints; and the servants of such a mistress must respect and conform to her style of manage. ment; otherwise they part company.

In looking over account books, it is easy to see where useless expenditures can be avoided in future, or a more economical method be instituted. The very fact of such a system of domestic book-keeping existing will ensure faithful attention to all the minor details, which, in the aggregate, amount to so much, and involve human happiness, as well as dollars and cents.

The following lines were written by one of the daughters of the late Lucretia Mott, the venerable and beloved Quaker teacher who, for more than half a century, labored as an active philanthropist, and a minister of the Society of Friends. That she belonged to a family of workers is evident from the " regulations," where even the aged grandmother is expected to sew and knit, make three beds daily, and "do the agreeable" for all. As a glimpse of the domestic life of a woman whose whole life was spent in the service of humanity, it is of interest to the public. The third verse details the mother's duties "when she's at home:"

RULES AND REGULATIONS FOR THE HOUSEHOLD.

Our grandmamma shall stately sit,
And, as it suits her, sew or knit;
Make her own bed—one for our mother,
And also one for Tom, our brother;
And when our aunt and cousins call,
Do the agreeable for all;
And sundry little matters tell,
In style that has no parallel.

Our father, daily at his store,
His work shall do, and when 'tis o'er
Return, behind him casting care;
And seated in his rocking chair,
With slippers on and lamp at hand,
Will read the news from every land.
Then quietly will take a book,
From which he'll sometimes slyly look,
And list to what the young folks say,
Or haply join them in their play.

Our mother's charge, when she's at home,
Shall be, bath, store, and dining-room.
Morning and night she'll wash the delf,
And place it neatly on the shelf.
To her own room she will attend.
And all the stockings she will mend;
Assist the girls on washing day,
And put the ironed clothes away;
And have a general oversight
Of things, to see that all goes right.

Thrice every week shall Edward go,
Through sun and rain, through frost and snow,
And, what the market can afford,
Bring home to grace our festal board;
Shall bring in coal, the fire to cover,
An go to bed when that is over.

Anna the lamps shall daily fill,
And wash the tumblers if she will;
Shall sweep her room and make beds, too—
One for herself, and one for Sue.
Make starch, and starch the ruffles, caps,
Collars and shirts, and other traps;
Sweep all the entries and the stairs,
And, added to these trifling cares,
Shall, as our mother sometimes goes
On little journeys, as she does,

Assume her duties, and shall try
If she can not her place supply.

Thomas shall close the house at night,
And see that all is safe and right.
When snow falls, paths make in the yard;
He can not call that labor hard.
Wait on the girls when'er they go
To lectures, unless other beau
Should chance his services to proffer,
And they should choose to accept the offer.

Our cousin and our sister Lizzie
Shall part of every day be busy.
Their own room they shall put in trim,
And keep our brother's neat for him.
The parlors they must take in care,
And keep all things in order there;
Must sweep and dust, and wash the glasses,
But leave for Anna all the brasses.
On wash-day set the dinner table,
And help fold clothes when they are able.
Shall lend their aid in ironing, too,
And aught else they incline to do;
And then, when they have done their share
Of work, if they have time to spare,
Assist their cousin A. C. T.,
'Till she's their cousin, A. C. B.

Dear little Sue shall be the runner,
Because our Patty, blessings on her,
To boarding-school has gone away,
Until bright spring returns to stay.
Her tireless kindness won each heart,
And we were grieved with her to part,
But in this case found case from pain,
That our great loss was her great gain.

Sarah shall in the kitchen be,
Preparing breakfast, dinner, tea,
And keeping free from dust the closets,
Where flour, etcetra, she deposits.
Anna shall on the table wait,
Attend the doors, see to the gate;
Clean the front steps and pavement too,
And many other things she'll do
That all may in such order be,
As each one of us likes to see.
Thus all their duty may fulfill,
And if 'tis done with cheerful will,
A sure reward to us will come,
In finding a most happy home.

ANNA MOTT HOPPER.

One is reminded, upon reading the poem, of the old adage, "Many hands make light work." I commend the regulations to the careful perusal of young housekeepers. They will find much to encourage and improve them in these simple verses breathing of home and its pleasant domestic duties.

The Rev Henry Hudson, the well-known Shakespearean scholar and author, says, regarding the education of women: "As for women, let it suffice that their rights and interests in this matter are co-ordinate with those of men; just that, and no more. Their main business, also, is to get an honest living, and the education that impairs them, or leaves them unprepared for this, is the height and folly of wrong. The greatest institution in the world is the family. The greatest art known among men is housekeeping, which is the life of the family. Housekeeping is the last thing that any lady can afford to be ignorant of."

WOMAN'S INVISIBLE WORK

Home means so much in this nineteenth century. It means all that makes life really worth the living. It means comfort, affection, sympathy, confidence, consolation, encouragement, rest, and peace. It is the object to which all unselfish endeavor is directed. It means the solitary spot in the desert of the world where all these principles and virtues taught us in infancy preserve their truthful, queen-like date-palms. It means one single link in the great chain of ethical knowledge, reaching out of the twilight of the past into the sungold of the future, preserving unbroken for generations to come the lessons of honor, affection, strong purpose, handed down to us through untold myriads of years.

When the head of the family returns home at night, after a weary day's endeavor, he is at once wrapped in a familiar atmosphere of comfort. There is a place for everything, and everything in its place—easy chairs offer themselves, sofas invite, fires shine clear, pictures smile, slippers line the tired feet, while the cozily spread social table offers a renewal of strength, and the closed blinds and zealous doors shut out even the noises of the outside world. All is bright, clear, warm, happy, and it is all woman's invisible work. It was she who arranged everything, brightened everything, placed necessary things ready to hand, and removed useless ones. The man of the house never saw her do these things—never will see her do them He is always absent when the household elves are busy. He is content without knowing why—without a thought of the thoughtfulness and constant labor required for his comfort.

But the day sometimes dawns when the invisible worker must cease to work. It is only then that her imperceptible labor is fully comprehended. Somehow every inanimate object rebels now that she is absent; nothing remains in place; bright things grow strangely dull; handy things are missing; locks get out of order; windows refuse to exclude the cold; noises will not be shut out; curtains will not obey the hand; familiar comforts flee away; the house becomes inexplicably void, and cold and dead; there is an aspect of ruin through all its riches; it lived before; it breathed; it spoke in a peculiar, pleasant, dumb way. Now its life has utterly departed from it; then does the invisible work make itself visible. But the gentle worker, being weary at last, has found a new home with that All-Comforter, whose palaces eternally silent, immeasurably vast, open their doors to guests only who may never depart.

WHY NOT SAVE MOTHER.

The farmer sat in his easy chair,
Between the fire and the lamplight's glare,
His face was ruddy and full and fair,
His three small boys in the chimney nook
Conned the lines of a picture book.
His wife, the pride of his home and heart
Baked the biscuit and made the tart—
Laid the table and steeped the tea—
Deftly, swiftly, and silently;
Tired and weary, weak and faint,
She bore her trials without complaint,
Like many another household saint—

Content, all selfish bliss above
In the patient ministry of love.

At last, between the clouds of smoke
That wreathed his lips, the farmer spoke:
" There's taxes to raise and inter'st to pay,
And if there should come a rainy day
'T would be mighty handy, I'm bound to say,
T' have something put by.   For folks must die
An there's funeral bills and gravestones to buy
Enough to swamp a man, purty nigh;
Besides, there's Edward an' Dick an' Joe
To be provided for when we go
So, if I were you, I'll tell you what I'd du;
I'd be savin' of wood as ever I could—
Extra fires don't do any good:
I'd be savin' of soap, and savin' of ile,
And run up some candles once in a while;
I'd rather be sparin' of coffee and tea
           For sugar is high,
           An' all to buy,
And cider is good enough drink for me;
I'd be kind o' careful about my clo'es
And look out sharp how the money goes—
Gewgaws is useless, nater knows;
           Extra trimmin'
           's the bane of women.
I'd sell the best of my cheese and honey,
An' eggs is as good, nigh 'bout as the money;
An' as tu the carpet you wanted new—
I guess we can make the old one du;
And as for th' washer, and sewin' machine,
Them smooth-tongued agents, so pesky mean,
You'd better get rid of 'em slick and clean.
What do they know 'bout women's work.
Do they calkilate women was made to shirk?"

Dick and Edward and little Joe
Sat in the corner in a row
They saw the patient mother go
On ceaseless errands to and fro;
They saw that her form was bent and thin,
Her temples grey, her cheeks sunk in;
They saw the quiver of lip and chin—
And then, with a wrath he could not smother,
Outspoke the youngest, frailest brother:
    " You talk of savin' wood an' ile
      And tea an' sugar all the while,
But you never talk of savin' mother!"

CHAPTER XXIII

A ⊛ Good ⊛ Manager.

R. Newton was looking over his cash account for the year.

"Well," asked his wife, "how do you come out?"

"I find," answered the husband, "that my expenses during the year have been thirty-seven cents over one thousand dollars."

"And your income has been one thousand dollars?"

"Yes; I managed pretty well, didn't I?"

"Do you think it managing well to exceed your income?" asked his wife.

"What's thirty-seven cents?"

"Not much, to be sure, but still, something. It seems to me that we ought to have saved from such an income, instead of falling behind."

"But how can we save on such a salary, Elizabeth? We haven't lived extravagantly, and yet it seems to have taken it all."

"Perhaps there is something in which we might retrench. Suppose you mention some of the items."

"The most important is house rent, one hundred and fifty dollars, and articles of food, five hundred dollars "

"Just half of the income?"

"Yes; and you admit you can not retrench them. I like to live well. I had enough of poor food before I was married. Now I mean to live as well as I can."

"Still, we ought to save something for a rainy day, Ezra."

"That would be like carrying an umbrella when the sun shines."

"Still, it is well to have an umbrella in the house."

"I can not controvert your logic, Elizabeth, but I am afraid I shall not be able to save anything this year. When I have my salary raised it will be time enough to think of that."

"Let me make a proposition to you," said Mrs. Newton. "You said that one-half of your income had been expended on articles of food. Are you willing to allow me that sum for that purpose?"

"Do you guarantee to pay all bills out of it?"

"Yes."

"Then I shift the responsibility upon you with pleasure. But I tell you beforehand, you wont be able to save much out of it, and I shouldn't relish having additional bills to pay As I am paid every month I will hand you the money "

The different characters of the husband and wife may be judged from the conversation which has been recorded. Mr. Newton had little prudence or foresight. He lived chiefly for the present, and seemed to fancy that whatever contingencies might arise in the future, he would somehow be provided for   Now, to trust to Providence is a proper way, but there is a good deal of truth in the adage, that "God helps those who help themselves "

Mrs. Newton, on the contrary. had been brought up in a family which was compelled to be economical, and though she was unwilling to deny herself comforts, yet she felt that it was desirable to procure them in a proper way.

The time at which this conversation took place was at the commencement of the second year of their married life.

The first step Mrs. Newton took, on accepting the charge of the household, was to commence the practice of paying cash for all articles that came under her department. She accordingly called on the butcher and inquired :

"How often have you been in the habit of presenting your bills, Mr. Wilson ?"

"Once in three months," was the reply.

" And I suppose you sometimes have bad bills."

"Yes; one-third of my profits, on an average, are swept off by them."

" I will set them an example, then," said Mrs. Newton. "Hereafter whatever articles shall be purchased will be paid for on the spot, and I shall expect you to sell them as reasonably as you can."

This arrangement was also made with the others, who, it is scarcely needful to say, were glad to enter into the arrangement. Ready money is a great supporter of trade, and a cash customer is worth two who purchase on credit. There are other ways in which a careful housekeeper is able to limit expenses, which Mrs. Newton did not overlook. With an object in view, she was always on the lookout to prevent waste—to get the full value of whatever was expended. The result was beyond her expectations.

At the close of the year, on examining her bank book —for she had regularly deposited whatever money she did not use—she found that she had one hundred and fifty dollars, besides reimbursing herself for the money spent during the first month, and had enough to last through the other.

" Well, Elizabeth, have you kept within your allowance," asked her husband at that time. " I imagine you have not found it as easy to save as you thought."

"I have saved something, however," said the wife. " How is it with you ?"

" 'That's more than I can say; however, I have not exceeded my income; that is one good thing. We have lived fully as well as last year, and I do not know but that we have lived better than when we spent the whole five hundred dollars.

" Its knack, Ezra," said his wife, smiling. She was not inclined to mention how much she had saved. She wanted some time or other to surprise him, when the amount would be of service.

"She may possibly have saved twenty-five dollars," thought Mr. Newton, or some trifle, and so dismissed the subject from his mind.

At the end of the second year Mrs. Newton's savings, including the interest, amounted to three hundred and fifty dollars, and she began to feel quite rich. Her husband did not think to inquire how much she had saved, supposing, as before, it could be but little. However, he had a piece of good news to communicate; his salary had been raised from one thousand to one thousand two hundred. He added:

"As I before allowed you one-half of my income for household expenses, it is no more than fair that I should do so now. That will give you a better chance to save part of it than before."

Mrs. Newton merely said she had saved something, without specifying the amount. Her allowance was increased to six hundred dollars, but her expenses were not increased at all, so that her savings for the third year swelled the aggregate sum in the savings bank to six hundred dollars.

Mr. Newton, on the contrary, in spite of his increased salary, was no better off at the end of his third year than before. His expenses had increased by one hundred dollars, though he would have found it difficult to tell in what way his comfort or happiness had been increased thereby.

In spite of his carelessness as to his own affairs, Mr. Newton was an excellent business man, and his services were valuable to his employers. They accordingly increased his salary from time to time until it reached one thousand six hundred dollars. He had continued his custom of giving his wife one-half, and this had become such a habit that he never thought to inquire whether she found it necessary to employ the whole or not.

Thus ten years rolled away. During all this time **Mr.**

Newton lived in the same hired house, for which he paid an annual rent of one hundred and fifty dollars. Latterly, however, he had become dissatisfied with it. It had passed into the hands of a new landlord, who was not disposed to keep it in the repair which the tenant considered desirable.

About this time a block of excellent houses was erected by a capitalist, who desired to sell or let them as he might have an opportunity. They were modern, and much better arranged than the one in which Mr. Newton lived, and he felt a strong desire to move into one of them. He mentioned it to his wife one morning.

"What is the rent?" asked Mrs. Newton. "Two hundred and twenty-five dollars for the corner house; two hundred for either of the others."

"The corner house would be preferable, on account of the side windows."

"Yes; and it has a large yard besides. I think we had better take one of them. I guess we'll engage one of them to-day. You know our year is up next week."

"Please wait until to-morrow before you engage one," urged Mrs. Newton.

"For what reason?"

"I should like to examine the house."

"Very well, I suppose to-morrow will do."

Soon after breakfast the next day Mrs. Newton called on the owner of the new block, and intimated her desire to be shown the corner house. Her request was readily complied with. Mrs. Newton was quite delighted with all the arrangements, and expressed her satisfaction.

"Are these houses for sale or to let?" she enquired.

"Either," replied the owner.

"The yearly rent is, I understand, two hundred and twenty-five dollars ?"

"Yes; I consider the corner house worth twenty-five dollars more than the others."

"And what do you charge for the house for a cash purchase ?" asked Mrs. Newton, with subdued eagerness.

"Four thousand dollars," was the reply, "and that is but a small advance on the cost."

"Very well, I will buy it of you," added Mrs. Newton, quietly.

"What did I understand you to say ?" asked the owner, scarcely believing his own ears.

"I will buy this house at your own price, and pay the money within a week."

"Then the house is yours. But your husband did not say anything of his intention, and in fact I did not know ——"

"That he had any money to invest, I suppose you would say. Neither does he know it, and I must ask you not to tell him at present."

The next morning Mrs. Newton invited her husband to take a walk, but without specifying the direction. They soon stood in front of the house in which he desired to live.

"Wouldn't you like to go in ?" she asked.

"Yes; it is a pity we did not get the key."

"I have the key," said his wife, and forthwith she walked up the steps and proceeded to open the door.

"When did you get the key ?" asked her husband.

"Yesterday, when I bought the house," said his wife, quietly.

"What *do* you mean?"

"Just what I say. This house is mine, and what is mine is yours. So this house is yours, Ezra."

"Where in the name of goodness did you raise the money?" asked Mr. Newton, his amazement as great as ever.

"I haven't been managing wife for ten years for nothing," said Mrs. Newton, smiling.

With some difficulty Mrs. Newton persuaded her husband that the price of the house was really the result of her savings. He felt, when he observed the commodious arrangements of the house, that he had reason to be grateful for the prudence of his managing wife.*

HOW A WORKING GIRL LIVES.

The story here told is that of a sensible, level-headed girl, who worked in an office in Cincinnati:

"My work is principally writing letters and helping to keep the books of my employer, who does a business of upwards of seventy-five thousand dollars a year. I receive seven dollars a

---

*The story of a good manager is a real incident, and offers a good moral, as well as pleasant reading; but I would not advise its readers to expect like results from a like experiment. Mrs. Newton had no children to divide her expenses with, no doctor's bills, did not make any journeys, and must have had either very little new clothing, or earned what she did have in some other way. The reader will, no doubt, have a burning curiosity to know what Mr. Newton did with his share of the money which must have been outside of his expenditures for rent and clothing—clear profit. The good management is evident in the fact that Mrs. Newton saved what she could easily have spent, without any noticeable decrease of comfort in her particular case, and so, in the end, realized a handsome home.

16

week for my work, and have no other means of support. My
parents are both dead, and they left no estate, above what was
necessary to pay a few debts. At the age of fifteen years I
started square with the world, and have held my own for five
years, although, I confess, it has been a continual struggle.

"There are a thousand girls in Cincinnati situated just as I
am, struggling on, day after day, to keep soul and body together,
with no future, as far as the human eye can discover, worth living for. There are many not half so well situated as I am, and
God only knows how they live. As long as I keep my health I
have enough, with none to spare; but that hundreds of poor
girls go to bed hungry every night in Cincinnati, I honestly
believe. I know girls who work for four dollars a week—servant girls often get more than this, and they have no board to
pay. It would be a sadly interesting chapter that would explain
just how a girl continues to keep herself in clothes, board herself, and pay rent on four dollars a week. Of the wages I
receive every penny has to count. A few girls of my acquaintance live at home, and have no rent to pay. There are others
who receive a little assistance from their fathers or brothers.
But there are many who live on this sum, and support themselves without assistance from any source. I know how some of
them manage it. Three or four, and in one case I know where
six girls have clubbed together and live in one room, thus
making the rent small to each one. They pretend to take their
meals at cheap restaurants, but really they are obliged to do
most of their own cooking. Economy could go no further than
is practiced by some of the working girls in large cities."

This young lady prepared an estimate of her expenses, which summed up as follows:

Salary one year (fifty-two weeks), at seven dollars a week,		$364 00
Deduct one week lost time,	$ 7 00	
Board and room,	· 208 00	
Coal extra,	10 00	
Clothing,	· 85 00	
Church,	10 00	
Car fare,	· 25 00	
		$345 00
Balance,		$19 00

"You can well imagine," concludes the writer, "that this balance of nineteen dollars is soon consumed in medicine or other necessary expenditures. Out of it I buy a paper, or drop an occasional nickel to some poor woman in the street, who seems to have a harder struggle with the world than I have myself."

The working girl who contributes this pathetic chapter to the literature of woman's work, would be surprised could she know how many girls live respectably, and even save a little for the "dark day," on seven dollars a week. A large family can live comfortably, pay house rent, and dress moderately well on twenty-eight dollars a week, or fourteen hundred and fifty-six dollars a year. Let four girls, then, club together, rent two rooms, and keep house on the co-operative plan, and they could not only live well but save something, and keep a cheap girl to do the house work. It would require good judgment and frugality in buying only what they actually needed—plain, wholesome food, that would nourish them and keep them in good health. Their washing would cost twenty-five cents each week, individually, and if employed in office work they can walk, and save car fare.

The girls who receive only four dollars weekly can make the same advantageous arrangements—one rent and one fire for four. Their food need not cost them over one shilling a day each, and rent and fire combined should not be more; or, at the most, four dollars a month. I admit that it will require the most rigid economy, but not actual hardship, to accomplish this result; but I actually believe our German friends, who have made economy a fine art, would get a small sum in the savings bank besides. It is a matter of constant surprise that people can live in a great city and manage on so little, and it is the only place where it can be done. The farmer's wife who throws a pan of milk away to get rid of it, could not believe that a pint of milk a day is a common quantity for families in the city who are far from poor. But they use it in the tea only, and that sparingly. The children drink water.

The hardest thing to do with these limited incomes is to keep out of debt. A slip-shod way of doing business, on the part of storekeepers, permits the running up of accounts, which worry and harass when they come due, worse than any other evil. "Hunger, cold, rags, suspicion, hard work, unjust reproach, are disagreeable," says Horace Greeley in his autobiography, "but debt is infinitely worse than them all. Avoid pecuniary obligations as you would pestilence or famine. If you have but fifty cents, and can get no more for a week, buy a peck of corn, parch it, and live on it, rather than owe any one a dollar."

CHAPTER XXIV

The ∗ Science ∗ of ∗ Cookery.

THERE is always a best way of doing anything, if it be but to boil an egg.—*Emerson.*

Learn the economy of the kitchen.—*Ruskin.*

A husband was once called upon to write an epitaph upon his departed wife. He was without education, and had few mental resources, but he had lived very comfortably with his wife and was deeply grieved at her loss, and at first he found it impossible to select one from any of her many virtues which would sufficiently commemorate her worth. The one he decided on at last was this:

"Her picked-up dinners were a perfect success."

Many a woman with a more pretentious epitaph has had a less satisfactory record. It is said of the modern belle:

"She had views on co-education,
 And the principal needs of the nation;
 And her glasses were blue, and the numbers she knew
 Of the stars in each high constellation.

And she wrote in a handwriting clerky,
And she talked with an emphasis jerky;
And she painted on tiles, in the sweetest of styles,
But she didn't know chicken from turkey.

Now, a woman who didn't know chicken from turkey would be a very poor housekeeper, and so the faculty of at least one college in the United States has decided. The girls of the junior class of the Iowa Agricultural College learn to cook in the most thorough manner, as the following description will show : Every girl in the class has learned to make good bread, and has put her knowledge into successful practice, each taking her turn in mixing, kneading, and baking, without other help from the teacher than the first lesson she received. Each has also been taught to make raised and baking-powder biscuit, pie crust, cake of various kinds, puddings—to cook a roast and broil a steak. All can tell which is the best cut of beef for roasting or broiling; how many minutes should be allowed for cooking a pound of roast mutton, beef, veal, or pork; how hot the oven should be for each; how to prepare it for the oven, and how to attend to it after it is put therein. They can give a clear and accurate description of the preliminary steps to be taken as a preparation for any sort of baking. They know how to stuff and roast a turkey, make oyster soup, prepare stock for other soups, steam and mash potatoes, so they will melt in the mouth, and, in short, can get up a palatable meal, combining both substantial and fancy dishes, in good style.

The class will be instructed in all the arts of canning fruits and vegetables; in preserving and making jellies;

and, if it is found to be impossible to give practical lessons in this department, the theoretical instruction will
be so carefully given that the members can be trusted to
can, pickle, and preserve by themselves.

The indication in connection with teaching the class
that gives the best promise for their future success as
cooks, is the genuine interest and enthusiasm they have
constantly manifested. The hard work has been cheerfully performed. Wood has been carried, fires kept up,
and dishes washed with unvarying good humor. Each
week's instruction has been eagerly received, and not an
unpleasant word, from first to last, has marred the good
feeling.

Outside of the instruction of the kitchen, these junior
girls have taken careful notes of lectures on many topics
connected with household management, such as house-
furnishing, care of beds and bedding, washing and ironing, care of the sick, care of children, etc. They have
prepared essays on similar topics, in a thoughtful manner, that has clearly proven that a genuine feeling of
appreciation of the tender and solemn responsibilities
devolving upon the wife and mother has been kindled in
their minds. The authorities of the college are thoroughly in earnest in trying to offer to girls a broad, sensible, and practical education. They give them now the
best possible instruction in science, mathematics, and
English literature, and mean that some day the department of domestic economy shall stand fairly abreast of
these in thoroughness and efficiency. If these girls can
carry into all their domestic experiences the same sunny
temper and the unfailing industry and perseverance that

they have evinced in the experimental kitchen, they will brighten and adorn any homes fortunate enough to secure them as mistresses.

TRAINING SCHOOL FOR COOKS.

It has often been said that while we have the best markets in the world, we have the worst and most wasteful cooking. And although within the last few years much interest has been felt in England, in the establishment of cooking schools, but little has been done in this country. Private classes were opened in Boston sixteen years ago, and were well patronized, but the expense of instruction was necessarily so large as to close them to persons of small means. Miss Carson, in New York, and Miss Parloa, of Boston, have met with good success in their cooking schools. It is now considered very desirable to bring such teaching within the reach of those who intend to become cooks, and of those girls who have left our grammar schools, and who, by learning to cook economically, and to become good housekeepers, may do much to keep their families above want.

Probably the best cooking school for an ignorant girl is the kitchen of a kind and intelligent mistress, who is willing to spend a large part of her life in that best missionary work—training Irish and German girls in ways of thrifty housewifery. But, since the days of our grandmothers, housekeeping has taken a new aspect. The young mother once had her kitchen within easy reach from her nursery, but now a separation, by long flights of stairs, makes it practically impossible that she shall spend much time in teaching her domestic to cook.

It is hoped that the cooking school, either as an adjunct to the college for educating women, or a separate establishment, may succeed and become a permanent institution of great value to families in providing good cooks; that it will be of still greater benefit to many unemployed and poorly paid women, by providing a way in which, at small expense, they can fit themselves to obtain comfortable homes, and to receive good wages. When shirts are sold for fifty cents, there must be many women working at extremely low wages. It will be well if these can be induced to fit themselves for domestic service.

The Grecians valued a cook so highly that the head of the kitchen department—the **archimageiros** as he was called—received the appointment of culinary artist, and presided at all public ceremonies. These officers received no salary as cooks; their fame was sufficient reward. "We alone," said they, "are entrusted by the gods with the secret of human happiness," and so they cheerfully resigned all emolument. It is hard for us to imagine such a condition of affairs! No salaries! No perquisites! But we must not credit them with utter disinterestedness, or forget that there were many prizes in the lottery for them. A successful dish, which pleased the palate of a senator, might, at any moment, procure for the cook a gift of priceless value; in any case, applause and a crown of flowers awaited him; and if he invented a new dish he received a sort of patent for it, no other cook dare make it for at least a twelvemonth, and he alone drew from it all honor and profit, until some rival successfully prepared another novelty.

When Mark Antony gave one of his famous and historic suppers to Cleopatra, and listened to the praises the Egyptian queen bestowed on the viands, he called for the cook and gave him a city as a recompense.

The head cook of Charles the VII. left to his descendants a valuable recipe for golden soup, which may interest the housewife of to-day : " Toast," he says, " slices of bread, then throw them into a jelly made of sugar, yolk of egg, white wine, and rose water. When they are well soaked try them, and then throw them again into rose water, and sprinkle well with sugar and saffron." Such a soup would hardly satisfy the esthetics of to-day.

Sicilians made the best cooks in olden times, and were enjoined to remain, while the Romans offered incredible sums for their services, the chief cook in a Roman household often receiving a salary equal to $4,000 a year. This, however, can be offset here in our own country, Mrs. Vanderbilt paying her head cook $7,000 yearly, while there are numerous instances among the wealthy where the cook is paid $3,000 and $4,000 a year. The ancients gave a great importance to the science of gastronomy. Their kitchen services were of silver, and each dish, sauce, and gravy had a special silver utensil. Forks were unknown to them, but silver spoons were abundant, and rich ladles of gold and silver, bronze chafing dishes, silver cups and saucers, rare porcelain, and all the luxurious dishes known to the present household, were in use. Many relics which we preserve as ornaments for our parlors were kitchen utensils of the ancient Greeks.

All was elegance, combined with utility, and the same feature of distinctive care in the arrangement of the kitchen is shown in pictures and sketches of the buried Pompeii; the kitchen floors were tiled, the doors were of rare woods, and the appurtenances were unique and costly. Cooking then ranked among the fine arts, while in this age of the world, and in America, it comes near being one of the lost arts.

May we not hope that in the coming time cards of invitation will be sent out which will read: "Drill exhibition by Mrs. Jones' class, in practical cooking, Dessert Day;" or, an advertisement of Roast beef, with clear gravy, by the young ladies of the Jones Cooking School." Doctor Johnson said of his friend Mrs. Carter, that she could both translate Epictetus and make a pudding. The widow of a courtier of Henry VIII. was rewarded with the gift of a dissolved priory, for some fine puddings she had presented his majesty. The great ladies of France have not only invented new dishes for the table, but have given their illustrious names to them, Bechamel sauce being a product of a marquise of that name, while Filets de Capereau a la Berry were named after the lady who invented them, the Duchess de Berry, daughter of the Regent Orleans. A writer on culture in cooking, says: "The daughters of the wealthy in this country often marry struggling men, and they know less about domestic economy than ladies of the highest rank abroad; not because English or French ladies take more part in housekeeping, but because they are at home all their lives. Ladies of the highest rank never go to a

boarding or any other school, and these are the women
who, with some few exceptions, know best how things
should be done." The same writer says: "Who does
not remember, with affectionate admiration, Charlotte
Brontë stealthily taking the eyes out of the potatoes
for fear of hurting the feelings of her purblind old ser·
vant, or, Margaret Fuller shelling peas."

One of the important features in the housekeeping
department is the kitchen library. Every kitchen
should have its books of reference—not the thin pam-
phlet, advertising some quack medicine, with a few haphazard recipes thrown in to command attention—but a
whole set of books, bound in oil-cloth, which can be
washed off — the cook-books of different countries —
ancient and modern cook-books, and curious dishes and
feasts, with historical descriptions of dinners, banquets,
etc., with the simple primary works of rudimentary
cooking. There are some twenty or thirty recipe books,
and as many more descriptive and anecdotal volumes,
out of which number a good selection might be made.
The Beecher family can furnish several. Miss Catharine
Beecher wrote a cook-book, Mrs. Henry Ward Beecher
has written two or three such domestic volumes, and
Marian Harland is an accepted authority on all cooking
and housekeeping topics, her books being in constant
demand. There are also some novels that are great helps
to young housekeepers, Mrs. Whitney's "We Girls"
being one of the most instructive. It is a delightful
book for young girls to read, its description of an art
kitchen being most fascinating, and its housekeeping

experiments of the most satisfactory kind. In regard to her cook-book, she says: "I revised that book with the proof in one hand and the cooking stove in the other;" and she tells a funny story of how, late one night, feeling a little troubled for fear the proportions in an Indian pudding were not exactly right, she came down stairs, built a fire, made and baked it, while the rest of the family were unconsciously asleep.

Add to these a book of domestic poems, and somewhere over the flour barrel or the piano—I am not sure but I would have a piano in every kitchen, as one of its attractive properties—let this verse, from grand George Herbert, be engraved, or embroidered, or frescoed:

> " A servant with this clause
> Makes drudgery divine,
> Who sweeps a roc n as for thy laws,
> Makes that and he action fine."

THE COOKING SCHOOL DRESS.

This costume consists of a neat, short dress, with an immense brown Holland or print over-apron, with waist, pockets and all conveniences. These aprons are inexpensive, and can, if necessary, be bought ready made at the Woman's Exchange, or in large dry goods stores, and keep the whole dress free of dust or spot. A cap of blue or pink cambric, or white muslin, protects the hair. These caps are simply large, round pieces of cloth, into which an elastic is shirred an inch or so from the edge, and they cost only a few cents. Some critical observer has said, that, as a general thing, female cooks are not expected to be fit to be seen, although male cooks have no such privileges of disorder allowed them. It is a new idea that women are less cleanly and tidy than men, but perhaps the truth may be found in the fact that women cooks are loaded with other duties. The artist in cooking will be also an artist in making of herself a picture, such as this description from a late novel, where the scenes are laid in France: "Rue's dress was tucked up and pinned behind, an immense coarse linen apron was tied over it, she had twisted a white handkerchief round her head to prevent the flour getting into her hair, and her sleeves were rolled above her elbows. But there were golden porte-bonhuers on the white and shapely arms, and the little feet, with their pink striped stockings and daintily buckled shoes, could not have belonged to a Bearnais peasant any more than could the aristocratic, delicately featured face."

IDEAL KITCHENS.

There are kitchens which resemble the ideal picture which is presented to us in the novel or on the stage, in real homes, and they are happy, comfortable places, where a neat, white-handed woman, in picturesque costume, moves with gracious ease among the pots and pans; where a white loaf is cut on a white table, such a place as we might imagine as that in which Werther's Charlotte "went on cutting bread and butter;" where golden pots of preserves are opened and inspected, and moulds of jelly turned out into crystal dishes; the presiding genius of such a place can not be otherwise than neat and daintly habited, for she understands the science of cooking, and invokes to her aid the principles of chemistry, and reduces all the forces of grease and dirt by a superior process of active absorption. Every pan has its place; each utensil its nail or closet; the holder is omnipresent; clean towels abound; neat mats are spread on the floor; there is a mirror on the wall; there are comfortable chairs to sit on; the kitchen is the heart of the house, and if there is disorder there it is felt through the entire system.

MRS. GARFIELD ON BREAD-MAKING.

Mrs. Lucretia Garfield, widow of the president, wrote to her husband, over twenty years ago, in the following strain :

"I am glad to tell you, that out of all the toil and disappointments of the summer just ended, I have risen up to a victory; that silence of thought, since you have been away, has won for my spirit a triumph. I read something like this the other day: 'There is no healthy thought without labor, and thought makes the labor happy.' Perhaps this is the way I have been able to climb up higher. It came to me this morning when I was making bread. I said to myself, 'Here I am compelled, by an inevitable necessity, to make our bread this summer. Why not consider it a pleasant occupation, and make it so, by trying to see what perfect bread I can make? It seemed like an inspiration, and the whole of my life grew brighter. The very sunshine seems flowing down through my spirit into the white loaves, and now I believe that my table is furnished with better bread than ever before; and this truth, old as creation, seems just now to have become fully mine, that I need not be the shrinking slave of toil, but its regal master, making whatever I do yield its best fruits.' "

The above quotation from Mrs. Garfield's letter was
read by Professor Hinsdale to the students at Hiram College, Ohio, as an incentive to more exalted work, and I
insert it here with the hope that some discouraged
worker, reading it, may take heart and rise nobly to
fresh endeavor. "Give us this day our daily bread," is
one of the beautiful petitions of Our Lord's Prayer.
How often have weary souls longed to add, with all due
reverence : "Give it to us white and light and sweet,
wholesome and digestible, that we may be comforted
and strengthened." The meaning of the word *lady* is
loaf-giver. Can there be a more acceptable priesthood
than this service of love and labor—the token of hospi-
tality—the badge of ladyhood ? Some one has curtly
said that it is not passion or ill-temper that drive men to
commit murder or suicide; it is heavy, sour bread, which
perverts the whole current of being, and transforms
human beings into demons. Every woman has a mission to learn to make good bread, if she would consider
the happiness of her family. The newspapers are fond
of disseminating such stories as the following, at the
expense of the girls who will not make bread :

"A fashionable young lady of this city visited a cooking
school the other afternoon, when her attention was equally
divided between a new dress, worn by an acquaintance, and the
directions for making cake. Upon returning home she under-
took to write down the recipe for cake-making for her mother,
who found that it read as follows:

"Take two pounds of flour, three rows of plaiting down the
front, the whites of two eggs, cut bias; a pint of milk, ruffle
around the neck, half a pound of currants, seven yards of bead

17

trimming, grated lemon peel, with Spanish lace fichu. Stir
well.''

Her mother said she thought these new-fangled ideas
on cooking ought to be frowned down.

''No, indeed, I'm not going to learn how to make
bread,'' said an Eastern belle, ''girls who know how to
make bread generally marry men who can not afford to
buy flour to make it with, and they have to work in a
millinery shop to help pay the board bill. I'll stick to
my fancy work.''

It is related of the Hon. Philetus Sawyer, a Wisconsin
senator, that he was so well pleased with a dinner prepared entirely for him by his two daughters, that he
gave to each of them a check for twenty-five thousand
dollars, a present quite within his gift, as he is a
millionaire.

The thrifty, economical German fathers have a quaint
and pretty way of interesting their young daughters in
bread-making, and, at the same time, reward them for
their industry. They conceal numerous small silver coin
in the flour, and the girl finds these in kneading the
bread.

There should be a cooking catechism published, with
such questions as these :

Can you make a clear gravy ?

Can you make good soups ?

Can you broil a beefsteak ?

In how many different ways can you cook potatoes ?

Do you know how to roast meats properly ?

Can you make puddings ?

Can you make sauces ?

Miss Julia Nast, the daughter of the well-known artist, Thomas Nast, has for some years presided over a young girl's cooking association, at her home in Morristown, New Jersey, where, as head cook, she displays true artistic talent, and offers an example worthy of emulation.

COOK INSTEAD OF CLERK.

A three line notice of the death of a lady, in the city papers, recently, is all the world will know of one whose life was crowded with strange vicissitudes.

Her family name was one of rare distinction in the record of the revolution. Her husband was a naval officer of merit, and she had been a society queen in the past administration. In the rebellion everything was swept from her family—husband, home, and money—as those of her kindred had chosen their part with the South. At the close of the war, friendless and penniless, so far as friends could help her—for they were all stranded together—she was not sufficiently educated to teach. She had no accomplishments, such as a knowledge of music or languages. She had always been fond of housekeeping, and possessed a practical knowledge of cooking in its higher branches. She found here a lady, unmarried, who had known her when fortune smiled, and there she served for sixteen years; this delicately nurtured lady performed the duties of cook. She hired a colored woman to do the washing and ironing, and other laborious duties, but cook she remained to the end.

The remarkable part of all this is, that had her history been known, and her grandfather's services to the country told, she would have been appointed to some position under the government; but she preferred to remain in the quiet and seclusion of her friend's kitchen. This woman, who had great claim upon the country for the deeds done by her ancestors, never paraded them, never hung about the Capitol or hunted down members. She never traded upon the renown of her grandfather, although his was one to be proud of. She went about her simple duties thankful that she could eat bread of her own earning, far from the madding crowd who hunt for and hold office. This brave, patient woman deserves a monument on which should be engraved: "Here rests one who chose rather to be a cook than a clerk."

⇥❖CHAPTER XXV.❖⇤

The ❋ New ❋ Cook.

We may live without poetry, music and art,
We may live without conscience and live without heart,
We may live without friends, we may live without books,
But civilized man can not live without cooks.

HERE is one thing you mustn't forget, Tom!"

"What's that, Emma?"

"Don't forget to go to the registry office and send me a cook. The new girl is good for nothing, and the old one can't do everything. Young or old, man or woman, I don't care, only send me up a competent cook by ten o'clock this morning."

"Don't look so desperate, Sis; I'll remember it. I want things in pretty good style for Maxwell; he is used to it—is fond of good dinners; and I guess I'll send you a good, smart man cook, Emma." Mr. Thomas Maye disappeared with a re-assuring nod. He had a proverbially bad memory; pretty Emma Maye knew it very well, yet in this desperate emergency she trusted him.

During the two years she had had charge of her wid-owed brother's family they had been blessed by the most skillful of cooks; but Joan had taken a fancy to get married, and her place was hastily supplied by one who soon proved incapable.

Just at this juncture Mr. Maye received tidings that his dead wife's favorite brother, Arthur Maxwell, just returned from abroad, would pay him a visit. From the first Emma had been nervous over the responsibility of entertaining this elegant young man, whom she had never seen. She was lovely and accomplished; but she could not cook—in fact, she had never tried.

It was half past seven o'clock when Mr. Maye went to town. He took nothing but a cup of coffee at seven o'clock, and lunched at his favorite restaurant at eleven o'clock. At half-past three o'clock the Mayes dined, and Mr. Maxwell was expected by the ten minutes past three o'clock train.

"There!" sighed Emma, when, two hours after her brother's departure, the house was in its usual exquisite order, and the viands and flowers sent up for dinner; "if Tom doesn't forget, and if he sends up a good cook, everything will be nice enough."

She did not dare think of the possibility of Tom's having forgotten, or that of the cook not coming for any other reason; but when, precisely at ten o'clock, the door-bell rang, a secret weight was lifted from her heart. She ran herself to answer the summons. A medium-sized, well-dressed, modest-looking young man stood at the entrance, and she brightened at sight of him.

"I am very glad you are so punctual; I was afraid I

should be disappointed," she said, leading the way to kitchen without an instant's delay. "Let me see—ten o'clock. I shall have to set you to work at once to prepare a first-class dinner. We are expecting company from London, my cook has left me, and I do not myself know anything about cooking. What is your name?" literally bereaving the young man of his hat and hanging it as high out of reach as possible.

His reply was rather faint, but she thought she caught it.

"Mac! You do not look like an Irishman. But it doesn't make any difference. Are you a good cook?"

The smile of the young man was rather puzzling. "I'll do my best," he said pleasantly.

"You see there's nothing in the house but cold chicken," continued Emma, unconsciously wringing her little hands as she continued to address the new cook, who certainly listened very attentively. "But my brother has sent us up some pigeons—to be roasted, I suppose."

"Yes'm."

"Can you make a celery salad?"

"I think I can."

"And Mayonnaise sauce for the cold chicken?"

"Yes'm."

"Can you make French soup?"

"I can."

"Oh, well, I think you will do" (beginning to look relieved).

"Be sure the vegetables are not overdone, and the coffee good—my brother is very particular about his coffee. And we will have a Florentine pudding?'' with an inquiring look.

" Yes'm,'' readily.

The new cook was already girding himself with one of the white towels that lay on the dresser, and casting a scrutinizing glance at the range fire.

Quite re-assured in spirit, Emma was turning away when she stopped to add :

"I will lay the table myself to-day, Mac, and fill the fruit-dishes and vases; but if you give satisfaction I will intrust you with the key of the china closet, and you will have the entire care of the table.''

And with a gracious nod the young lady withdrew from the kitchen.

She piled the fruit dishes with rosy pears, golden oranges and white grapes; filled the vases with roses, lilies and ferns; set clusters of dainty glasses, filled with amber jelly, among the silver and china, and then, with a sigh of satisfaction at the result, ran away to dress.

" I'll not go near the kitchen to even smell the dinner. I don't know anything about cooking it, and will trust to luck. I have an idea that Mac is really capable—is going to prove a treasure. His dress was so neat, and he was so quiet and respectful,'' concluded Emma, leisurely arranging her hair.

Her new dress, with its abundant lace and cardinal ribbons, was very becoming, and fitted the petite, round figure so perfectly, that Emma felt at peace with all the world.

" I have heard that Mr. Arthur Maxwell is very fastidious in the matter of ladies' dress,'' mused Emma, twisting

her head over her shoulder to see the effect of her sash. ,
"I wonder what his first impression of me will be? I
should like to have poor Ally's brother like me."

At length the last bracelet was clasped, the last touch
given, and, retiring backward from the mirror with a
radiant face, Emma turned and ran up to the nursery to
see the children dressed for company, and also to speak
with the boys—and, it must be confessed, flirt a little
with Mr. Vincent, the tutor, who was always at her service for this exercise.

There was a delightfully savory odor pervading the
house, when she came down and set out the fruits and
ice, and made a few additions to the table.

She looked at her watch—five minutes past three.
Then she went softly to the end of the hall, and listened
to the lively clatter in the kitchen. She could hear Mac
chatting pleasantly with the little housemaid, Nanny,
and all seemed to be well in that direction.

At ten minutes past three she repaired to the drawing-
room and took a seat overlooking the street.

Carriages came and carriages went, but none stopped
at the entrance.

The little girls, brave in new ribbons, came down.

The boys and Mr. Vincent came down.

Mr. Maye's latch-key rattled in the door, the dinner-
bell rang.

"Not come?" asked Mr. Maye, at sight of Emma's
disappointed face.

"No," she pouted, "and such a nice dinner!"

"Very strange!" mused that gentleman, now leading
the way into the dinner-room. "I hadn't the least

doubt—Why, my dear fellow," seizing by the shoulders the new cook, who, acting also as butler, had just placed the soup-tureen upon the table—"my dear fellow, why, how is this? Emma declared you hadn't come!"

That young lady grew as white as the table cloth, and grasped a chair for support.

"That Mr. Arthur Maxwell? I—I thought it was the cook."

"I came earlier than I expected, and in time to make myself useful to Miss Emma," laughed Mr. Maxwell, divesting himself of his white towel and bowing with grace to that young lady.

How could she have fallen into such an error?

"I was so terribly anxious—I didn't look at you twice. Mr. Maxwell, I hope you will forgive me!" stammered Emma, as red now as she had been pale.

"There is nothing to forgive, if my dinner turns out well," he added, laughing, evidently the sweetest tempered man in the world. "I learned to cook when I was a student in Paris—a Frenchman taught me. I have been rather proud of my culinary skill, but I am a little out of practice now, and am not quite sure of the Florentine."

"Emma," cried Mr. Maye, "what does this mean?"

"Why, John, you promised to send me up a man cook."

Mr. Maye clasped his hands tragically.

"Emma, I forgot it."

"Well, he came just at ten o'clock. I thought he was the cook; I ushered him into the kitchen, among the pots and pans. I questioned him as to what he knew about cooking. I urged him to make all haste and serve the dinner; and—and I called him an Irishman!" sobbed Emma, hysterically.

"No offense, Miss Emma. My grandfather, on my mother's side — Maj. Trelawny — was an Irishman," observed Mr. Maxwell, coolly. "And, since I have done my best, won't you try the soup before it is cold?"

The others stared and Emma cried, but Mr. Maye laughed—laughed uproariously.

"The best joke of the season! Sit down, everybody! Emma, you foolish girl, don't cry. Arthur doesn't care. And, as for your Florentine—Arthur, tell Nanny to bring it in. The proof of the pudding is the eating, you know."

"Miss Emma won't cry when she tastes my soup," remarked Arthur, ladling it out promptly, with an air of pride.

And then they fell to tasting and praising, and urging Emma to taste and praise, until she laughed and cried all together.

But Mr. Arthur was so delightful, so winning and so witty, so kind to his agitated young hostess, and had cooked such an excellent dinner—from the pigeons to the pudding, everything was perfect.

By-and-by Emma was herself again.

"This has taught me a lesson," she said. "I never will be so desperately situated again. I will learn to cook."

"Let me teach you," said Arthur.

He did

❧ CHAPTER XXVI. ❧

Keeping ❖ Boarders.

HERE is no doubt that the boarding-house business is a popular one, look at it from whatever side we may, for it gives the woman incapable of doing anything else, a chance to earn a respectable living, and it gives the people who are without homes or means to establish them a chance to live respectably. Like all other business, it is overdone, and it often proves a dismal failure in the hands of incompetent people, just as any other enterprise does. There are people who are well adapted to keeping boarders, and making money out of them, in a proper and legitimate way, and they are not the most agreeable characters to know, either, for entertaining guests at so much a head is certainly a rather demoralizing business. A woman needs to be sharp and shrewd who can cater successfully to a half hundred different tastes, serve them all with equal partiality, listen to their tales of woe, take sides in their domestic differences, and not let her left hand lodger know what the right hand lodger does or says. She must be blind to

frowns and sneers, and deaf to complaints, and able to
read character at a glance, so that she may not be
cheated out of board bills by some systematic Micawber;
she must harden her heart against stories of unpaid salaries and delayed remittances, or be unjust to herself
and her other boarders, who pay promptly. It is folly
to talk about model boarding houses, unless there is a
community of model boarders to fill it. In all boarding
houses the guests are served with what the best judgment of the landlady has dictated. It would be a most
delightful state of things if one could have broiled
chicken and another broiled steak, according to their
individual tastes; but this is only possible in restaurants
conducted on the European style, where each article is
paid for at its individual price. The wise landlady
studies the tastes of her boarders as far as she can; she
gives them each day a comfortable spread of such things
as are in the market and within the limits of the price
she pays for them, and a majority of the guests are satisfied. But there are some—and the captious critic
will at once cry out that these are women; yes, my dear
sir, I am afraid they are, with the exception of an old-
maidish man, with the tastes of an invalid—who always
want something that is not on the table or bill of fare,
such as toasted bread at dinner, or hot meats at supper.
If these things are not immediately forthcoming there
are complaints long and loud, and the grumbling individual infects the whole table with the same spirit.
There must be a little wise management here, and, if
within the bounds of reason, the boarder's tastes should
be consulted and the favorite dish prepared, for this

involves the principle of home. One man or woman can
not eat hot bread, so a plate of the cold article is placed
near. It gives a little more work to the tired waiters,
but, to look at it financially, it will probably pay in the
end. "But," says some envious boarder, "this is being
partial."

Not at all; because *you* can not get home to dinner a
plate of hot viands is in the oven for you, and the balance is struck.

Nearly all boarding houses are kept by women. It
is an established fact, that men are unsuccessful and
unpopular in the business. They have neither the prudence or the patience to contend with the many difficulties in the way. In the best kept boarding house the
landlady is never seen, except when business requires
her. She has her own room, which is also her office,
and boarders go there to see her, engage board, pay bills,
or make complaints. She takes no one without special
reference, and aims at having her people of a social
equality, and of such financial standing as will ensure
their bills being promptly paid. She will be able to
cater to their wants much easier if free from anxiety on
this head; and if she has discrimination she will soon
learn what kind of a table to set. If they pay handsomely she can have her house well furnished, and keep
it in repair; but the average boarder pays only for what
there is to eat: the price does not include new Brussels
carpet in the halls every spring, and a luxurious air of
hot house prosperity. The thread-bare carpets and worn
furniture, familiar to all who have ever lived in large
boarding houses, are not the results of a penurious dis-

position, but of actual necessity. There is nothing left when the rent, fuel, and food, with gas, wages, and incidental expenses, to which the arrears of impecunious boarders must be added, not even enough to give the patient, over-worked landlady a new dress. She is only too thankful that she has earned food and shelter for herself and family, and not run in debt. Boarders seldom take this into consideration.

If a woman owns her house she has a better chance to make a little profit; and if she is unscrupulous and cheats her trades-people, she saves enough to retire upon, but the actual experience of all boarding house keepers is about the same. If, by the closest good management, they can pay expenses, they consider themselves fortunate. There are some people who always manage to get their board at cost price, and these are usually the ones who, after a while, neglect to pay at all. Every landlady suffers from these irregular people, who expect to live comfortably at the expense of others, and usually manage to do so.

Having decided that there must be a certain uniform system about the table, on the basis which is equally removed from niggardliness or extravagance, the next item of regard is the cooking, and this can give a character to a boarding house just as decidedly as the guests. Eternal vigilance is the price of a good table, as much as it is of liberty. The table cloths and napkins must be spotless for the dinner table—if they can not be changed at each meal—the silver and glasses highly polished, the food well cooked and savory. The vegetables cooked in boarding houses are usually abominable, and an investi-

gation into the matter discloses the fact that in nine
times out of ten the vegetable cook is a slatteringly girl
who knows nothing about the business, and is hardly
competent to wash a pan full of potatoes properly. She
pares the potatoes without washing them first, to save
trouble, and puts them on in cold water, to soak and
simmer, or else she hurries them over the fire and cooks
them at a galloping boil, taking them off with a "bone
in the middle." There are as many different ways of
cooking potatoes as there are days in the week, but the
average boarding house finds it too much trouble, or,
rather, the servants do. It is certainly one woman's
work to attend to the vegetables alone and cook them as
they should be cooked. Who does not recall the mashed
potatoes of home as compared with those of the boarding
house, with a yearning sense of loss. And how different
the black, soggy mass called fried potatoes from the
crisp, brown slices that mother cooked. True, there
are a great many more to cook for, but the one woman
can easily do it. And the strong grease in which they
are usually cooked is one of the penny-wise-pound-
foolish habits of the woman who despises the day of
small things.

Marketing judiciously is another of the branches
which a woman, who would be successful in it, must
study and understand. The woman who pays ready
money for all she buys will save a large per centage on
her purchases. She should have her marketing always
done a week in advance, or nearly so; that is, she should
select her steaks and roasts of beef for Thursday on Monday, and have it hung in the ice-room. The fish for Wed-

nesdays and Fridays should be decided on the same day. The poultry for Thursdays and Sundays engaged regularly from a poulterer who knows his customer and dare not supply an inferior article, and so on with all other supplies. And let her vary the monotony of a uniform day for fish and fowl, by giving her boarders a surprise. A supper of tenderloin steaks and escalloped potatoes, or a New England Sunday breakfast of baked beans and brown bread, with baked apples and fried mush, or a dinner course of oysters and celery, on some day that is not Sunday. Instead of the stewed prunes, prunelles, dried peaches and apple sauce, which figure over and over on the boarding house table, let her have fresh canned peaches and cream, preserves, apples quartered and dropped into a boiling syrup of white sugar, flavored with lemon, and some of the home dishes, custards and floating islands that are so grateful to the eyes and delicious to the taste. A house that has a reputation of this kind is always filled with boarders. Hot Graham gems and a cup of fragrant, yellow coffee for supper will prove a great innovation upon bakers' toast and weak, sloppy tea. It will require more labor and forethought, but when that woman wants to sell the good will of the business she will realize its full value in dollars and cents, and she will never need to advertise for boarders. A mechanics' boarding house frequently pays better than the aristocratic one which has a high rent and much style to contend with. Clean beds and a good table are the principal requisites; the cooking good but plain. The men usually have good appetites and make a vigorous attack on the substantials,

18

and care more for quantity than quality. They have been used to homes, and like the landlady to preside in the dining room and look after their comfort herself, and they are usually good pay. In all large cities where rent is high, a few boarders are taken in the family to help out. It is not, as a general thing, pleasant to board in a private family where the boarder is one of themselves and has "*all the comforts of a home.*" It means going without fire in one's room and feeling like an intruder in the family circle—to taking pot-luck on Mondays and Saturdays, and getting dinner down town whenever the girl leaves or has the sulks. There is also a certain amount of patronage bestowed on the family boarder, who is made to feel the great privilege of being received into the bosom of so highly respected a family, who only take boarders for company. This method of doing business is as silly as the announcement of the young man who desires to enter a home where his society will be an equivalent for his board. Boarders are not guests. If they could not pay for the privilege of being one of the family they would soon be required to leave.

Business principles should control in this matter. If the boarder grows into the family and finds a place in the regard of its members, it will be the happy result of good sense and congeniality between them, and thrice happy is the wayworn wanderer who finds such a haven of rest.

The ideal boarding house is the one where the landlady has no time to gossip about her boarders; where she does not assume the management of their domestic affairs; where the elements of tattling and backbiting never gain entrance; in short, where a community of ladies and gentlemen manage their housekeeping on the co-operative plan and meet at one common table, where they can enjoy each other's company socially. Every room is a home—a castle to its temporary owner. The landlady is the queen of the realm, and she needs to be wise and gracious in her rule if she would have loyal subjects.

Much has been said about the lack of home comfort in a boarding house, and the meagre furniture of rooms offered for inspection. But it remains for the boarder who takes possession to transform the bare room into a home, to magnetize the walls with an atmosphere of love and contentment. The landlady who furnishes her house does not know whom she is furnishing for, what style of chairs and sofas the new comers would prefer, or if she may not be obliged to hustle her own furniture into the attic to make room for the household goods of the new boarders. It is desirable that the room should be clean —thoroughly clean, and the bed in good order—plenty of towels and fresh water, and a cake of genuine soap. Any attempt at parsimony will be a bad stroke of policy to begin with. As heaven has never yet been realized upon earth, it would be vain to look for it even in the ideal boarding house, the projector of which has an urgent need of dollars and cents as a basis on which to found it. The only way in which she can realize success is to conduct it on the best business system, making her labor yield a fair profit. There is no doubt that there is money in it.

CHAPTER XXVII

Story of a Summer Boarder.

I T was a scandal," the neighbors said, "that Miss Delia should be obliged to take boarders, after all she'd been through; and Heaven knows, boarders did not help a body to work out her salvation. And so much money in the family, too, taking it by small and large. Wasn't her uncle Eben, over at Dover, well-to-do, and not a chick of his own to care for except the boy he had adopted, who was no credit to him? It was odd, now, that a man with poor relations should take to a stranger when his own flesh and blood was needy; but sometimes it does seem as if folks had more feeling for others than for their own kith and kin. Then there were cousins in the city, forehanded and fashionable, who were never worth a row of pins to Delia, and there was her great-uncle John's widow a-larkin' on the continent, a-gamin' at Baden-Baden, and trying the waters of every mineral spring in the three kingdoms, for no disease under the sun but old age. She had been known to say that her folks were too rich already, and probably she would endow some hospital with her property." Evidently, wealthy relatives were of no value to Miss Delia. To be sure, she had never seen her great-aunt since she was a child, when her uncle John had brought her into their simple life for a month's visit. with her French maid and dresses, her jewels and fallals, w ich won the heart of her namesake. Since then uncle John's widow had become a sort of gilded creation, always young and beautiful; for, though Delia had received little gifts from time to time across the seas for the last fifteen years, she had neither heard nor seen anything of the being who had inspired her youthful imagination, and was quite uncertain if such a person as Mrs. John Rogerson was in the land of the living. Dead or alive, she seemed to have made no material difference to Delia's humdrum life. After having nursed her father through a long sickness, Delia found that he had left a heavy mortgage on the homestead, and her mother and herself on the high road to the poorhouse, unless they should bestir themselves. As her mother was already bedridden, the stirring naturally fell upon Delia, and she advertised for summer boarders:

> GOOD BOARD in the country near the river side, at $7 a week. Large chambers, broad piazzas, fine views, berries and new milk. One mile from the station.
>
> Address DELIA ROGERSON,
> *Croftsborough, Me.*

"Cheap enough!" commented an elderly lady who happened upon it. "Delia Rogerson. An old maid, I

suppose, obliged to look out for herself. I've a good
mind to try her broad piazzas and new milk. If I don't
like it there'll be no harm done.''

And so Delia's first boarder arrived—an old lady with
false front hair, brown wrinkled skin, faded eyes, a black
alpaca gown and a hair trunk. Delia made her as welcome as if she had been a duchess; lighted a fire in Mrs.
Clement's room, as the night was damp, and brought out
her daintiest cup and saucer, with the fadeless old roses
wreathing them. ''Wonderfully kind,'' reflected Mrs.
Clement, as she combed out her wisps of gray hair and
confided the false front to a box. ''Wonderful kindness for $7 a week. She's new to the trade. She'll
learn better. Human nature doesn't change with lati-
tudes. She'll find it doesn't pay to consider the comforts of a poverty-stricken old creature.'' But in spite
of her worldly wisdom, Mrs. Clement was forced to confess that Delia had begun as she meant to hold out,
though other boarders came to demand her attention
and to multiply her cares. The fret and jar of conflict-
ing temperaments under her roof was a new experience
to Delia. When Mrs. Griscome complained of the mos-
quitoes, with an air as if Miss Rogerson were responsible
for their creation; of flies, as if they were new acquaint-
ances; of want of appetite, as though Delia had agreed
to supply it along with berries and new milk; of the
weather, as if she had pledged herself there would be
no sudden changes to annoy her boarders; of the shabby
house and antiquated furniture, ''too old for comfort,
and not old enough for fashion''—then Delia doubted if
taking boarders was her mission. ''What makes you

keep us, my dear?" asked Mrs. Clement, after a day when everything and everybody had seemed to go wrong. "Why didn't you ever marry? You had a lover, I dare say?"

"Yes, a long, long time ago."

"Tell me about him—it?"

"There isn't much to tell. He asked me to marry him. He was going to Australia. I couldn't leave father and mother, you know (they were both feeble), and he couldn't stay here. That's all.'

"And you—you?"

"Now all men beside are to me like shadows."

"And have you never heard of him since?"

"Yes. He wrote; but where was the use? It could never come to anything. It was better for him to forget me and marry. I was a millstone about his neck. I didn't answer his letter."

"And supposing he should return some day, would you marry him?"

"I dare say," laughed Delia, gently, as if the idea were familiar, "let the neighbors laugh ever so wisely, I've thought of it sometimes sitting alone, when the world was barren and commonplace. One must have recreation of some kind, you know. Everybody requires a little romance, a little poetry, to flavor everyday thinking and doing. I am afraid you think me a silly old maid, Mrs. Clement."

"No. The heart never grows old. The skin shrivels, the color departs, the eyes fade, the features grow pinched; but the soul is heir of eternal youth—it is as beautiful at fourscore as at 'sweet twenty.' Time

makes amends for the ravages of the body by developing the spirit. You didn't tell me your lover's name.
Perhaps you would rather not."

"His name was Stephen Langdon. Sometimes Capt.
Seymour runs against him in Melbourne, and brings me
word how he looks and what he is doing, though I never
ask, and Stephen never asks for me that I can hear."

Delia's summer boarders were not a success, to be
sure. If they took no money out of her pocket, they
put none in. She was obliged to eke out her support by
copying for lawyer Dunmore, and embroidering for Mrs.
Judge Door. One by one her boarders dropped away
like autumn leaves; all but old Mrs. Clement.

"I believe I'll stay on," she said. "I'm getting too
old to move often. Perhaps you take winter boarders
at reduced rates. Eh ?"

"Do you think my rates high ?"

"By no means. But when one's purse is low—"

"Yes; I know. Do stay at your own price. I can't
spare you." She had grown such a fondness for the old
lady that to refuse her at her own terms would have
seemed like turning her own mother out of doors;
besides, one mouth more would not signify. But she
found it hard to make both ends meet, and often went
to bed hungry, that her mother and Mrs. Clement might
enjoy enough, without there appearing to be "just a
pattern." At Christmas, however, came a ray of sunshine for Delia, in the shape of a $100 bill from an
unknown friend.

"It can't be meant for me," she cried.

"It's directed to Delia Rogerson," said her mother;

"and there's nobody else of that name, now that your, Aunt Delia's dead."

"We are not sure she's dead," objected Delia.

"Horrors! Don't you know whether your aunt is dead or alive?" asked Mrs. Clement, in a shocked tone.

"It isn't our fault. She is rich and lives abroad. I was named for her. I used to look in the glass and try to believe I'd inherit her beauty with the name, though she was only our great-uncle's wife."

"She ought to be doing something for you."

"How can she if she is dead? I don't blame her, anyway. Her money is her own, to use according to her pleasure. Uncle John made it himself and gave it to her."

"But if she should come back to you, having run through with it, you'd divide your last crust with her, I'll be bound."

"I suppose I should," replied Delia.

The winter wore away as winters will, and the miracles of spring began in fields and wayside, and Delia's boarders returned with the June roses, and dropped away again with the falling leaves, and still Mrs. Clement stayed on. Just now she had been some weeks in arrears with her reduced board. No money had been forthcoming for some time, and she was growing more feeble daily, needed the luxuries of an invalid and the attention of a nurse, both of which Delia bestowed upon her, without taking thought of the morrow.

"I must hear from my man-of-business to-morrow, Delia; I'm knee-deep in debt to you," she began one night.

"Don't mention it," cried Delia. "I'd rather never see a cent of it than have you take it to heart. You are welcome to stay and share pot-luck with us, you are such company for mother and me."

"Thank you, my dear. I've grown as fond of you as if you were my own flesh and blood. There, turn down the light. Draw the curtain, dear, and put another stick on the fire, please. It grows chilly, doesn't it? You might kiss me just once, if you wouldn't mind. It's one hundred years or so since any one kissed me."

And next morning when Delia carried up Mrs. Clement's breakfast her boarder lay cold and still upon the pillows.

The first shock over, Delia wrote to the lawyer of whom she had heard Mrs. Clement speak as having charge of her affairs, begging him to notify that lady's relatives, if she had any. In reply, Mr. Wills wrote:

"The late Mrs. Clement appears to have no near relatives. Some distant cousins, who have an abundance of the world's goods, yet served her shabbily when she tested their generosity as she has tried yours, are all that remain of her family. In the meantime I enclose you a copy of her last will and testament, to peruse at your leisure."

"What interest does he think I take in Mrs. Clement's will," thought Delia, but she read, nevertheless:

Being of sound mind, this, the 16th day of June, 18—, I, Delia Rogerson Clement, do hereby leave $100 to each of my cousins; and I bequeath the residue of my property, viz., $30,000 invested in the Ingot Mining Company, $50,000 in United States bonds, $20,000 in the For-

tunate Flannel Mills, and my jewels, to the beloved
niece of my first husband, John Rogerson, Delia Rogerson, of Croftsborough, Me.

For I was a stranger and ye took me in; hungry, and
ye fed me; sick and ye ministered unto me.

"Goodness alive!" cried the neighbors, when the fact
reached their ears, "what a profitable thing it is to take
boarders. Everybody in town will be trying it. Of
course Steve Langdon will come and marry her, if she
were forty old maids. You may stick a pin in there!"

Delia did not open her house to boarders the next season. She found enough to do in looking after her money
and spending it; in replying to letters from indigent people, who seemed to increase alarmingly; in receiving old
friends, who suddenly found time to remember her existence. And, sure enough, among the rest appeared Steve
Langdon, and all the village said: "I told you so."

"It's not my fault that you and I are single yet,
Delia," he said.

"And we are too old to think of it now, Steve."

"Nonsense! It's never too late to mend. I'm not
rich, Delia, but I've enough for two and to spare."

"I wouldn't be contented not to drive in my carriage
and have servants under me now," laughed Delia.

"Indeed! Then, perhaps, you have a better match in
view. Capt. Seymour asked me, by the way, if I had
come to interfere with Squire Jones' interest."

"Yes, Squire Jones proposed to me last week."

"Now, see here, Delia. Have I come all the way from
Melbourne on a fool's errand? There I was growing used
to my misery and loneliness, when the mail brings me a

letter in a strange hand, which tells me that my dear love, Delia Rogerson, loves and dreams of me still, is poor and alone, and needs me—me! And the letter is signed by her aunt, Mrs. Clement, who ought to know. I packed my household goods and came."

"I'm glad that you did."

"In order that I may congratulate 'Squire Jones?'"

"But I haven't accepted him. In fact, I've refused him—because—because—"

"Because you will marry your old love, like the lass in the song, Delia?"

In Croftsborough, people are not yet tired of telling how a woman made money by taking boarders.

CHAPTER XXVIII

The · Value · of · Personal · Appearance.

A YOUNG woman entering upon a business life must ask and answer one question almost at its outset: "Shall she go into society or not?" By society I mean the parties, weddings, receptions, dinners, and lunches, which make up the existence of merely fashionable women. If she has a large and influential acquaintance she will necessarily be invited out a great many times, she will be obliged to dress correspondingly well, and her dress will naturally demand some time and attention, as well as a good deal of money. Social life, parties and balls will keep her up late at night and tax her strength, and the question to herself will be, whether she will be able to meet the demands of society and of business, and preserve her health? Here, again, the frequent theory of women's ability to overwork intrudes itself. There can be no possible doubt that if she is engaged eight hours a

285

day, in any kind of work, she will do better to ignore society, and rest in the evenings; but if

> All work and no play
> Makes Jack a dull boy,

will it not apply equally well to Jill? Only Jack has the strength and Jill has not.

A compromise can be made by going out occasionally, and not attempting to compete with the women who have nothing to do, and by not keeping excessively late hours. One rich, dark silk, made with an evening waist and worn with a change of laces and flowers, a cream-white dotted muslin and an illusion over-dress will be all sufficient for a season, with a supply of fresh gloves, and will look much better, even if worn frequently, than a new, cheap, hastily gotten together evening dress. When there is only one silk it should be either black or a dark olive or blue, as a vivid, new color will be so conspicuous that the wearer will soon be known by it, and there will be some one ill-natured enough to say, "There goes that everlasting sunflower yellow silk of Miss ——'s." Black can be worn with masses of pink garniture, upon one occasion, with pink gloves; with white upon another with white gloves; with masses of mixed flowers and deep orange gloves; and it will always look handsome. Then it can be a dead black toilet—quantities of black lace, black gloves, and coral or gold jewelry as an effect. One of the most elegant toilets I ever saw was a black silk, draped and trimmed with water lilies, and worn with pale green gloves that reached above the elbows. It is by no means the expense of a costume that makes it elegant. There are hundreds of

dowdy women at parties who are elaborately dressed
and loaded with diamonds, and there are ladies who are
regally beautiful in severely plain toilets. Some ladies
need very little adornment. This is especially the case
with young women who have dark hair and eyes, and a
fresh color. If they wear much jewelry, or dress in high
colors, they are at once commented on with unfriendly
criticism. Miss Oakey, who is an authority on beauty
in dress, and the author of a book with that title, says:
"The object of dress may be said to be threefold—to
cover, to warm, to beautify. Beauty in dress, as in
other things, is largely relative." To admit this, is to
admit that a dress which is beautiful upon one woman
may be hideous worn by another. Each should understand her own style, accept it, and let the fashion of her
dress be built upon it. Because my dark, slender friend
looks well in a heavy velvet with a high ruff, her rival,
who is short and blonde, tries to outshine her in a heavier
velvet, with a higher ruff. It is reason enough that the
last should look ill in the dress, because the first looks
well in it.

ELOQUENCE OF DRESS.

Not every woman can dress well with the most reckless expenditure; but a clever woman can dress well with
intelligent economy and an artistic taste. Let women
remember that it is harmony of color and grace of cut
that makes a dress beautiful, and its fitness to the style
and needs of the wearer, not richness of material or cost-
liness of ornament. No material is more beautiful than
a cashmere, which is one of the most truly economic
dresses that one can wear, as it both washes and dyes,

without loss of beauty, and wears well and long. The dress should always be harmonious with one's surroundings. Sometimes a woman is more elegant in a plain dress, when a richer dress, being out of place, would be vulgar. Let the dress be so simply an expression of the woman that she is unconscious of it when she has put it on. Let the thinking come before the dressing. Thus, alone, can she be harmonious, and possess the graceful attributes that form the highest beauty.

Another high authority on all that pertains to the well being of true womanhood, Mrs. Julia Ward Howe, thus writes:

"If dress can heighten the whole sense of what is really beautiful in womanhood, it is certainly a power, and a great one. Surely, one of the first conditions to this end would be, that dress should represent womanly reserve. It should clothe, not disguise or deform. The lines of beauty should be preserved—colors should be modest beside the coloring of nature. Let no glaring tints disturb the harmony of the delicately-blended lines. The gold in a young girl's hair, the evanescent roses in her cheeks, glowing and paling with the rhythm of her pulse, is a silent eloquence, or, rather, a light-and-shadow utterance. Never profane or frizzle the one out of all color, or place beside the other any brilliant ornament which can conflict with its perfect charm."

Every year that a woman lives the more pains she should take with her dress. The dress of elderly ladies ought to be more of a science than it is. How often one hears a woman of fifty say, "Oh, my dressing days are past;" when, if she thought about it, they have only well begun. At least, the time has come when dress is

more to her than ever. Remember, that from forty to
sixty-five is a quarter of a century—the third of a long
life. It is the period through which the majority of
grown-up people pass. And yet how little pride women
take—how little thought beforehand—to be charming
then.

THE OTHER EXTREME.

But she must be equally careful to avoid a foolish
assumption of youth, which will be even more unbecoming. The well-known saying, that a woman is no older
than she looks, amiable and consoling as it is, has not
been altogether harmless. Acting upon this assumption, and losing sight of the eternal fitness of things,
many a woman has arrayed herself in a manner which is
not only entirely unbecoming to her face, but has a tendency to make her ridiculous. Who has not trembled
for a friend when the mania seized her to color her hair;
and then, as her good sense admonished her never to do
it again, walked trembling by her side while she wore
the changing hues from black to greenish white; and
who does not rejoice at the decree which makes it possible for gray hair to be not only honorable, but beautiful and fashionable also? There are other things which
need the strong light of common sense thrown upon
them—the colors chosen for dresses, the style of the
hats and bonnets, the dressing for the neck demand
attention. What a pity it is that women with thin
faces and necks do not understand the softening effect of
lace—white next the throat and black outside of that.
Plain, rich dresses emphasize the grace which should, at
fifty, be even more admirable than at twenty-five or
19

thirty. One is disposed to wonder at, if not to criticize, Thackeray severely for making Henry Esmond marry Lady Castlewood, whose daughter was his first love; and he is pardoned only when we remember that her lovely character and the beauty of her face are represented as existing without the aid of those artificial appliances which disfigure some women even at the present day, when good sense is the rule and not the exception. The "eternal fitness of things" should be studied by every woman; and she might make a sort of golden text of this sentence. No woman looks so old as one who tries to look young. The little girl who tries on her mother's apron, and so has a long dress in front, and the traditional ostrich which hides its head in the sand, are not more absurd than the woman who persuades herself at forty that she looks eighteen. If she would only stop a moment and reason with herself, she would know that she is infinitely more handsome as she is. Would she exchange the lines of intelligence, of thought, of knowledge, for the mere simper of youth? Her face that has bent over the cradled babe night after night has the holy seal of motherhood to beautify it; the eyes that have looked into the faces of the dying have a tender light in their depths; love has glorified the quivering mouth with its sacred pathos; the faded complexion is lighted by the immortal glow of life's western sky.

> " Would you be young again?
> So would not I;
> One tear to memory given,
> Onward we hie.

Life's dark stream forded o'er,
Almost at rest on shore.
Say, would you plunge once more,
   With home so nigh?"

There are some old ladies who are grandly beautiful. I recall such a one, with snowy white hair, dressed fashionably; with a rich, black velvet dress, and masses of real old lace and blonde at the throat. And when she went to parties she wore pink roses in her hair and in her bosom, and to some one who criticized her she said: " Did you never hear how the roses grow over old ruins, showing the triumph of nature over art ?" and went on her way with stately step and a sad, sweet smile on her grand, old face.

Some writer has said that a woman's power in the world is measured by her power to please. Whatever she may wish to accomplish she will best manage it by pleasing. A woman's grand social aim should be to please. And let me tell you how that is to be done. A woman can please the eye by her appearance, her dress, her face, her figure. A plain woman can never be pretty. She can always be fascinating, if she takes pains. I well remember a man, who was a great admirer of our sex, telling me that one of the most fascinating women he had ever met with was not only not pretty, but, as to her face, decidedly plain—ugly, only the word is rude. How, then, did she fascinate ? I well remember his reply : " Her figure," said he, " was neat, her dressing was faultless, her every movement was graceful, her conversation was clever and animated, and she always tried to please. It was not I alone who called her fasrinating. She was one of the most acceptable women in society I ever knew. She married brilliantly, and her husband, a lawyer in large practice, was much devoted to her.

A BUSINESS DRESS.

Much has been said about a distinctive dress for ladies who are engaged in business pursuits, but as the sisterhood has never taken kindly to a uniform, and there is a more definite style about the individual in the ranks of women than in those of men, it would be hard to decide on any one particular costume that will please all. Some little black-eyed, trim-figured woman will sheath herself in a neat-fitting black dress, with a segment of white linen at the neck and cuffs, cover her smooth hair with a close Turban hat, draw on a pair of dog-skin gloves, and look essentially refined and lady-like, while another in the same suit would be intolerably loud and ungraceful in appearance. Water-proofs, Ulsters, gossamers, and similar garments are worn almost universally on the street, but in shops, offices, the school-room, and other commercial resorts where women are to be found, the dress will remain a matter of individual taste. Custom makes laws as irrevocable as those of legislatures, and the time has not yet come, possibly never will, when a girl can snatch her hat from its nail and get out into the open air as quickly as her brother. There must necessarily be certain restrictions of sex, and no amount of reform will change the laws of nature. The matter is already simplified by the short, scant dress, and the absence of trails, hoops, and bustles, and it is to be hoped these will never be resumed to such an extent by our fashionable women that the others will feel obliged to adopt them. The working dress of American ladies to-day is a happy compromise between the despotic fashions of a court and the severe bigotry of a reform costume of the coat and trowsers pattern. The absence of voluminous skirts of white goods, starched and fluted, is not to be deplored, when a single yoked garment, depending from the shoulder, can happily replace them. A dark, neat color, such as navy blue, or a rich brown, in a soft woolen goods that drapes artistically, and follows the outlines of the form in classic folds, is preferable to the wash lawns and percales of the past, and saves much time and money over laundrying, etc. Thus one vexed question has adjusted itself, and we will not ask whether it came through the reformer or the fashion inventor; it is enough to know that a woman can dress prettily and in accordance with the laws of health at the same time, and that time is the present.

DRESS REFORMERS.

Miss Oakey voices the opinion of all sensible women when she says, in one of her essays: "It appears to us that the failure of the 'dress reformers' to find acceptance, except at the hands of a few enthusiasts, arises from two causes: First. That their object has no relation to beauty; and, secondly, because they defeat their own purpose by a superficial knowledge of the true formation of the body. A dress reform that opposes itself to beauty, deserves to be stamped out by every reasonable woman in the land, just as a fashion that, in its blind search for beauty, destroys the most beautiful work of the Creator, deserves the same fate. The human being was meant to be beautiful. It is always an accident or mistake, or blind or willful disregard of the laws of nature when the human being is ugly as an individual or as a race. The highest beauty is elevating and refining in its influence on the individual and on the home. It is the natural object of the desire of humanity. The infant, who can not speak, delights in it. The most cultured man uses it to express his highest aspiration. The Creator sows it broadcast over nature. Even the dumb animals have some sense of it; and here starts up a little band of 'reformers,' so-called, doubtless as sincere as they are misguided, and they say that beauty is a mistake, a delusion, and a snare; that what we shall seek is use—simply use—as if, forsooth, use and beauty were at war with each other. We might say that use demands beauty almost, though we can not reverse the saying, and assert that beauty demands use, for 'beauty is its own excuse for being,' our wise and honored sage has said in one of his deepest moments; and yet this beauty, that exists as it were for very pleasure, has, perhaps, the highest use—that of lifting us for the time quite out of all doctrines of expediency, and floating us in the purely ideal world.''

Emerson wrote of Margaret Fuller: ''She was always dressed neatly and becoming.'' Even a philosopher, writing of so eminent a woman as Miss Fuller, could remember that. The fact is, that the more prominently a woman is before the world, or in any kind of semi-public work, such as a professional and literary life really is, the more scrupulously should she insist on perfect taste of toilet.

"WHERE IS YOUR HOME?" "WHERE MOTHER IS."

CHAPTER XXIX.

The Kingdom of Home.

"Domestic Happiness, thou only bliss
Of Paradise that has survived the fall."

"Our wives are as comely
And our home is still home, be it ever so homely."

—Dibdin.

IN speaking of his home to a friend, a child was asked, "Where is your home?" Looking with loving eyes at his mother, he replied, "Where mother is."

"Home," says a celebrated divine, "should be the center of joy, equatorial and tropical. A man's house should be on the hill-top of cheerfulness and serenity so high that no shadows rest upon it, and where the morning comes so early and the evening tarries so late that the day has twice as many golden hours as those of other men. He is to be pitied whose house is in some valley of grief between the hills, with the longest night and the shortest day."

It is the woman in the house who makes the home,

not always an easy or a comfortable task to do, but most satisfactory when accomplished.

THE INFLUENCE OF THE WIFE AND MOTHER

in the domestic world is unquestioned, her sway is absolute; she can make all who come within her reach happy and contented or she can render them miserable. She can rule with an iron rod or lead with a silken string. "When you want to get the grandest idea of a queen," says a modern writer, "you do not think of Catherine of Russia, or of Anne of England, or of Marie Theresa of Germany; but when you want to get your *grandest* idea of a queen you think of the plain woman who sat opposite your father at the table, or walked with him arm-in-arm down life's pathway, sometimes to the thanksgiving banquet, sometimes to the grave, but always together—soothing your petty griefs, correcting your childish waywardness, joining in your infantile sports, listening to your evening prayers, toiling for you with needle or at the spinning-wheel, and on cold nights wrapping you up snug and warm. And then at last, on that day when she lay in the back room dying, and you saw her take those thin hands with which she had toiled for you so long and put them together in a dying prayer that commended you to the God whom she had taught you to trust—oh, she was the queen! The chariots of God came down to fetch her, and as she went in all heaven rose up. You cannot think of her now without a rush of tenderness that stirs the deep foundations of your soul, and you feel as much a child again as when you cried on her lap; and if you could bring her back again to speak just once more your name as tenderly as she used to speak it, you would be willing to throw yourself on the ground and kiss the sod that covers her, crying, 'Mother! Mother!' Ah, she was the queen! She was the queen!''

AN IDEAL WOMAN.

She was my peer;
No weakling girl, who would surrender will
And life and reason, with her loving heart,
To her possessor; no soft, clinging thing
Who would find breath alone within the arms
Of a strong master, and obediently
Wait on his will in slavish carefulness;
No fawning, cringing spaniel to attend
His royal pleasure, and account herself
Rewarded by his pats and pretty words,
But a sound woman, who, with insight keen,
Had wrought a scheme of life, and measured well
Her womanhood; had spread before her feet
A fine philosophy to guide her steps;
Had won a faith to which her life was brought
In strict adjustment—brain and heart meanwhile
Working in conscious harmony and rhythm
With the great scheme of God's great universe
On toward her being's end.

.—*Holland.*

HOME EDUCATION.

Teach children to eat properly and speak correctly in the home circle. Many a young man has gone out of his father's home into the world, who has been mortified and embarrassed by the criticism of strangers on his table manners and conversation. Children acquire a habit of using slip-shod expressions, such as, "I ain't

got it," "I don't want nothing;" of using the knife
instead of the fork ; of eating in a loud and noisy manner,
with their elbows extended as if they were birds feeding
on the wing ; of making uncouth sounds in breathing,
and of acting in other careless ways which are exceed-
ingly annoying to older and well-bred people. These
are all indications of lack of home breeding. Parents
who have been neglected themselves in their early years
have no right to transmit their careless habits to their
children, or send them out into the world to learn in
manhood or womanhood the primary laws of social
ethics. It has been wisely said that education does not
begin with the alphabet. It commences with a mother's
look, with a father's nod of approval or his sign of
reproof ; with a sister's gentle pressure of the hand, or a
brother's noble act of forbearance ; with a handful of
flowers in green and daisied meadows ; with a bird's
nest admired but not touched ; with pleasant walks in
shady lanes, and with thoughts directed, in sweet and
kindly tones and words, to nature, to beauty, to acts of
benevolence, to deeds of virtue. To every parent, to
every influential member of a household, there is com-
mitted a charge which can be shifted to no one else.
There can be no model system grafted upon the family
tree. The children of one family cannot be brought up
successfully by the same method. There must be kisses
for one and discipline for another. In this connection an
incident suggests itself. A mother of my acquaintance
had two little girls—one a healthy, strong child, without
nerves ; the other a delicate, sensitive, shrinking little
one, with a shy and timid nature. The mother had one

set of rules for the two children ; they ate the same food,
and were sent to bed at exactly the same hour, immediately after a light supper. The younger and healthier one went to sleep at once ; the other begged for a light to be kept burning, and when this was denied would be found sitting in the passage-ways in a tremor of fright, which no amount of reasoning would control. Cold hands and feet and a burning head resulted. The doctor was constantly in attendance upon the little one, who could not go to school without getting a severe cold, though both wore the same amount of clothing and were equally well guarded from the weather. The mother took counsel with herself, and wisely adopted a different method of treatment with the child. She put her bed in her own chamber, kept a night-lamp burning, and sat in the room with the little girl telling her soothing stories until she fell quietly to sleep. Believing that her child's interests were superior to all others, she never allowed anything to interfere with her evening work, until the time came when the little girl could be safely left alone, her thoughts composed and her nerves tranquil. Had the mother persisted in her first attempt to bring up the two children on the same hygienic and mental plans, one would probably have been a peevish invalid for life, with impaired mental faculties. If it is necessary for us to respect each other's prejudices, how much more important that we conciliate infirmities of temperament which are so closely allied with our personal welfare.

HAPPY SLUMBERS.

There is one rule that it is always safe to enforce in

the family—the rule of love which will send each child
to bed with a smile on its lips and peace in its heart.
Fretful mothers have much to excuse them, for there is
an accumulation of work and responsibility in the home,
of which they bear the chief burden, but it will pay
them infinitely well in the end to send the children to
bed happy. They will be more tractable and useful in
the morning; they will have happier memories of their
childhood when they have gone out from the home nest
into the world, and they will enshrine in their hearts, as
household saints, the mothers who gave them a good-
night kiss with smiles and benedictions every night of
their young lives. Mothers seem to think often that
childhood is eternal—that the little one will always be
there to kiss and caress; but it is inevitable that the
child is with us but a few years, and the mother who
neglected the opportunity of going into the next room
to press the rosy cheek with a good-night kiss, sits alone
and asks in sadness and solitude, "Where is my boy
to-night?" "Where is my girl to-night?"

THE VALUE OF "MOTHER."

A father, talking to his careless daughter, said: "I
want to speak to you of your mother. It may be that
you have noticed a careworn look upon her face lately.
Of course, it has not been brought there by any act of
yours, but still it is your duty to chase it away. I want
you to get up to-morrow morning and get breakfast; and
when your mother comes and begins to express her surprise, go right up and kiss her on the cheek. You can't
imagine how it will brighten her dear face. Besides,

you owe her a kiss or two.   Away back, when you were
a little girl, she kissed you when no one else was tempted
by your fever-tainted breath and swollen face.   You
were not as attractive then as you are now.   And
through those years of childish sunshine and shadows
she was always ready to cure, by the magic of a mother's
kiss, the little dirty, chubby hands whenever they were
injured in those first skirmishes with the rough old
world.   And then the midnight kiss with which she
routed so many bad dreams, as she leaned above your
restless pillow, have all been on interest these long, long
years.   Of course, she is not so pretty and kissable as
you are ; but if you had done your share of work during
the last ten years the contrast would not be so marked.
Her face has more wrinkles than yours, far more, and
yet if you were sick that face would appear more beautiful than an angel's as it hovered over you, watching
every opportunity to minister to your comfort, and
every one of those wrinkles would seem to be bright
wavelets of sunshine chasing each other over the dear
face.   She will leave you one of these days.   These bur-
dens, if not lifted from her shoulders, will break her
down.   Those rough, hard hands, that have done so
many necessary things for you, will be crossed upon her
lifeless breast.   Those neglected lips, that gave you your
first baby kiss, will be forever closed, and those sad
tired eyes will have opened in eternity, and then you
will appreciate your mother ; but it will be too late.''

MY MOTHER'S HYMN.

Like patient saint of olden time,
With lovely face almost divine,

So good, so beautiful and fair,
Her very attitude a prayer:
I heard her sing so low and sweet,
" His loving-kindness—oh, how great! "
Turning, behold the saintly face,
So full of trust and patient grace.

" He justly claims a song from me,
His loving-kindness—oh, how free! "
Sweetly thus did run the song,
" His loving-kindness " all day long,
Trusting, praising, day by day,
She sang the sweetest roundelay—
" He near my soul hath always stood,
His loving-kindness—oh, how good! "

" He safely leads my soul along,
His loving-kindness—oh, how strong! "
So strong to lead her on the way
To that eternal better day,
Where safe at last in that blest home,
All care and weariness are gone,
She " sings, with rapture and surprise,
His loving-kindness in the skies."

FEEDING THE SICK.

Four causes of suffering among the sick occur to us as worth considering. First, a poor choice of diet; secondly, a poor way of preparing it; thirdly, an improper time for serving it; and fourthly, the bad habit of retaining it within the patient's recognition by the sense of sight or smell. The purpose of feeding the well or ill is to supply the demand for nourishment and not the gratification of the appetite. Still, the latter result has its value, in that we digest more readily and perfectly those articles of nutrition that we like.

It may be well even for the sick to have regular times

for taking nourishment; still, very sick persons can take so little nutriment of any kind that their needs and wants must be consulted. The general rule must be that the smaller the quantity that can be taken the oftener it may be given. And a second rule should be, never to offer a patient the same dish of food that he has once refused. If it has stood long it is not fresh and nice. A third rule founded on experience is, always make the food of the sick *palatable*.

In the course of a severe sickness discretion in many things is valuable. It is needed in measuring out the food. A teaspoonful of any proper liquid every half hour or more may be all that the sufferer can bear. If he is stupid or delirious, rub his lips gently with a spoon to notify him that he must now be ready to swallow what you present. You may tenderly press down the lower lip with your finger, slowly introduce the spoon to attract his attention, so that he may swallow the liquid almost unconsciously, and yet with safety. The sick may suffer from thirst, and still be unable to announce it. Small bits of ice enclosed in a soft linen rag may meet his needs and be eagerly received. Some slightly acid drinks, as lemonade, will demand his gratitude.

The kind of food should be easy of solution in the patient's mouth and in the gastric sack. The taste of the sick is easily offended, so that proper and agreeable food only should be offered ; otherwise, the patient's stomach will loathe and utterly reject it—even if once well down it will soon come up again. No nurse, then, is well educated and fitted for the practice of her profession, who does not know how to select proper food, how

to prepare it, and how to serve it.   What food a sick
person really needs, and how it can be rendered palatable and easily digestible, must be learned by observation and experience.

The temperature of food renders it hard or easy of
digestion.   If it be lower than the temperature of the
stomach, the digestion will be more or less delayed.   It
should be as warm at least as the temperature of the gastric sack in which it must be dissolved, or it may induce
temporary indigestion.   Tea, coffee, toast or bits of beef
should be hot when presented to the invalid or convales-
cent, because time will cool them to suit his taste.   The
cups for tea or coffee or chocolate need no warming, but
the plates on which he carves his meat or toast often do.

The physician, as a part of his duty, may prescribe
the amount of food the patient may safely take, but
still the nurse should be able to vary his directions when
circumstances occur to warrant it.   A nurse should
never urge the sick person to eat more than he really
wants.

The idea of having a certain article of food long enter-
tained will inevitably impair the appetite for it.   It is a
careless and disagreeable practice to fill a cup so full
that its contents will run over and partially fill the saucer.   The nurse should never taste the tea or coffee or
broth in the presence of the patient.   It makes him feel
that he is to drink only slops remaining in the nurse's
cup.   Be considerate enough to know what the sick one
may need.   Have everything placed in tasteful order on
a waiter—salt, pepper, fork and knife, extra cup and
spoons.   A neat bouquet will make your patient smile

and increase his appetite. A loving tone and a few tender words are often worth more than stimulants.

THE GIRL IN THE HOUSEHOLD.

As the march of civilization renders the art of living more complicated, the question of how we shall be served increases in importance. Untrained peasants, direct from Europe, invade our homes, spoil our dinners, destroy our delicate china and bric-a-brac, and rule us with a rod of iron. We pay them high wages, and only complain when goaded to desperation. Many of these girls are good-natured, quick-witted, and easily taught the manifold duties of the average household. But how many women are willing to convert their tastefully furnished homes into training-schools for ignorant servants? No doubt there are some admirable housekeepers who prefer taking a raw girl just from the ship, and training her into the ways of their households. If they can at the same time inculcate habits of order and system, they are doubly to be blessed. While this course of education is going on, however, the same wages are demanded in many cases as after the girl has graduated and received her diploma. At any time during her tutelage the offer of an additional dollar per month will induce the average girl to leave her kind instructor and palm off her incompetency on some other mistress. How is this unjust state of affairs to be remedied?

A thoroughly good servant, one who understands her duties and attends to them properly, deserves to be well paid. A skilled workman can always command good wages, and there is no reason why a woman's skill in

domestic duties should not have a marketable value.
But this will never be the case until ladies absolutely
refuse to pay high wages for poor work. There are
thousands of households in this city to-day, where the
ladies themselves do much of the dirty and disagreeable
work, for fear of offending Bridget by asking her to
attend to it. Instead of keeping a general supervision
over the various departments of household labor, they
are constantly employed in doing up the little odds and
ends of work which their hired "help" have purposely
neglected. Of course, in families where only one servant is kept, who is expected to do washing, ironing,
cooking and cleaning, a great deal devolves upon the
mistress. In such cases the lady of the house should
take upon herself certain departments of work, and
attend to them regularly. Many ladies do the up-stairs
work themselves, except on Fridays, when the girl gives
the bedroom a thorough sweeping. Other ladies wash
the fine china and silver, and brush up and dust the dining room after breakfast is over, while the girl makes
the beds up-stairs. Some such arrangement is absolutely necessary where the family is large. In such
cases the girl is not expected to do much baking. Either
the mistress makes pies, cakes and desserts herself or
has recourse to the bakery. When hiring a girl for general housework, a lady should always specify exactly
what the girl will be expected to do, and state what
work she will herself attend to. After this she should
never do Bridget's work for her. If in setting the table
she forgets something, and the mistress gets it herself,
the girl will invariably forget it the next time. If called

herself and asked to fetch it, it will not again be missing. The ironing drags and looks as if there was no
prospect of it being finished. The lady foresees confusion, takes a hand, and works until she has a headache.
Next week the same scene is repeated, only if the mistress goes out calling, instead of giving the desired help,
black, sullen looks are the result. Never give a girl too
much work for her strength, but on no account accept
less than the work she is engaged to do.

Ladies who take ignorant girls just landed, to teach
in their families, should pay them no more than a reasonable sum a month while learning. If they would
refuse to pay more, a reform would soon be effected.
The matter lies in the hands of the mistresses themselves.
Servant-girls who are assisted by the lady of the house,
and who only do a part of the work themselves, are not
worth as high wages as those who are competent cooks,
laundresses and chamber-maids. The latter ought to
command higher wages than those who only do one
thing.

Many families, who find two girls in a house apt to
disagree, either put out their entire washing and ironing
or have a woman come in every week to do it, and keep
one good general servant. Under these circumstances
there is often more real comfort than when two or three
girls are kept.

Of course, the mistress of a household must understand and act upon the principle that duty is two-fold—
that she as well as the servant must keep watch and
ward over her temper and her actions, that she has no
more right to shirk that share of the household duties

she has assumed than the family servant, and finally that the relation of mistress and servant is purely a business one and warrants no personal liberties, no unkindness of speech or discourtesy of action on the one side or on the other.

SECRET OF A TRUE LIFE.

Dr. Arnold, of Rugby, gives in one of his letters an account of a saintly sister. For twenty years, through some disease, she was confined to a kind of crib; never once could she change her position for all that time. "And yet," said Dr. Arnold (and I think his words are very beautiful), "I never saw a more perfect instance of the power of love and a sound mind. Intense love, almost to the annihilation of selfishness; a daily martyrdom for twenty years, during which she adhered to her early formed resolution of never talking about herself; thoughtful about the very pins and ribbons of my wife's dress, about the making of a doll's cap for a child, but of herself—save as regarded her improvement in all goodness — wholly thoughtless, enjoying everything lovely, grand, beautiful, high-minded, whether in God's works or man's, with the keenest relish; inheriting the earth to the fullness of the promise; and preserved through the valley of the shadow of death from all fear or impatience, and from every cloud of impaired reason which might mar the beauty of Christ's glorious work. May God grant that I might come within one hundred degrees of her place in glory!"

Such a life was true and beautiful. But the radiance of such a life never cheered this world by chance. A sunny patience, a bright-hearted self-forgetfulness, a sweet and winning interest in the little things of family intercourse, the divine lustre of a Christian peace, are not fortuitous weeds carelessly flowering out of the life-garden. It is the internal which makes the external. It is the force residing in the atoms which shapes the pyramid. It is the beautiful soul within which forms the crystal of the beautiful life without.

> "Be what thou seemest; live thy creed;
>   Hold up to the earth the torch divine;
> Be what thou prayest to be made;
>   Let the great Master's steps be thine.
>
> "Sow love, and taste its fruitage pure;
>   Sow peace, and reap its harvest bright;
> Sow sunbeams on the rock and moor,
>   And find a harvest home of light."

THE "LITTLE PITCHERS."

It is rather a sad fact, nevertheless it is true, that chil dren are often necessary in the household to act as scav. engers and keep the moral air pure. Often it happens that when a party of older people are telling some doubtful bit of gossip, or relating a story too salacious for dainty palates, the earnest, interrogative gaze of a little child produces a sudden hush, and some one invariably remarks, "Little pitchers have long ears," a phrase older than the oldest memory and singularly attractive to the little folk. "Where are the little pitchers?" ask these innocent ones, taking the words literally; but the conversation takes another turn—the "child in their midst" has been a purifying influence.

and they restrain the tide of gossip or slander, conscious that it is potent for evil.

It is a pity if there are any families where this nursery rhyme is unknown, where the "little pitchers" are filled with words of profanation, and scoldings and contradiction are poured daily into the "long ears" that should be filled only with the dews of heaven. Children are so quick to learn, and no word they hear is ever lost, but reverberates in memory until years have passed and father and mother gone, and the boy or girl grown to maturity, when it all comes back, "Mother used to say," "I have heard my father tell," etc. Oh, if they were words of wisdom, of love and kindly counsel, how sweet to remember and reproduce them—how precious the draught which, distilled in the "little pitcher," refreshes like the fountain of pure cold water in the desert. Every parent is a future historian. Teachers and playmates may be forgotten, but the first lesson learned from the lips of a parent is immortal in its power. Fill up the "little pitchers," then, with the milk and honey that nourish unto a perfect growth— make them vessels of honor in the home and the world.

☞ CHAPTER XXX. ☜

Women as Poets.

BATTLE HYMN OF THE REPUBLIC.

By Mrs. Julia Ward Howe

Mrs. Howe was born in New York in 1819. She was the daughter of Samuel Ward, a banker of that city, and in 1843 was married to Samuel G. Howe, of Boston. Her first volume was a book of poems called Passion Flowers, published in 1854. It was in 1866, after the close of the war, that she published the Battle Hymn in her volume Later Lyrics. Mrs. Howe is a grand woman, a poet and philanthropist, and a worker in every good cause that furthers the advancement of women. She is also the author of several prose works commemorative of her travels abroad.

MINE eyes have seen the glory of the coming of the Lord.
 He is trampling out the vintage where the grapes of
wrath are stored;
He hath loosed the fateful lightning of His terrible swift sword.
  His truth is marching on.

I have seen him in the watch-fires of a hundred circling camps;
They have builded him an altar in the evening dews and damps.
I can read his righteous sentence by the dim and flaring lamps.
  His day is marching on.

I have read a fiery gospel writ in burnished rows of steel:
As ye deal with my contemners, so with you my grace shall
deal.
Let the Hero, born of woman, crush the serpent with his heel—
  Since God is marching on.

He has sounded forth the trumpet that shall never call retreat;
He is sifting out the hearts of men before his judgment seat.
Oh, be swift, my soul, to answer him! be jubilant, my feet!
      Our God is marching on.

In the beauty of the lilies, Christ was born across the sea,
With a glory in his bosom that transfigures you and me.
As he died to make men holy, let us die to make men free—
      While God is marching on.

ROCK ME TO SLEEP.

By Mrs. Elizabeth Akers Allen.

The author of this beautiful and favorite poem, Mrs. Allen, was born
October 9th, 1832, in Strong, Franklin Co., Maine, and at an early period
was married to Paul Akers, the sculptor, who died in the following year.
She afterwards married Mr. E. M. Allen, a resident of New York City,
and under the *nom-de-guerre* of Florence Percy, wrote many beautiful and
touching poems, none of which have attained to such popular fame as
Rock Me to Sleep, which is claimed by as many authors as Beautiful
Snow.

BACKWARD, turn backward, O Time, in your flight—
     Make me a child again just for to-night.
Mother, come back from the echoless shore;
Take me again to your heart as of yore;
Kiss from my forehead the furrows of care,
Smooth the few silver threads out of my hair;
Over my slumbers your loving watch keep—
Rock me to sleep, mother, rock me to sleep.

Backward, flow backward, O tide of the years,
I am so weary of toil and of tears—
Toil without recompense, tears all in vain—
Take them and give me my childhood again.

I have grown weary of dust and decay--
Weary of flinging my soul wealth away;
Weary of sowing for others to reap—
Rock me to sleep, mother, rock me to sleep.

Tired of the hollow, the base, the untrue,
Mother, O mother, my heart calls for you.
Many a summer the grass has grown green,
Blossomed and faded, our faces between;
Yet, with strong yearning and passionate pain,
Long I to-night for your presence again.
Come from the silence so long and so deep—
Rock me to sleep, mother, rock me to sleep.

Over my heart in the days that are flown,
No love like mother-love ever has shone;
No other worship abides and endures—
Faithful, unselfish, and patient, like yours;
None like a mother can charm away pain
From the sick soul and the world-weary brain.
Slumber's soft calms o'er my heavy lids creep—
Rock me to sleep, mother, rock me to sleep.

Come, let your brown hair, just lighted with gold,
Fall on your shoulders again as of old;
Let it drop over my forehead to-night,
Shading my faint eyes away from the light;
For, with its sunny-edged shadows once more,
Haply will throng the sweet visions of yore.
Lovingly, softly, its bright billows sweep—
Rock me to sleep, mother, rock me to sleep.

Mother, dear mother, the years have been long
Since I last listened your lullaby song:

Sing, then, and unto my soul it shall seem
Womanhood's years have been only a dream.
Clasped to your heart in a loving embrace,
With your light lashes just sweeping my face,
Never hereafter to wake or to weep—
Rock me to sleep, mother, rock me to sleep.

ANSWER TO ROCK ME TO SLEEP.

MY child, ah my child! thou art weary to-night,
Thy spirit is sad and dim is the light;
Thou wouldst call me back from the echoless shore,
To the trials of life, to thy heart as of yore;
Thou longest again for my fond loving care,
For my kiss on thy cheek, for my hand on thy hair;
But angels around thee their loving watch keep,
And angels, my darling, will rock thee to sleep.

"Backward?"   Nay, onward, ye swift rolling years!
Gird on thy armor, keep back thy tears;
Count not thy trials nor efforts in vain—
They'll bring thee the light of thy childhood again.
Thou shouldst not weary, my child, by the way,
But watch for the light of that brighter day;
Not tired of "sowing for others to reap,"
For angels, my darling, will rock thee to sleep.

Tired, my child, of the "base, the untrue!"
I have tasted the cup they have given to you—
I've felt the deep sorrow in the living green
Of a low mossy grave by a silvery stream.
But the dear mother I then sought for in vain
Is an angel presence and with me again,

And in the still night, from the silence so deep,
Come the bright angels to rock me to sleep.

Nearer thee now than in days that are flown,
Purer the love light encircling thy home;
Far more enduring the watch for to-night,
Than ever earth worship away from the light.
Soon the dark shadows will linger no more,
Nor come to thy call from the opening door;
But know thou, my child, that the angels watch keep,
And soon, very soon, they'll rock thee to sleep.

They'll sing thee to sleep with a soothing song,
And waking, thou'lt be with a heavenly throng;
And thy life, with its toil and its tears and pain,
Thou wilt then see has not been in vain.
Thou wilt meet those in bliss whom on earth thou didst love,
And whom thou hast taught of the "mansions above."
" Never hereafter to suffer or weep,"
The angels, my darling, will rock thee to sleep.

KENTUCKY BELLE.

BY CONSTANCE F. WOOLSON.

This lady is a magazine writer of great power and originality. Her most popular novel is Anne, a tale of Mackinac, which was published in Harper's Magazine in 1881. She is unmarried, and an artist as well as an author and poet. The poem we append is an especial favorite in public readings.

SUMMER of 'sixty-three, sir, and Conrad was gone away—
Gone to the country-town, sir, to sell our first load of hay—
We lived in the log house yonder, poor as ever you've seen;
Röschen there was a baby, and I was only nineteen.

Conrad, he took the oxen, but he left Kentucky Belle.
How much we thought of Kentuck, I couldn't begin to tell—
Came from the Blue-Grass country; my father gave her to me
When I rode North with Conrad, away from the Tennessee.

Conrad lived in Ohio—a German he is, you know—
The house stood in broad corn-fields, stretching on row after
　　row.
The old folks made me welcome: they were kind as kind
　　could be;
But I kept longing, longing, for the hills of the Tennessee.

Oh, for a sight of water, the shadowed slope of a hill!
Clouds that hang on the summit, a wind that never is still!
But the level land went stretching away to meet the sky—
Never a rise, from north to south, to rest the weary eye.

From east to west, no river to shine out under the moon,
Nothing to make a shadow in the yellow afternoon:
Only the breathless sunshine, as I looked out, all forlorn,
Only the "rustle, rustle," as I walked among the corn.

When I fell sick with pining, we didn't wait any more,
But moved away from the corn-lands, out to this river-shore—
The Tuscarawas it's called, sir—off there's a hill, you see—
And now I've grown to like it next best to the Tennessee.

I was at work that morning.　Some one came riding like mad
Over the bridge and up the road—Farmer Rouf's little lad.
Bareback he rode; he had no hat; he hardly stopped to say,
"Morgan's men are coming, Frau; they're galloping on this
　　way.

"I'm sent to warn the neighbors.　He isn't a mile behind;
He sweeps up all the horses—every horse that he can find.

Morgan, Morgan the raider, and Morgan's terrible men,
With bowie-knives and pistols, are galloping up the glen!"

The lad rode down the valley, and I stood still at the door;
The baby laughed and prattled, playing with spools on the floor;
Kentuck was out in the pasture; Conrad, my man was gone.
Near, nearer, Morgan's men were galloping, galloping on!

Sudden I picked up baby, and ran to the pasture-bar.
"Kentuck!" I called—"Kentucky!" She knew me ever so far!
I led her down the gully that turns off there to the right,
And tied her to the bushes; her head was just out of sight.

As I ran back to the log house, at once there came a sound—
The ring of hoofs, galloping hoofs, trembling over the ground—
Coming into the turnpike out from the White-Woman Glen—
Morgan, Morgan the raider, and Morgan's terrible men.

As near they drew and nearer, my heart beat fast in alarm;
But still I stood in the door-way, with baby on my arm.
They came; they passed; with spur and whip in haste they sped
        along—
Morgan, Morgan the raider, and his band, six hundred strong.

Weary they looked and jaded, riding through night and through
        day;
Pushing on east to the river, many long miles away,
To the border-strip where Virginia runs up into the west,
And fording the Upper Ohio before they could stop to rest.

On like the wind they hurried, and Morgan rode in advance;
Bright were his eyes like live coals, as he gave me a sideways
        glance;
And I was just breathing freely, after my choking pain,
When the last one of the troopers suddenly drew his rein.

Frightened I was to death, sir; I scarce dared look in his face,
As he asked for a drink of water, and glanced around the place.
I gave him a cup and he smiled—'twas only a boy, you see,
Faint and worn, with dim-blue eyes; and he'd sailed on the
    Tennessee.

Only sixteen he was, sir—a fond mother's only son—
Off and away with Morgan before his life had begun !
The damp drops stood on his temples; drawn was the boyish
    mouth;
And I thought me of the mother waiting down in the South.

Oh, pluck was he to the backbone, and clear grit through and
    through;
Boasted and bragged like a trooper; but the big words wouldn't
    do—
The boy was dying, sir, dying, as plain as plain could be,
Worn out by his ride with Morgan up from the Tennessee.

But when I told the laddie I too was from the South,
Water came in his dim eyes, and quivers around his mouth.
"Do you know the Blue-Grass country?" he wistful began to
    say;
Then swayed like a willow-sapling, and fainted dead away.

I had him into the log house, and worked and brought him to;
I fed him, and I coaxed him, as I thought his mother'd do;
And when the lad got better, and the noise in his head was
    gone,
Morgan's men were miles away, galloping, galloping on.

"Oh, I must go," he muttered; "I must be up and away!
Morgan—Morgan is waiting for me! Oh, what will Morgan
    say?"

"I HAD HIM INTO THE LOG HOUSE, AND WORKED AND BROUGHT HIM THROUGH;
I FED HIM, AND I COAXED HIM. AS I THOUGHT HIS MOTHER 'D DO."

But I heard a sound of tramping and kept him back from the
    door—
The ringing sound of horses' hoofs that I had heard before.

And on, on came the soldiers—the Michigan cavalry—
And fast they rode, and black they looked, galloping rapidly,—
They had followed hard on Morgan's track; they had followed
    day and night;
But of Morgan and Morgan's raiders they had never caught a
    sight.

And rich Ohio sat startled through all those summer days;
For strange, wild men were galloping over her broad highways:
Now here, now there, now seen, now gone, now north, now east,
    now west,
Through river-valleys and corn-land farms, sweeping away her
    best.

A bold ride and a long ride!   But they were taken at last,
They almost reached the river by galloping hard and fast;
But the boys in blue were upon them ere ever they gained the
    ford,
And Morgan, Morgan the raider, laid down his terrible sword.

Well, I kept the boy till evening—kept him against his will—
But he was too weak to follow, and sat there pale and still.
When it was cool and dusky—you'll wonder to hear me tell—
But I stole down to that gully, and brought up Kentucky Belle.

I kissed the star on her forehead—my pretty, gentle lass—
But I knew that she'd be happy back in the old Blue-Grass.
A suit of clothes of Conrad's, with all the money I had,
And Kentuck, pretty Kentuck, I gave to the worn-out lad.

I guided him to the southward as well as I knew how;
The boy rode off with many thanks, and many a backward bow;
And then the glow it faded, and my heart began to swell,
As down the glen away she went, my lost Kentucky Belle!

When Conrad came in the evening, the moon was shining high;
Baby and I were both crying—I couldn't tell him why—
But a battered suit of rebel gray was hanging on the wall,
And a thin old horse, with drooping head, stood in Kentucky's
    stall.

Well, he was kind, and never once said a hard word to me;
He knew I couldn't help it—'twas all for the Tennessee.
But, after the war was over, just think what came to pass—
A letter, sir; and the two were safe back in the old Blue-Grass.

The lad had got across the border, riding Kentucky Belle;
And Kentuck she was thriving, and fat, and hearty, and well;
He cared for her, and kept her, nor touched her with whip or
    spur.
Ah, we've had many horses since, but never a horse like her!

DEATH AND THE YOUTH.

By Letitia E. Landon.

The beautiful, gifted, and most unhappy L. E. L., as she signed herself
in her first youthful poems, was the daughter of an army agent, and was
born in Chelsea, England, in 1802, and died in 1838. She acquired a brief
and splendid popularity, but her sad domestic life tinged her later poems
with its melancholy. Letitia E. Landon, afterwards Mrs. Madeau, died in
the same year that she was married.

NOT yet—the flowers are in my path,
    The sun is in the sky;
Not yet—my heart is full of hope,
    I cannot bear to die.

Not yet—I never knew till now,
How precious life could be;
My heart is full of love—O Death,
I cannot come with thee!

But love and hope, enchanted twain,
Passed in their falsehood by;
Death came again, and then he said,
"I'm ready now to die."

AFTER THE BALL

BY NORA PERRY.

Miss Perry, who has written many golden poems, is a resident of Boston, Mass., and has published a couple of volumes of sweet and graceful verse. As she is still writing and has an exuberant fancy, coupled with a gentle poetic nature, pure and bird-like in its simplicity, we may expect much good work to succeed the exquisite love romances she has already written.

THEY sat and combed their beautiful hair,
Their long bright tresses one by one,
As they laughed and talked in the chamber there,
After the revel was done.

Idly they talked of waltz and quadrille;
Idly they laughed like other girls,
Who, over the fire, when all is still,
Comb out their braids and curls.

Robe of satin and Brussels lace,
Knots of flowers and ribbons, too,
Scattered about in every place,
For the revel is through.

21

And Maud and Madge, in robes of white,
   The prettiest night-gowns under the sun,
Stockingless, slipperless, sit in the night,
   For the revel is done.

Sit and comb their beautiful hair,
   Those wonderful waves of brown and gold,
Till the fire is out in the chamber there,
   And the little bare feet are cold.

Then out of the gathering winter chill—
   All out of the bitter St. Agnes weather,
While the fire is out and the house is still,
   Maud and Madge together—

Maud and Madge, in robes of white,
   The prettiest night-gowns under the sun,
Curtained away from the chilly night
   After the revel is done,

Float along in a splendid dream,
   To a golden gittern's tinkling tune,
While a thousand lustres shimmering stream,
   In a palace's grand saloon.

Flashing of jewels and flutter of laces,
   Tropical odors sweeter than musk—
Men and women with beautiful faces,
   And eyes of tropical dusk.

And one face shining out like a star;
   One face haunting the dreams of each,
. And one voice sweeter than others are,
   Breaking in silvery speech.

Telling through lips of bearded bloom,
  An old, old story over again,
As down the royal bannered room,
  To the golden gittern's strain,

Two and two they dreamily walk,
  While an unseen spirit walks beside,
And, all unheard in the lover's talk,
  He claimeth one for a bride.

O Maud and Madge! dream on together,
  With never a pang of jealous fear;
For, ere the bitter St. Agnes weather
  Shall whiten another year,

Robed for the bridal, and robed for the tomb,
  Braided brown hair and golden tress,
There'll be only one of you left for the bloom
  Of the bearded lips to press.

Only one for the bridal pearls,
  The robe of satin and Brussels lace—
Only one to blush through her curls,
  At the sight of a lover's face.

O beautiful Madge, in your bridal white,
  For you the revel has just begun;
But for her who sleeps in your arms to-night
  The revel of life is done!

But robed and crowned with your saintly bliss,
  Queen of Heaven and bride of the sun,
O beautiful Maud, you'll never miss
  The kisses another hath won!

LAMENT OF THE IRISH EMIGRANT.

By Lady Dufferin.

The sweet pathos of this sadly-worded song has never been rivaied by any poem of exile ever written or sung, and it will always be just as touch-ing to the homesick heart as now. The writer, Lady Dufferin, is the mother, and not the wife, as erroneously stated, of the former Governor-general of Canada. It was published originally in the year 1838, and was set to music and sung in every drawing-room in the United Kingdom, and became espe-cially a favorite in America during the year of the Irish famine, 1848.

I'M sittin' on the stile, Mary,
    Where we sat side by side,
On a bright May mornin' long ago,
    When first you were my bride;
The corn was springin' fresh and green,
    And the lark sung loud and high,
And the red was on your lip, Mary,
    And the love-light in your eye.

The place is little changed, Mary,
    The day is bright as then,
The lark's loud song is in my ear,
    And the corn is green again;
But I miss the soft clasp of your hand,
    And your breath warm on my cheek,
And I still keep listenin' for the words
    You never more will speak.

'Tis but a step down yonder lane,
    And the little church stands near,—
The church where we were wed, Mary,
    I see the spire from here;

But the graveyard lies between, Mary,
  And my step might break your rest,—
For I've laid you, darling, down to sleep
  With your baby on your breast.

I'm very lonely now, Mary,
  For the poor make no new friends;
But, oh, they love the better still
  The few our Father sends;
And you were all I had, Mary—
  My blessin' and my pride;
There's nothing left to care for now,
  Since my poor Mary died.

Yours was the good, brave heart, Mary,
  That still kept hoping on,
When the trust in God had left my soul,
  And my arm's young strength was gone;
There was comfort ever on your lip,
  And the kind look on your brow,—
I bless you, Mary, for that same,
  Though you cannot hear me now.

I thank you for the patient smile
  When your heart was fit to break—
When the hunger-pain was gnawin' there,
  And you hid it for my sake;
I bless you for the pleasant word,
  When your heart was sad and sore,—
Oh, I'm thankful you are gone, Mary,
  Where grief can't reach you more!

I'm bidding you a long farewell,
  My Mary, kind and true!

But I'll not forget you, darling,
  In the land I'm going to.
They say there's bread and work for all,
  And the sun shines always there,—
But I'll not forget old Ireland,
  Were it fifty times as fair!

And often in those grand old woods
  I'll sit and shut my eyes,
And my heart will travel back again
  To the place where Mary lies;
And I'll think I see the little stile
  Where we sat side by side,
And the springin' corn and the bright May morn,
  When first you were my bride.

ON THE SHORES OF TENNESSEE.

By Mrs. Ethel Lynn Beers.

The writer of this beautiful song was born in Goshen, Orange Co., N. J.,
in 1827, and was very popular as a contributor to the New York Ledger,
Harper's Weekly, and other papers, under the pseudonym of Ethel Lynn,
to which she added afterwards her married name. She died in 1879. The
old slave-days are recalled with vivid earnestness by her stirring lines.

" MOVE my arm-chair, faithful Pompey,
    In the sunshine bright and strong,
For this world is fading, Pompey—
    Massa won't be with you long;
And I fain would hear the south wind
    Bring once more the sound to me,
Of the wavelets softly breaking
    On the shores of Tennessee.

"Mournful though the ripples murmur,
　As they still the story tell,
How no vessel floats the banner
　That I've loved so long and well;
I shall listen to their music,
　Dreaming that again I see
Stars and Stripes on sloop and shallop,
　Sailing up the Tennessee.

" And, Pompey, while Ole Massa's waiting
　For death's last dispatch to come,
If that exiled starry banner
　Should come sailing proudly home,
You shall greet it, slave no longer,
　Voice and hand shall both be free,
That shout and point to Union colors
　On the waves of Tennessee."

"Massa's berry kind to Pompey,
　But ole darkey's happy here,
Where he's tended corn and cotton
　For dese many a long gone year.
Over yonder Missis' sleeping,
　No one tends her grave like me,
Mebbe she would miss the flowers
　She used to love in Tennessee."

" 'Pears like she was watching Massa,
　If Pompey should beside him stay,
Mebbe she'd remember better
　How for him she used to pray,
Telling him that way up yonder
　White as snow his soul would be,

If he served the Lord of Heaven
  While he lived in Tennessee."

Silently the tears were rolling
  Down the poor old dusky face,
As he stepped behind his master,
  In his long accustomed place.
Then a silence fell around them,
  As they gazed on rock and tree,
Pictured in the placid waters
  Of the rolling Tennessee.

Master dreaming of the battle,
  When he fought by Marion's side—
When he bid the haughty Tarlton
  Stoop his lordly crest of pride;
Man, remembering how yon sleeper
  Once he held upon his knee,
Ere she loved the gallant soldier,
  Ralph Vervair of Tennessee.

Still the south wind fondly lingers
  'Mid the veteran's silver hair;
Still the bondsman, close beside him,
  Stands beside the old-arm chair,
With his dark-hued hand uplifted,
  Shading eyes he bends to see
Where the woodland, boldly jutting,
  Turns aside the Tennessee.

Thus he watches cloud-born shadows
  Glide from tree to mountain crest,
Softly creeping, aye and ever,
  To the river's yielding breast.

"POMPEY, HOLD ME ON YOUR SHOULDER,
HELP ME STAND ON FOOT ONCE MORE."

Ha, above the foliage yonder,
　Something flutters wild and free!
" Massa! Massa! Hallelujah!
　The flag's come back to Tennessee!"

" Pompey, hold me on your shoulder,
　Help me stand on foot once more,
That I may salute the colors
　As they pass my cabin door.
Here's the paper, signed, that frees you,
　Give a freeman's shout with me!
God and Union! be our watchword
　Evermore in Tennessee!"

Then the trembling voice grew fainter,
　And the limbs refused to stand;
One prayer to Jesus—and the soldier
　Glided to the better land.
When the flag went down the river,
　Man and master both were free,
While the ring-dove's note was mingled
　With the rippling Tennessee.

BRAVE KATE SHELLEY.

BY MRS. M. L. RAYNE.

It will be remembered that Kate Shelley, a young girl of fifteen years, on that terrible night of July 6, 1881, walked five miles, crossing in the darkness and storm a long dangerous bridge, to warn the night express on the Chicago and Northwestern Railway of a wrecked train. When the story of her heroic behavior spread throughout the State, several funds for her benefit were started, and, so far as money can pay for such devotion, she has been well rewarded for her night's work. At the session of the Iowa Legislature, that winter, it was ordered that a medal commemorative of the girl's bravery be struck, and a committee was appointed to present it to her. Her heroism was made the theme of many eloquent speeches

"How far that little candle throws its beams.
So shines a good deed in a naughty world."

THROUGH the whirl of wind and water parted by the
rushing steel,
Flashed the white glare of the headlight, flew the swift revolv-
ing wheel,
As the midnight train swept onward, bearing on its iron wings
Through the gloom of night and tempest, freightage of most
precious things.

Little children by their mothers nestle in unbroken rest,
Stalwart men are dreaming softly of their journey's finished quest,
While the men who watch and guard them, sleepless stand at
post and brake;
Close the throttle! draw the lever! safe for wife and sweet-
heart's sake.

Sleep and dream, unheeding danger; in the valley yonder lies
Death's debris in weird confusion, altar fit for sacrifice!
Dark and grim the shadows settle where the hidden perils wait;
Swift the train, with dear lives laden, rushes to its deadly fate.

Still they sleep and dream unheeding.　Oh, thou watchful One
above,
Save Thy people in this hour! save the ransomed of Thy love!
Send an angel from Thy heaven who shall calm the troubled air,
And reveal the powers of evil hidden in the darkness there.

Saved! ere yet they know their peril, comes a warning to alarm;
Saved! the precious train is resting on the brink of deadly harm.
God has sent his angel to them, brave Kate Shelley, hero-child!
Struggling on, alone, unaided through that night of tempest wild.

Brave Kate Shelley! tender maiden, baby hands with splinters torn,
Saved the lives of sleeping travelers swiftly to death's journey
borne.
Mothers wept and clasped their darlings, breathing words of
grateful prayer;
Men with faces blanched and tearful thanked God for Kate
Shelley there.

Greater love than this hath no man. When the Heavens shall
    unfold,
And the judgment books are opened, there in characters of gold
Brave Kate Shelley's name shall center, mid the pure, the brave
    and good,
That of one who crowned with glory her heroic womanhood.

LABOR IS WORSHIP.

BY FRANCIS SARGENT OSGOOD.

Mrs. Osgood struck a popular vein in writing her poems, and they have
made themselves a permanent place in the hearts of the people. This is
particularly true of the one below, which glorifies the humblest mission of
labor into a heroic achievement. Mrs. Osgood was born in Boston in 1812,
and was the daughter of a merchant named Locke. In 1834 she married
S. S. Osgood, an artist. She died in 1850.

PAUSE not to dream of the future before us;
    Pause not to weep the wild cares that come o'er us.
Hark, how creation's deep musical chorus
    Unintermitting goes up into Heaven.
Never the ocean wave falters in flowing;
Never the little seed stops in its growing;
More and more richly the rose-heart keeps glowing,
    Till from its nourishing stem it is riven.

"Labor is worship!"—the robin is singing;
"Labor is worship!"—the wild bee is ringing;
    Listen! that eloquent whisper upspringing
        Speaks to thy soul from out Nature's great heart.
From the dark cloud flows the life-giving shower;
From the rough sod blows the soft-breathing flower;
From the small insect, the rich coral bower;
    Only man, in the plan, ever shrinks from his part.

Labor is life! 'Tis the still water faileth;
Idleness ever despaireth, bewaileth;
Keep the watch wound, for the dark rust assaileth:
   Flowers droop and die in the stillness of noon.
Labor is glory!—the flying cloud lightens;
Only the waving wing changes and brightens;
Idle hearts only the dark future frightens;
   Play the sweet keys, wouldst thou keep them in **tune.**

Labor is rest from the sorrows that greet us,
Rest from all petty vexations that meet us,
Rest from sin-promptings that ever entreat us,
   Rest from world-sirens that lure us to ill.
Work—and pure slumbers shall wait on thy pillow;
Work—thou shalt ride over Care's coming billow;
Lie not down wearied 'neath Woe's weeping-willow;
   Work with a stout heart and resolute will!

Labor is health! Lo, the husbandman reaping,
How through his veins goes the life current leaping!
How his strong arm, in its stalwart pride sweeping,
   True as a sunbeam the swift sickle guides.
Labor is wealth! In the sea the pearl groweth;
Rich the queen's robe from the frail cocoon floweth;
From the fine acorn the strong forest bloweth;
   Temple and statue the marble block hides.

Droop not, though shame, sin, and anguish are round **thee;**
Bravely fling off the cold chain that hath bound thee;
Look to yon pure heaven smiling beyond thee;
   Rest not content in thy darkness—a clod.
Work for some good, be it ever so slowly;
Cherish some flower, be it ever so lowly;
Labor! all labor is noble and holy;
   Let thy great deeds be thy prayer to thy God.

THE YOUTHFUL PILOT.

By Miss Julia Pleasants.

[Written on the death of Robert A. Whyte.]

About forty years ago George D. Prentice, of the Louisville Journal, was receiving poetic contributions from a number of young lady writers of rare merit, whom he pleasantly termed his "staff of young lady poets." Among these was "Amelia," who, under his kindly criticism and fostering poetic care, became famous.

Miss Julia Pleasants (the "Amelia" mentioned), then in her teens, and residing in Huntsville, Ala., was a leading favorite of his, and she contributed the poem in question. Prentice, in his editorial comment on publishing it, remarked that "one might not unwillingly contract to die on stipulation of such a poem *in memoriam.*"

Miss Pleasants subsequently married Judge David Creswell, a prominent civil law jurist, who died a few years since in this State (Louisiana); and so the authoress became known as Mrs. Julia Pleasants Creswell.

Alas! the sweet bells that chimed so harmoniously were destined to jangle sadly out of tune. The fancy that wrought this beautiful pen picture became tossed and driven by the weird fantasies of a mind diseased. Mrs. Julia Pleasants Creswell died at the State Lunatic Asylum, Jackson, La., June 9, 1886.

O**N the bosom of a river,**
      Where the sun unbinds its quiver,
Or the starlight streams forever,
      Sailed a vessel light and free.
Morning dewdrops hung like manna
On the bright folds of her banner,
While the zephyrs rose to fan her
      Safely to the radiant sea.

At her prow a pilot, beaming
In the flush of youth, stood dreaming,
And he was in glorious seeming,
      Like an angel from above;

Through his hair the breezes sported,
And, as on the waves he floated,
Oft that pilot, angel-throated,
    Warbled lays of hope and love.

Through those locks so brightly flowing
Buds of laurel bloom were blowing,
And his hands anon were throwing
    Music from a lyre of gold.
Swiftly down the stream he glided,
Soft the purple waves divided,
And a rainbow arch abided
    O'er his canvas' snowy fold.

Anxious hearts, with fond devotion,
Watched him sailing to the ocean,
Praying that no wild commotion
    Midst the elements might rise;
And he seemed some young Apollo
Charming summer winds to follow,
While the water-flags corolla
    Trembled to his music-sighs.

But those purple waves enchanted
Rolled beside a city haunted
By an awful spell that daunted
    Every comer to her shore;
Night shades rank the air encumbered,
And pale marble statues numbered
Lotos-eaters, where they slumbered
    And awoke to life no more.

Then there rushed with lightning quickness
O'er his face a mortal sickness,
And death-dews in fearful thickness
 Gathered o'er his temples fair;
And there swept a mournful murmur
Through the lovely Southern summer,
As the beauteous pilot comer
 Perished by that city there.

Still rolls on that radiant river,
And the sun unbinds its quiver,
Or the starlight streams forever
 On its bosom, as before;
But that vessel's rainbow banner
Greets no more the gay savannah,
And that pilot's lute drops manna
 On the purple waves—no more!

OVER THE RIVER.

By Mrs. Nancy Priest Wakefield.

The writer of this representative poem was born in 1834, and died in 1870. Royalston and Winchendon, Mass., both claim the honor of her birth. Her maiden name was Nancy Amelia Woodbury, and she married Lieutenant A. C. Wakefield in 1865. Her poem is considered one of the finest inspirational lyrics in the English language.

OVER the river they beckon to me,
 Loved ones who've crossed to the farther side;
The gleam of their snowy robes I see,
 But their voices are drowned in the rushing tide;
There's one with ringlets of sunny gold,
 And eyes the reflection of Heaven's own blue;

He crossed in the twilight gray and cold,
  And the pale mist hid him from mortal view;
We saw not the angels who met him there,
  The gates of the city we could not see;
Over the river, over the river,
  My brother stands waiting to welcome me.

Over the river, the boatman pale
  Carried another,—the household pet;
Her brown curls waved in the gentle gale,
  Darling Minnie, I see her yet.
She crossed on her bosom her dimpled hands,
  And fearlessly entered the phantom bark;
We watched it glide from the silver sands,
  And all our sunshine grew strangely dark;
We know she is safe on the farther side,
  Where all the angels and ransomed be;
Over the river, the mystic river,
  My childhood's idol is waiting for me.

For none return from those quiet shores,
  Who cross with the boatman, cold and pale;
We hear the dip of the golden oars,
  We catch a gleam of the snowy sail—
And lo! they have passed from our yearning heart;
  They cross the stream and are gone for aye;
We may not sunder the veil apart
  That hides from our vision the gates of day;
We only know that their barks no more
  May sail with us over Life's stormy sea;
Yet, somewhere I know, on the unseen shore,
  They watch and beckon and wait for me.

And I sit and think when the sunset's **gold**
  Is flushing river and hill and shore,
I shall one day stand by the water cold,
  And list for the sound of the boatman's oar;
I shall watch for a gleam of the flapping sail,
  I shall hear the boat as it gains the strand,
I shall pass from sight with the boatman pale
  To the better shore of the spirit land;
I shall know the loved who have gone before,
  And joyfully sweet will the meeting be,
When over the river, the peaceful river,
  The Angel of Death shall carry me.

IF.

By MAY RILEY SMITH.

The writer of this pathetic poem is Mrs. Albert Smith, of Chicago, Ill.,
but formerly May Louise Riley, of Brighton, New York, where she was
born in 1842. She is a magazine writer, and excels in descriptive poems of
a personal nature.

IF, sitting with this little worn-out shoe
  And scarlet stocking lying on my knee,
I knew the little feet had pattered through
  The pearl-set gates that lie 'twixt heaven and me,
I could be reconciled and happy, too,
  And look with glad eyes toward the Jasper sea.

If, in the morning, when the song of birds
  Reminds me of a music far more sweet,
I listen for his pretty, broken words,
  And for the music of his dimpled feet,
I could be almost happy, though I heard
  No answer, and but saw his vacant seat.

22

I could be glad if, when the day is done,
    And all its cares and heartaches laid away,
I could look westward to the hidden sun,
    And, with a heart full of sweet yearnings, say:
" To-night I'm nearer to my little one,
    By just the travel of a single day."

If I could know these little feet were shod
    In sandals wrought of light in better lands,
And that the foot-prints of a tender God
    Ran side by side with him in golden sands,
I could bow cheerfully and kiss the rod,
    Since Benny was in safer, wiser hands.

If he were dead I would not sit to-day
    And stain with tears the wee sock on my knee;
I would not kiss the tiny shoe and say,
    " Bring back again my little boy to me!"
I would be patient, knowing it was God's way,
    And wait to meet him o'er death's silent sea.

But, oh, to know the feet once pure and white,
    The haunts of vice had boldly ventured in;
The hands that should have battled for the right,
    Had been wrung crimson in the clasp of sin,
And, should he knock at Heaven's gate to-night,
    To fear my boy could hardly enter in!

SENT TO HEAVEN.

By Adelaide Ann Procter.

Miss Procter was born in Bedford Square, London, on the 30th of October, 1825, and died on the 2d of February, 1864. Her father was distinguished in literature, under the *nom-de-plume* of Barry Cornwall, and was the intimate friend of Charles Dickens. She was highly educated, of a serious, sensitive nature, and sacrificed her strength in a round of benevolent pursuits, under the conviction that her life must be devoted to mitigating the sufferings of mankind. Her poems are comprised in one small volume, edited by Charles Dickens, and are greatly quoted and admired The one given here is set to music, and sung under the title of **The Message**. It is popular, both as a poem and a concert piece.

I HAD a message to send her—
  To her whom my soul loved best,
But I had my task to finish,
  And she was gone home to rest.

To rest in the far bright Heaven,
  Oh, so far away from here,
It was vain to speak to my darling,
  For I knew she could not hear.

I had a message to send her,
  So tender and true and sweet;
I longed for an angel to bear it,
  And lay it down at her feet.

I placed it, one summer evening,
  On a cloudlet's fleecy breast,
But it faded in golden splendor,
  And died in the crimson west.

I gave it the lark next morning,
  And I watched it soar and soar,
But its pinions grew faint and weary,
  And it fluttered to earth once more.

To the heart of a rose I told it,
  And the perfume sweet and rare,
Growing faint on the blue, bright ether,
  Was lost in the balmy air.

I laid it upon a censer,
  And I saw the incense rise,
But its clouds of rolling silver
  Could not reach the far blue skies.

I cried in my passionate longing;—
  "Has the earth no Angel friend
Who will carry my love the message
  That my heart desires to send?"

Then I heard a strain of music
  So mighty, so pure, so clear,
That my very sorrow was silent,
  And my heart stood still to hear.

And I felt in my soul's deep yearning
  At last the sure answer stir—
The music will go up to Heaven
  And carry my thought to her."

It rose in harmonious rushing
  Of mingled voices and strings,
And I tenderly laid my message
  On the music's outspread wings.

I heard it float farther and farther,
  In sound more perfect than speech,
Farther than sight can follow,
  Farther than soul can reach.

And I know that at last my message
Has passed through the golden gate,
So my heart is no longer restless,
And I am content to wait.

SOMEBODY'S DARLING.

By Maria R. La Caste.

This exquisite ballad is usually published as anonymous. Like Beautiful Snow, it has had a number of claimants, but no name has remained attached to it until Epes Sargent rescued it in 1880, and published it in his collection, with extracts from letters written by Miss La Caste. The poem was first published, with her name attached, in the Southern Churchman. She was living in Savannah, Georgia, when she published it. She is of French parentage, and dislikes anything like notoriety. She is an attractive lady, accomplished, and of superior mental qualifications, but has no desire to shine in the world of letters.

INTO a ward of the white-washed walls
    Where the dead and the dying lay,
Wounded by bayonets, shells, and balls,
    Somebody's darling was borne one day.
Somebody's darling, so young and so brave,
    Wearing yet on his pale, sweet face—
Soon to be hid by the dust of the grave—
    The lingering light of his boyhood's grace.

Matted and damp are the curls of gold
    Kissing the sun of that fair young brow;
Pale are the lips of delicate mold—
    Somebody's darling is dying now.
Back from the beautiful blue-veined brow
    Brush all the wandering waves of gold;

Cross his hands on his bosom now,
  Somebody's darling is still and cold.

Kiss him once for somebody's sake,
  Murmur a prayer soft and low;
One bright curl from its fair mates take;
  They were somebody's pride you know.
Somebody's hand hath rested there—
  Was it a mother's soft and white—
And have the lips of a sister fair
  Been baptized in those waves of light?

God knows best!   He was somebody's love;
  "Somebody's" heart enshrined him there;
"Somebody" wafted his name above,
  Morn and night on the wings of prayer.
"Somebody" wept when he marched away,
  Looking so handsome, brave, and grand;
"Somebody's" kiss on his forehead lay,
  "Somebody" clung to his parting hand.

"Somebody's" watching and waiting for him,
  Yearning to hold him again to their heart;
And there he lies with his blue eyes dim,
  And the smiling, child-like lips apart.
Tenderly bury the fair young dead,
  Pausing to drop on his grave a tear,
Carve on the wooden slab at his head,
  "Somebody's darling slumbers here."

DRIVING HOME THE COWS.

BY KATE P. OSGOOD.

Kate Putnam Osgood has written many touching and pretty poems on homely, familiar subjects. She was born in Fryeburg, Maine, in 1840, and has done a great deal of miscellaneous literary work that is far above mediocrity.

OUT of the clover and blue-eyed grass
    He turned them into the river lane;
One after another he let them pass,
    Then fastened the meadow bars again.

Under the willows and over the hill,
    He patiently followed their sober pace;
The merry whistle for once was still,
    And something shadowed the sunny face.

Only a boy!—and his father had said
    He never could let his youngest go;
Two already were lying dead
    Under the feet of the trampling foe.

But after the evening work was done,
    And frogs were loud in the meadow swamp,
Over his shoulder he slung his gun,
    And stealthily followed the foot-path damp.

Across the clover and through the wheat,
    With resolute heart and purpose grim;
Though cold was the dew on his hurrying feet,
    And the blind bat's flitting startled him.

Thrice since then had the lanes been white,
    And the orchards sweet with apple-bloom;

And now, when the cows came back at night,
   The feeble father drove them home.

For news had come to the lonely farm
   That three were lying where two had lain,
And the old man's tremulous, palsied arm
   Could never lean on a son's again.

The summer day grew cool and late—
   He went for the cows when the work was **done;**
But down the lane, as he opened the gate,
   He saw them coming one by one.

Brindle, Ebony, Speckle, and Bess,
   Shaking their horns on the evening wind,
Cropping the butterflies out of the grass,
   But who was it following close behind.

Loosely swung in the idle air
   The empty sleeve of army blue;
And worn and pale from the crisping air,
   Looked out a face that the father knew.

For Southern prisons will sometimes yawn
   And yield their dead unto life again,
And the day that comes with a cloudy dawn
   In golden glory at last may wane.

The great tears sprang to their meeting eyes,
   For the heart must speak when the lips are **dumb,**
And under the silent evening skies
   Together they followed the cattle home.

"THE GREAT TEARS SPRANG TO THEIR MEETING EYES,
FOR THE HEART MUST SPEAK WHEN THE LIPS ARE DUMB."

THE OLD ARM-CHAIR.

By Eliza Cook.

This favorite English writer was born in 1817, in Southwark, London. Her poems are mostly on homely household topics, and are written with but little exercise of the power of imagination, but they have always pleased a large class of people. It is nearly half a century since The Old Arm-Chair was a popular song. It is now found in many of our best collections of fireside poetry.

I LOVE it, I love it, and who shall dare
    To chide me for loving the old arm-chair;
I've treasured it long as a sainted prize;
I've bedewed it with tears, and embalmed it with sighs;
'Tis bound by a thousand ties to my heart—
Not a tie will break, not a link will start;
Would ye learn the spell, a mother sat there,
And a sacred thing is that old arm-chair.

In childhood's hour I lingered near
The hallowed seat with listening ear,
And gentle words that mother would give
To fit me to die and teach me to live;
She told me shame would never betide,
With truth for my creed and God for my guide;
She taught me to lisp my earliest prayer,
As I knelt beside that old arm-chair.

I sat and watched her many a day,
When her eye grew dim, and her locks were gray,
And I almost worshipped her when she smiled,
And turned from her Bible to bless her child.

Years rolled on, but the last one sped—
My idol was shattered, my earth star fled;
I learned how much the heart can bear,
When I saw her die in that old arm-chair.

'Tis past! 'tis past! but I gaze on it now
With quivering breath and throbbing brow;
'Twas there she nursed me, 'twas there she died,
And memory flows with lava tide;
Say it is folly and deem me weak,
While the scalding drops start down my cheek;
But I love it, I love it, and cannot tear
My soul from a mother's old arm-chair.

PHILIP, MY KING.

By Miss Mulock.

Miss Mulock is better known as the author of John Halifax, and other popular novels, than as a poet; yet, there is hardly a collection of fine poems to be found which does not include one from her pen. As a writer she has been before the public for nearly half a century. Miss Mulock was born in 1826, and married to Mr. Craik in 1865. John Halifax was written in 1857. She contributes to English and American periodicals, and is popular with all classes of readers. As a writer she is best known by her maiden name, Dinah Maria Mulock; her poem and song, Philip, my King, is the best known of her verses. Miss Mulock was born in England, at Stoke-upon-Trent, Staffordshire.

> " Who bears upon his baby brow the round
> And top of sovereignty."

LOOK at me with thy large brown eyes,
          Philip, my king.
Round whom the enshadowing purple lies
Of babyhood's royal dignities.

Lay on my neck thy tiny hand
With love's invisible sceptre laden,
I am thine Esther to command
Till thou shalt find a queen-handmaiden,
    Philip, my king.

Oh, the day when thou goest a-wooing,
    Philip, my king,
When those beautiful lips 'gin suing,
And some gentle heart's bars undoing,
Thou dost enter love-crowned, and there
Sittest love-glorified. Rule kindly,
Tenderly over thy kingdom fair,
For we that love, ah! we love so blindly,
    Philip, my king.

Up from thy sweet mouth—up to thy brow,
    Philip, my king,
The spirit that there lies sleeping now
May rise like a giant and make men bow,
As to one heaven-chosen amongst his peers.
My Saul, than thy brethren taller and fairer,
Let me behold thee in future years—
Yet thy head needeth a circlet rarer,
    Philip, my king.

A wreath, not of gold, but of palm—one day,
    Philip, my king.
Thou, too, must tread as we trod, a way
Thorny and cruel, and cold and gray;
Rebels within thee, and foes without,
Will snatch at thy crown. But march on, glorious
Martyr, yet monarch, till angels shout,
As thou sit'st at the feet of God, victorious,
    "Philip, the king!"

THE LEGEND OF THE STORKS AND THE BABIES.

By Ella Wheeler.

Mrs. Ella Wheeler Wilcox is a native of Wisconsin, and is still a comparatively young woman. She has published a volume of poems, on the passions and affections, which has been received with much favor, and upon her donating a copy to the public library at Milwaukee, Wis., the citizens presented her with a purse of $500 in gold, as a testimonial of their esteem. Mrs. Wilcox has made literature her profession since she was fifteen years old.

HAVE you heard of the valley of Babyland,
    The realm where the dear little darlings stay,
Till the kind storks go, as all men know,
    And oh, so tenderly bring them away?
The paths are winding and past all finding
    By all save the storks, who understand
The gates and the highways, and the intricate byways
    That lead to Babyland.

All over the valley of Babyland
    Sweet flowers bloom in the soft green moss,
And under the blooms fair, and under the leaves there,
    Lie little heads like spools of floss.
With a soothing number, the river of slumber
    Flows o'er a bed of silver sand;
And angels are keeping watch o'er the sleeping
    Babes of Babyland.

The path to the valley of Babyland
    Only the kingly white storks know.
If they fly over mountains or wade thro' fountains—
    No man sees them come and go;

But an angel, maybe, who guards some baby,
　Or a fairy, perhaps, with her magic wand,
Brings them straightway to the wonderful gateway
　That leads to Babyland.

And there in the valley of Babyland,
　Under the mosses and leaves and ferns,
Like an unfledged starling, they find the darling,
　For whom the heart of a mother yearns.
And they lift him lightly and tuck him tightly
　In feathers as soft as a lady's hand,
And off with a rock-a-way step they walk away
　Out of Babyland.

As they go from the valley of Babyland
　Forth into the world of great unrest,
Sometimes weeping he wakes from sleeping
　Before he reaches his mother's breast.
Oh, how she blesses him, how she caresses him:—
　Bonniest bird in the bright home band,
That o'er land and water the kind stork bro't her
　From far off Babyland.

MEASURING THE BABY.

By Emma Alice Browne.

Emma Alice Browne (Mrs. E. A. Bevar) was for years a resident of Danville, Ill., where, in a quiet home, she devoted her life to literary pursuits. The sweet, pathetic little poem on "Measuring the Baby" was written during a night's vigil at the cradle of a beloved child, "sick unto death." Mrs. Bevar kindly wrote this poem especially for this publication, and alluded to it in touching language as a real incident in her own life. The lady was a Southerner, the daughter of a clergyman, the Rev. William A.

Browne, who died when his gifted daughter was still very young. In a private letter Mrs. Bevar said: "At thirteen I was a regular and paid contributor to the Louisville (Ky.) Journal, the New York Ledger, Philadelphia Saturday Evening Post, and other current publications." Mrs. Bevar was a lineal descendant of Mrs. Hemans, the English poetess, whose maiden name was Browne, and had much of that graceful style of writing pathetic verse with a delicacy of poetic fervor that is wholly original.

W E measured the riotous baby
    Against the cottage wall;
A lily grew at the threshold,
    And the boy was just so tall!
A royal tiger lily,
    With spots of purple and gold,
And a heart like a jeweled chalice,
    The fragrant dews to hold.

His eyes were wide as blue-bells,
    His mouth like a flower unblown,
Two little bare feet, like funny white mice,
    Peep'd out from his snowy gown;
And we thought, with a thrill of rapture,
    That yet had a touch of pain,
When June rolls around with her roses
    We'll measure the boy again!

Ah, me! In a darkened chamber,
    With the sunshine shut away,
Thro' tears that fell like a bitter rain,
    We measured the boy to-day!
And the little bare feet, that were dimpled
    And sweet as a budding rose,
Lay side by side together,
    In the hush of a long repose!

"We measured the riotous baby
  Against the cottage wall;
A lily grew at the threshold,
  And the boy was just so tall."

Up from the dainty pillow,
    White as the rising dawn,
The fair little face lay smiling,
    With the light of Heaven thereon!
And the dear little hands, like rose-leaves
    Dropt from a rose, lay still—
Never to snatch at the sunbeams
    That crept to the shrouded sill!

We measured the sleeping baby
    With ribbons white as snow,
For the shining rose-wood casket
    That waited him below;
And out of the darkened chamber
    We went with a childless moan:—
To the height of the sinless Angels
    Our little one had grown!

FAITH AND REASON.

By Lizzie York Case.

Mrs. Lizzie York Case is a Southern lady, a resident of Baltimore and vicinity for many years, and subsequently living at Mobile, Alabama, where her husband, Lieutenant J. Madison Case, was stationed in the service of the United States Navy. Mrs. Case is descended from Quaker ancestry, and much of the grace and versatility of character she possessed was derived from that source. Many of her poems have been published in household collections and school readers, and are much admired for their high educational standard.

TWO travelers started on a tour
    With trust and knowledge laden;
One was a man with mighty brain,
And one a gentle maiden.

They joined their hands and vowed to be
Companions for a season.
The gentle maiden's name was Faith,
The mighty man's was Reason.

He sought all knowledge from this world,
And every world anear it;
All matter and all mind were his,
But hers was only spirit.
If any stars were missed from Heaven,
His telescope could find them;
But while he only found the stars,
She found the GOD behind them.

He sought for truth above, below,
All hidden things revealing;
She only sought it woman-wise,
And found it in her feeling.
He said, "This Earth 's a rolling ball."
And so doth science prove it;
He but discovered that it moves,
She found the springs that move it.

He reads with geologic eye
The record of the ages;
Unfolding strata, he translates
Earth's wonder-written pages.
He digs around a mountain base
And measures it with plummet;
She leaps it with a single bound
And stands upon the summit.

He brings to light the hidden force
In nature's labyrinths lurking,

And binds it to his onward car
To do his mighty working.
He sends his message 'cross the earth,
And down where sea gems glisten;
She sendeth hers to GOD himself,
Who bends His ear to listen.

All things in science, beauty, art,
In common they inherit;
But he has only clasped the form,
While *she* has clasped the spirit.

He tries from Earth to forge a key
To ope the gate of Heaven!
That key is in the maiden's heart,
And back its bolts are driven.
They part! Without her all is dark;
His knowledge vain and hollow.
For Faith has entered in with GOD,
Where Reason may not follow.

REQUIESCAM.

Mrs. Robert S. Howland, an American lady, who is not known as a writer, is the author of this beautiful poem, said to have been found under the pillow of a wounded soldier near Port Royal, 1864.

I LAY me down to sleep,
   With little thought or care
Whether my waking find
   Me here or there.

A bowing, burdened head,
   That only asks to rest

Unquestioningly upon
  A loving breast.

My good right hand forgets
  It's cunning now—
To march the weary march
  I know not how.

I am not eager, bold,
  Nor strong—all that is past.
I am ready not to do
  At last ! at last !

My half-day's work is done,
  And this is all my part;
I give a patient God
  My patient heart.

And grasp his banner still
  Though all its blue be dim;
These stripes, no less than stars,
  Lead after Him.

HANNAH BINDING SHOES.

By Lucy Larcom.

POOR, lone Hannah,
  Sitting at the window binding shoes,
    Faded, wrinkled,
  Sitting, stitching in a mournful muse;
    Bright-eyed beauty once was she
    When the bloom was on the tree.
      Spring and winter
  Hannah's at the window binding shoes.

Not a neighbor
Passing, nod or answer will refuse
   To her whisper,
Is there from the fishers any news?
   Oh, her heart's adrift with one
   On an endless voyage gone.
      Night and morning
Hannah's at the window binding shoes.

   Fair young Hannah!
Ben, the sun-burned fisher, gayly wooes;
   Hale and clever,
For a willing heart and hand he sues.
   May-day skies are all aglow,
   And the waves are laughing so,
      For her wedding,
Hannah leaves her window and her shoes.

   May is passing.
'Mid the apple-boughs a pigeon coos.
   Hannah shudders,
For the mild south-wester mischief brews.
   Round the rocks of Marblehead,
   Outward bound a schooner sped,
      Silent—lonesome,
Hannah's at the window binding shoes.

   'Tis November;
Now no tear her wasted cheek bedews.
   From Newfoundland
Not a sail returning will she lose,
   Whispering hoarsely, "Fishermen,
   Have you, have you heard of Ben."
      Old with watching,
Hannah's at the window binding shoes.

Twenty winters
Bleach and tear the ragged shore she views;
Twenty seasons,
Never one has brought her any news.
Still her dim eyes silently
Chase the white sail o'er the sea.
Hopeless, faithful,
Hannah's at the window binding shoes.

CURFEW MUST NOT RING TO-NIGHT.

By Mrs. Rosa Hartwick Thorpe.

ENGLAND'S sun was slowly setting o'er the hill-tops far
away,
Filling all the land with beauty at the close of one sad day;
And its last rays kissed the forehead of a man and maiden fair,—
He with steps so slow and weary; she with sunny, floating hair;
He with bowed head, sad and thoughtful; she with lips so cold
and white,
Struggled to keep back the murmur, " Curfew must not ring to-
night."

" Sexton," Bessie's white lips faltered, pointing to the prison old,
With its walls so tall and gloomy,—moss-grown walls dark,
damp, and cold,—
" I've a lover in that prison, doomed this very night to die,
At the ringing of the curfew, and no earthly help is nigh.
Cromwell will not come till sunset," and her lips grew strangely
white,
As she spoke in husky whispers, " Curfew must not ring
to-night."

" Bessie," calmly spoke the sexton (every word pierced her
  young heart
Like a gleaming death-winged arrow—like a deadly poisoned
  dart,
"Long, long years I've rung the curfew from that gloomy,
  shadowed tower;
Every evening, just at sunset, it has tolled the twilight hour.
I have done my duty ever, tried to do it just and right;
Now I'm old, I will not miss it. Curfew bell must ring
  to-night !"

Wild her eyes and pale her features, stern and white her
  thoughtful brow;
And within her heart's deep centre Bessie made a solemn vow.
She had listened while the judges read, without a tear or sigh,
" At the ringing of the Curfew Basil Underwood *must die.*"
And her breath came fast and faster, and her eyes grew large
  and bright;
One low murmur, faintly spoken, " Curfew *must not* ring
  to-night !"

She with quick step bounded forward, sprang within the old
  church-door,
Left the old man coming slowly, paths he'd trod so oft before;
Not one moment paused the maiden, but with cheek and brow
  aglow,
Staggered up the gloomy tower, where the bell swung to and
  fro;
As she climbed the slimy ladder, on which fell no ray of
  light,
Upward still, her pale lips saying, " Curfew *shall not* ring
  to-night !"

She has reached the topmost ladder; o'er her hangs the great
dark bell;
Awful is the gloom beneath her, like the pathway down to hell.
See! the ponderous tongue is swinging; 'tis the hour of curfew
now,
And the sight has chilled her bosom, stopped her breath and
paled her brow.
Shall she let it ring? No, never! her eyes flash with sudden
light,
As she springs, and grasps it firmly: "Curfew *shall not* ring
to-night!"

Out she swung, far out,—the city seemed a speck of light
below—
There, 'twixt heaven and earth suspended, as the bell swung to
and fro.
And the Sexton at the bell-rope, old and deaf, heard not the bell,
Sadly thought that twilight curfew rang young Basil's funeral
knell;
Still the maiden clinging firmly, quivering lip and fair face
white,
Stilled her frightened heart's wild beating: "*Curfew shall not
ring to-night.*"

It was o'er—the bell ceased swaying; and the maiden stepped
once more
Firmly on the damp old ladder, where for hundred years before
Human foot had not been planted. The brave deed that she
had done
Should be told the long ages after. As the rays of setting sun
Light the sky with golden beauty, aged sires, with heads of
white,
Tell the children why the Curfew did not ring that one sad night.

O'er the distant hills comes Cromwell.   Bessie sees him; and her
    brow,
Lately white with sickening horror, has no anxious traces now.
At his feet she tells her story, shows her hands all bruised and
    torn;
And her sweet young face still haggard, with the anguish it had
    worn,
Touched his heart with sudden pity, lit his eyes with misty
    light,
" Go ! your lover lives," cried Cromwell, " Curfew *shall not* ring
    to-night."

Wide they flung the massive portals, led the prisoner forth to
    die,
All his bright young life before him, 'neath the darkening
    English sky.
Bessie came, with flying footsteps, eyes aglow with lovelight
    sweet,
Kneeling on the turf beside him, laid his pardon at his feet.
In his brave strong arms he clasped her, kissed the face upturned
    and white,
Whispered, "Darling, you have saved me, Curfew will not ring
    to-night."

THE GUEST.

By Harriet McEwan Kimball.

Miss Kimball is best known as a writer of devotional verse, her first published work being a book of hymns.   She has the true inspirational quality
which distinguishes the poet, and her poems are much admired by thoughtful and intellectual readers.   She is a native of this country, and was born
in New Hampshire in 1834.

SPEECHLESS sorrow sat with me,
    I was sighing heavily;
Lamp and fire were out; the rain
Wildly beat the window-pane.
In the dark we heard a knock,
And a hand was on the lock,
One in waiting spake to me,
    Saying sweetly,
"I am come to sup with thee."

All my room was dark and damp;
"Sorrow" said I, "trim the lamp;
Light the fire and cheer thy face;
Set the guest-chair in its place."
And again I heard the knock;
In the dark I found the lock;
"Enter! I have turned the key,
    Enter stranger,
Who art come to sup with me."

Opening wide the door he came;
But I could not speak his name;
In the guest-chair took his place;
But I could not see his face,—
When my cheerful fire was beaming,
When my little lamp was gleaming,
And the feast was spread for three—
    Lo, my Master
Was the Guest that supped with me!

THE VOICE OF THE POOR.

By Lady Wilde (Speranza).

Lady Wilde, at present a resident of London, England, was born in Ireland about the year 1830. She is the mother of Oscar Wilde, who has achieved almost a world-wide celebrity as the apostle of beauty. Many years ago Lady Wilde contributed to the Dublin Nation poems which attracted attention, over the name of "Speranza," which poems have since been issued in book form. She is in sympathy with all political movements which are for the good of her native country, and is impulsive and patriotic.

WAS ever sorrow like to our sorrow,
    O, God above?
Will our night never change into a morrow
    Of joy and love?
A deadly gloom is on us waking, sleeping,
    Like the darkness at noontide
That fell upon the pallid mother weeping
    By the Crucified.

Before us die our brothers of starvation,
    Around are cries of famine and despair;
Where is hope for us, or comfort, or salvation—
    Where—oh where?
If the angels ever hearken downward bending,
    They are weeping, we are sure,
At the litanies of human groans ascending
    From the crushed hearts of the poor.

When the human rests in love upon the human,
    All grief is light;
But who lends one kind glance to illumine
    Our life-long night?

The air around is ringing with their laughter—
    God only made the rich to smile;
But we in our rags and want and woe—we follow after,
    Weeping the while.

And the laughter seems but uttered to deride us,
    When, oh, when
Will fall the frozen barriers that divide us
    From other men?
Will ignorance forever thus enslave us?
    Will misery forever lay us low?
All are eager with their insults; but to save us
    None, none we know.

We never knew a childhood's mirth and gladness,
    Nor the proud heart of youth free and brave;
Oh, a death-like dream of wretchedness and sadness,
    Is life's weary journey to the grave.
Day by day we lower sink, and lower,
    Till the God-like soul within
Falls crushed beneath the fearful demon power
    Of poverty and sin.

So we toil on, on with fever burning
    In heart and brain;
So we toil on, on through bitter scorning,
    Want, woe and pain.
We dare not raise our eyes to the blue heaven,
    Or the toil must cease—
We dare not breathe the fresh air God has given
    One hour in peace.

We must toil, though the light of life is burning
    Oh, how dim;

We must toil on our sick-bed, feebly turning
    Our eyes to Him
Who alone can hear the pale lips faintly saying,
    With scarce moved breath,
While the pale hands, uplifted, aid the praying:
    " Lord, grant us *death!*"

THE BETTER LAND.

By Mrs. Felicia D. Hemans.

Mrs. Hemans was born in Liverpool, England, in 1793, and died in 1835. Her maiden name was Felicia Dorothea Browne. She married Captain Hemans in 1812, but it was an unhappy marriage, and in the latter part of her life they separated, and she devoted her time to the education of her five sons, and her poetical work. The tenderness and pathos of her poems, give them a charm that their mere intellectual merit would not have achieved, and they will always be popular in the household.

I HEAR thee speak of the better land,
    Thou call'st its children a happy band;
Mother! Oh, where is that radiant shore ?
Shall we not seek it and weep no more ?
Is it where the flower of the orange blows,
And the fire-flies glance through the myrtle boughs ? "
    Not there, not there, my child ! "

" Is it where the feathery palm trees rise,
And the date grows ripe under sunny skies ?
Or, midst the green islands of glittering seas,
Where fragrant forests perfume the breeze,
And strange bright birds on their starry wings
Bear the rich hues of all glorious things ?
    Not there, not there, my child !

Is it far away in some region old,
Where the rivers wander o'er sands of gold,
Where the burning rays of the ruby shine,
And the diamond lights up the secret mine,
And the pearl gleams forth from the coral strand?
Is it there, sweet mother, that better land?
   "Not there, not there, my child!"

Eye hath not seen it, my gentle boy,
Ear hath not heard its deep sounds of joy;
Dreams cannot picture a world so fair—
Sorrow and death may not enter there;
Time doth not breathe on its fadeless bloom
Far beyond the clouds and beyond the tomb.
   "It is there, it is there, my child!"

GONE IS GONE, AND DEAD IS DEAD.

BY MISS LIZZIE DOTEN.

Miss Lizzie Doten was born in Plymouth, Massachusetts, about the year 1820. She is what is known as an inspirational writer, and has published two volumes of poems which have attracted much attention in England, as well as here. Her poetry is the rapid verse of the improvisator, produced without any intellectual purpose or mental labor, but with certain peculiar qualities of strength and plaintiveness.

"On the returning to the inn, he found there a wandering minstrel—a woman—singing, and accompanying her voice with the music of a harp. The burden of the song was, "Gone is gone, and dead is dead."—*Jean Paul Richter.*

"GONE is gone, and dead is dead;"
 Words to hopeless sorrow wed;
Words from deepest sorrow wrung,
Which a lonely wanderer sung,

While her harp prolonged the strain,
Like a spirit's cry of pain
When all hope with life is fled.
"Gone is gone, and dead is dead."

Mournful singer ! hearts unknown
Thrill responsive to that tone,
By a common weal and woe
Kindred sorrows all must know.
Lips all tremulous with pain
Oft repeat that sad refrain
When the fatal shaft is sped.
"Gone is gone, and dead is dead."

Pain and death are everywhere;
In the earth, and sea, and air,
And the sunshine's golden glance,
And the Heaven's serene expanse.
With a silence calm and high,
Seem to mock that mournful cry
Wrung from hearts by hope unfed
"Gone is gone, and dead is dead."

As the stars which one by one,
Lighted at the central sun,
Swept across ethereal space
Each to its predestined place,
So the soul's Promethean fire
Kindled never to expire,
On its course immortal sped,
Is not gone and is not dead !

By a Power to thought unknown,
Love shall ever seek its own,

Sundered not by time or space,
With no distant dwelling-piace,
Soul shall answer unto soul
As the needle to the pole;
Leaving grief's lament unsaid.
" Gone is gone, and dead is dead."

Evermore Love's quickening breath
Calls the living soul from death,
And the resurrection's power
Comes to every dying hour,
When the soul, with vision clear,
Learns that Heaven is always near,
Nevermore shall it be said
" Gone is gone, and dead is dead."

THE TWO MYSTERIES.

By Mary Mapes Dodge.

Mary Mapes Dodge is the editor of the St. Nicholas Magazine, and the
writer of numerous pleasing poems, and various successful works for the
young. Mrs. Dodge is a daughter of the late Professor Mapes, and resides
with her family in the city of New York.

"In the middle of the room in its white coffin lay the dead child, the
nephew of the poet. Near it, in a great chair, sat Walt Whitman, surrounded by little ones, and holding a beautiful little girl on his lap. She
looked wonderingly at the spectacle of death, and then enquiringly into the
old man's face. " You don't know what it is, do you, my dear? " said he,
and added " we don't either."

WE know not what it is, dear, this sleep so deep and still;
      The folded hands, the awful calm, the cheek so pale
and chill,

The lids that will not lift again, though we may call and call;
The strange white solitude of peace that settles over all.

We know not what it means, dear, this desolate heart-pain,
This dread to take our daily way and walk in it again;
We know not to what other sphere the loved who leave us go,
Nor why we're left to wonder still, nor why we do not know.

But this we know, our loved and dead, if they should come this
    day,
Should come and ask us, what is life? not one of us could say.
Life is a mystery, as deep as ever death can be;
Yet, oh, how dear it is to us, this life we live and see!

Then might they say—those vanished ones,—and blessed is the
    thought,
"So death is sweet to us, beloved! though we may show you
    nought;
We may not to the quick reveal the mystery of death —
Ye cannot tell us if ye would the mystery of breath."

The child who enters life comes not with knowledge or intent,
So those who enter death must go as little children went.
Nothing is known. But I believe that God is overhead,
And as life is to the living, so death is to the dead.

HEARTBREAK HILL.

By Celia Thaxter.

Mrs. Thaxter is an American writer, a native of the Isle of Shoals, where
she lives in a pleasant home surrounded by the beauty of nature, and rich
in historic lore. She has published several volumes of poetry and prose,
and is a popular contributor to the leading magazines.

IN Ipswich town, not far from sea,
   Rises a hill which the people call
Heartbreak Hill, and its history
   Is an old, old legend, known to all.

The selfsame dreary, worn-out tale
   Told by all people in every clime,
Still to be told till the ages fail,
   And there comes a pause in the march of time.

It was a sailor who won the heart
   Of an Indian maiden, lithe and young;
And she saw him over the sea depart,
   While sweet in her ear the promise rung;

For he cried as he kissed her wet eyes dry,
   "I'll come back, sweetheart, keep your faith!"
She said, "I will watch while the moons go by."—
   Her love was stronger than life or death.

So this poor dusk Ariadne kept
   Her watch from the hill-top rugged and steep:
Slowly the empty moments crept
   While she studied the changing face of the deep,

Fastening her eyes upon every speck
   That crossed the ocean within her ken:—
Might not her lover be walking the deck,
   Surely and swiftly returning again?

The Isles of Shoals loomed, lonely and dim,
   In the northeast distance far and gray,
And on the horizon's uttermost rim
   The low rock-heap of Boon Island lay.

And north and south and west and east
  Stretched sea and land in the blinding light,
Till evening fell, and her vigil ceased,
  And many a hearth-glow lit the night,

To mock those set and glittering eyes
  Fast growing wild as her hope went out;
Hateful seemed earth, and the hollow skies,
  Like her own heart, empty of aught but doubt.

Oh, but the weary, merciless days,
  With the sun above, with the sea afar,—
No change in her fixed and wistful gaze
  From the morning red to the evening star !

Oh, the winds that blew, and the birds that sang,
  The calms that smiled, and the storms that rolled,
The bells from the town beneath, that rang
  Through the summer's heat and the winter's cold!

The flash of the plunging surges white,
  The soaring gull's wild, boding cry,—
She was weary of all; there was no delight
  In heaven or earth, and she longed to die.

What was it to her though the dawn should paint
  With delicate beauty skies and seas ?
But the swift, sad sunset splendors faint
  Made her soul sick with memories,

Drowning in sorrowful purple a sail
  In the distant east, where shadows grew,
Till the twilight shrouded it cold and pale,
  And the tide of her anguish rose anew.
24

Like a slender statue carved of stone
  She sat, with hardly motion or breath,
She wept no tears and she made no moan,
  But her love was stronger than life or death.

He never came back ! Yet faithful still,
  She watched from the hill-top her life away:
And the townsfolk christened it Heartbreak Hill,
  And it bears the name to this very day.

THE HIGH TIDE ON THE COAST OF LINCOLNSHIRE, 1571.

By Jean Ingelow.

Miss Ingelow is an English poet, born at Ipswich, and is now about sixty
years old. She has written some interesting literature for children, one or
two novels, and a volume of poems. The one given here is the most popu
lar of all her writings. It is much admired as a recitation.

THE old mayor climbed the belfry tower,
    The ringers rang by two, by three;
" Pull, if ye never pulled before;
    Good ringers, pull your best," quoth he,
" Play uppe, play uppe, O Boston Bells !
  Play all your changes, all your swells,
    Play uppe, the Brides of Enderby."

Men say it was a stolen tyde—
  The Lord that sent it, He knows all;
But in mine ears doth still abide
  The message that the bells let fall;
And there was naught of strange beside
The flight of mews and peewits pied
  By millions crouched on the old sea-wall.

I sat and spun within the doore,
  My thread brake off, I raised my eyes,
The level rim, like ruddy ore
  Lay sinking in the barren skies;
And dark against day's golden death
She moved where Lindis wandereth,—
My sonne's faire wife, Elizabeth.

" Cusha! cusha! cusha! " calling,
  For the dews will soon be falling.
Farre away I heard her song,
" Cusha! cusha! " all along
  Where the reedy Lindis floweth,
      Floweth, floweth,
  From the meads where melick groweth,
  Faintly came her milking song—

" Cusha! cusha! cusha! " calling,
  For the dews will soon be falling;
Leave your meadow-grasses mellow,
      Mellow, mellow;
Quit your cowslips, cowslips yellow;
Come uppe Whitefoot, come uppe Lightfoot,
Quit the stalk of parsley hollow,
      Hollow, hollow;
Come uppe Jetty, rise and follow!
From the clovers lift your head;
Come uppe Whitefoot, come uppe Lightfoot,
Come uppe Jetty, rise and follow
Jetty to the milking shed."

If it be long—ay, long ago,
  When I beginne to think howe long

Againe I hear the Lindis flow
　　Swift as an arrow, sharp and strong;
And all the aire it seemeth mee
Bin full of floating bells (sayth shee),
That ring the tune of Enderby.

Alle fresh the level pasture lay,
　　And not a shadow mote be scene
Save where, full fyve good miles away,
　　The steeple towered from out the greene,
And lo! the great bell far and wide
Was heard in all the country-side
That Saturday at eventide.

The swanherds, where their sedges are,
　　Moved on in sunset's golden breath;
The shepherde lads I heard afarre,
　　And my sonne's wife, Elizabeth;
Till floating o'er the grassy sea
Came downe that kyndly message free
The " Brides of Mavis Enderby."

Then some looked up into the sky,
　　And all along where Lindis flows
To where the goodly vessels lie
　　And where the lordly steeple shows;
They sayde, " And why should this thing be?
What danger lowers by land or sea ?
They ring the tune of Enderby! "

For evil news from Mablethorpe,
　　Of pyrate galleys warping downe—
For shippes ashore beyond the scorpe,
　　They have not spared to wake the towne;

But while the west bin red to see,
And storms be none and pyrates flee,
Why ring "The Brides of Enderby?"

I looked without, and lo! my sonne
   Came riding down with might and main;
He raised a shout as he drew on,
   Till all the welkin rang again:
" Elizabeth! Elizabeth!
(A sweeter woman ne'er drew breath
Than my son's wife, Elizabeth.)

" The old sea-wall (he cryed) is downe,
   The rising tide comes on apace,
And boats adrift in yonder towne
   Go sailing uppe the market-place."
He shook as one that looks on death,
" God save you, mother," straight he sayeth,
" Where is my wife, Elizabeth ? "

" Good sonne, where Lindis winds away,
   With her two bairns I marked her long,
And ere yon bells began to play
   Afar I heard her milking-song."
He looked across the grassy lea,
To right, to left, " Ho Enderby!"
They rang " The Brides of Enderby!"

With that he cried and beat his breast,
   For lo! along the river's bed
A mighty eygre reared his crest,
   And uppe the Lindis raging sped;
It swept with thunderous noises loud,
Shaped like a curling snow-white cloud,
Or like a demon in a shroud.

And rearing Lindis backward pressed,
 Shook all her trembling banks amaine,
Then madly at the eygre's breast
 Flung uppe her weltering walls again;
Then bank came downe with ruin and rout,
Then beaten foam flew round about,
Then all the mighty floods were out.

So farre, so fast the eygre drave
 The heart had hardly time to beat
Before a shallow seething wave
 Sobbed in the grasses at our feet;
The feet had hardly time to flee
Before it brake against the knee,
And all the world was in the sea.

Upon the roofe we sat that night;
 The noise of bells went sweeping by;
I marked the lofty beacon light
 Stream from the church tower, red and high,
A lurid mark and dread to see;
And awesome bells they were to me
That in the dark rung " Enderby!"

They rang the sailor lads to guide
 From roofe to roofe, who fearless roved,
And I—my sonne was at my side—
 And yet the ruddy billow glowed;
And yet he moaned beneath his breath,
" Oh, come in life, or come in death,
Oh, lost! my love, Elizabeth! "

And didst thou visit him no more?
 Thou didst, thou didst, my daughter dear;

The waters laid thee at his doore
　Ere yet the early dawn was clear;
Thy pretty bairns in fast embrace
The lifted sun shone on thy face,
Downe drifted to thy dwelling-place.

That flow strewed wrecks about the grass,
　That ebb swept out the flocks to sea;
A fatal ebbe and flow, alas!
　To manye, more than myne and niee;
But each will mourn her own (she sayth),
And sweeter woman ne'er drew breath,
Than my sonne's wife, Elizabeth.

THE SLEEP.
["He giveth His beloved sleep."—Psalms cxxvii, 2.]

BY ELIZABETH BARRETT BROWNING.

Elizabeth Barrett was born in London, in 1806, married to Robert Browning, the poet, in 1846, and died at Florence, Italy, in 1851. Her poems are characterized by a high intellectual attainment, and a great interest in the political events of the day. She was deeply religious, and of exquisite delicacy of imagination. "The Sleep" is one of her finest religious poems, and has been extensively published. She takes a position, independent of sex, among the foremost writers of the century.

OF all the thoughts of God that are
　Borne inward unto souls afar,
　　Along the psalmists' music deep,
Now tell me if there any is
For gift or grace surpassing this?
　　"He giveth His beloved sleep!"

What would we give to our beloved?
The hero's heart to be unmoved,
  The poet's star-tuned harp to sweep,
The patriot's voice to teach and rouse,
The monarch's crown to light the brows;
  " He giveth His beloved sleep!"

What do we give to our beloved?
A little faith all undisproved,
  A little dust to overweep,
And bitter memories to make
The whole earth blasted for our sake;
  '" He giveth His beloved sleep!"

"Sleep soft, beloved!" we sometimes say,
But have no tune to charm away
  Sad dreams that through the eyelids creep.
But never doleful dream again
Shall break the happy slumber, when
  " He giveth His beloved sleep!"

O, earth! so full of dreary noises;
O, men, with wailing in your voices;
  O, delv'ed gold, the wailers heap;
O, strife! O, curse that o'er it fall!
God makes a silence through it all,
  And " giveth His beloved sleep."

His dews drop mutely on the hill;
His cloud above it saileth still,
  Though on its slope men sow and reap.
More softly than the dew is shed,
Or cloud is floated overhead;
  " He giveth His beloved sleep!"

Yea ! men may wonder while they scan
A living, thinking, feeling man,
　　Confirm'd in such a rest to keep.
But angels say—and through the Word
I think their happy smile is *heard*,
　　" He giveth His beloved sleep ! "

For me, my heart that erst did go
Most like a tired child at a show,
　　That tries through tears the juggler's leap—
Would now its wearied vision close;
Would childlike on His love repose
　　Who " giveth His beloved sleep."

And friends, dear friends—when it shall be
That this low breath has gone from me,
　　And 'round my bier ye come to weep;
Let one most loving of you all,
Say, " Not a tear must o'er her fall,
　　' He giveth His beloved sleep !' "

ONLY WAITING.

By Frances Laughton Mace.

　　Frances Laughton (Mace) is a name almost wholly unknown to fame, although one of the tenderest poems in the English language originated from her pen; one, too, that has had a world-wide circulation in the annals of literature. This little poem, " Only Waiting," is constantly published and credited as anonymous. It was written by Miss Laughton when she was but eighteen years old, and first saw the light in the Waterville (Me.) Mail of September 7th, 1854. It has been used with great success as a hymn.

Some visitors at an almshouse noticed a very old man sitting in the door-way. When they asked him what he was doing there, he answered, "Only Waiting."

"ONLY waiting till the shadows
    Are a little longer grown,
Only waiting till the glimmer
    Of the day's last beam is flown;
Till the night of earth is faded
    From this heart once full of day,
Till the dawn of Heaven is breaking
    Through the twilight, soft and gray.

"Only waiting till the reapers
    Have the last sheaf gathered home,
For the Summer-time hath faded
    And the autumn winds are come;
Quickly reapers! gather quickly
    The last ripe hours of my heart,
For the bloom of life is withered
    And I hasten to depart.

"Only waiting till the angels
    Open wide the mystic gate,
At whose feet I long have lingered,
    Weary, poor and desolate.
Even now I hear their footsteps
    And their voices far away—
If they call me, I am waiting,
    Only waiting to obey.

"Only waiting till the shadows
    Are a little longer grown,
Only waiting till the glimmer
    Of the day's last beam is flown;

"ONLY WAITING, TILL THE SHADOWS ARE A LITTLE LONGER GROWN."

When from out the folded darkness,
Holy, deathless stars shall rise,
By whose light my soul shall gladly
Wing her passage to the skies."

LIFE.

By Charlotte Brontë.

Charlotte Brontë is best known to the world as the author of the popular novel, Jane Eyre. She was born in 1816, and died in 1855. Her famous story was published in 1847. She was one of three remarkable and gifted sisters, daughters of the Rev. Patrick Brontë, who lived at Haworth, in Yorkshire, England. The Rev. Robert Collyer was a neighbor of Charlotte, and can remember her as a slim, pale girl, when he worked at the forge. She married a Mr. Nicholls, her father's curate, and died after one year of happiness.

L IFE, believe, is not a dream
So dark as sages say;
Oft a little morning's rain
Foretells a pleasant day;
Sometimes there are clouds of gloom,
But these are transient all;
If the shower will make the roses bloom,
Oh! why lament its fall?
Rapidly, merrily,
Life's sunny hours flit by;
Gratefully, cheerfully,
Enjoy them as they fly.

What though death at times steps in
And calls our last away?

What though sorrow seems to win
O'er hope a heavy sway ?
Yet hope again elastic springs
Unconquered though she fell.
Still buoyant are her golden wings,
Still strong to bear us well.
Manfully, fearlessly,
The day of trial bear,
For gloriously, victoriously,
Can courage quail despair.

PRAYER OF MARY STUART, QUEEN OF SCOTS.

This beautiful, accomplished and most unfortunate queen was beheaded at Fothingay, February 8, 1587, at the command of her cousin, Queen Elizabeth, who feared her power, and accused her of complicity in a plot against her life. Mary died like a queen, inspiring her enemies with a fervent admiration of her beauty and heroic powers of endurance. We give a translation from the original Latin, in which the Queen wrote it in her book of devotions shortly before she was executed.

" O DOMINE Deus! speravi in te;
O care mi Jesu! nunc libera me
In dura catena, in misera pœna,
Desidero te;
Languendo, gemendo, et genuflectendo,
Adoro, imploro, ut liberes me."

[TRANSLATION.]

O, Master and Maker! my hope is in thee;
My Jesus, dear Saviour! now set my soul free
From this my hard prison, my spirit uprisen
Soars upward to thee.
Thus moaning, and groaning, and bending the knee,
I adore and implore that thou liberate me.

THE GRAY SWAN.

By Alice Cary.

The Carey sisters are as inseparable in literature as they were in their lives. Alice was born in 1820, and died in 1871. Phœbe was born in 1824, and died in 1871. They were born on a farm eight miles from Cincinnati, Ohio, and died in New York City, in the same year. They wrote verses from childhood, and their poems are published together in one volume. They were the center of a refined literary circle in New York when they died. Horace Greeley was a frequent and welcome visitor at their home.

"O TELL me, sailor, tell me true,
  Is my little lad, my Elihu,
    A-sailing with your ship?"
  The sailor's eyes were dim with dew,
 "Your little lad, your Elihu?"
    He said with trembling lip,—
    " What little lad? what ship?"

 "What little lad! as if there could be
  Another such a one as he!
    What little lad, do you say?
  Why, Elihu, that took to the sea
  The moment I put him off my knee!
    It was just the other day
    The *Gray Swan* sailed away."

 "The other day?" the sailor's eyes
  Stood open with a great surprise,—
    " The other day? the *Swan?*"
  His heart began in his throat to rise.
 "Ay, ay, sir, here in the cupboard lies
    The jacket he had on."
    " And so your lad is gone?"

"Gone with the *Swan*." "And did she stand
With her anchor clutching hold of the sand,
   For a month, and never stir?"
"Why, to be sure! I've seen from the land,
Like a lover kissing his lady's hand,
   The wild sea kissing her,—
    A sight to remember, sir."

"But, my good mother, do you know
All this was twenty years ago?
   I stood on the *Gray Swan's* deck,
And to that lad I saw you throw,
Taking it off, as it might be, so,
   The kerchief from your neck."
    "Ay, and he'll bring it back!"

"And did the little lawless lad
That has made you sick and made you sad,
   Sail with the *Gray Swan's* crew?"
"Lawless! the man is going mad!
The best boy ever mother had,—
   Be sure he sailed with the crew!
    What would you have him do?"

"And he has never written line,
Nor sent you word, nor made you sign
   To say he was alive?"
"Hold! if 'twas wrong, the wrong is mine;
Besides, he may be in the brine,
   And could he write from the grave?
    Tut, man, what would you have?"

"Gone twenty years—a long, long cruise,
'Twas wicked thus your love to abuse
   But if the lad still live,

And come back home, think you you can
Forgive him?"—"Miserable man,
   You're mad as the sea—you rave,—
   What have I to forgive?"

The sailor twitched his shirt so blue,
And from within his bosom drew
   The kerchief. She was wild.
"My God! my Father! is it true
My little lad, my Elihu?
    My blessed boy, my child!
    My dead,—my living child!"

HAPPY WOMEN.

By Phœbe Cary.

IMPATIENT women, as you wait
  In cheerful homes to-night, to hear
The sound of steps that soon or late
Shall come as music to your ear;

Forget yourselves a little while,
And think in pity, of the pain
Of women who will never smile
To hear a coming step again.

With babes that in their cradles sleep,
Or cling to you in perfect trust,
Think of the mothers left to weep
Their babies lying in the dust.

And when the step you wait for comes,
And all your world is full of light;
O, women! safe in happy homes,
Pray for all lonesome souls to-night!

"LIFE! I KNOW NOT WHAT THOU ART."

By Mrs. L. A. Barbauld.

Mrs. Letitia Aikin Barbauld was born in 1743, and died in 1825. She was a native of Tibworth, Leicestershire, and the daughter of a gentleman who was principal of an Academy for the education of boys. Mrs. Barbauld was the favorite poetess of the English youth of half a century ago. The little poem we publish here is an abbreviation of a longer poem, which is a favorite in its present condensed form.

LIFE! I know not what thou art,
    But know that thou and I must part;
And when, or how, or where we met
I own to me's a secret yet.

Life! we've been long together
Through pleasant and through cloudy weather;
'Tis hard perhaps to part when friends are dear,—
Perhaps t'will cost a sigh, a tear;
Then steal away, give little warning,
Choose thine own time;
Say not Good Night,—but in some brighter clime
Bid me Good Morning.

ROBIN ADAIR.

By Lady Caroline Keppel.

Lady Caroline Keppel, daughter of the second Earl of Albemarle, was born in 1735. Robin Adair was the name of an Irish surgeon whom she loved and married, and whose memory she has perpetuated in undying verse. He survived his loving wife many years, remaining constant to her image. This favorite song is set to a plaintive Irish air.

WHAT'S this dull town to me?
    Robin's not here:

He whom I wished to see,
  Wished for to hear!
Where's all the joy and mirth
Made life a heaven on earth?
Oh, they're all fled with thee
    Robin Adair!

What made the assembly shine?
    Robin Adair.
What made the ball so fine?
    Robin was there!
What when the play was o'er,
What made my heart so sore?
Oh, it was parting with
    Robin Adair!

But now thou'rt far from me,
    Robin Adair;
But now, I never see
    Robin Adair;
Yet he I loved so well
Still in my heart shall dwell;
Oh, I can ne'er forget
    Robin Adair!

Welcome on shore again,
    Robin Adair;
Welcome once more again,
    Robin Adair;
I feel thy trembling hand,
Tears in thy eyelids stand
To greet thy native land,
    Robin Adair.

25

Long I ne'er saw thee, love,
　　Robin Adair;
Still I prayed for thee, love,
　　Robin Adair.
When thou wert far at sea
Many made love to me;
But still I thought on thee,
　　Robin Adair.

Come to my heart again,
　　Robin Adair;
Never to part again,
　　Robin Adair!
And if thou still art true
I will be constant, too,
And will wed none but you,
　　Robin Adair!

KNOCKING*.
"Behold! I stand at the door and knock."

By HARRIET BEECHER STOWE.

It seems almost superfluous to give a memoir of the author of "Uncle Tom's Cabin;" her name is a household word, and she belongs as imperishably to the present century, and the American people, as the record of their liberties. A sister of the famous divine, Henry Ward Beecher, she is a year or two older than he, and singularly like him in disposition and peculiarities of temperament, but very unlike in personal appearance. Born in 1812, at Litchfield, Connecticut, she was almost the eldest of that large Beecher family, remarkable for their talents and idiosyncrasies of character. In 1836 Miss Beecher was married to the Rev. Calvin E. Stowe. She is still living at Hartford, Connecticut, where their pleasant home is located. Mrs. Stowe gave to the world in 1852, the book that made her famous,—

* Suggested by Hunt's picture "Light of the World."

" Uncle Tom's Cabin,"—which had for many years a phenomenal sale, it being difficult to supply the demand for it.   Mrs. Stowe told her publishers she hoped to make a new black silk out of the profits.   Her first check was for $10,000, and she and her husband were so bewildered by the receipt of such a large sum that they had to be instructed how to take care of it.

K NOCKING, knocking, ever knocking!
   Who is there?
'Tis a pilgrim, strange and kingly,
 Never such was seen before;
Ah, sweet soul; for such a wonder,
   Undo the door!

No! that door is hard to open;
Hinges rusty, latch is broken;
   Bid Him go.
Wherefore, with that knocking dreary,
Scare the sleep from one so weary?
   Say Him, no.

Knocking, knocking, ever knocking!
   What! still there?
Oh, sweet soul, but once behold Him,
 With the glory-crowned hair;
And those eyes, so true and tender,
   Waiting there!
Open, open, once behold Him—
   Him so fair!

Ah, that door! why wilt thou vex me—
Coming ever to perplex me?
For the key is stiffly rusty;
And the bolt is clogged and dusty;

Many fingered ivy vine
Seals it fast with twist and twine;
Weeds of years and years before,
Choke the passage of that door.

Knocking, knocking! What! still knocking?
    He still there?
What's the hour? The night is waning;
In my heart a drear complaining,
    And a chilly, sad interest.
Ah, this knocking! it disturbs me—
Scares my sleep with dreams unblest.
      Give me rest—
      Rest—ah, rest!

Rest, dear soul, He longs to give thee;
Thou hast only dreamed of pleasure—
Dreamed of gifts and golden treasure;
Dreamed of jewels in thy keeping,
Waked to weariness of weeping;
Open to thy soul's one Lover,
And thy night of dreams is over;
The true gifts He brings have seeming
More than all thy faded dreaming.

Did she open? Doth she—will she?
So, as wondering we behold,
Grows the picture to a sign,
Pressed upon your soul and mine;
For in every breast that liveth
Is that strange, mysterious door,—
The forsaken and betangled,
Ivy-gnarled and weed bejangled

Dusty, rusty, and forgotten;—
There the pierced hand still knocketh,
And with ever patient watching,
With the sad eyes true and tender,
With the glory-crowned hair,
Still a God is waiting there.

THE EARLY BLUE-BIRD.

By Mrs. Lydia H. Sigourney.

Mrs. Sigourney was a profuse and valuable writer for the young, when the age dealt in fact rather than fiction, and religion was believed to be a stronger power than morality. Many of her poems are devotional hymns in their character, and no doubt they had a salutary influence in molding the lives of the young of that period. Mrs. Sigourney was born in 1791. and died in 1865. She was an American writer, her birth-place being Norwich, Conn. Her style is similar to that of Mrs. Hemans.

BLUE-BIRD on yon leafless tree,
    Dost thou carol thus to me?
"Spring is coming! spring is here!
Sayest thou so, my birdie dear?
What is that in misty shroud
Stealing from the darkened cloud?
Lo! the snow-flakes, gathering mound
Settles o'er the whitened ground.
Yet thou singest, blithe and clear,
"Spring is coming! Spring is here!"

Strikest thou not too loud a strain?
Winds are piping o'er the plain;
Clouds are sweeping o'er the sky
With a black and threatening eye;

Urchins, by the frozen rill
Wrap their mantles closer still;
Yon poor man, with doublet old,
Doth he shiver at the cold?
Hath he not a nose of blue?
Tell me birdling, tell me true.

Spring's a maid of mirth and glee,
Rosy wreaths and revelry;
Hast thou woo'd some winged love
To a nest in verdant grove?
Sung to her of greenwood bower,
Sunny skies that never lower?
Lured her with thy promise fair
Of a lot that knows no care?
Prythee hid in coat of blue,
Though a lover, tell her true.

Ask her if when storms are long,
She can sing a cheerful song?
When the rude winds rock the tree
If she'll closer cling to thee?
Then the blasts that sweep the sky,
Unappalled shall pass thee by;
Through thy curtained chamber show
Sifting of untimely snow;
Warm and glad thy heart shall be,
Love shall make it spring for thee.

RELEASED.

By Mrs. A. D. T. Whitney.

Mrs. Whitney was born in Boston, in 1824, and married to Seth D. Whitney in 1843. She is best known as a writer of popular novels, her works being singularly felicitous in character and sentiment for the young. "Pansies" and "Footsteps on the Seas," her poetical effusions, were published in 1857. Her poetry has the same charm that her prose has, that of dealing gracefully and tenderly with homely subjects, and elevating the commonest daily toil to ennobling heights. Mrs. Whitney is still engaged in writing for the public.

A little low-ceiled room. Four walls
    Whose blank shut out all else of life,
And crowded close within their bound
    A world of pain, and toil and strife.

Her world. Scarce furthermore she knew
    Of God's great globe that wondrously
Outrolls a glory of green earth,
    And frames it with the restless sea.

Four closer walls of common pine;
    And therein lying, cold and still,
The weary flesh that long hath borne
    Its patient mystery of ill.

Regardless now of work to do,
    No queen more careless in her state,
Hands crossed in an unknown calm;
    For other hands the work may wait.

Put by her implements of toil;
    Put by each coarse, obtrusive sign;
She made a sabbath when she died,
    And round her breathes a rest divine.

Put by, at last, beneath the lid,
    The exempted hands, the tranquil face;
Uplift her in her dreamless sleep,
    And bear her gently from the place.

Oft has she gazed, with wistful eyes,
    Out from that threshold on the night;
The narrow bourn she crosseth now;
    She standeth in the eternal light.

Oft she has pressed, with aching feet,
    Those broken steps that reach the door;
Henceforth, with angels, she shall tread
    Heaven's golden stair, for evermore!

THE LAND OF THE LEAL.

By Lady Caroline Nairne.

This exquisitely simple and pathetic poem was written by Lady Caroline
Nairne, who was born in 1766, and died in 1845. Caroline Oliphant was a
native of Perth, Scotland, and married Major Nairne, who afterwards was
raised to the peerage, when she became Baroness Nairne. This poem, and
another, "Would you be young again," gave Lady Nairne a rank among
the best English poets, but they are often published anonymously, or credited to older Scottish poets. They can both be found in her poems and
memoirs, edited by Dr. Charles Rogers, and published in 1868.

I'M WEARIN' awa', Jean,
    Like snaw-wreaths in thaw, Jean,
I'm wearin' awa'
    To the land of the leal.

There's nae sorrow there, Jean,
There's neither cauld nor care, Jean,
The day is aye fair
    In the land of the leal.

Our bonnie bairn's there, Jean,
She was baith gude and fair, Jean,
And oh! we grudged her sair
    To the land of the leal.

But sorrow's sel' wears past, Jean,
And joy's a-comin' fast, Jean,
The joy that's aye to last
    In the land of the leal.

Sae dear that joy was bought, Jean,
Sae free the battle fought, Jean,
That sinful man e'er brought
    To the land of the leal.

Oh! dry your glistening e'e, Jean,
My soul langs to be free, Jean,
An angel beckons me
    To the land of the leal.

Oh! haud ye leal and true, Jean,
Your day it's wearin' thro', Jean,
And I'll welcome you
    To the land of the leal.

Now fare ye weel, my ain Jean,
This warld's cares are vain, Jean,
We'll meet and we'll be fain,
    In the land of the leal.

A MOTHER'S DAY.

By Mrs. C. D. Spencer.

Mrs. C. D. Spencer, at present a resident of Centralia, Wash., was born at Naples, Ontario Co., New York, in 1839. Her maiden name was Lovica Ingraham. Mrs. Spencer has for many years contributed short stories and poems to the best periodicals and magazines of the country. She takes special delight in entertaining the young in her short stories, and has brightened many homes and faces by them. This poem was written one short cold winter's day while her husband was pastor of a country church It touches an answering chord in many a mother's heart.

WHEN the bustle all was over,
    And the last hood snugly tied,
And the eager, dancing children,
    Fearful lest they lose their ride,
Rushed away to join their playmates
    In the sleigh now running o'er
With its freightage, to be emptied
    Safely at the schoolroom door,

Then I turned, and looked around me
    At the work that must be done
Ere these children, tired and hungry,
    Should at last come trooping home.
And the task seemed but a burden
    I had little heart to bear;
And, with thoughts despondent, bitter,
    Sank into an easy chair.

And it seemed to me my children
    Ne'er so careless were before;
Even husband's coat and slippers
    Had been left upon the floor.

And they would expect that mother
All these things would put to rights,
And have smiles and supper ready
When they should return at night.

And with hands all idly folded
Thus my bitter thoughts ran o'er:
All the duties of my household
Which had blessings seemed before,
Duties which as wife and mother
Daily, hourly, I must do.
Time must not be idly wasted,
If to these trusts I prove true.

I must keep my house so "homelike"
That to all these precious ones
There would be no place so pleasant,
None where they so loved to come.
There must be the constant watching
Lest the evil enter there,
Earnest, loving, prayerful shielding
From the wily tempter's snare.

I must reprimand when wayward;
I must praise when they do well;
I must heal each head and heart ache;
Hear each tale they have to tell;
I must teach them to be helpful;
Guide their feet and hands aright;
I must help them weave their life web,
With no respite day or night.

I must tread the daily routine
Of my housework o'er and o'er,

For the Father had not given
To me much of earthly store;
So the planning and the working
My own head and hands must do,
Even though those hands grow weary,
And my head and heart ache too.

And not even with my home work—
Still my bitter thoughts ran on—
Can I stop, for other duties
Press my mind and time upon;
Sabbath school, and mission circle,
Temperance lodge and Christmas tree,
Concert, meeting and church social—
Everything must call on me.

Why need I help do the planning,
Urge the pressing need of work,
Spend my time and strength in doing,
When so many others shirk?
Others with so much more leisure,
More ability to do,
Who should feel it was a pleasure
And an urgent duty, too.

Others with more means for giving
That the story may be told—
Ah! of whom? The blessed Saviour—
To my vision there arose
Suddenly a striking picture
Of the scene on Calvary,
Of the precious, patient Jesus
Bleeding, dying, there for me.

And I seemed to hear him saying,
"I will give my life for thee,
I am bearing this great burden,
Canst not thou bear aught for me?
I have given thee home and husband,
And these precious children, too;
Given thee church and Sabbath priv'lege,
Given thee this *work* to do."

Still my hands lay idly folded,
But the bitter thoughts were gone;
And I turned, subdued and thankful,
To the duties of my home.
Would I give unto another
My place in my husband's heart,
Desecrate the name of Mother,
By not bearing well my part!

Would I give up the dear church home
Where I love so well to meet
With the followers of my Saviour,
Worshiping at his dear feet?
And would I have any other
Bear my cross and wear my crown,
And not hear the voice of Jesus
Say to me, "Thou hast well done"?

Of the struggle and the victory
None but Jesus ever knew;
But I gained new strength and courage
My life duties to renew.
And all day my hands were busy
Putting all the things to rights,
And, with smiles and supper ready,
Greeted the loved ones at night.

OLD AGE COMING.

By Elizabeth Hamilton.

Elizabeth Hamilton, a Scotch writer, author of "The Cottagers of Glen-burnie," and several other sensible and interesting works. She died, unmarried, about fifty years ago, nearly sixty years old. These lines were written in such very broad Scotch, that we have taken the liberty to render them in English, making no changes, except a few slight variations, which the necessities of rhyme required.

IS that Old Age, who's knocking at the gate?
   I trow it is. He sha'n't be asked to wait.
You're kindly welcome, friend! Nay, do not fear
To show yourself! You'll cause no trouble here.
I know there 're some who tremble at your name,
As though you brought with you reproach or shame;
And who of thousand lies would bear the sin,
Rather than own you for their kith and kin.
But far from shirking you as a disgrace,
Thankful I am to live to see your face.
Nor will I e'er disown you, or take pride
To think how long I might your visit hide.
I'll do my best to make you well respected,
And fear not for your sake to be neglected.
Now you have come, and, through all kinds of weather
We're doomed from this time forth to jog together,
I'd fain make compact with you, firm and strong,
On terms of give and take, to hold out long.
If you'll be civil, I will liberal be;
Witness the list of what I'll give to thee.
First then, I here make o'er, for good and aye,
All youthful fancies, whether bright or gay.

Beauties and graces, too, might be resigned,
But much I fear they would be hard to find;
For 'gainst your daddy Time they could not stand,
Nor bear the grip of his relentless hand.
But there's my skin, which you may further crinkle,
And write your name, at length, on ev'ry wrinkle.
On my brown locks your powder you may throw,
And bleach them to your fancy, white as snow.
But look not, Age, so wistful at my mouth,
As if you longed to pull out ev'ry tooth!
Let them, I do beseech you, keep their places!
Though, if you like, you're free to paint their faces.
My limbs I yield you; and if you see meet
To clap your icy shackles on my feet,
I'll not refuse; but if you drive out gout,
Will bless you for 't, and offer thanks devout.
So much I give to you with free good-will;
But, O, I fear that more you look for still.
I know, by your stern look and meaning leers,
You want to clap your fingers on my ears.
Right willing, too, you are, as I surmise,
To cast your misty powder in my eyes.
But, O, in mercy, spare my little twinklers!
And I will always wear your crystal blinkers.
Then 'bout my ears I'd fain a bargain strike,
And give my hand upon it, if you like.
Well, then—would you consent their use to *share?*
'T would serve us both, and be a bargain rare.
I'd have it thus,—When babbling fools intrude,
Gabbling their noisy nonsense for no good;
Or when ill-nature, well brushed up with wit,
With sneer sarcastic, takes its aim to hit;

Or when detraction, meanest sort of pride,
Spies out small faults, and seeks great worth to hide;
Then make me deaf as ever deaf can be !
At all *such* times, my ears I lend to thee.
But when, in social hours, you see combined
Genius and wisdom, fruits of heart and mind,
Good sense, good nature, wit in playful mood,
And candor, e'en from ill extracting good;
O, then, old friend, I *must* have back my hearing !
To want it then would be an ill past bearing.
I'd rather sit alone, in wakeful dreaming,
Than catch the sound of words without their meaning.
You will not promise?   O, you're very glum !
Right hard to manage, you're so cold and dumb !
No matter.—Whole and sound I'll keep my *heart.*
Not from one crumb on't will I ever part.
Its kindly warmth shall ne'er be chilled by all
The coldest breath that from your lips can fall.
You needn't vex yourself, old churl, nor fret !
My kindly feelings you shall never get.
And though to take my hearing you rejoice,
In spite of you, I'll still hear friendship's voice.
And though you take the rest, it shall not grieve me;
For gleams of cheerful spirits you *must* leave me.
But let me whisper in your ear, Old Age,
I'm bound to travel with you but one stage.
Be 't long or short, you cannot keep me back;
And when we reach the *end* on 't, you must pack !
Be 't soon or late, we part forever there !
Other companionship I then shall share.
This blessed change to me you're bound to bring.
You need not think I shall be loath to spring

From your poor feeble side, you churl uncouth !
Into the arms of Everlasting Youth.
All that your thieving hands have stolen away
He will, with interest, to me repay.
Fresh gifts and graces freely he'll bestow,
More than the heart has wished, or mind can know.
You need not wonder then, nor swell with pride.
That I so kindly welcomed you as guide
To one who's far your better.   Now all's told.
Let us set out upon our journey cold.
With no vain boasts, no vain regrets tormented.
We'll quietly jog on our way, contented.

IDA LEWIS.

By Miss Alice E. Ives.

Miss Ives has had considerable success as a writer of verse and short stories, also as a dramatic and art critic. Her stories, written for New York and Detroit papers, have been quite extensively copied.   One which appeared several years ago in the "Detroit Free Press" went the rounds of different journals, and reached as far as New Zealand.   Her verses have appeared in many of the most prominent journals of the country.   As a dramatic writer she bids fair to obtain prominence, some of her plays having been accepted by leading companies.   She wrote a play for a Detroit company last winter.   Miss Ives is a resident of Detroit, which is her birthplace.

THE lighthouse keeper's daughter
   With wind-toss'd rippling hair,
And eyes bright as the sea-gull's,
   Stands tall, and strong, and fair.

As out her frail skiff plunges
　From shade of Lime Rock Light,
Across the angry breakers
　On through the stormy night,

Fearless as some wild water sprite,
　Her white, round arms of steel
Fling foam and spray from flashing **oar**
　And from the dancing keel.

Within her blue eye gleams the light
　Of purpose calm and bold,
Such as made knights and martyrs
　In saintly days of old.

Her quick ear strains to catch the sound—
　As swift she guides her barque—
Of cries above the tempest,
　That wail out through the dark.

For never boom of signal gun
　Nor aid comes from afar,
As she through mountain billows
　Steers for the floating spar;

Steers for the clinging, dying man,
　Who sees no help in sight;
When suddenly the little skiff
　Dawns like a beam of light.

It speeds like sea-bird on the blast,
　On, on, and still more near,
Till, through the storm, the maiden's **voice**
　Rings out with words of cheer.

And as the strong arms pull each **stroke,**
   The gulf of death is spanned,
And life comes to the shudd'ring **soul,**
   Brought by a *woman's* hand.

So ever as the years go by,
   On errands swift to save,
The angel of the Lighthouse
   Still braves the wind and wave.

O woman soul, so true and strong !
   No marble shaft is thine,
But in a nation's heart thy deeds
   Shall shine with light divine.

And when in after ages
   They ask of her fair fame,
The very waves 'round old Lime Rock
   Shall sing the maiden's name.

THE STORY OF IDA LEWIS.

That our readers may better appreciate the **beautiful** poem of Miss Ives (written especially for this work), we give here some of the facts pertaining to the bravery of Ida Lewis, the Newport heroine, appropriately called by some "The Grace Darling of America."

Ida Lewis is the daughter of Captain Hosea Lewis, of Higham, Mass., and was born on February 25, 1842. She attended the public school at Newport until she was fifteen years of age, when her parents moved to Lime Rock Lighthouse ; soon after their removal to the lighthouse her father was stricken down with paralysis, and

Ida was obliged to accustom herself to the use of the oars, and bring all the supplies to the lighthouse, and row her smaller brothers and sisters to and from school; she soon became an expert—as much at home on the water as on the land. Her philanthropic nature was first gratified in the fall of 1858, when she won a place among the brave by rescuing from drowning four young men whose pleasure boat had been upset; at this time she was but sixteen. Eight years later she saved a soldier from a neighboring fort from drowning. In 1867 three Irishmen saw a sheep drifting off at sea, and started after it in a small row boat; they had gone but a short distance, when, amid the white-capped billows of the ocean, their courage failed them, and, on turning round, they found they were powerless to reach the shore. The heroine of old Lime Rock took them from their sinking boat, and brought them safely to shore, after which she returned and brought the sheep to land also. Two weeks later she saved a man whose boat, having sprung a leak from striking a rock, had sunk and left him up to his chin in water, while the rising tide was threatening to engulf him. On March 29, 1869, Ida was sitting in her favorite chair, beside the warm fire, finishing some needlework before preparing the family's evening meal. Her mother, sitting near the window, suddenly discovered a capsized boat, to which two soldiers from the garrison at Fort Adams were clinging. She had scarcely made known the facts, when her daughter, catching only the words "drowning men," sprang to her feet, prompt and eager to save them. In spite of her invalid father's entreaties (for the old sailor knew the danger), she is at the door. All thoughts of the warmth and comfort within have vanished now, and the patient, toiling girl has become a heroine, flying, with dauntless soul, to save the perishing. She has no shoes upon her feet, no hat upon her head, and no outer garments to protect her from the storm, with only a towel, hastily seized and knotted about her neck, her stocking-clad feet speed her away over sharp rocks to her ever-ready boat. A younger brother, at her request, accompanies her to assist in dragging the drowning men into the boat; but to Ida's skill and willing arms must be trusted the plying of those oars upon whose dexterous use depends the saving of those lives, now so sorely threatened. Never before were her hands so tried, or the strength of woman's arm so tested. Though the green billows, crested with white foam, came flying over the open boat, nearly filling it with water, she heeds them not. Fame, success and a nation's encomiums wait upon her exertions, or, it may be, a watery grave beside those she is trying to save. Her mother stands upon the rock, wildly gesticulating and endeavoring to encourage the drowning men to continue their efforts for life; it is all the aged woman can do, but she does it well. The race for life is accomplished, our heroine reaches the drifting wreck, the exhausted men are brought safely to the lighthouse, and new laurels are added to Ida's well-earned wreath of fame. One of the rescued men, Sergeant Adams, is barely able to totter to the house, while his companion, but an hour ago a picture of strength and vigor, required united strength to remove him from the boat.

Thus ends the story of Ida Lewis's exploits—deeds worthy of emulation, which, in the grand old days of Greece and Rome, would have gained the applause of Senates, and have been perpetuated in the sculptor's marble and upon the historian's tablet of brass.

The Life Saving Benevolent Association of New York awarded her a silver medal and one hundred dollars, and the General Assembly of her own State (Rhode Island) passed resolutions acknowledging her brave and valuable services. These resolutions were formally communicated to her by a document from the Secretary of State, and with the State seal affixed. The officers and soldiers of the fort sent her their thanks, accompanied by the more substantial reward of a purse containing two hundred and eighteen dollars, and from all parts of the country letters and valuable gifts were sent to her as tokens of regard.

Through the heroic deeds of Ida Lewis, Lime Rock Lighthouse has become famous, and many noted persons have since then visited the place.

There are many philanthropic women who, in Christian faith and love have done noble deeds, but it is doubtful if any have become so famous as Ida Lewis for handling the oars, and with such noble results ; but all true women will delight to honor one who reflects so much honor on her sex and humanity, and who has so clearly demonstrated *what a woman can do.*

CHAPTER XXXI

Friendship ✽ Among ✽ Women.

OMEN feel friendship insipid after love, says that dogmatic Frenchman, La Rochefoucauld. And Swift, who ought to have known better, with the example right under his eyes of the life-long affection of Esther Johnson and Lady Gifford, wrote: "To speak the truth, I never yet knew a tolerable woman to be fond of her own sex."

It would scarcely be worth while to attempt to controvert the sweeping assertions of a cynic and a satirist, were it not that even in this advanced age we occasionally hear people of considerable sense advance a like opinion, with every appearance of believing it themselves. Very sad, indeed, must be the private experience of any of us who cannot furnish at least one refutation of this charge against womankind.

But if the genuine friendship which exists between women who are unknown to the public, like the testimonials attached to patent medicines, is not likely to be taken as very authentic proof of the value of the article, at least a few instances, of which there is abundant corroboration, in the lives of world-renowned and illustrious women, may serve to prove the truth of our argument.

What devotion could be more lasting and heroic than that of the Princess Lamballe for her unfortunate friend, Marie Antoinette? They had shared each other's confidences in the happy days of prosperity, and, when evil days came upon the queen, the princess could not be persuaded to seek her own safety by leaving the palace. When at last she was summoned to the bedside of a dying relative, Marie Antoinette sent her a letter begging her not to return. "Your heart," she wrote, "would be too deeply wounded; you would have too many tears to shed over my misfortunes, you who love me so tenderly. Adieu, my dear Lamballe; I am always thinking of you, and you know I never change!" But the princess hastened back to her imperiled friend, and all through those terrible last days of the sack, the pillage, and the prison, clung to her with a devotion as tender as it was heroic. When they strove to draw from her at the trial something prejudicial to the royal victim, when the mob which had lost the semblance of humanity, with wild, red eyes, howled like wolves for blood, she preferred death to treachery, and her beautiful head, with its wealth of golden locks, in which was concealed this last letter from Marie Antoinette, was elevated on a pike before the prison window of the woman for whom she had died.

Whatever may have been said derogatory to this daughter of Maria Theresa, the fact stands proved that a woman who could inspire and hold such a devoted and noble friendship must have had elements of character equally lofty and beautiful.

Scarcely less touching and heroic was the attachment of Catharine Douglass to Lady Jane Beaufort, consort of James I. of Scotland, to whom she was maid of honor. On that terrible night of February 20, 1437, when three hundred assassins, led by the earl of Athole, "were forcing their way into the royal chamber, Catharine thrust her beautiful arm into the stanchion of the door as a bolt, and held it there till it was broken."

The poet Chaucer had good cause to lament the presence of a powerful lady rival in the affections of his intended bride, who for this reason kept him waiting eight years for her hand. Philippa Picard was the favorite of the queen of Edward the Third, and, being warmly attached to her royal friend, she vowed she would not marry while the latter lived ; and so the father of English poetry was forced to possess his soul in patience until the death of the queen set his affianced free.

Mary Stuart's four maids of honor, Mary Fleming, Mary Beton, Mary Livingston, and Mary Seton, "the Queen's Marys," as they were called, with the exception of one who through illness was obliged to retire to a convent, never left their royal mistress while she lived, but supported and comforted her even to the block.

A friendship which provoked the good-natured ridicule of the day was that of Madame Salvage de Faverolles for Hortense, daughter of Josephine, and queen of Holland. Madame was jocosely called the queen's bodyguard, as she seemed to be her shadow on all occasions. But when in the last illness of Hortense she still remained her shadow, never leaving her day or night, and after her friend's death faithfully carried out the instructions of the will, the jokers were silent.

Hannah More, who wrote the tragedy of Percy for David Garrick, and whose fame as a dramatist was wide in her day, became so attached to Mrs. Garrick after the tragedian's death that the widow fondly called Miss More her chaplain.

Miss Elizabeth Carter, who enjoyed the friendship of Dr. Johnson and other great men of that time, had a devoted confidante in the person of Miss Catherine Talbot. They shared their secrets, and corresponded regularly for thirty years. Never in all that time was there one instance of betrayal or misunderstanding. Think of that, ye croakers and cynics, who are forever saying "a woman can't keep a secret!" Think of keeping hundreds of secrets, and for thirty years, too! If there are any men who can boast of a more extended confidence and friendship, we have never known them.

Anna Seward, admired in her generation as a beauty and a writer, was the devoted friend of the lovely Honora Sneyd, of whom Major André was the rejected lover. "Ah," writes Miss Seward, "how deeply was I a fellow sufferer with Major André, on her marriage! We both lost her forever."

Miss Seward's once famous "Monody on Major André," in which she severely censured Washington for his part in the execution of the unfortunate young officer, was the source of so much grief and mortification to the general that, after peace was concluded between this country and Great Britain, he sent an officer to the

English lady, with papers showing how he had labored to save André. "On examining them," she writes to the Ladies of Llangollen, "I found they entirely acquitted the general. They filled me with contrition for the rash injustice of my censure."

The Ladies of Llangollen, above referred to, were perhaps the most romantic and remarkable instances of single-hearted devotion on record. William R. Alger has given a most delightful account of them, from which we condense the following: In the latter part of the eighteenth century Lady Eleanor Butler and Miss Sarah Ponsonby conceived for each other such a violent affection that they determined to forsake the social world, and pass the remainder of their lives together. Accordingly they departed to an obscure retreat in the country, but their relatives, strongly objecting to such an eccentric proceeding, traced out their hiding-place, and succeeded in separating and bringing them back. Opposition in nowise dampened their ardor, and they determined that their second elopement should be a more successful one. Confiding their secret only to a single faithful servant, they fled. They chose the romantic valley of Llangollen, in Wales, one of the quietest and loveliest spots in the world. Here they bought a tiny cottage, which they fitted with every comfort, and furnished with books, pictures, and all the necessities of two elegant, cultured women. Their neighbors, ignorant of their names, called them "the Ladies of the Vale." "For a quarter of a century, it is said, they never spent twenty-four hours at a time out of their happy valley." They seem never to have wearied of each other, or to have had even the slightest misunderstanding.

A faithful servant, who had been much attached to them, set out several times to search for the young ladies in vain. They, happening to hear of her unsuccessful attempts, sent for the woman, and she lived and died of old age in their service.

After a time the story of this romantic friendship began to be noised abroad, and brought many distinguished visitors to the little cottage in Llangollen. Quite a number of these guests became sincerely attached to their entertainers, and an extensive correspondence was the result. Madame de Genlis wrote enthusiastically of her stay with them. She spoke of the exquisite taste of their tiny establishment, and especially of the Æolian harp they had in the library window, which she then heard for the first time. Both of the ladies read and spoke most of the modern languages, and Miss Seward, in describing the library of "the two Minervas," speaks of the finest editions, superbly bound, of the best authors of prose and verse in the English, French and Italian languages. They were especially admirers of Dante. Miss Seward paid many tributes in verse to their charming retreat, which she called the "Cambrian Arden," and the two ladies "the Rosalind and Celia of real life."

Miss Martineau visited them in their old age, and describes as something unique these ancient dames in their riding habits, with the rolled and powdered hair, and stately manners of a past century. They declared that they had never, even in the long winters of imprisoning snows, felt a desire to return to the world they had abandoned. Miss Sarah Ponsonby lived to be seventy-six years of age, and Lady Eleanor Charlotte Butler to be ninety. Their deaths were only two years apart. Thus for nearly three score years lived together two of the most devoted friends the world has ever known. Their last resting-place, with that of the faithful servant, can be seen to-day, marked by a marble tombstone, in the old churchyard of the little Welsh village, set in the velvety green of its valley, and shadowed by the rugged hills of Llangollen.

A world-renowned friendship was that of the brilliantly-gifted Madame de Stael and the most celebrated beauty of her time, Madame Récamier. Margaret Fuller, after seeing an engraving of the latter, records in her diary the following: "I have so often thought over the intimacy between her and Madame de Stael. It is so true that a woman may be in love with a woman, and a man with a man." Madame Récamier had an enthusiastic appreciation of the genius of her friend, and Madame de Stael in return felt a sort of intoxication of happiness in the society of the beautiful young creature, whose sincerity, purity and loftiness of character, together with other charming attributes, never failed to attract and fascinate. Sainte Beuve said that she brought the art of friendship to perfection, and Luyster that she "seemed to possess some talisman by whose spell she disarmed envy and silenced detraction." It need scarcely be hinted that the talisman was innate unselfishness, sweet kindliness and tact. Of the first meeting of these two remarkable women Madame Récamier says: "That day was an epoch in my life."

On the banishment of Madame de Stael, Madam-Récamier risked the displeasure of Napoleon in order to visit her friend, for which action she also was banished. During this sad period the two kept up an incessant correspondence. On one occasion, after receiving a present from her "dear Juliette," Madame de Stael writes: "Dear friend, how this dress has touched me! I shall wear it on Tuesday in taking leave of the court. I shall tell everybody that it is a gift from you, and shall make all the men sigh that it is not you who are wearing it."

Again she writes from Blois: "Dear Juliette—Our stay here is drawing to a close. I cannot conceive of either country or home life without you. I know that certain sentiments seem to be more necessary to me; but I also know that everything falls to pieces when you leave." In another letter she says: "Your friendship is like the spring in the desert that never fails; and it is this which makes it impossible not to love you."

That Madame de Stael's estimate of her friend was correct, subsequent events most unmistakably demonstrated. Death only ended this beautiful attachment. The devotion of Madame Récamier to the memory of the illustrious author, and her efforts to disseminate her writings were not less earnest and genuine than had been her affection for her living friend.

The fascination of this delightful subject might make one, like the brook, "go on forever," were it not for a wholesome fear of readers less enthusiastic on this point than the writer. But certainly examples similar to the foregoing might be multiplied to fill volumes. How much might be said of such pairs of friends as Elizabeth

Barrett Browning and Mary Mitford, Joanna Baillie and Miss Aiken, Mrs. Hemans and Miss Jewsbury, Madame Swetchim and Romandra Stourdza, Margaret Fuller and the Marchioness Arconati, L. Maria Child and Lucy Osgood, and Sarah Austin and the Duchess of Orleans.

It seems as if each and every one of these said to us: "Dear sister woman, you cannot afford to do without such a necessity as a true, devoted friend. You cannot afford to forego the uplifting of soul, the broadening and sweetening of your life, which such an experience brings. They who are forever sufficient unto themselves must be either gods or fiends; they are not human. The most shrinking, sensitive temperament that shuns all social life has need of one friend, as Michael Angelo had of Vittoria Colonna. Do not expect perfection, but cover small faults with the mantle of sweet charity, and don't lift up the corner of the mantle to see if they are still thriving; search, search, search for what is nobler. As elevating and beautiful as are these friendships we have been considering, be sure that one breath of envy, petty spite, narrowness, or uncharitableness would have killed them as dead as an Easter lily under the hot blast of the desert. "Do men gather grapes of thorns?"

—ALICE E. IVES.

❖CHAPTER XXXII.❖

Unmarried Women.

OWARDS civilization society moves slowly, but when we compare epochs half a century, or even quarter of a century apart, we perceive many signs that progress *is* made. Among these pleasant indications is the fact that the phrase "old maid" has gone well nigh out of fashion; that jests on the subject are no longer considered witty, and are never uttered by gentlemen. In my youth, I not unfrequently heard women of thirty addressed in this style: "What, not married yet? If you don't take care, you will outstand your market." Such words could never be otherwise than disagreeable, nay, positively offensive, to any woman of sensibility and natural refinement; and that not merely on account of wounded vanity, or disappointed affection, or youthful visions receding in the distance, but because the idea of being in the *market*, of being a *commodity*, rather than an individual, is odious to every human being.

I believe a large proportion of unmarried women are so simply because they have too much conscience and

delicacy of feeling to form marriages of interest or con-
venience, without the concurrence of their affections and
their taste. A woman who is determined to be married,
and who "plays her cards well," as the phrase is, usually
succeeds. But how much more estimable and honorable
is she who regards a life-union as too important and
sacred to be entered into from motives of vanity or
selfishness.

To rear families is the ordination of Nature, and where
it is done conscientiously it is doubtless the best education that men or women can receive. But I doubt the
truth of the common remark that the discharge of these
duties makes married people less selfish than unmarried
ones. The selfishness of single women doubtless shows
itself in more petty forms; such as being disturbed by
crumbs on the carpet, and a litter of toys about the
house. But fathers and mothers are often selfish on a
large scale, for the sake of advancing the worldly prosperity or social condition of their children. Not only is
spiritual growth frequently sacrificed in pursuit of these
objects, but principles are trampled on, which involve
the welfare of the whole human race. Within the sphere
of my own observation, I must confess that there is a
larger proportion of unmarried than married women
whose sympathies are active and extensive.

I have before my mind two learned sisters, familiar
with Greek, Latin, and French, and who, late in life,
acquired a knowledge of German also. They spent more
than sixty years together, quietly digging out gold, silver, or iron from the rich mines of ancient and modern

literature, and freely imparting their treasures wherever
they were called for. No married couple could have been
more careful of each other in illness, or more accom-
modating toward each other's peculiarities; yet they
were decided individuals; and their talk never wanted

> "An animated No,
> To brush its surface, and to make it flow."

Cultivated people enjoyed their conversation, which was
both wise and racy; a steady light of good sense and
large information, with an occasional flashing rocket of
not ill-natured satire. Yet their intellectual acquisitions
produced no contempt for the customary occupations of
women. All their friends received tasteful keepsakes of
their knitting, netting, or crocheting, and all the poor of
the town had garments of their handiwork. Neither
their sympathies nor their views were narrowed by celibacy. Early education had taught them to reverence
everything that was established; but with this reverence
they mingled a lively interest in all the great progressive
questions of the day. Their ears were open to the recital
of everybody's troubles and everybody's joys. On New
Year's day, children thronged round them for books and
toys, and every poor person's face lighted up as they
approached; for they were sure of kindly inquiries and
sympathizing words from them, and their cloaks usually
opened to distribute comfortable slippers, or warm stockings of their own manufacture. When this sisterly bond,
rendered so beautiful by usefulness and culture, was
dissolved by death, the survivor said of her who had
departed: "During all her illness she leaned upon me as

a child upon its mother; and O, how blessed is now the
consciousness that I never disappointed her!'' This
great bereavement was borne with calmness, for loneliness
was cheered by hope of reunion. On the anniversary of
her loss the survivor wrote to me: "I find a growing
sense of familiarity with the unseen world. It is as if
the door were invitingly left ajar, and the distance were
hourly diminishing. I never think of *her* as alone. The
unusual number of departed friends for whom we had
recently mourned seem now but an increase to her happiness.''

I had two other unmarried friends, as devoted to each
other, and as considerate of each other's peculiarities as
any wedded couple I ever knew. Without being learned,
they had a love of general reading, which, with active
charities, made their days pass profitably and pleasantly.
They had the orderly, systematic habits common to single
ladies, but their sympathies and their views were larger
and more liberal than those of their married sisters.
Their fingers were busy for the poor, whom they were
always ready to aid and comfort, irrespective of nation
or color. Their family affections were remarkably strong,
yet they had the moral courage to espouse the unpopular
cause of the slave, in quiet opposition to the prejudices
of beloved relatives. Death sundered this tie when both
were advanced in years. The departed one, though not
distinguished for beauty during her mortal life, had,
after her decease, a wonderful loveliness, like that of an
angelic child. It was the outward impress of her interior life.

Few marriages are more beautiful or more happy than

these sisterly unions; and the same may be said of a brother and sister, whose lives are bound together. All lovers of English literature know how charmingly united in mind and heart were Charles Lamb and his gifted sister; and our own poet, Whittier, so dear to the people's heart, has a home made lovely by the same fraternal relation of mutual love and dependence.

A dear friend of mine, whom it was some good man's loss not to have for a life-mate, adopted the orphan sons of her brother, and reared them with more than parental wisdom and tenderness, caring for all their physical wants, guiding them through precept and example by the most elevated moral standard, bestowing on them the highest intellectual culture, and studying all branches with them, that she might in all things be their companion.

Nor is it merely in such connections, which somewhat resemble wedded life, that single women make themselves useful and respected. Many remember the store kept for so long a time in Boston by Miss Ann Bent.

Her parents being poor, she early began to support herself by teaching. A relative subsequently furnished her with goods to sell on commission; and in this new employment she manifested such good judgment, integrity, and general business capacity, that merchants were willing to trust her to any extent. She acquired a handsome property, which she used liberally to assist a large family of sisters and nieces, some of whom she established in business similar to her own. No mother or grandmother was ever more useful or beloved. One of her nieces said: "I know the beauty and purity of my aunt's character, for I lived with her forty years, and I never knew her to say or do anything which might not have been said or done before the whole world."

I am ignorant of the particulars of Miss Bent's private history; but doubtless a woman of her comely looks, agreeable manners, and excellent character, might have found opportunities to marry, if that had been a paramount object with her. She lived to be more than eighty-eight years old, universally respected and beloved; and the numerous relatives, toward whom she had performed a mother's part, cheered her old age with grateful affection.

There have also been instances of single women who have enlivened and illustrated their lives by devotion to the beautiful arts. Of these none are perhaps more celebrated than the Italian Sofonisba Angusciola and her two accomplished sisters. These three "virtuous gentlewomen," as Vasari calls them, spent their lives together in most charming union. All of them had uncommon talent for painting, but Sofonisba was the most gifted. One of her most beautiful pictures represents her two sisters playing at chess, attended by the faithful old duenna, who accompanied them everywhere. This admirable artist lived to be old and blind; and the celebrated Vandyke said of her, in her later years: "I have learned more from one blind old woman in Italy, than from all the masters of the art."

Many single women have also employed their lives usefully and agreeably as authors. There is the charming Miss Mitford, whose writings cheer the soul like a meadow of cowslips in the springtime. There is Fred-

erica Bremer, whose writings have blessed so many souls.
There is Joanna Baillie, Maria Edgeworth, Elizabeth
Hamilton, and our own honored Catherine M. Sedgwick,
whose books have made the world wiser and better
than they found it.

I am glad to be sustained in my opinions on this subject by a friend whose own character invests single life
with peculiar dignity. In a letter to me, she says: " I
object to having single women called a *class*. They are
individuals, differing in the qualities of their characters,
like other human beings. Their isolation, as a general
thing, is the result of unavoidable circumstances. The
Author of Nature doubtless intended that men and
women should live together. But, in the present state
of the world's progress, society has, in many respects,
become artificial in proportion to its civilization ; and
consequently the number of single women must constantly increase. If humanity were in a state of natural,
healthy development, this would not be so ; for young
people would then be willing to begin married life with
simplicity and frugality, and real happiness would
increase in proportion to the diminution of artificial
wants. This prospect, however, lies in the future, and
many generations of single women must come and go
before it will be realized.

"But the achievement of *character* is the highest end
that can be proposed to any human being, and there is
nothing in single life to prevent a woman from attaining
this great object ; on the contrary, it is in many respects
peculiarly favorable to it. The measure of strength in
character is the power to conquer circumstances when

they refuse to co-operate with us. The temptations peculiarly incident to single life are petty selfishness, despondency under the suspicion of neglect, and *ennui* from the want of interesting occupation. If an ordinary, feeble-minded woman is exposed to these temptations, she will be very likely to yield to them. But she would not be greatly different in character, if protected by a husband and flanked with children ; her feebleness would remain the same, and would only manifest itself under new forms.

"Marriage, under favorable circumstances, is unquestionably a promoter of human happiness. But mistakes are so frequently made by entering thoughtlessly into this indissoluble connection, and so much wretchedness ensues from want of sufficient mental discipline to make the best of what cannot be remedied, that most people can discover among their acquaintance as large a proportion of happy single women as they can of happy wives. Moreover, the happiness of unmarried women is as independent of mere gifts of fortune, as that of other individuals. Indeed, all solid happiness must spring from inward sources. Some of the most truly contented and respectable women I have ever known have been domestics, who grew old in one family, and were carefully looked after, in their declining days, by the children of those whom they faithfully served in youth.

"Most single women might have married, had they seized upon the first opportunity that offered; but some unrevealed attachment, too high an ideal, or an innate fastidiousness, have left them solitary ; therefore, it is fair to assume that many of them have more sensibility and true tenderness than some of their married sisters. Those who remain single in consequence of two much worldly ambition, or from the gratification of coquettish vanity, naturally swell the ranks of those peevish, discontented ones, who bring discredit on single life in the abstract. But when a delicate gentlewoman deliberately prefers passing through life alone, to linking her fate with that of a man toward whom she feels no attraction, why should she ever repent of so high an exercise of her reason? This class of women are often the brightest ornaments of society. Men find in them calm, thoughtful friends, and safe confidants, on whose sympathy they can rely without danger. In the nursery, their labors, being voluntary, are less exhausting than a parent's. When the weary, fretted mother turns a deaf ear to the twenty-times-repeated question, the baffled urchins retreat to the indulgent aunt, or dear old familiar friend, sure of obtaining a patient hearing and a kind response. Almost everybody can remember some samples of such *Penates*, whose hearts seem to be too large to be confined to any one set of children.

"Some of my fairest patterns of feminine excellence have been of the single sisterhood. Of those unfortunate ones who are beacons, rather than models, I cannot recall an individual whose character I think would have been materially improved by marriage. The faults which make a single woman disagreeable would probably exist to the same degree if she were a wife; and the virtues which adorn her in a state of celibacy would make her equally beloved and honored if she were married. The human soul is placed here for development and progress;

and it is capable of converting all circumstances into means of growth and advancement.

"Among my early recollections is that of a lady of stately presence, who died while I was still young, but not till she had done much to remove from my mind the idea that the name of 'old maid' was a term of reproach. She was the daughter of Judge Russell, and aunt to the late Reverend and beloved Dr. Lowell. She had been one of a numerous family of brothers and sisters, but in my childhood was sole possessor of the old family mansion, where she received her friends and practiced those virtues which gained for her the respect of the whole community. Sixty years ago it was customary to speak of single women with far less deference than it now is; and I remember being puzzled by the extremely respectful manner in which she was always mentioned. If there were difficulties in the parish, or if any doubtful matters were under discussion, the usual question was 'What is Miss Russell's opinion?' I used to think to myself, 'She is an old maid, after all, yet people always speak of her as if she were some great person.'

"Miss Burleigh was another person of whom I used to hear much through the medium of mutual friends. She resided with a married sister in Salem, and was the 'dear Aunt Susan,' not only of the large circle of her own nephews and nieces, but of all their friends and favorites. Having ample means, she surrounded herself with choice books and pictures, and such objects of art or nature as would entertain and instruct young minds. Her stores of knowledge were prodigious, and she had such a happy way of imparting it, that lively boys were glad to leave their play, to spend an hour with Aunt Susan. She read to her young friends at stated times, and made herself perfectly familiar with them ; and as they grew older she became their chosen confidant. She was, in fact, such a centre of light and warmth, that no one could approach her sphere without being conscious of its vivifying influence.

" 'Aunt Sarah Stetson,' another single lady, was a dear and honored friend of my own. She was of masculine size and stature, gaunt and ungainly in the extreme. But before she had uttered three sentences, her hearers said to themselves, ' Here is a wise woman ! ' She was the oldest of thirteen children, early deprived of their father, and she bore the brunt of life from youth upward. She received only such education as was afforded by the public school of an obscure town seventy years ago. To add to their scanty means of subsistence, she learned the tailor's trade. In process of time, the other children swarmed off from the parental hive, the little farm was sold, and she lived alone with her mother. She built a small cottage out of her own earnings, and had the sacred pleasure of taking her aged parent to her own home, and ministering with her own hands to all her wants. For sixteen years she never spent a night from home, but assiduously devoted herself to the discharge of this filial duty, and to the pursuance of her trade. Yet in the midst of this busy life, she managed to become respectably familiar with English literature, especially with history. Whatever she read, she derived from it healthful aliment for the growth of her mental powers. She was full of wise maxims and rules of life ; not doled out with see-saw prosiness, but with strong common sense, rich and racy, and frequently flavored with the keenest satire. She had a flashing wit, and wonderful power of detecting shams of all sorts. Her religious opinions were orthodox, and she was an embodiment of the Puritan character. She was kindly in her feelings, and alive to every demonstration of affection, but she had a granite firmness of principle, which rendered her awful toward deceivers and transgressors. All the intellectual people of the town sought her company with avidity. The Unitarian minister and his family, a wealthy man, who happened to be also the chief scholar in the place, and the young people generally, took pleasure in resorting to Aunt Sarah's humble home, to minister to her simple wants, and gather up her words of wisdom. Her spirit was bright and cheerful to the last. One of her sisters, who had been laboring sixteen years as a missionary among the southwestern Indians, came to New England to visit the scattered members of her family. After seeing them in their respective homes, she declared : ' Sarah is the most light-hearted of them all ; and it is only by *her* fireside that I have been able to forget past hardships in merry peals of laughter.'

"During my last interview with Aunt Sarah, when she was past seventy years of age, she said, 'I have lived very agreeably single; but if I become infirm, I suppose I shall feel the want of life's nearest ties.' In her case, however, the need was of short duration, and an affectionate niece supplied the place of a daughter.

"Undoubtedly, the arms of children and grandchildren form the most natural and beautiful cradle for old age.   But loneliness is often the widow's portion, as well as that of the single woman ; and parents are often left solitary by the death or emigration of their children.

"I am tempted to speak also of a living friend, now past her sixtieth year. She is different from the others, but this difference only confirms my theory that the mind can subdue all things to itself. This lady is strictly feminine in all her habits and pursuits, and regards the needle as the chief implement of woman's usefulness. If the Dorcas labors performed by her one pair of hands could be collected into a mass, out of the wear and waste of half a century, they would form an amazing pile. In former years, when her health allowed her to circulate among numerous family connections, her visits were always welcomed as a jubilee; for every dilapidated wardrobe was sure to be renovated by Aunt Mary's nimble fingers. She had also a magic power of drawing the little ones to herself. Next to their fathers and mothers, she was the best beloved. The influence which her loving heart gained over them in childhood increased with advancing years. She is now the best and dearest friend of twenty or thirty nephews and nieces, some of whom have families of their own.

"A large amount of what is termed mother-wit, a readiness at repartee, and quickness in seizing unexpected associations of words or ideas, rendered her generally popular in company ; but the deep cravings of her heart could never be satisfied with what is termed success in society. The intimate love of a few valued friends was what she always coveted, and never failed to win. For several years she has been compelled by ill health to live entirely at home. There she now is, fulfilling the most important mission of her whole beneficent life, training to virtue and usefulness five motherless children of her brother. Feeble and emaciated, she lives in her chamber surrounded by these orphans, who now constitute her chief hold on life. She shares all their pleasures, is the depositary of their little griefs, and unites in herself the relations of aunt, mother, and grandmother. She has faith to believe that her frail thread of existence will be prolonged for the sake of these little ones. The world still comes to her, in her seclusion, through a swarm of humble friends and dependents, who find themselves comforted and ennobled by the benignant patience with which she listens to their various experiences, and gives them kindly, sympathizing counsel, more valuable to them than mere pecuniary aid. Her spirit of self-abnegation is carried almost to asceticism; but she reserves her severity wholly for herself; toward others she is prodigal of indulgence. This goodly temple of a human soul was reared in these fair proportions upon a foundation of struggles, disappointments, and bereavements. A friend described her serene exterior as a 'placid, ocean-deep manner'; under it lies a silent history of trouble and trial, converted into spiritual blessings.

"The conclusion of the matter in my mind is, that a woman may make a respectable appearance as a wife, with a character far less noble than is necessary to enable her to lead a single life with usefulness and dignity. She is sheltered and concealed behind her husband; but the unmarried woman must rely upon herself; and she lives in a glass house, open to the gaze of every passer-by.

To the feeble-minded, marriage is almost a necessity, and if wisely formed it doubtless renders the life of any woman more happy. But happiness is not the sole end and aim of this life. We are sent here to build up a character; and sensible women may easily reconcile themselves to a single life, since even its disadvantages may be converted into means of development of all the faculties with which God has endowed them."

—L. MARIA CHILD.

EPITAPH ON THE UNMATED.

No chosen spot of ground she called her own.
In pilgrim guise o'er earth she wandered on ;
Yet always in her path some flowers were strown.
No dear ones were her own peculiar care,
So was her bounty free as heaven's air ;
For every claim she had enough to spare.
And, loving more her heart to *give* than lend,
Though oft deceived in many a trusted friend.
She hoped, believed, and trusted to the end.
She had her joys ;—'t was joy to her to love,
To labor in the world with God above,
And tender hearts that ever near did move.
She had her griefs ;—but they left peace behind,
And healing came on every stormy wind,
And still with silver every cloud was lined.
And every loss sublimed some low desire,
And every sorrow taught her to aspire,
Till waiting angels bade her " Go up higher."

CHAPTER XXXIII.

IF this latent power could be aroused! If woman would shake off this slumber, and put on her strength, her beautiful garments, how would she go forth conquering and to conquer! How would the mountains break forth into singing, and the trees of the field clap their hands! How would our sin-stained earth arise and shine, her light being come, and the glory of the Lord being risen upon her!

One cannot do the world's work; but one can do one's work. You may not be able to turn the world from iniquity; but you can, at least, keep the dust and rust from gathering on your own soul. If you cannot be directly and actively engaged in fighting the battle, you can, at least, polish your armor and sharpen your weapons, to strike an effective blow when the hour comes. You can stanch the blood of him who has been wounded in the fray—bear a cup of cold water to the thirsty and fainting—give help to the conquered, and smiles to the victor.

You can gather from the past and the present, stores of

431

wisdom, so that, when the future demands it, you may bring forth from your treasures things new and old. Whatever of bliss the "Divinity that shapes our ends" may see fit to withhold from you, you are but very little lower than the angels, so long as you have the

"Godlike power to do—the godlike aim to know."

You can be forming habits of self-reliance, sound judgment, perseverance, and endurance, which may, one day, stand you in good stead. You can so train yourself to right thinking and right acting, that uprightness shall be your nature, truth your impulse. His head is seldom far wrong, whose heart is always right. We bow down to mental greatness, intellectual strength, and they are divine gifts; but moral rectitude is stronger than they. It is irresistible—always in the end triumphant.

There is in goodness a penetrative power that nothing can withstand. Cunning and malice melt away before its mild, open, steady glance. Not alone on the fields where chivalry charges for laurels, with helmet and breastplate and lance in rest, can the true knight exultingly exclaim,

"My strength is as the strength of ten,
Because my heart is pure;"

but wherever man meets man, wherever there is a prize to be won, a goal to be reached. Wealth, and rank, and beauty, may form a brilliant setting to the diamond; but they only expose more nakedly the false glare of the paste. Only when the king's daughter is all glorious within, is it fitting and proper that her clothing should be of wrought gold.

From the great and good of all ages rings out the same monotone. The high-priest of Nature, the calm-eyed poet who laid his heart so close to hers, that they seemed to throb in one pulsation, yet whose ear was always open to the "still sad music of humanity," has given us the promise of his life-long wisdom in these grand words:

> " True dignity abides with him alone
>   Who, in the silent hour of inward thought,
>   Can still suspect and still revere himself."

Through the din of twenty rolling centuries, pierces the sharp, stern voice of the brave old Greek: "Let every man, when he is about to do a wicked action, above all things in the world, stand in awe of himself, and dread the witness within him." All greatness, and all glory, all that earth has to give, all that Heaven can proffer, lies within the reach of the lowliest as well as the highest; for He who spake as never man spake, has said that the very "kingdom of God is within you."

Born to such an inheritance, will you wantonly cast it away? With such a goal in prospect, will you suffer yourself to be turned aside by the sheen and shimmer of tinsel fruit? With earth in possession, and Heaven in reversion, will you go sorrowing and downcast, because here and there a pearl or a ruby fails you? Nay, rather forgetting those things which are behind, and reaching forth unto those which are before, press forward :

Discontent and murmuring are insidious foes; trample them under your feet. Utter no complaint, whatever betide; for complaining is a sign of weakness. If your trouble can be helped, help it; if not, bear it. You can be whatever you will to be. Therefore, form and accomplish worthy purposes.

If you walk alone, let it be with no faltering tread. Show to an incredulous world

> " How grand may be Life's might,
> Without Love's circling crown."

Or, if the golden thread of love shine athwart the dusky warp of duty, if other hearts depend on yours for sustenance and strength, give to them from your fullness no stinted measure. Let the dew of your kindness fall on the evil and the good, on the just and on the unjust.

Compass happiness, since happiness alone is victory. On the fragments of your shattered plans, and hopes, and love—on the heaped-up ruins of your past, rear a stately palace, whose top shall reach unto heaven, whose beauty shall gladden the eyes of all beholders, whose doors shall stand wide open to receive the way worn and weary. Life is a burden, but it is imposed by God. What you make of it, it will be to you, whether a millstone about your neck, or a diadem upon your brow. Take it up bravely, bear it on joyfully, lay it down triumphantly.

—GAIL HAMILTON.

HILE at a station the other day I had a little sermon preached in the way I like, and I'll report it for your benefit, because it taught me one of the lessons which we all should learn, and taught it in such a natural, simple way that no one could forget it.

It was a bleak, snowy day. The train was late; the ladies' room dark and smoky, and the dozen women, old and young, who sat waiting impatiently, all looked cross, low-spirited, or stupid. I felt all three, and thought, as I looked around, that my fellow-beings were a very unamiable, uninteresting set.

Just then a forlorn old woman, shaking with palsy, came in with a basket of wares for sale, and went about mutely offering them to the sitters. Nobody bought anything, and the poor old soul stood blinking at the door a minute, as if reluctant to go out into the bitter storm again.

She turned presently and poked about the room as if trying to find something; and then a pale lady in black,

who lay as if asleep on a sofa, opened her eyes, saw the
old woman, and instantly asked in a kind tone, "Have
you lost anything ma'am?"

"No, dear. I'm looking for the heatin' place to have
a warm 'fore I goes out again. My eyes is poor, and I
don't seem to find the furnace nowheres."

"Here it is;" and the lady led her to the steam
radiator, placed a chair, and showed her how to warm
her feet.

"Well, now, is not that nice?" said the old woman,
spreading her ragged mittens to dry. "Thank you, dear;
this is comfortable, isn't it? I'm mos' froze to-day, bein'
lame and wimbly, and not selling much makes me kind
of down-hearted"

The lady smiled, went to the counter, bought a cup of
tea and some sort of food, carried it herself to the old
woman, and said as respectfully and kindly as if the
poor woman had been dressed in silk and fur, "Won't
you have a cup of hot tea? It's very comforting such a
day as this."

"Sakes alive! do they give tea to this depot?" cried
the old lady in a tone of innocent surprise that made a
smile go round the room, touching the gloomiest face
like a stream of sunshine. "Well, now, this is jest
lovely," added the old lady, sipping away with a relish.
"This does warm my heart."

While she refreshed herself, telling her story meanwhile, the lady looked over the poor little wares in the
basket, bought soap and pins, shoe-strings and tape, and
cheered the old soul by paying well for them.

As I watched her doing this I thought what a sweet

face she had, though I'd considered her rather plain before. I felt dreadfully ashamed of myself that I had grimly shaken my head when the basket was offered to me; and as I saw the look of interest, sympathy, and kindliness come in to the dismal faces all around me, I did wish that I had been the magician to call it out.

It was only a kind word and a friendly act, but somehow it brightened that dingy room wonderfully. It changed the faces of a dozen women, and I think it touched a dozen hearts, for I saw many eyes follow the plain, pale lady with sudden respect; and when the old woman got up to go, several persons beckoned to her and bought something, as if they wanted to repair their first negligence.

Old beggar-women are not romantic, neither are cups of tea, boot-laces and colored soap. There were no gentlemen present to be impressed with the lady's kind act, so it wasn't done for effect, and no possible reward could be received for it except the ungrammatical thanks of a ragged old woman.

But that simple little charity was as good as a sermon to those who saw it, and I think each traveler went on her way better for that half hour in the dreary station. I can testify that one of them did, and nothing but the emptiness of her purse prevented her from "comforting the heart" of every forlorn old woman she met for a week after.

-LOUISA M. ALCOTT.

CHAPTER XXXV.

HREE of the most beautiful words in the English language, says a writer, are "Mother, Home and Heaven." And truly they may well be called so. What force upon the human heart has the word mother! Coming from childhood's lips, it has a sweet charm, for it speaks of one to whom they look in trust for protection; coming from older lips, it betokens affection and filial regard.

A mother is the truest friend we have on earth. What one like her will cling to us, and by kind counsels and precepts dissipate the clouds of darkness, and cause peace to return to our hearts, when friends who rejoiced with us in the sunshine of our success desert us, when, like a dense cloud, troubles thicken around us; when prosperity gives place to adversity; when trials suddenly fall heavily upon us! No voice is so potent as hers in reclaiming an erring one from the path of unrighteousness to a life of prosperity and happiness.

Even the lonely convict in his dreary cell, though

438

other friends forsake him, finds consolation in thinking of the innocent days of his childhood, when he played by his mother's knee; he realizes that he has still a guardian angel watching over him who will forgive and forget, however dark his sins may have been.

What a sweet name is mother, and what a high station she occupies! In her hands minds are molded almost at her will, for to her belongs the privilege of planting in the hearts of her children those seeds of love, which, nurtured and fostered, will bear the fruit of earnest and useful lives, and fit them for the enjoyment of the eternal home in heaven.

Home! The dearest spot on earth! That which seems to imprint itself most indelibly upon the memory is the recollection of home. All delight to dwell upon the happy days spent in the home of their childhood, when, like the joyous songsters of the woods, they whiled away the happy moments with never a thought of care.

How many hearts are gladdened by the thought that, amid all the troubles and anxieties of busy life, there is one spot to which they can come and forget all care, and let peace and joy reign supreme.

Heaven! The home of the just beyond the grave, that awaits the storm-tossed mariner upon the sea of life, who realizes more and more its beauties as he approaches the golden gates, and experiences the vanity of all earthly things. There no sorrow shall come, partings shall be no more, and the friends who on earth found many a cloud to dim their joys, now are reunited, never again to be separated.

It is God's reward for those who have made a life-long effort for right—the home of "just men made perfect."

There are three words that sweetly blend,
   That on the heart are graven;
A precious, soothing balm they lend—
   They're mother, home and heaven.

They twine a wreath of beauteous flowers,
   Which, placed on memory's urn,
Will e'en the longest, gloomiest hours
   To golden sunlight turn.

They form a chain whose every link
   Is free from base alloy;
A stream where whosoever drinks
   Will find refreshing joy.

They build an altar where each day
   Love's offering is renewed;
And peace illumes with genial ray
   Life's darkened solitude.

If from our side the first has fled,
   And home be but a name,
Let's strive the narrow path to tread,
   That we the last may gain.

—MARY J. MUCKLE.

CHAPTER XXXVI

Influence * of * Wife * and * Mother.

N O human being can come into this world without increasing or diminishing the sum total of human happiness, not only of the present but of every subsequent age of humanity. No one can detach himself from this connection, there is no sequestered spot in the universe, no dark niche along the disc of non-existence to which we can retreat from our relations to others—where we can withdraw the influence of our existence upon the moral destiny of the world; everywhere our presence or absence will be felt—everywhere we will have companions who will be better or worse for our influence. It is an old saying, and one of fathomless import, that we are forming characters for eternity. Forming characters! Whose? our own or others? Both; and in that momentous fact lies the peril and responsibility of our existence. Who is sufficient for the thought? Thousands of our fellow beings will yearly enter eternity with characters differing from those they would have carried had we never lived to exert our influence. The sunlight of that world will reveal many finger marks in their primary formation and in their successive strata of thought and life.

Every individual is a missionary for good or evil. He may be a blot extending his dark influence outward to the very circumference of society, or he may be a star of blessing spreading benediction over the length and breadth of the world ; but a blank he cannot be—there are no moral blanks—no neutral characters. The christian and the pagan alike wield their influence. The refined, cultured man of society, and the uncouth, uncultured cowboy of the plains are possessed of and susceptible to the same influence. Perhaps none wield so great an influence over a man as the wife and family. We believe that no man, whatever his occupation, is so hardened but that, under some circumstances, his better nature and judgment will give way to the gentle influences of wife and mother. An incident, a Texas story, which bears testimony that all may be influenced for good, seems applicable here. One hot evening in July, 1860, a herdsman near Helena, Texas, was moving his cattle to a new ranch further north, and passing down the banks of a stream his herd became mixed with other cattle that were grazing in the valley, and some of them failed to be separated. The next day about noon, a band of a dozen mounted Texan Rangers overtook the herdsman and demanded their cattle, which they said were stolen.

It was before the days of law and court houses in Texas, and one would better kill five men than steal a mule worth five dollars, and the herdsman knew it. He tried to explain, but they told him to cut his story short. He offered to turn over all the cattle not his own, but they laughed at his proposition, and hinted that they usually confiscated the whole herd, and left the thief hanging to a tree as a warning to others in like cases.

The poor fellow was completely overcome. They consulted apart a few moments, and then told him if he had any explanation to make or business to do they would allow him ten minutes to do so and defend himself.

He turned to the rough faces, and commenced: "How many of you men have wives?" Two or three nodded. "How many of you have children?" They nodded again.

"Then I know who I am talking to, and you'll hear me," and he continued: "I never stole any cattle; I have lived in these parts over three years. I came from New Hampshire; I failed there in the fall of '57, during the panic. I have been saving; I have lived on hard fare; I ·have slept out on the ground; I have no home here. My family remain east, for I go from place to place. These clothes are rough, and I am a hard looking customer; but this is a hard country. Days seem like months to me and months like years; married men, you know, that but for the letters from home (here he pulled out a handful of well-worn envelopes and letters from his wife) I should get discouraged. I have paid part of my debts. Here are the receipts (and he unfolded the letters of acknowledgment). I expected to sell and go home in November. Here is the testament my good mother gave me; here is my little girl's picture, God bless her!" and he kissed it tenderly and continued: "Now, men, if you have decided to kill me for what I am innocent of, send these home, and send as much as you can from the cattle when I am dead. Can't you send half their value?—my family will need it."

"Hold on, now; stop right thar!" said a rough Ranger. "Now I say boys," he continued; "I say let him go. Give us your hand, old boy; that pictur and them letters did the business. You can go free; but you're lucky, mind ye."

"We'll do more'n that," said a man with a big heart, in Texan garb, and carrying the customary brace of pistols in his belt, "let's buy his herd and let him go home now."

They did, and when the money was paid over, and the man about to start, he was too weak to stand. The long strain of hopes and fears, his being away from home under such trying circumstances, and the sudden delivery from death, had combined to render him help-less as a child. He sank to the ground completely overcome. An hour later, however, he left on horseback for the nearest stage route, and, as they shook hands and bade him good-bye, they looked the happiest band of men ever seen.

Little did this wife and mother dream of the influence in those magic letters, which she had sealed and sent hundreds of miles away. They and the family pictures carried by the faithful husband, had their daily influ-ence upon his life and courage, and no doubt made his banished home one of endurance. A mother's love and influence is never exhausted, it never changes, it never tires. A father may turn his back on his child, brothers and sisters may become enemies, but a mother's love endures through all, and she never ceases to exert her influence for good over that wayward son who, perhaps, has abused and disgraced her ; but night after night she sends up anxious prayers for his safety and reformation. Can he repay her for the many anxious hours and sleepless nights that she has watched over him, from the time he was but a helpless infant nestling in her bosom until death has removed her from all care and anxiety ? We would answer, yes.

Next to the love of her husband, nothing so crowns the mother's life with honor as the devotion of a son to her. We never knew a boy to turn out badly who began by falling in love with his mother. Any boy may fall in love with a fresh-faced girl, and may neglect the poor, weary wife in after years. But the big boy who is a lover of his mother is a true knight who will love his wife in sere leaf autumn as he did in the daisied spring. There is nothing so beautifully chivalrous as the love of a big boy for his mother.

✦CHAPTER XXXVII.✦

Mother at the Helm.

HE mother should try, above every thing, for respectful servants. She should demand that quality, even before efficiency, as the one great desideratum. She must not allow herself to be treated with disrespect. The little creature sitting on her lap is to be influenced for life by that hour in the nursery when he sees her authority outraged. For, before the lips speak, the brain is working, the bright eyes are taking in the situation, and the baby is sitting in judgment on his mother. She must be worthy of that judgment.

Above all things, let him never see her lose her temper. The nurse will then have an advantage which will strike the impartial judge. A woman at the head of the house should be as calm and as imperturbable and as immovable as Mount Blanc, to be the model mistress. Of course, this is often difficult, but it is not impossible. Again, when she has given an order, she must see that it is obeyed, even if it costs her a great deal of trouble   It is worth the trouble to be disagreeably pertinacious on this point, and inflexible, even to the degree of being tiresome, as it establishes a precedent. A lady who was a pattern housekeeper made a rule that her waitress should bring her a glass of water at six o'clock every morning, and no woman who disregarded that rule was allowed to stay in her house. Every one thought this very unnecessary; but they admired the punctuality with which the eight-o'clock breakfast was served. "Do you not know," said the wise housekeeper, "that my inflexible rule brings about the certainty of her early rising?" And as nothing conduces so thoroughly to the health and welfare of children as regularity, this was an admirable beginning for the young mother.

It is almost impossible, with some families, to have young children at the table with their parents; they are left almost necessarily to the care of nurses at meal-time. The result is, of course, that they get bad manners at the table. A mother should try to eat at least one meal a day with her child, so as to begin at the beginning with his table manners.

And those important things, accent and pronunciation! What sins do not Americans commit in their slovenly misuse of their own tongue? Educated men, scientific men, often so mispronounce their words, or speak with so palpable a Yankee twang, that they are unfitted to become public speakers. It would be a good thing for every American household, could they employ one English girl, with the good pronunciation which is the common inheritance of all the well-trained servants in those parts of rural England where the ladies take an interest in the peasantry. A mother should be very careful to talk much to her children; to watch their earliest accent as they begin to go to school; and to try and impress a good pronunciation upon them in their first lisping talk.

It is very much the fashion now even for people of wealth to have a polyglot family of servants—a German nurse and a French governess, an English maid and a Spanish waiter—thinking that their children will pick up a dozen languages with their playthings. But, although they do learn a smattering, children rarely learn a language well in this way; and it is quite certain that they will never know their own language as correctly as if they *learned that first*, and perfectly. To learn to spell in English correctly, English must be taught before the other languages come in to confuse the mind.

A mother should try to be at home when her children return from the school. She must of course be out sometimes; but that hour she should try to be in, to receive the little fatigued, miserable child, who has endured the slavery of desks and books, classes, bad air, and enforced tasks which we call "school."

If we called it racks, thumb-screws, the boot, the pulleys, and the torture, as they did similar institutions in the Middle Ages, we should be more true to the facts. The modern teacher extorts confessions of how much is eight times eight, or what are the boundaries of Pennsylvania, or some other country, in the midst of heat, bad air, and general oppression and suffering such as few chambers of torture ever equaled. The boy comes home with burning brow, perhaps with a headache; tired, angry, and depressed, to know that all is to be repeated

on the morrow   If his mother is at home he rushes to
her room.   Let her have patience and sympathy, for it is
his crucial hour.   Let her bathe his head and hands;
give him a good lunch, at which she presides herself;
hear all his grievances, and smooth them over; and then
send him out to play for an hour or two in the open air.
When he *must* study in the evening, both father and
mother should tackle the arithmetic and the geography
with the boy, and, if possible, smooth the thorny road
which leads else to despair.

The animals know how to take care of their young better than we do.   The human race has no inspiration on
the subject.   A young fox is educated for his sphere in
life much more easily than is a human boy.   We have
not conquered the secrets of doing the best for our children, or else we certainly should have learned how to
make education more agreeable.   Perhaps the Kindergarten is the first move in the right direction, for we find
children very happy there.   Certainly a boys' school or
a girls' school, with bad air and enforced tasks, is not a
happy place.   Dickens had a realizing sense of the mis-
eries of school, and has painted for us the tragedy of
Paul Dombey in colors which will never fade.

Now, in the education of children with a view toward
the amenities, does it seem probable that a child who is
struck and whipped, will become as gentle and amiable
as one who is always treated with a firm and consistent
and equable kindness?   The "sparing the rod and spoil-
ing the child" question is one which has not been
answered.

The violent-tempered and easily irritated child is often

29

'apparently much relieved by what is called, in familiar parlance, a "good whipping." It seems to carry off a certain "malaise" which he is glad to get rid of. Whether a ride on donkey-back, a row on the river, or a hearty run would not do it as well, there are no possible means of deciding. But to cuff a child's ears, to shake him, to whip him often, is to arouse all that is worse in his nature. The human body is sacred, and a parent should hesitate to outrage that natural dignity which is born in every sensible child.

If the amenities of home are to begin early, we should recommend a great prudence as to the administration of corporal punishment; but, that it should be entirely banished, no one can say. There are all sorts of children born into this world. No one can decide as to what sort of treatment would have made Jesse James a better boy, as he seems to have been born a fiend. No one can, on the other hand, recommend the conduct of the clergyman who whipped his child to death because the little frightened creature would not say his prayers. The kind and good mother will be apt to find the mean between the two.

The other point of which we are reminded by the account of the French Familistere is the influence of music.

Every mother learns that, from the cradle-song up to the dancing tune which she plays on the piano, her great help in the work of education, and in her attempt at the amenities, is music. Nothing is so perfect as the work and aim of this divine messenger in the otherwise insoluble problem of the nursery. A song often puts a sick baby to sleep. It is sure, if it is a simple ballad, and if it tells a story, to interest the boys and girls. What mother who can sing has not felt her deep indebtedness to the "Heir of Linn," "Young Lochinvar," "The Campbells are Coming," "Lizzie Lindsay," "What's a' the steer, Kimmer?" "Auld Robin Grey," and even to the homely "Old Grimes is Dead," and the familiar nursery rhymes of Mother Goose set to the simplest of tunes?

A famous statesman and orator said, in one of his best speeches, that he could never think of "Kathleen O'Moore" as his mother sang it, without the tears coming to his eyes, and he often wondered what power of oratory she possessed that he had not inherited, what nerve she contrived to reach which none of his polished periods could conquer. He should have remembered that the "hearer's mood is the speaker's opportunity," and he should thank her that she aroused in him the early softer emotion which the battle of life has not quite rubbed out.

Children like to march. The rhythmic instinct is inborn; they like to dance, to move in phalanxes. The French have caught this element of concord, and have utilized it. It is introduced here into our public schools, and to any one who has seen the the Normal College, where a regiment as large as the Seventh—a regiment of girls—marches in to music, the story need not be told of the influence of music upon order. At home, the evening dance by the firelight, the mother playing for her children, is always a picture of happiness and glee.

Boys, as well as girls, should be taught to play upon some musical instrument. It has the most admirable effect upon the amenities of home. No more soothing or more refining influence can be introduced than the home concert. To vary the usual custom and to give variety, let a girl learn the violin and a boy the piano. It is very interesting to see the usual position occasionally reversed, and there is nothing ungraceful or unfeminine in the use of the violin. Very few natures are so coarse or so fierce that they can not be reached by music.

"I had," said a woman who was famed for her lovely manners, "the good fortune to have a musical papa. He used to wake me in the morning by playing Mozart's 'Batti, Batti' on the flute, and he always, although a busy lawyer, gave us an hour in the evening with his violin. I am sure Strauss, with his famous Vienna Orchestra, and his world-renowned waltzes, has never put such a thrill into my nerves, or such quicksilver into my heels as did my father's playing of the Virginia Reel and the first movement of Von Weber's 'Invitation á la Valse,' nor have I ever heard such solemn notes as those which came from his violoncello, as he accompanied my mother in the Funeral March in the 'Seventh Symphony.' Their music made home a more attractive spot than any theatre or ball. They were neither of them great musicians. I dare say their playing would have been considered very amateurish in these days of musical excellence. But it served the purpose of making home a very peaceful spot to their boys and girls, and of keeping it a memory of delight through much that was trying in the way of small income, personal self-sacrifice, and ill-health. We had our trials, but everything vanished when father began to play."

We can not, in our scheme of life, always command a musical papa, but this testimony is invaluable. Children should always be taught to sing, unless hopelessly defective in musical organization—a fact which can only be ascertained by trial. The great use of the Kindergarten is perhaps in this unconscious development of a voice, and the power of keeping time and tune. Many a child, whose musical gift would have remained unknown, suddenly develops a beautiful voice in the chorus of the school.

Here the mother should be the first teacher, and the world is now happily full of books to help her. The " Songs of Harrow," edited by the head-master, contain beautiful simple part-songs for boys, and there are hundreds of such compilations for girls. To the Countess of Dufferin we owe the introduction of the singing quadrilles, where, to the Mother Goose poems of " Mary, Mary, quite contrary," and " Ride a Cock-horse to Banbury Cross," have been married to certain very good old English tunes, which the dancers sing in different parts as they dance, making a charming effect. The Christmas Carols, the English Madrigals, Song of the Waits, Old English glees and ballads, are simple, delightful, pure, and elevating. The mother need not be afraid of these aids to the home amenities. They may not do all that she may wish to make her children cultivated musicians, but they will do much. The opportunities for musical culture are very great in our cities now, and we should not forget that, in giving our children a musical education, we are giving them a defense against ennui, a new and undying means of amusing themselves, but also a means of making their own future homes happy, that we aid them in an accomplishment which will be always useful, often also remunerative, and with which they can help to swell the praises of our Lord, and to cheer the bedside of the sick and dying.

It is not, of course, universal that the manners of musicians are perfect, but it has never been urged against music that it injured the manners. Certainly, in a household, music when once learned, can help to increase the cheerfulness of home.

❖CHAPTER XXXVIII.❖

Education ✳ and ✳ Manners ✳ of ✳ Our ✳ Girls.

E come now to the subject which perhaps has little connection with the nature of this work, but much to do with the welfare of the state. We must consider the two extremes which are now being brought about by the emancipation of young women. One is, their higher education, the other is, the growing "fastness" of manner.

One can scarcely imagine amenity of manner without education, and yet we are forced to observe that it can exist, as we see the manners of highly educated and what are called strong-minded women. Soft, gentle, and feminine manners do not always accompany culture and education. Indeed, pre-occupation in literary matters used to be supposed to unfit a woman for being a graceful member of society, but *nous avons changé tout cela;* and we are now in the very midst of a well-dressed and well-mannered set of women who work at their pen as Penelope at her web.

The home influence is, however, still needed for those

young daughters who begin early to live in books; and neatness in dress and order should be insisted upon by the mother of a bookish, studious girl. All students are disposed to be slovenly, excepting an unusual class, who, like the Count de Buffin, write in lace ruffles and diamond rings. Books are apt to soil the hands, and libraries, although they look clean, are prone to accumulate dust. Ink is a very permeating material, and creeps up under the middle finger-nail. To appear with such evidences of guilt upon one would make the prettiest woman unlovely.

The amenities of manner are not quite enough considered at some of our female colleges. With the college course the young graduates are apt to copy masculine manners, and we have heard of a class who cheered from a boat their fellow-students at West Point. This is not graceful, and to some minds would more than balance the advantages of the severe course of study marked out and pursued at college. A mother with gentle and lady-like manners would, however, soon counteract these masculine tendencies and overflow of youthful spirits. We all detest a man who copies the feminine style of dress, intonation and gesture. Why should a girl be any more attractive who wears an ulster, a Derby hat, and who strides, puts her hands in her pockets, and imitates her brother's style in walk and gesture?

However, to a girl who is absorbed in books, who is reading, studying, and thinking, we can forgive much if she only will come out a really cultivated woman. We know that she will be a power in the state, an addition to the better forces of our government; that she will be not only happy herself, but the cause of happiness in others. The cultivated woman is a much more useful factor in civilization than the vain, silly, and flippant woman, although the latter may be prettier. But it is a great pity that, having gone so far, she should not go further, and come out a cultivated flower, instead of a learned weed.

Far more reprehensible and destructive of all amenities, is the growing tendency to "fastness," an exotic which we have imported from somewhere; probably from the days of the Empire in Paris.

It seems hardly possible that the "fast" woman of the present, whose fashion has been achieved by her questionable talk, her excessive dress, her doubtful manners, can have grown out of the same soil that produced Priscilla Mullins. The old Puritan Fathers would have turned the helm of the Mayflower the other way if they could have seen the product of one hundred years of independence. Now all Europe rings with the stories of American women, young, beautiful, charmingly dressed, who live away from their husbands, flirt with princes, make themselves the common talk of all the nations, and are delighted with their own notoriety. To educate daughters to such a fate seems to recall the story of the Harpies. Surely no mother can coolly contemplate it. And the amenities of home should be so strict and so guarded that this fate would be impossible.

In the first place, young girls should not be allowed to walk in the crowded streets of a city alone; a companion, a friend, a maid, should always be sent with them. Lady Thornton said, after one year's experience of Washington, "I must bring on a very strict English governess to walk about with my girls." And in the various games so much in fashion now, such as skating and lawn-tennis, there is no doubt as much necessity for a chaperon as in attending balls and parties. Not alone that impropriety is to be checked, but that manners may be cultivated. A well-bred woman who is shocked at slang, and who presents in her own person a constant picture of good manners, is like the atmosphere, a presence which is felt, and who unconsciously educates the young persons about her.

"I have never gotten over Aunt Lydia's smile," said a soldier on the plains, who, amid the terrible life of camp and the perils of Indian warfare, had never lost the amenities of civilized life. "When a boy I used to look up at the table, through a long line of boisterous children clamoring for food, and see my Aunt Lydia's face. It never lost its serenity, and when things were going very wrong she had but to look at us and smile, to bring out all right. She seemed to say with that silent smile, 'Be patient, be strong, be gentle, and all will come right.'"

The maiden aunt was a perpetual benediction in that house, because of her manner; it was of course, the out-crop of a fine, well-regulated, sweet character; but sup-posing she had had the character with a disagreeable manner? The result would have been lost.

We have all visited in families where the large flock of children came forward to meet us with outstretched hand and ready smile. We have seen them at table, peaceful and quiet, waiting their turn. We have also visited in other houses where we have found them discourteous,

sullen, ill-mannered and noisy.   We know that the latter
have all the talent, the good natural gifts, the originality,
and the honor of the former.   We know that the parents
have just as much desire in the latter case to bring up
their children well, but where have they failed?   They
have wanted firmness and an attention to the amenities.

~*CHAPTER XXXIX.*~

The Model Girl.

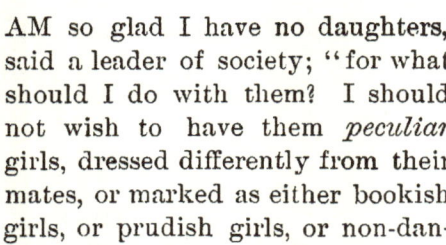

AM so glad I have no daughters, said a leader of society; "for what should I do with them? I should not wish to have them *peculiar* girls, dressed differently from their mates, or marked as either bookish girls, or prudish girls, or non-dancing girls, or anything queer; and yet I could never permit them to go out on a coach, be out to the small hours of the night with no chaperon but a woman no older than themselves. I could not allow them to dance with notorious drunkards, men of evil life, gamblers, and betting men; I could not let them dress as many girls do whom I know and like; so I am sure it is fortunate for me that I have no daughters. I could not see them treat my friends as so many of my friends' daughters treat me—as if I were the scum of the universe. I am glad I have no daughters; for a modern daughter would kill me."

Perhaps this lady but elaborated the troublesome problem which has tried the intellects of all observant women —how to make the proper *medium girl;* not the "fast"

400

THE MODEL GIRL

girl; still again, not the "slow" dowdy girl; not the
exceptional girl, but the girl who shall be at once good
and successful—that is the question?

The amenities of home, the culture of the fireside, the
mingled duty and pleasure which come with a life which
has already its duties before its pleasures—this would
seem to make the model girl. The care and interest in
the younger sisters and brothers; a comprehension and a
sympathy with her mother's trials; a devotion to her
hard-worked father; a desire to spare him one burden
more, to learn the music he loves, to play to him of an
evening; to be not only the admired belle of the ball-
room, but also the dearest treasure of home; to help
along the boys with their lessons, to enter into those trials
of which they will not speak; to take the fractious baby
from the patient or impatient nurse's arms, and to toss it
in her own strong young hands and smile upon it with
her own pearly teeth and red lips; to take what comes to
her of gayety and society as an outside thing, not as the
whole of life; to be not heart-broken if one invitation fail,
or if one dress is unbecoming; to be cheerful and watchful; to be fashionable enough, but neither fast nor furi-
ous; to be cultivated and not a blue-stocking; to be artistic, but not eccentric or slovenly; to be a lovely woman
whom men love, and yet neither coquette nor flirt—such
would seem to be the model girl.

And it is home and its amenities which must make her.
School cannot do it; society cannot and will not do it;
books will not do it, although they will help.

And here we have much to say on the books which
should surround a girl. We must seek, and watch, and

try to find the best books for our girls. But we can no more prevent a bad French novel from falling into their hands than we can prevent the ivy which may poison them, from springing up in the hedge. The best advice we can give, is to let a girl read as she pleases in a well-selected library; often reading with her, recommending certain books, and forming her taste as much as possible; then leaving her to herself, to pick out the books she likes. Nothing will be so sure to give a girl a desire to read a book as to forbid it, and we are now so fortunate in the crowd of really good novels and most unexceptional magazines which lie on our tables that we are almost sure that her choice will be a good one; for she can find so much more good than bad.

It is unwise to forbid girls to read novels. They are to-day the best reading. Fiction, too, is natural to the youthful mind. It is absurd to suppose that Heaven gave us our imagination and rosy dreams for nothing. They are the drapery of fact, and are intended to soften for us the dreary outlines of duty. No girl was ever injured, if she were worth saving, by a little novel-reading. Indeed, the most ethical writers of the day have learned that, if a fact is worth knowing, it had better be conveyed in the agreeable form of a fiction. What girl would ever learn so much of Florentine history in any other way as she learns by reading " Romola?" What better picture of the picturesque past than " The Last Days of Pompeii?" Walter Scott's novels are the veriest mine of English and Scotch history; and we might go on indefinitely.

As for studies for girls, it is always best to teach them

Latin, as a solid foundation for the modern languages, if for nothing else; as much arithmetic as they can stand; and then go on to the higher education and the culture which their mature minds demand, if they desire it and are equal to it.

But no mother should either compel or allow her daughter to study to the detriment of her health. The moment a girl's body begins to suffer, then her mind must be left free from intellectual labor. With some women, brain-work is impossible. It produces all sorts of diseases, and makes them at once a nervous wreck. With other women intellectual labor is a necessity. It is like exercise of the limbs. It makes them grow strong and rosy. No woman who can study and write, and at the same time eat and sleep, preserve her complexion and her temper, need be afraid of intellectual labor. But a mother must watch her young student closely, else in the ardor of emulation amid the excitements of school she may break down, and her health leave her in an hour. It is the inexperienced girl who ruins her health by intellectual labor.

To many a woman intellectual labor is, however, a necessity. It carries off nervousness; it is a delightful retreat from disappointment; it is a perfect armor against *ennui*. What the convent life is to the devotee, what the fashionable arena is to the belle, what the inner science of politics is to the European women of ambition, literary work is to certain intellectual women. So a mother need not fear to encourage her daughter in it, if she sees the strong growing taste, and finds that her health will bear it.

But we fear that certain fashionable schools have ruined the health of many a girl, particularly those where the rooms are situated at the top of a four-story building, as they generally are. A poor, panting, weary girl mounts these cruel steps to begin the incomprehensibly difficult service of a modern school. "Why do you never go out at recess?" said a teacher to one of her pupils. "Because it hurts my heart so much to come up the stairs," said the poor girl. "Oh! but you should take exercise," said the teacher; "look at Louisa's color!" .

That teacher knew as much of pathology as she did of Hottentot; and the pupil thus advised lies to-day a hopeless invalid on her bed.

CHAPTER XL

The · Manners · of · Our · Boys.

UT, if the amenities of home are thus hopefully to direct our daughters in the right way, what will they do for our sons?

Of one thing we may be certain, there is no royal road by which we can make "good young men." The age is a dissolute one. The story of temptation and indulgence is not new or finished. The worst of it is that women feed and tempt the indulgence of the age. Women permit a lack of respect. Even young men who have been well brought up by their mothers, become careless when associating with girls who assume the manners and customs of young men. And when it is added that some women in good society hold lax ideas, talk in *double entendre*, and encourage instead of repressing license, how can young men but be demoralized?

If women show disapproval of coarse ideas and offensive habits, men drop those ideas and habits. A woman is treated by men exactly as she elects to be treated. There is a growing social blot in our society. It is the

complacency with which women bear contemptuous
treatment from men. It is the low order at which they
rate themselves, the rowdiness of their own conduct, the
forgiveness on the part of women of all masculine sins of
omission, that injures men's manners irretrievably.

Fast men and women, untrained boys and girls, people
without culture, are doing much to injure American
society. They are injuring the immense social force of
good manners. Women should remember this part of
their duty. Men will not be chivalrous or deferential
unless women wish them to be.

The amenities of home are everything to a boy. Without them very few men can grow to be gentlemen. A
man's religion is learned at his mother's knee; and often
that powerful recollection is all that he cares for on a
subject which it is daily becoming more and more of a
fashion for men to ignore. His politeness and deference
are certainly learned there, if anywhere. A mother must
remember that all hints which she gives her son, as to a
graceful and gentlemanly bearing, are so many powerful
aids to his advancement in the world. A clergyman who
did not approve of dancing still sent his son to dancing-
school, because, as he said, he wished "him to learn to
enter a drawing-room without stumbling over the piano."

The education of the body is a very important thing.
The joints of some poor boys are either too loosely or too
tightly hung, and they find it difficult to either enter or
leave a room gracefully. "Don't you know how hard
it is for some people to get out of a room after their visit
is really over? One would think they had been built in
your parlor or study, and were waiting to be launched,"

says Dr. Holmes. This is so true that one almost may suggest that it be a part of education to teach a boy how to go away. The "business of salutation" and leave-taking is really an important part of education.

One great argument for a military exercise is that it teaches the stooping to stand up, the lagging to walk, the awkward to be graceful, the shambling to step accurately. Lord Macauley in his old age wished that he had had a military training, as he "never had known which foot to start with."

There are some persons born into the world graceful, whose bodies always obey the brain. There are far more who have no such physical command. To those who have it not, it must be taught. The amenities of home should begin with the morning salutation, a graceful bow from the boy to his mother, as he comes in to breakfast.

And table manners, what a large part they play in the amenities of home! A mother should teach her boy to avoid both greediness and indecision at table. He should be taught to choose what he wants at once, and to eat quietly, without unnecessary mumbling noise. Unless she teaches him such care early, he will hiss at his soup through life. She must teach him to hold his fork in his right hand, and to eat with it, and to use his napkin properly. If Dr. Johnson had been taught these accomplishments early, it would have been more agreeable for Mrs. Thrale. Teach your boy the grace of calmness. Let the etiquette of the well-governed, well-ordered table be so familiar to him that he will not be flustered if he upsets a wine-glass, or utterly discomposed if a sneeze or a choking fit require his sudden retreat behind his napkin, when, after he leaves you, he essays to dine abroad.

Life in America is in a great hurry, and the breakfast before school or business can not be in most families the scene of much instruction. We are accused by foreigners of bolting our food, and we are supposed to be dyspeptic in consequence. It is no doubt true that we do eat too fast and too much. Seneca tells us that "our appetite is dismissed with small payment, if we only give it what we owe it," and not what an ungoverned appetite craves. It is a debt which we should pay slowly, and by installments. But, if breakfast is hurried, dinner can be quiet and well ordered, be it ornate or simple.

Nothing is better for the practice of the amenities of home than a rigorous determination to dress for dinner. This does not mean that we should be expensively or showily dressed, but that every member of the family should appear clean and brushed, and with some change of garment. A few minutes in the dressing-room is not too much of a task to even the busiest man, and he comes down much refreshed to his meal.

A lady hardly needs any urging on this point; but, if any one does need urging, it is certainly worth mentioning.

Several years ago a growing family of boys and girls were taken by their parents, who had experienced a reverse of fortune, to the neighborhood of the oil-wells to live. It was about the time they were growing up, and their mother was in despair as she thought of the lost opportunities of her children. Nothing about them but

ignorance.   No prospect, no schools, no anything.   But
in the depth of her love she found inspiration.

Out of the wreck of her fortunes she had saved enough
to furnish parlor and dining room prettily, and to buy a
few handsome lamps. Books were there in plenty, for old
books sell for very little; so she had been able to save
that important factor of civilization.

Every evening her lamps were lighted and her dinner
spread as if for a feast; and every member of the family
was made to come in as neatly dressed as if it were a
party.   The father and mother dressed carefully, and the
evening was enlivened by music and reading.

She attended to their education herself, although not
fitted for it by her own training.   She did as well as she
could.   She taught them to bow and to courtesy, to
dance, to draw, to paint, to play and sing; that is, she
started them in all these accomplishments. In five years,
when better fortunes brought them to the city again, they
were as well-bred as their city cousins, and all her friends
applauded her spirit.   This was done, too, with only
the assistance of one servant, and sometimes with not
even that.

It required enormous courage, persistence, and belief
in the amenities of home. How many women, under such
doleful circumstances, would have sunk into slovenli-
ness and despair, and would have allowed their flock to
run wild, like the neighboring turkeys!

There is great hope for country children who are surrounded by a certain prosperity and agreeable surroundings.   They see more of their parents than city children
can; and perhaps the ideal home is always in the coun-

try. Those small but cultivated New England villages, those inland cities, those rural neighborhoods, where nature helps the mother, where the natural companionship of animals is possible for the boys, and the pony comes to the door for the girls; where water is near for boating and fishing, and in winter for the dear delights of skating—such is the beautiful home around which the memory will for ever cling. The ideal man can be reared there, one would think—that ideal man whom Richter delighted to depict, one whose loving heart is the beginning of knowledge.

We could paint the proper place for the ideal man to be born in, if, alas! for all our theories, he did not occasionally spring out of the slums, ascend from the lowest deeps, and confute all our theories by being nature's best gem, without ancestry, without home, without help, without culture.

The education of boys in cities is beset with difficulties; for the fashionable education may lead to self-sufficiency and conceit, with a disdain of the solid virtues; or it may lead to effeminacy and foppishness—the worst faults of an American. These two last faults are, however, not fashionable or common faults in our day. There is a sense of superiority engendered in the "smart young man," so called, which is very offensive. All snobs are detestable; the American snob is preëminently detestable.

A young man of fashion in New York is apt to get him a habitual sneer, which is not becoming, and to assume an air of patronage, which is foolish. He has a love for discussing evil things, which has a very poor effect on his mind; he has no true ideas of courtesy or good-breeding; he is thoroughly selfish, and grows more and more debased in his pleasures, as self-indulgence becomes the law of his life.

His outward varnish of manner is so thin that it does not disguise his inner worthlessness. It is like that varnish which discloses the true grain of the wood. Some people of showy manners are thoroughly ill-bred at heart. None of these men have the tradition of fine manners, that old-world breeding of which we have spoken. They would be then able to cover up their poverty; but they have not quite enough for that; and they truly believe—these misguided youths—that a rich father, a fashionable mother, an air of ineffable conceit, will carry them through the world. It is astonishingly true that it goes a great way, but not the whole way.

No youth, bred in a thoroughly virtuous and respectable family, grows up to be very much of a snob, let us hope. Alas! he may become a drunkard, a gambler, a failure. And then we come up standing against that great cruel stone wall, that unanswered question, "Why have I wrought and prayed to no purpose?" And who shall answer us?

It is the one who sins least who is found out, and who gets the most punishment.

There is a pathetic goodness about some great sinners which they never lose. We love the poor fallen one whom we try to save. Never are the amenities of home more precious, more sacred, more touching, than when they try to help the faltering, stumbling footstep; to hide the disgrace, to shelter the guilty, to ignore, if possible, the failing which easily besets the prodigal son; to welcome him back when society has discarded him; to be patient with his pettishness, and to cover his faults with the mantle of forgiveness; all these are too tragic, too noble, too sacred for us to dilate upon. They are the amenities of heaven.

Society makes no explanations and asks none, else we might ask why some men and women are tolerated, and why others are cast out? Why some young man who had once forgotten himself after dinner is held up to scorn, and why another is forgiven even through the worst scandal? Why is injustice ever done?

Many a young man, having experienced injustice at the hands of society, goes off and deliberately commits moral suicide. The conduct of society is profoundly illogical, and we cannot reform it.

⟶✦CHAPTER XLI.✦⟵

A ✦ Profession ✦ for ✦ Our ✦ Boys.

HANCELLOR Kent said, in his wise way, that the citizen who did not give his son a profession or a trade, was wronging the state. Every one must have something to do. The idle man is a dangerous man. It is a pity that every boy cannot learn a profession and a trade. In the troublous times which we have just gone through, we have seen how much better it was to be a shoemaker than to be a lawyer. The professional men nearly starved.

Madame de Genlis said that she knew seventy trades, by any one of which she could have earned a living. She taught the sons of Philip Egalité to make shoes, pocket-books, brooms, brushes, hats, coats, and all sorts of cabinet-work. She taught them literature, science, and music; had them instructed in watch-making and clock-making, and even in the arts of killing and cutting up a sheep. They found many of these resources valuable in exile; and it is strange that it has not occurred to those who have boys who are not princes, to do the same. A boy could learn to be a carpenter while preparing for college, and could study his Latin, Greek, and mathematics with a better brain for the exercise.

It is to be regretted that gentlemen's sons deem certain trades beneath their notice. For all labor is honorable, and all cannot succeed as lawyers, doctors, clergymen, or merchants. There is great need of the handicraft so honorably considered in the middle ages. Every gift bestowed upon us by Providence, whether of mind or body, is a talent to be grateful for. Arthur can write verses; Jack can cut down a tree; Sam can reason; Edmund can do a sum; Peter can measure and saw boards; Henry can tame animals and make all nature his tributary; James likes to sit and work at some thoughtful, sedentary task; Horatio is speculative, active, courageous—he aims at Wall street. Alas! they *all* aim at Wall street, that fairy street lined with gold. They go there, most of them, to find only Peter Goldthwaite's "treasure," if, indeed, they do not find something worse.

In the forming of character, the father and mother should try to make headway against this national mistake, that to rush headlong into money-making is the end of life. A boy should be taught to respect the day of small things; to work honestly for every dollar he gets; and to let that dollar represent something given back for the worth of it. It would be a very good thing for all young men if there were a law that they should enter no profession or business, until they had proved that they could earn their living by their hands.

Casimir Périer said, when accused of being an aristo-crat: "My only aristocracy is the superiority which industry, frugality, perseverance, and intelligence will insure to every man in a free state of society; and I belong to those privileged classes of society to which you may all belong in your turn. Our wealth is our own; we have gained it by the sweat of our brows or by the labor of our minds. Our position in society is not conferred upon us, but purchased by ourselves with our own intellect, application, zeal and knowledge, patience and industry. If you remain inferior to us, it is because you have not the talent, the industry, the zeal or the sobriety, the patience or the application, necessary to your advancement. You wish to become rich as some do to become wise, but there is no royal road to wealth any more than there is to knowledge."

These are sentences which should be engraved on the walls of every college and schoolhouse. Young men should learn to look to patient labor as their lot in life. The feverish and sudden success of a few, wrecks a thousand yearly.

"There is Charley, who has made his pile in Wall street in six months. Why should I work all my life for what he gains in half a year?" asks visionary and lazy Fred, not counting the thousand failures in Wall street, including failures to be honest.

There is, however, a growing taste for agriculture in our country which is most hopeful. The earth owes us all a living, and if we will "tickle her with a hoe she will laugh with a harvest."

There is now living in the State of New York a young farmer who went from the ranks of a fashionable career right into the fields. Inheriting a farm which was worth nothing unless he worked it himself, he determined to study scientific farming at an agricultural college in England; and came home armed with useful knowledge and with practical ideas. He had learned to be a very good blacksmith, carpenter, saddler, and butcher — for a farmer should know how to mend his farm-wagon, stitch his harness, shoe his horse, and kill his calves—according to the economical English fashion.

And he had great good luck, this young farmer, in that he found a wife who, like himself, had been reared in "our best society," but who was willing to leave all for his sake, and to learn to pickle and preserve, to bake and brew, to attend to the dairy, and to get up at five o'clock in the morning to give her working husband his breakfast, and he learned that,

> ' He who by the plow would thrive,
> Must either hold himself or drive."

So this jolly farmer is always at it, and drives his team afield himself at daybreak.

The old farmers wonder as they see this handsome young fellow, beautifully dressed, on Sunday, driving his pretty wife to church, that he can make more money than they can. His butter is better, and brings more a pound; his wheat is more carefully harvested; his breed of pigs is celebrated; his chickens are wonderful—for the books tell him the best to buy. He has learning and science to hitch to his cart, and they " homeward from the field " bring him twice the crop that ignorance and prejudice draw.

Above all, he is leading a happy, healthy, and independent life. To be sure, his hands are hard and somewhat less white than they were. But polo and cricket would have ruined his hands. His figure is erect, and his face is ruddy. He has not lost his talent in the elegant drawing room, but can still dance the German to admiration. He is doing a great work and setting a good example; for he is, as we Americans say, "making it pay." To be sure, he has a great taste for a farmer's life. No one should go into it who has not. But what a certainty it is! Seed-time and harvest never fail. Wall street sometimes does.

It would seem, while there is so much to be done in America with her railroads, oil-wells, mines, farms, and wheat-fields, her numerous industries and requirements, that no man need be poor. Our sons can find something to do, something to turn a hand to.

The teaching of home should be in this particular age of the world to inculcate "plain living and high thinking" in our sons. That is what they need to be great and good men, and useful citizens.

⊸✣CHAPTER XLII.✣⊸

The · Good · Wife.

WIFE, is said to be the most agreeable and delightful name in nature. A woman indeed ventures much when she assumes it, for it is to her the final throw for happiness or unhappiness. Be she ever so good, so gifted, so true, so noble, she may marry a man who will disgrace her and make her unhappy; she has no security whatever against the most cruel fate.

And home must be her battle-ground. The man has the world before him, where to choose; therefore, an unhappy marriage is but one bitter drop in his full cup. With the wife, it is the whole draught. Let her weigh well the dangers of the future; even with prudence she may not escape misfortune.

It is well if she can always think her husband wise, whether he is or not. She is a happy woman who can make her husband always a hero. She is happiest who is humblest, and who takes a pleasure in looking up. Not that we would ignore or despise the moral beauty of great courage in women or a proper belief in themselves.

473

MRS. POTTER PALMER.

The rare heights which women have reached through their struggles, and by means of their self-dependence and courage, are to be regarded with awe and admiration.

The trouble is, that women have not quite the courage of their opinions. They have a certain degree of courage, and then they halt. This often puts a woman in a perilous attitude of indecision. A woman may wish to keep her manners at the true level of social restriction, and yet she may have longings for a higher sphere.

This very ambition to be better, wiser, more free to act out her own character, may in the attitude of wife make her uneasy and uncomfortable. There are great characters who are cheerful in a lonely adherence to the right. There are others which must have the sympathy and love and admiration of those near them, or they are miserable.

They can not help this uneasiness, this belief that they were born for other duties than the chronicling of small beer, and yet they do not like to move out of the beaten track, knowing very well that the people who govern the world, and who are respected, are those who move in the conventional track, shocking nobody—souls which find their highest aspirations satisfied with the making of afghans and the embroidery of tidies.

Women, however, are obliged, like men, to live out their own natures, and to use their talents as men are. Talent and spirit will not slumber or sleep. Irrespective of ridicule and regardless of happiness, a great woman must manifest her intellectual or moral supremacy. Happy for the gifted woman, if there be a vital refinement in her mind which keeps her from making her gifts but illustrations of her weaknesses.

A good wife, if it ever occurs to her that her husband is her inferior, conceals the fact religiously; many a witty wife has put good stories into her husband's lips—a forgivable deceit. Women have the talent of ready utterance to much greater perfection than men; they are quicker-witted; they have more ready tact. A wife's mind has traveled over the whole journey, and started home again, often before the husband has gone ten miles; but she has (or should have) the sense to keep silent until he has caught up with her.

No women are so detestable as those who make "game" of their husbands in public, who show them up to the world, and exhibit their defects. If a husband speaks bad grammar, his wife should ignore the fact, and bid him discourse as if he were a nightingale. She honors herself by concealing his defects. She degrades herself if she lowers him. There are disinterestedness and self-devotion in a woman's character, sometimes, of which a man seems incapable. She should show it all as a wife.

However badly wives behave in prosperity, the authors and philosophers do give them credit for behaving well in adversity. They show then that in the vainest and most frivolous heart "there is a spark of heavenly fire which beams and blazes in the dark hours of adversity."

"Women are in their natures far more gay and joyous than men, whether it be that their blood is more refined, their fibers more delicate, and their animal spirits more light and volatile, or whether, as some have imagined, there may not be a kind of sex in the very soul. As vivacity is the gift of women, so is gravity that of man.''

Women are very fond of admiration. They love flattery and fine clothes, and grow frivolous, almost from the very necessity of the case. The worst faults of women are fed by the admiration of men, for the very youngest girl is not long in seeing that her prettiest and most frivolous companion is assured of the highest social success.

As a wife, she must sometimes observe that her husband is attracted by the very faults which he most deprecates in her, and that, if his homage can be won from her, it is by the exhibition of qualities which her own self-respect would prevent her from exhibiting.

So, from first to last, a good wife has need of all her virtue, all her strength, and all her good sense. She must put a thousand disappointments and little injuries and small injustices in her pocket. She may be very much assured, if she keeps up an imperturbable good temper, serenity, and composure, that Monsieur will be won back at last, and admire her more than he has done Madam Fugatif.

The good wife accepts her husband's dictum as to the scale of splendor on which she shall arrange her house. She learns from him how much she shall spend; she helps him to economize; she even sometimes restricts his too ardent fancy in the way of opera-boxes and pictures. A wife of frugal mind is a great help to a man, if she be not mean. A miserly woman is a contradiction in terms, for women should be "*loving and giving.*"

As a good wife, a woman brings up her children to
31

respect their father, to obey him, to accept his advice rather than her own; to be the vice-regent in the house is her chosen position.   Never does she secretly, as some bad wives do, plot against his known wishes.   Religion, politics, business, social position, expenditure, — she allows him to decide all these things, if he wishes to do so.   It is a man's prerogative.

She reserves the right to think for herself; to, in a measure, lead her own life, choose her own books, her own amusements, and her own friends; and her home is a much happier one if she brings into it some element of variety, for, as we have said, each member of the home should be an individual.

Society is in the hands of the women almost exclu- sively in this country.   Most men like to see their wives shine in society; it gratifies their pride.   Good company, lively conversation, brightening up the wits, makes a wife twice as agreeable a companion.   Society, too, is the true sphere of many women; they are lost out of it. Without carrying it too far, women are much better for a social taste.   They get moody else.   In social life diffi- culties are met and conquered, restraints of temper become necessary, and striving to behave rightly in these emergencies will help to fit a woman to behave rightly at home.   She is useful to others, and is improving herself. If she is always at home, she is apt to become morbid and introspective.

She should be at home when her husband wants her. He is the first society which she should seek, nor should she ever accept with patience any indignity to him.   He may not be as great an ornament to society as she is, no matter; he must go with her, and to him she always shows a most respectful observance. And she must not break her heart if, after treating her like a goddess, he comes down and treats her like a woman. It is not in the nature of man to keep up on the highest stilts of admiration and love all the time. She must accept his more commonplace liking.

And let her preserve a disposition to be pleased, not slighting the humble blessing of an every-day good fellowship.

A good wife remembers her husband's dignity, and is more than ever careful not to compromise it. She is more careful than when she was a girl, because then laughter, playfulness, and coquetry were allowable; now, for every fault of hers, husband and children must suffer. She can not be too considerate of them.

A man of wit and sense, who looks upon his wife with pleasure, confidence, and admiration, will have few comments to make on the amount of pleasure she may take in the company of other men. A jealous husband is a tyrant, whom no propriety of conduct can appease. The races of the Othellos, the Borgias, and the Cencis are not extinct. A woman cannot supply all the failings of the man who loves her and whom she loves, but it is her duty to try to do so.

A good wife who is married to a great man—the "people's idol," a favorite clergyman, a noted orator, or an Adonis—has a hard part to act. The world owns her idol, and she has to accept the quota which the world leaves. She has to see him adored by other women; to know that, officially, he must accept the confidences of

other women which do not come to her; she sees the
world seeking him first, and her perhaps not at all. This
is a very trying position. The wives of noted authors,
particularly in England, where the wife is not always
invited with her husband, have had some rather trying
experiences of this kind. Would that they could all
behave as well as did Moore's Bessy !

It is the glory of woman that she was sent into the
world to live for others rather than herself, to live, yes,
and to die for them. Let her never forget that she was
sent here to make man better, to temper his greed, control his avarice, soften his temper, refine his grosser
nature, and teach him that there is something better than
success. These thoughts will come to help her in the
lonely hours when he is receiving homage and she is not.
She may be apt to remember, too, that she has been his
inspiration, his guiding star, that but for her he would
not have been the poet, the orator, or the preacher.

There is said to be no burden on earth like the foolish
woman tied to the competent man, with the one exception of the false woman. No good wife would care to fill
either of these disagreeable alternatives. But many
women, otherwise good wives, have allowed wounded
vanity to come in and wreck the happiness of home.

More than one literary lion has cursed his celebrity
when it has brought to him the unhappiness of home.
It is said to have been one of the reasons of the separation of Mr. and Mrs. Dickens.

The wife may find that her ideal is made of clay, and
of very poor clay at that. But she only makes herself
ridiculous by showing up his faults to the world. What-

ever else he is, he is *her husband*, and there are but few faults which he can commit of which she should speak. A wife, who finds that as years go on she and her husband are drifting farther and farther apart, is indeed to be pitied.

As we grow old, we shall need each other more and more, the faltering steps down the hill should be taken hand in hand, and we should invoke all the amenities of home and all its capabilities to draw us together again. We should purify the current of earthly affection, which is growing turbid by the water of life, remembering that true passion comes first, but true *love* last.

⊷CHAPTER XLIII.⊷

The ⋅ Good ⋅ Father.

I T is one of the misfortunes of our American way of living, that the head of the house, the father—he who is the support, the mainstay, the highest central figure—should be scarcely able to live with his family at all. If he is a busy man, earning their daily bread, he must leave them after a hasty breakfast, to meet them again at a late dinner with a chance of seeing them in the evening; but, if a club man, or anxious for the opportunity of going out in the evening for improvement or change, he does not see much of his family even then. The younger children get to regard him as a feature of Sundays, and perhaps associate him with the unpleasant slavery of sitting still in church. A loving and kind father will, of course, impress himself upon his family and earn their affection and respect even in these brief intervals; but it is too little for the proper emphasis of an affection which should be almost the first in our hearts.

There must be something radically wrong in the

arrangements of life when this can happen. Either women should enter more into the business of life or man should work less, for a father is the natural teacher, guardian, and companion of his family. We will, for the moment, ignore the fact that he may desire the rest and the comforts of the home which he supports but scarcely enjoys; we will consider only the loss to his children of his society.

The father is, of course, the natural and the best companion for his boys; to teach them to swim, to ride, to master the common knowledge and accomplishments of life, should be his pleasure. He should be their teacher in the arts of gunnery and the noble science of the fishing-rod. They ought to be able to remember him as the story-teller and companion of their sports, the best guide, and the most agreeable company that they will ever know. How they hang on his lips as he tells them of his own boyhood, his sufferings at the poorly fed boarding-school, where he had to gather raw turnips in the field! How they like to hear of the size of his first trout; how magnificent he looks to them as he tells of his shooting a deer! How much, as they grow older, they enjoy his college stories! His early struggles and conquests give them heart for the same strife and victory which they are about to plunge into.

It is a very happy circumstance also for the grown daughters if their father, after having petted them as little girls, after helping to solve the difficult question in arithmetic, after construing the Latin, and giving them a little sweep of his strong penmanship, is still young and fresh enough to go out into society with them. A young-minded papa is a great boon to a daughter.

But here again comes in a national mistake. Our best men will rarely go to parties; they leave all that work to the mamma. Fatigued they no doubt are by their hard fight with the world, and society offers them no seat, no welcome.

When our middle-aged men will make a point of going into society, then, and not till then, will they become a part of it, and the women will find, what many of them have already found, that they are much better worth talking to than the boys.

A good father owes it to his wife and children to thus keep pace with them in their amusements, not allowing himself to get rusty, or to have an entirely different set of ideas and occupations. They cannot enter into his professional or business life. When he leaves after breakfast, he becomes a mystery to them. But he can, on his return, go with them to the theatre, the party, or the concert, and should try to do so to make himself a part of them.

They, in their turn, the sons and daughters, should have every delicate attention, every agreeable accomplishment, ready to make home delightful to the father who works for them. There is something pathetic in the idea of the chained slave, chained to the oar, to whom all look for money, clothing, food. If he is a millionaire, all goes well, but if he is a struggling man, threatened with ruin, knowing that so long as he lives he must pull up the stony hill, the only reward when he reaches the top, the going down the other side, it is sad enough. It

is wonderful that so many bear it patiently, and accept
it as the inevitable doom!

What fireside can be made too easy for such a man?
What good dinners, cheerful faces, what voices full of
obedience, should greet the hard-working, patient man!
His newspaper should be aired, his slippers ready, his
particular magazine in waiting. All the disagreeable
remarks about bills and the coal should be deferred until
after breakfast next morning—that moment conceded by
all for disagreeable communications. He should be forgiven if he is abstracted and silent. His cares may be
greater than he can bear, but he should be tenderly
moved to talk, and be merry, at least cheerful.

We all know families in which the mother and daughters are in conspiracy against the father, where he is
looked upon simply as a bank to be robbed, where the
buying of expensive dresses must go on, whether they
can be paid for or not, and where the asking for and
obtaining of money is all the need they have of him.
Henry James, Jr., has drawn the picture in "The Pension Beauregard," his companion-piece to "Daisy Mil-
ler." Such rapacity and vulgarity are too common.
They belong to the abuses of home.

But we know many another home where there are
silent economies practiced, heart-breaking ones sometimes, rather than to "ask father for money;" where
each one feels a personal indebtedness to the hard-working head of the house, and where each one sighs for the
time when he or she can help along.

The household is the home of the man as well as of
the child. To it he should bring all that is best in him:

his culture, if he has any, at least, his lofty, true thoughts, his benevolence and refinement. He should not, in getting rich, sacrifice himself. This is too great a price to pay for bread and lodging, fine hangings and fine clothes. A business man should take time to read, else when he becomes a man of leisure, he will find that he cannot read. He must bring into his household that spirit which is understanding, health and self-help. There was never a country which offered to the working man, the business man, the true man, such opportunity for a happy home as this. He can, in the first place, be educated without money; he can go to work without it. He can begin without patronage; the field is as open to the poor boy as to the rich one. It is character which determines everything.

It is sad to be obliged to confess that many a home, full of prosperity, full of rosy children, is still unhappy because of some mistake of father or mother, or both, some unruly tongue, some implacable temper! It seems as if a demon stood at the door and warned happiness away. Nothing can be urged in such a case but the old, old remedy of good manners, manners which shall compel an outward decency, and which will make one hesitate to exhibit the shame of an open quarrel. To see one's parents quarrel is the most dreadful suffering, the most acute mortification, to a family of children.

"Many a marriage has commenced, like the morning, red, and perished like a mushroom. Wherefore? Because the married pair neglected to be as agreeable to each other after their union as they were before it," says that intelligent old maid Fredrika Bremer. Old maids always write well about marriage and the education of children. Perhaps the looker-on is the best judge of the game.

The quarrels of married people who really love each other, and which come from irritated temper, are soon healed, and the daily life goes on without a sensible break between them. But, for the sake of their home, these dissensions should be avoided as much as possible. They both lose dignity and place in the ideas of their family, and the servants are not as apt to obey.

A father should never under any circumstances permit his children to treat him with disrespect. *They* will never forgive him for it even if he forgives. Nor should he desert his post as captain of the ship. In those unhappy families, where, as in the tragedy of "King Lear," we see the result of power given away, there is a perpetual lesson of the folly of a father's renunciation of his power. Happy for him if in his group of daughters there be one Cordelia to balance Regan and Goneril.

The wise father will so graduate his expenditure, if living on an income, that his expected expenditure will reach but two-thirds of his income, knowing well that the unexpected will consume the other third. The trouble is, in America, that no one knows exactly what his income is. In England he can tell to the quarter of a penny, even for his great-grandchildren. But here, where by far the largest number live from hand to mouth, thorough economy is almost impossible. Things look well one year, and a hospitable table, good clothes, and fine carriages are not impossible. Things look very much less well the next year, and these now necessaries of life become impossible; so the business of making one's house a scene of consistent expenditure, without miserly prudence or injudicious luxury, is a very difficult one. Our exchequer resembles our climate—heavy rains or a long drought. We do not know which to calculate upon.

All these facts work against a thoroughly understood and possible economy. All that the good father can do is to aim at making his children feel that home is the happiest place in the world, as he and their mother should aim at making it the best.

LOOKING TOWARD SUNSET.

—⋆✣ CHAPTER XLIV. ✣⋆—

Looking ✴ Toward ✴ Sunset.

TRYING crisis in life is to feel that you have had your fair half at least of the ordinary term of years allotted to mortals; that you have no right to expect to be any handsomer, or stronger, or happier than you are now; that you have climbed to the summit of life, whence the next step must necessarily be decadence. The air may be as fresh, the view as grand, still you know that, slower or faster, you are going down hill. It is not a pleasant descent at the beginning. It is rather trying, when, from long habit, you unwittingly speak of yourself as a " girl," to detect a covert smile on the face of your interlocutor; or, when led by some chance excitement to deport yourself in an ultra-youthful manner, some instinct warns you that you are making yourself ridiculous; or, catching in some strange looking-glass the face you are too familiar with to notice much, ordinarily, you suddenly become aware that it is not a young face, and will never be a young face again. With most people, the passing from maturity to middle age is so gradual as to be almost

imperceptible to the individual concerned. There is no denying this fact, and it ought to silence many an ill-natured remark upon those unlucky ones who insist upon remaining "young ladies of a certain age." It is very difficult for a woman to recognize that she is growing old; and to all, this recognition cannot but be fraught with considerable pain. Even the most sensible woman cannot fairly put aside her youth, with all it has enjoyed, or lost, or missed, and regard it as henceforth to be considered a thing gone by, without a momentary spasm of the heart.

To "grow old gracefully" is a good and beautiful thing; to grow old worthily is a better. And the first effort to that end is to become reconciled to the fact of youth's departure; to have faith in the wisdom of that which we call change, but which is in truth progression; to follow openly and fearlessly, in ourselves and our daily life, the same law which makes spring pass into summer, summer into autumn, and autumn into winter, preserving an especial beauty and fitness in each of the four.

If women could only believe it, there is a wonderful beauty even in growing old. The charm of expression, arising from softened temper or ripened intellect, often atones amply for the loss of form and coloring; consequently, to those who could never boast of either of these latter, years give much more than they take away. A sensitive person often requires half a lifetime to get thoroughly used to this corporeal machine; to attain a wholesome indifference both to its defects and perfections; and to learn at last what nobody would acquire from any teacher but experience, that it is the *mind* alone which is of any consequence. With good temper, sincerity, and a moderate stock of brains, or even with the two former only, any sort of a body can in time be made a useful, respectable, and agreeable traveling-dress for the soul. Many a one who was absolutely plain in youth, thus grows pleasant and well-looking in declining years. You will seldom find anybody, not ugly in mind, who is repulsively ugly in person after middle life.

So it is with character. However we may talk about people being "not a whit altered," "just the same as ever;" the fact is, not one of us is, or can be, for long together, exactly the same. The body we carry with us is not the identical body we were born with, or the one we supposed ours seven years ago; and our spiritual self, which inhabits it, also goes through perpetual change and renewal. In moral and mental, as well as in physical growth, it is impossible to remain stationary. If we do not advance, we retrograde. Talk of being "too late to improve," "too old to learn!" A human being should be improving with every day of a lifetime; and will probably have to go on learning throughout all the ages of immortality.

One of the pleasures of growing old is to know, to acquire, to find out, to be able to appreciate the causes of things; this gradually becomes a necessity and an exquisite delight. We are able to pass out of our own small daily sphere, and to take interest in the marvellous government of the universe; to see the grand workings of cause and effect; the educing of good out of apparent evil; the clearing away of the knots in tangled destinies, general or individual; the wonderful agency of time,

change, and progress in ourselves, in those surrounding
us, and in the world at large.   In small minds, this feeling expends itself in meddling, gossiping, scandal-mon-
gering; but such are merely abortive developments of a
right noble quality, which, properly guided, results in
benefits incalculable to the individual and to society.
Undoubtedly the after-half of life is the best working-
time.   Beautiful is youth's enthusiasm, and grand are
its achievements; but the most solid and permanent
good is done by the persistent strength and wide experience of middle age.   Contentment rarely comes till
then; not mere resignation, a passive acquiescence in
what cannot be removed, but active contentment.   This
is a blessing cheaply bought by a personal share in that
daily account of joy and pain, which the longer one lives
the more one sees is pretty equally balanced in all lives.
Young people enjoy " the top of life " ecstatically, either
in prospect or fruition; but they are very seldom contented.   It is not possible.   Not till the cloudy maze is
half traveled through, and we begin to see the object
and purpose of it, can we be really content.

The doubtful question, to marry or not to marry, is by
this time generally settled.   A woman's relations with
the other sex imperceptibly change their character, or
slowly decline.   There are exceptions; old lovers who
have become friends, or friends whom no new love could
make swerve from the fealty of years; still it usually
happens so.   The society of honorable, well-informed
gentlemen, who meet a lady on the easy neutral ground
of mutual esteem, is undoubtedly pleasant, but the time
has passed when any one of them is *the* one necessary to

her happiness. If she wishes to retain influence over mankind, she must do it by means different from those employed in youth. Even then, be her wit ever so sparkling, her influence ever so pure and true, she will often find her listener preferring bright eyes to intellectual conversation, and the satisfaction of his heart to the improvement of his mind. And who can blame him? The only way for a woman to preserve the unfeigned respect of men, is to let them see that she can do without either their attention or their admiration. The waning coquette, the ancient beauty, as well as the ordinary woman, who has had her fair share of both love and liking, must show by her demeanor that she has learned this.

It is reckoned among the compensations of time that we suffer less as we grow older; that pain, like joy, becomes dulled by repetition, or by the callousness that comes with years. In one sense this is true. If there is no joy like the joy of youth, the rapture of a first love, the thrill of a first ambition, God's great mercy has also granted that there is no anguish like youth's pain ; so total, so hopeless, blotting out earth and heaven, falling down upon the whole being like a stone. This never comes in after life ; because the sufferer, if he or she have lived to any purpose at all, has learned that God never meant any human being to be crushed under any calamity, like a blind worm under a stone.

For lesser evils, the fact that our interests gradually take a wider range, allows more scope for the healing power of compensation. Also our loves, hates, sympa-

3.

thies, and prejudices, having assumed a more rational and softened shape, do not present so many angles for the rough attrition of the world. Likewise, with the eye of faith we have come to view life in its entireness, instead of puzzling over its disjointed parts, which were never meant to be made wholly clear to mortal eye. And that calm twilight, which, by nature's kindly law, so soon begins to creep over the past, throws over all things a softened coloring, which transcends and forbids regret.

Another reason why woman has greater capacity for usefulness in middle life than in any previous portion of her existence, is her greater independence. She will have learned to understand herself, mentally and bodily ; to be mistress over herself. Nor is this a small advantage ; for it often takes years to comprehend, and to act upon when comprehended, the physical peculiarities of one's own constitution. Much valetudinarianism among women arises from ignorance or neglect of the commonest sanitary laws ; and from indifference to that grand preservative of a healthy body, *a well-controlled and healthy mind.* Both of these are more attainable in middle age than in youth ; and therefore the sort of happiness they bring, a solid, useful, available happiness, is more in her power then than at any earlier period. And why ? Because she has ceased to think principally of herself and her own pleasures ; because happiness has itself become to her an accidental thing, which the good God may give or withhold, as He sees most fit for her, and most adapted to the work for which he means to use her in her generation. This conviction of being at once an active and a passive agent is surely consecration enough to form the peace, nay, the happiness, of any good woman's life; enough, be it ever so solitary, to sustain it until the end. In what manner such a conviction should be carried out, no one individual can venture to advise. In this age, woman's work is almost unlimited, when the woman herself so chooses. She alone can be a law unto herself; deciding and acting according to the circumstances in which her lot is placed. And have we not many who do so act? There are women of property, whose names are a proverb for generous and wide charities; whose riches, carefully guided, flow into innumerable channels, freshening the whole land. There are women of rank and influence, who use both, or lay aside both, in the simplest humility, for labors of love, which level all classes, or rather raise them all, to one common sphere of womanhood.

Many others, of whom the world knows nothing, have taken the wisest course that any unmarried woman can take; they have made themselves a home and a position; some as the Ladies Bountiful of a country neighborhood; some, as elder sisters, on whom has fallen the bringing up of whole families, and to whom has been tacitly accorded the headship of the same, by the love and respect of more than one generation thereof. There are some who, as writers, painters, and professional women generally, make the most of whatever special gift is allotted to them; believing that, whether it be great or small, it is not theirs, either to lose or to waste, but that they must one day render up to the Master his own, with usury.

I will not deny that the approach of old age has its sad

aspect to a woman who has never married ; and who, when her own generation dies out, no longer retains, or can expect to retain, any flesh-and-blood claim upon a single human being.   When all the downward ties, which give to the decline of life a rightful comfort, and the interest in the new generation which brightens it with a perpetual hope, are to her either unknown, or indulged in chiefly on one side.   Of course there are exceptions, where an aunt has been almost like a mother, and where a loving and lovable great-aunt is as important a person-age as any grandmother.   But, generally speaking, a single woman must make up her mind that the close of her days will be more or less solitary.

Yet there is a solitude which old age feels to be as nat-ural and satisfying as that rest which seems such an irk-someness to youth, but which gradually grows into the best blessing of our lives ; and there is another solitude, so full of peace and hope, that it is like Jacob's sleep in the wilderness, at the foot of the ladder of angels.

The extreme loneliness, which afar off appears sad, may prove to be but as the quiet, dreamy hour "between the lights," when the day's work is done, and we lean back, closing our eyes, to think it all over before we finally go to rest, or to look forward, with faith and hope, unto the coming Morning.

A life in which the best has been made of all the materials granted to it, and through which the hand of the Great Designer can be plainly traced, whether its web be dark or bright, whether its pattern be clear or clouded, is not a life to be pitied ; for it is a completed life.   It has fulfilled its appointed course, and returns to the Giver of all breath, pure as he gave it.   Nor will he forget it when he counteth up his jewels.

—MISS MULOCH.

⟡CHAPTER XLV.⟡

Thoughts ⁎ About ⁎ Women ⁎ by ⁎ Notable ⁎ Writers.

ABILITY.

EN need not try where women fail.—*Euripides.*

There are many more clever women in the world than men think for; our habit is to despise them; we believe they do not think because they do not contradict us, and they are weak because they do not struggle and rise up against us. A man only begins to know women as he grows old; and, for my part, my opinion of their cleverness rises every day.—*Thackeray.*

When I see the elaborate study and ingenuity displayed by women in the pursuit of trifles, I feel no doubt of their capacity for the most herculean undertakings.—*Julia Ward Howe.*

Women have more of common sense, though less of acquired capacity, than men.—*Hazlett.*

This I set down as a positive truth: a woman with fair opportunities, and without an absolute hump, may marry whom she likes. Only let us be thankful that the darlings are like the beasts of the field, and don't know their own power.—*Thackeray.*

AFFECTIONS.

A wise woman confides in few persons, a cunning one in none.—*Ninon de Lenclos.*

A supreme love, a motive that gives a sublime rhythm to a woman's life, and exalts habit into partnership with the soul's highest needs, is not to be had where and how she wills ; to know that high initiation, she must often tread where it is hard to tread, and to feel the chill air, and watch through darkness.—*George Eliot.*

A woman's whole life is a history of affections.— *Washington Irving.*

Beneath the odorous shade of the boundless forests of Chili, the native youth repeats the story of love as sincerely as it was ever chanted in the valley of Vaucluse. The affections of family are not the growth of civilization.—*Bancroft.*

No padlock, bolts, or bars can secure a maiden so well as her own reserve.—*Cervantes.*

Our own capacity for loving, be it pure and good, will make us beloved.—*Mrs. L. H. Sigourney.*

Men are misers, and women prodigal in affection.— *Lamartine.*

Is not the life of woman all bound up in her affections ? What hath she to do in this bleak world alone ? It may be well for man, on his triumphal course, to move uncumbered by soft bonds ; but we were born for love and grief.—*Mrs. Hemans.*

Affection is woman's native atmosphere.—*Lamartine.*

AFFLICTIONS.

There is strength deep-bedded in our hearts, of which we reck but little, till the shafts of heaven have pierced its fragile dwelling. Must not earth be rent before her gems are found?—*Mrs. Hemans.*

The sorrows of beautiful women draw tears from our purses.—*Alphonse Karr.*

No man knows what the wife of his bosom is—no man knows what a ministering angel she is—until he has gone with her through the fiery trials of this world.—*Washington Irving.*

For women are by nature formed to feel some consolation when their tongue gives utterance to the afflictions they endure.—*Euripides.*

AMBITION.

It is true that men not unfrequently sacrifice love to ambition, but few women have ever done this voluntarily. Love with them, as weighed against all things else, will kick the beam. Horace says that an ambitious man will storm heaven itself in his folly.—*Bayard Taylor.*

It is not love that steals the heart from love ; it is the hard world and its perplexing cares, its petrifying selfishness, its pride, its low ambition, and its paltry aims.—*Charlotte Bowles.*

AMIABILITY.

That you may be beloved, be amiable.—*Ovid.*

A modest woman is ever amiable ; a reserved one is only prudent.—*Rivarol.*

The loveliest faces are to be seen by moonlight, when one sees half with the eye and half with the fancy.—*Bovee.*

How very easy it is to be amiable in the midst of happiness and success.—*Mme. Swetchine.*

A virtuous mind in a fair body is, indeed, a fine picture in a good light, and therefore it is no wonder that it makes the beautiful sex all over charms.—*Addison.*

Amiable people, while they are more liable to imposition in their casual contact with the world, yet radiate so much of mental sunshine that they are always reflected in all appreciative hearts.—*Mme. Deluzy.*

ART.

Moral beauty is the basis of all true beauty. This foundation is somewhat covered and veiled in nature. Art brings it out and gives it more transparent forms. It is here that art when it knows well its power and resources, engages in a struggle with nature in which it may have the advantage.—*Victor Cousin.*

The slight that can be conveyed in a glance, in a gracious smile, in a wave of the hand, is often the *ne plus ultra* of art. What insult is so keenly felt as the polite insult, which it is impossible to resent.—*Julia Kavanagh.*

ATTRIBUTES.

Men, being stronger, are larger in all things, even in their love. When they love, they love better than we love, but less absorbingly. We give the whole of our lives to love ; they keep one portion of theirs for work, and another for ambition. Still, the half measure of a gallon is more than the full measure of a pint, and, weight for weight, the man's love is greater than the woman's.—*E. Lynn Lynton.*

Every woman is a volume within herself if you but know how to read her.—*Chamfort.*

No woman is all sweetness ; even the rose has thorns.— *Mme. Récamier.*

Woman is rather made to be loved than to love, like the flowers which feel nothing of the perfume, but yield it to be felt by others.—*Alphonse Esquiros.*

The crimson hue and silver tears become her better than any ornament of gold and pearls. These may hang on the neck of a wanton, but those are never seen disconnected with moral purity.—*Gotthold.*

The bread of life is love, salt of life is work, the sweetness of life is poesy, and the water of life faith. A true woman is a compound of them all.—*Mrs. Jameson.*

A little acidity is not objectionable in a woman of spirit ; we add lemon to make punch more palatable.— *Bayard Taylor.*

A great woman not imperious, a fair woman not vain, a woman of common talents not jealous, an accomplished woman not eager to shine, are four wonders great enough to be divided among the four quarters of the globe.— *Lavater*

Women live only in the tender emotions.—*Fontenelle.*

BEAUTY.

A handsome woman is a jewel ; a good woman is a treasure.—*Saadi.*

Beauty is like an almanac ; if it lasts a year it is well.—*Rev. T. Adams.*

Beauty draws us with a single hair.—*Pope.*

Even virtue is more fair when it appears in a beautiful person.—*Virgil.*

Affect not to despise beauty,—no one is free from its dominion ; but regard it not a pearl of price ; it is fleeting as the bow in the clouds.—*Tupper.*

All orators are dumb when beauty pleadeth.—*Shakspeare.*

The influence of great personal beauty, unless supported by force of character, is ever short-lived.—*Harriet Martineau.*

BEHAVIOR.

A woman is more considerate in affairs of love than a man, because the love is more the study and business of her life.—*Washington Irving.*

The coy mistress, who makes her lover wrest every favor from her, is the successful one.—*Ninon de Lenclos.*

Women should be doubly careful of their conduct, since appearances often injure them, as much as faults.—*Abbé Girard.*

Venus herself, if she were bold, would not be Venus.—*Apuleius.*

BRAVERY.

There is no love-broker in the world can more prevail in man's commendation with woman than report of valor.—*Shakspeare.*

What will not woman, gentle woman, dare when strong affection stirs her spirit up ?—*Southey.*

CHARACTERISTICS.

All women are, in some degree, poets in imagination, angels in heart, and diplomatists in mind.—*Emanuel Gonzales.*

Just corporeal enough to attest humanity, yet sufficiently transparent to let the celestial origin shine through.—*Ruffini.*

Men at most, differ as heaven and earth ; but women, worst and best, as heaven and hell.—*Tennyson.*

O woman, in ordinary cases so mere a mortal, how, in the great and rare events of life, dost thou swell into the angel !—*Bulwer-Lytton.*

It is easier for a woman to defend her virtue against men than her reputation against women.—*Rochebrune.*

It is beauty that doth oft make women proud ; it is virtue that doth make them most admired ; it is modesty that makes them seem divine.—*Shakspeare.*

I think man will always lead in affairs of intellect, of reason, imagination, understanding,—he has the bigger brain ; but that women will always lead in affairs of emotion, moral, affectional, religious,—she has the better heart, the truer intuition of the right, the lovely, the holy.—*Theodore Parker.*

CHARITABLENESS.

A woman who wants a charitable heart wants a pure mind.—*Haliburton.*

Large charity doth never soil, but only whitens, soft hands.—*Lowell.*

The ideal woman feels that all the children of want,—

bodily, mental, moral want, the infant of days or the man bowed with age,—all are children whom the Lord has given her, and over a wide and ever-widening circle beams the radiance of her spotless motherhood.—*Gail Hamilton.*

If a woman were to try to do the very best for herself in a worldly sense, she could take no surer course than by fitting herself to confer the largest benefits on those around her. For her, then, I ask that she shall be trained so to be best able to do good.—*John Boyd Kinnear.*

CHEERFULNESS.

Sighs and groans are as disenchanting as freckles, while good cheer is the natural ally of beauty.—*Mme. de Lambert.*

Those there are whose hearts have a look southward, and are open to the whole noon of nature ; be thou of such.—*Bailey.*

Cheerfulness becomes a woman at all times ; mirthfulness requires a proper occasion.—*Mme. Necker.*

Cheerfulness will render the face of a plain woman handsome, if it be coupled with intellect.—*Rivarol.*

Women wish to make themselves agreeable ; there is no harm in that. It is part of their nature. But how do they expect to continue so, when the attractions of youth forsake them ? Let them make trial of the temper that looks on the bright side of things ; let them put on the spectacles that discern the bright side of character. The smile of such a temperament is always admired.—*Mrs. L. H. Sigourney.*

A wise woman will at all times cultivate a cheerful expectation of the best, and thus become a fountain of joy to all with whom she associates.—*Lady Blessington.*

Dance, dance as long as you can; we must travel through life, but why make a dead march of it.—*Eliza Cook.*

CONTENT.

The most delicate beauty in the mind of women is, and ever must be, an independence of artificial stimulants for content. It is not so with men. The link that binds men to capitals belongs to the golden chain of civilization.—the chain which fastens all our destinies to the throne of Jove.—*Bulwer-Lytton.*

To be content smilingly to lie on a bed of roses while they know that thousands around them sleep on thorns,—this is represented by all around them as constituting pretty nearly the whole duty of woman. Thus practicing meekly an aimless and unmeaning patience and self-repression, they dwindle down year by year into pettiness and inanity.—*Frances Power Cobbe.*

Very few men understand the true significance of contentment; women alone illustrate it.—*Mme. Deluzy.*

Let woman at once reject the absurd notion that she was created for happiness; let her constitute herself instead a creator of it; let her accept with joy the fact this is a working-day world; then she will no longer strive to escape from labor, discipline, or sorrow, but will gladly hail each in its turn as part of God's appointed teaching, a shadow crossing the sunshine to show that it is bright.—*Caroline H. Dall.*

COUNSEL.

Let no man value at a little price a virtuous woman's counsel; her winged spirit is feathered oftentimes with heavenly words, and, like her beauty, ravishing and pure.—*Chapman.*

Always man needs woman for his friend. He needs her clearer vision, her subtler insight, her softer thought, her winged soul, her pure and tender heart. Always woman needs man to be her friend. She needs the vigor of his purpose, the ardor of his will, his calmer judgment, his braver force of action, his reverence, and his devotion.—*Mary Clemmer.*

When I read history and am impressed with any great deed, I feel as if I should like to see the woman who is concealed behind it, as the secret incentive.—*Heinrich Heine.*

Sweet is the voice of a sister in the season of sorrow, and wise is the counsel of those who love us.—*Beaconsfield.*

Aspasia did not leave any philosophical writings; but it is an admitted fact that Socrates resorted to her for instruction, and avowed himself to have obtained it.—*J. Stuart Mill.*

The counsel of a woman is not worth much, but he who does not take it is more worthless still.—*Cervantes.*

We have a wise saying, "Take a woman's first advice," which is supplemented by the Italian maxim, "Women are wise off-hand, and fools on reflection."—*Alfred de Musset.*

DELICACY.

Delicacy in woman is strength.—*Lichtenberg.*

Delicacy is to affection what grace is to beauty.— *Mme. de Maintenon.*

An appearance of delicacy, and even of fragility, is almost essential to beauty.—*Burke.*

Woman could take part in the processions, the songs, the dances of old religion; no one fancied her delicacy was impaired by appearing in public for such a cause.— *Margaret Fuller Ossoli.*

To a woman of delicate feeling the most persuasive declaration of love consists in the embarrassment of the lover.—*Laténa.*

The commonest man, who has his ounce of sense and feeling, is conscious of the difference between a lovely, delicate woman and a coarse one. Even a dog feels a difference in her presence. The man may be no better able than the dog to explain the influence the more refined beauty has on him, but he feels it.—*George Eliot.*

Woman, the precious porcelain of human clay!— *Jeremy Taylor.*

DEVOTION.

The best part of woman's love is worship; but it is hard to be sent away with her precious spikenard rejected, and her long tresses, too, that were let fall ready to soothe the wearied feet.—*George Eliot.*

To feel, to love, to suffer, to devote herself, will always be the text of the life of woman.—*Balzac.*

That perfect disinterestedness and self-devotion of

which men seem incapable, but which is sometimes found in women.—*Macaulay.*

Man may content himself with the applause of the world and the homage paid to his intellect, but woman's heart has holier idols.—*Miss Evans.*

Oh, only those whose souls have felt this one idolatry can tell how precious is the slightest thing affection gives and hallows.—*L. E. Landon.*

DUTIES.

Can man or woman choose duties? No more than they can choose their birthplace, or their father and mother.—*George Eliot.*

To the honor, to the eternal honor, of the sex, be it stated that in the path of duty no sacrifice is to them too high or too dear. Nothing is with them impossible, but to shrink from love, honor, innocence, and religion. The voice of pleasure or of power may pass by unheeded ; but the voice of affliction never.—*Balfour.*

She is so free, so kind, so apt, so blessed a disposition, she holds it a vice in her goodness not to do more than she is requested.—*Shakespeare.*

A woman's duties are clearly defined by her own instinct.—*Mme. Necker.*

We must educate our maidens into what is far better than any blind clamor for ill-defined "rights,"—into what ought to be the foundation of rights,—duties.— *Miss Muloch.*

O woman ! thou knowest the hour when the good man of the house will return, when the heat and burden of the day are past ; do not let him at such time, when he

is weary with toil, and jaded with discouragement, find
that the foot which should hasten to meet him is wandering at a distance, that the soft hand which should wipe
the sweat from his brow is knocking at the door of other
houses.— *Washington Irving.*

The true way to render ourselves happy is to love our
duty and find in it our pleasure.—*Mme. de Mottville.*

EDUCATION.

Man forms and educates the world, but woman educates
man.—*Julie Buron.*

I believe that for one woman whom the pursuits of
literature, the ambition of authorship, and the love of
fame, have rendered unfit for home-life, a thousand have
been made thoroughly undomestic by poor social striv-
ings, the follies of fashion, and the intoxicating distinction which mere personal beauty confers.—*Grace Greenwood.*

School is no place of education for any children whatever till their minds are well put in action. This is the
work which has to be done at home, and which may be
done in all homes where the mother is a sensible woman.
This done, a good school is a sort of inestimable advantage for cultivating the intellect, and aiding the acquisition of knowledge.—*Harriet Martineau.*

Bonaparte asked Madame de Staël in what manner he
could best promote the happiness of France. Her reply
is full of political wisdom. She said, "Instruct the
mothers of the French people."—*Daniel Webster.*

We claim for women a share of the educational opportunities offered to man, because we believe that they
₃₃

will never be thoroughly taught until they are taught at the same time, and in the same classes.—*Caroline H. Dall.*

The same education and opportunity for self-development which makes man a good guardian will make a woman a good guardian ; for their original nature is the same.—*Plato.*

EMPLOYMENT.

People cry out and deplore the unremunerative employment of women. The true want is the other way. Woman really trained and capable of good work can command any wages or salaries.—*Gail Hamilton.*

The question of woman's work in its economic aspect is really one not so much now of woman's *rights* as of woman's *mights.* Pretty much anything she wants to do, a resolute girl may now do.—*R. H. Newton.*

Let us candidly confess our indebtedness to the needle. How many hours of sorrow has it softened, how many bitter irritations calmed, how many confused thoughts reduced to order, how many life-plans sketched in purple.—*Caroline H. Dall.*

At present the most valuable gift which can be bestowed on woman is something to do, which they can do well and worthily and thereby maintain themselves.—*James A. Garfield.*

As well I remember the long afternoon buzz of the wheel that turned the white rolls into yarn in the chamber where I was born, so I know how woman stands by the distaff, whence man receives the precious stuff so painfully wrought.—*Bartol.*

ENDURANCE.

I have often had occasion to remark the fortitude with which women sustain the most overwhelming reverses of fortune. Those disasters which break down the spirit of a man and prostrate him in the dust seem to call forth all the energies of the softer sex, and give such intrepidity and elevation to their character that at times it approaches to sublimity.— *Washington Irving.*

Through suffering and sorrow thou hast passed to show us what a woman true can be.—*Lowell.*

To the disgrace of men it is seen that there are women both more wise to judge what evil is expected, and more constant to bear it when it happens.—*Sir P. Sidney.*

The burden becomes light that is shared by love.— *Ovid.*

The women of the poorer classes make sacrifices, and run risks, and bear privations, and exercise patience and kindness, to a degree that the world never knows of, and would scarcely believe even if it did know.—*Samuel Smiles.*

FACES.

Features,—the great soul's apparent seat.— *W. C. Bryant.*

The face of a woman, whatever be the force or extent of her mind, whatever be the importance of the object she pursues, is always an obstacle or a reason in the story of her life.—*Mme. de Staël.*

Men talk in raptures of youth and beauty, wit and sprightliness ; but after seven years of union, not one of them is to be compared to good family management, which is seen at every meal, and felt every hour in the husband's purse. — *Witherspoon.*

Quite the ugliest face I ever saw was that of a woman whom the world called beautiful. Through its "silver veil" the evil and ungentle passions looked out, hideous and hateful. On the other hand, there are faces which the multitude at first glance pronounce homely, unattractive, and such as "Nature fashions by the gross," which I always recognize with a warm heart-thrill. Not for the world would I have one feature changed; they please me as they are; they are hallowed by kind memories, and are beautiful through their associations.— *Whittier.*

What furniture can give such finish to a room as a tender woman's face? And is there any harmony of tints that has such stirring of delight as the sweet modulation of her voice?—*George Eliot.*

Those faces which have charmed us the most escape us the soonest.— *Walter Scott.*

The cheek is apter than the tongue to tell an errand.— *Shakespeare.*

Some women's faces are, in their brightness, a prophecy, and some, in their sadness, a history.—*Dickens.*

FAME.

In the career of female fame, there are few prizes to be obtained which can vie with the obscure state of a beloved wife or a happy mother.—*Jane Porter.*

She is best who is least spoken of among men, whether for good or evil.—*Pericles.*

Neglect is worse than death to most of us, and notoriety is our version of fame, as admiration is the sum of our ambition. Even Madame de Staël would have exchanged her brains for Madame de Récamier's beauty; poll the world of woman honestly and not one in a thousand would dissent from her choice.—*E. Lynn Lynton.*

Before entering upon a career of fame, women should reflect that, even for fame itself, they must renounce the happiness and repose destined for their sex, and that in this career there are few situations that can compare with the obscure life of an adored wife and happy mother.—*Mme. de Staël.*

Public praise has no power to fill up a woman's heart. She wants home love, and duties, and sympathy; all the rest is worth nothing without them.—*Florence Marryat.*

FASCINATIONS.

But common clay taken from the common earth, moulded by God, and tempered by the tears of angels, to the perfect form of woman.—*Tennyson.*

The most fascinating women are those that can most enrich the every-day moments of existence. In a particular and attaching sense, they are those that can partake our pleasures and our pains in the liveliest and most devoted manner. Beauty is little without this; with it she is indeed triumphant.—*Leigh Hunt.*

In the age of chivalry it was the beauty of woman alone that wrestled successfully against barbarism. She softened the rude manners of the warrior, and inspired the valorous knight with courage, generosity, and honor; thus civilizing by the influence of her charms those whose hearts could not be touched by any other human power.—*Alexander Walker.*

Without the smile from partial beauty won, oh, what were man ?—a world without a sun.—*Campbell.*

How much wit, good nature, indulgence, how many good offices and civilities, are required among friends to accomplish in some years what a lovely face or a fine hand does in a minute.—*Bruyère.*

FORGIVENESS.

Women do not often have it in their power to forgive like men, but they forgive like Heaven.—*Mme. Necker.*

Only a woman will believe in a man who has once been detected in fraud and falsehood.—*Dumas Père.*

She hugged the offender and forgave the offense,—sex to the last.—*Dryden.*

Receive no satisfaction for premeditated impertinence ; forget it, forgive it, but keep him inexorably at a distance who offered it.—*Lavater.*

FRIENDSHIP.

Female friendships are of rapid growth.—*Beaconsfield.*

Women, like princes, find few real friends.—*Lord Littleton.*

Perhaps there is nothing more lovely than the love of two beautiful women, who are not jealous of each other's charms.—*Beaconsfield.*

In the forming of female friendships, beauty seldom recommends one woman to another.—*Fielding.*

The chief thing wanting between men and women, as it seems to me, is friendship. Of love and poetic admiration there is an abundance, of course, and to spare. The world could not go on without these pretty amenities, but we want friendship far more than all these.—*E. Lynn Lynton.*

A female friend, amiable, clever, and devoted, is a possession more valuable than parks and palaces; and, without such a muse, few men can succeed in life, none be content.—*Beaconsfield.*

GENTLENESS.

With all women gentleness is the most persuasive and powerful argument.—*Théophile Gautier.*

In families well ordered there is always one firm, sweet temper, which controls without seeming to dictate. The Greeks represented Persuasion as crowned.—*Bulwer-Lytton.*

Gentleness in the gait is what simplicity is in the dress. Violent gestures or quick movements inspire involuntary disrespect.—*Balzac.*

The best and simplest cosmetic for women is constant gentleness and sympathy for the noblest interests of her fellow creatures. This preserves and gives to her features an indelibly gay, fresh and agreeable expression. If women would but realize that harshness makes them ugly, it would prove the best means of conversion.—*Auerbach.*

A woman's strength is most potent when robed in gentleness.—*Lamartine.*

Fearless gentleness is the most beautiful of feminine attractions, born of modesty and love.—*Mrs. Balfour.*

GIRLHOOD.

She was in the lovely bloom and spring-time of woman-hood; at that age when, if ever angels be for God's good purpose enthroned in mortal forms, they may be, without impiety, supposed to abide in such as hers. Cast in so slight and exquisite a mold, so mild and gentle, so pure and beautiful, that earth seemed not her element, nor its rough creatures her fit companions.—*Dickens.*

The presence of a young girl is like the presence of a flower; the one gives its perfume to all that approach it, the other her grace to all who surround her.—*L. Desnoyers.*

Girls we love for what they are; young men for what they promise to be.—*Goethe.*

Girls at an early age are not content with being pretty; they wish to be thought so. We see by their little airs that this care already occupies them; and scarcely are they capable of understanding what is said, when they may be governed by telling them what is thought of them. The same motive very indiscreetly proposed to little boys has no influence over them.—*Rousseau.*

A lovely girl is above all rank.—*Charles Buxton.*

One must always regret that law of growth which renders necessary that kittens should spoil into demure cats, and bright joyous school-girls develop into the spiritless, crystallized beings, denominated young ladies.—*Abba Goold Woolson.*

Signs are small, measurable things, but interpretations are illimitable, and in girls of sweet, ardent nature, every sign is apt to conjure up wonder, hope, belief, vast as a sky, and colored by a diffused thimbleful of matter in the shape of knowledge.—*George Eliot.*

GRACE AND GOODNESS.

They are as Heaven made them, handsome enough if they be good enough; for handsome is that handsome does.—*Goldsmith.*

Her form was fresher than the morning rose when the dew wets its leaves; unstained and pure as is the lily or the mountain snow.—*Thomson.*

The hand that hath made you fair hath made you good; the goodness that is cheap in beauty makes beauty brief in goodness; but grace, being the soul of your complexion, should keep the body of it ever fair.—*Shakespeare.*

The loveliest hair is nothing, if the wearer is incapable of a grace. The finest eyes are not fine if they say nothing.—*Leigh Hunt.*

What is good looking, as Horace Smith remarks, but looking good? Be good, be womanly, be gentle, generous in your sympathies, heedful of the well-being of all around you, and, my word for it, you will not lack kind words of admiration. Loving and pleasant associations will gather about you. Never mind the ugly reflection which your glass may give you. The mirror has no heart; but quite another picture is yours on the retinas of human sympathy.— *Whittier.*

Grace has been defined the outward expression of the inward harmony of the soul.—*Hazlitt.*

HAPPINESS.

The most happy women in the interior of their houses
are those who have married sensible men. The latter
suffer themselves to be governed with so much the more
pleasure, as they are always masters of themselves.—
Prince de Ligne.

The happiness which we enjoy is realized in anticipation,
not in fruition. Landor has said very finely, "Happiness
is like the statue of Isis, whose veil no mortal ever
raised."—*Anna Cora Mowatt.*

Our happiness in this world depends upon the affections we are enabled to inspire.—*Duchesse de Praslin.*

Happiness is woman's rarest cosmetic.—*G. J. W. Mel-
ville.*

The happiness that is quite understood at last becomes
tiresome; to give it zest we must have ups and downs;
the difficulties which are usually mingled with love
awaken passion and increase pleasure.—*Molière.*

Happy in this, she is not yet so old but she may learn;
and happier than this, she is not bred so dull but she
can learn; happiest of all is, that her gentle spirit commits itself to yours, to be directed.—*Shakespeare.*

HEALTH.

Our dainty notions have made women such hot-house
plants that one half the sex are invalids.—*Wendell Phil-
lips.*

Doubtless there are few things more important to a
community than the health of its women. The Sand-
wich Island proverb says: "If strong is the frame of

the mother, the son will give laws to the people." And in nations where all men give laws, all men need mothers of strong frames.—*Higginson.*

Michelet tells the sentimental world that woman is an exquisite invalid, with a perennial headache and nerves perpetually on the rack. It is a mistake. When I gaze upon German and French peasant-women, I ask Michelet which is right, he or nature.—*Kate Field.*

Gracefulness cannot subsist without ease; delicacy is not debility; nor must a woman be sick in order to please. Infirmity and sickness may excite our pity, but desire and pleasure require the bloom and vigor of health.—*Rosseau.*

The requirements of health and the style of female attire which custom enjoins are in direct antagonism to each other.—*Abba Goold Woolson.*

American ladies are known abroad for two distinguishing traits (besides, possibly, their beauty and self-reliance), and these are their ill-health and their extravagant devotion to dress.—*Abba Goold Woolson.*

HEARTS.

Oh, if the loving, closed heart of a good woman should open before a man, how much controlled tenderness, how many veiled sacrifices and dumb virtues, would be seen reposing there —*Richter.*

A human heart can never grow old if it takes a lively interest in the pairing of birds, the reproduction of flowers, and the changing tints of autumn leaves.—*Mrs., Lydia M. Child.*

There is in the heart of women such a deep well of love that no age can freeze it.—*Bulwer-Lytton.*

A womans heart is just like a lithographer's stone, what is once written upon it cannot be rubbed out.—*Thackeray.*

Where there is room in the heart, there is always room in the house.—*Moore.*

There are no little events with the heart. It magnifies everything ; it places in the same scale the fall of an empire and the dropping of a woman's glove, and almost always the glove weighs more than the empire.—*Balzac.*

The more heart, the more sorrow ; the less heart, the less of tender sensibility to loveliness.—*Mme. Necker.*

The human heart has of course its pouting fits ; it determines to live alone ; to flee into desert places ; to have no employment, that is, to love nothing ; but to keep on sullenly beating, beating, beating, until death lays his little finger on the sulky thing, and all is still. It goes away from the world, and straightway, shut from human company, it falls in love with a plant, a stone ; yea, it dandles cat or dog, and calls the creature darling. Yes, it is the beautiful necessity of our nature to love something.—*Douglas Jerrold.*

Without hearts there is no home.—*Byron.*

HOME.

A house is no home unless it contains food and fire for the mind as well as for the body. For human beings are not so constituted that they can live without expansion. If they do not get it in one way, they must in another, or perish.—*Margaret Fuller Ossoli.*

Our natural and happiest life is when we lose ourselves in the exquisite absorption of home, the delicious retirement of dependent love.—*Miss Muloch.*

Home is the grandest of all institutions.—*Spurgeon.*

In family government let this be always remembered, that no reproof or denunciation is so potent as the silent influence of a good example.—*Hosea Ballou.*

It is a woman, and only a woman,—a woman all by herself, if she likes, and without any man to help her,—who can turn a house into a home.—*Frances Power Cobbe.*

I value this delicious home-feeling as one of the choicest gifts a parent can bestow.— *Washington Irving.*

INFLUENCE.

If you would know the political and moral condition of a people, ask as to the condition of its women.—*Aimé Martin.*

All amusements of youth to which virtuous women are not admitted are, rely on it, deleterious in their nature. All men who avoid female society have dull perceptions and are stupid, or have gross tastes and revolt against what is pure.— *Thackeray.*

Men make laws ; women make manners.—*De Ségur.*

If woman lost us Eden, such as she alone can restore it.— *Whittier.*

Women govern us ; let us render them perfect ; the more they are enlightened, so much the more shall we be. On the cultivation of the mind of women depends the wisdom of men. It is by women that nature writes on the hearts of men.—*Sheridan.*

Few great men have flourished who, were they candid, would not acknowledge the vast advantage they have experienced in the earlier years of their career from the spirit and sympathy of woman.—*Beaconsfield.*

LITERARY PURSUITS.

Women excel more in literary judgment than in literary production,—they are better critics than authors.—*Lady Blessington.*

The purity and goodness of woman have done their proper work in the literature of the times. They have greatly contributed to chasten the morals of literature, and establish a code of laws by which offenses against decency are condemned as offenses against taste. While she uses the pen, she must always use it to inculcate the graces which she loves, and in which she herself excels. —*F. W. P. Greenwood.*

MOTHER.

I think it must somewhere be written that the virtues of mothers shall, occasionally, be visited on their children, as well as the sins of the fathers.—*Dickens.*

Stories first heard at a mother's knee are never wholly forgotten,—a little spring that never quite dries up in our journey through scorching years.—*Ruffini*

The future destiny of the child is always the work of the mother.—*Napoleon.*

Mothers, when your children are irritable, do not make them more so by scolding and fault-finding, but correct their irritability by good nature and mirthfulness. Irritability comes from errors in food, bad air, too little sleep, a necessity for change of scene and surroundings; from confinement in close rooms, and lack of sunshine. —*Herbert Spencer.*

Men are what their mothers made them. You may as well ask a loom which weaves huckabuck why it does not make cashmere, as to expect poetry from this engineer, or a chemical discovery from that jobber.— *Emerson.*

Youth fades; love droops; the leaves of friendship fall; a mother's secret hope outlives them all.—*Holmes.*

I believe I should have been swept away by the flood of French infidelity if it had not been for one thing: the remembrance of the time when my sainted mother used to make me kneel by her side, taking my little hands folded in hers, and cause me to repeat the Lord's Prayer. —*Thomas Randolph.*

The mother's heart is the child's school-room.— *Beecher.*

Even He that died for us upon the cross, in the last hour, in the unutterable agony of death, was mindful of his mother, as if to teach us that this holy love should be our last worldly thought,—the last point of earth from which the soul should take its flight for heaven.—*Longfellow.*

Holy as heaven a mother's tender love,—the love of many prayers and many tears, which changes not with dim, declining years.—*Mrs. Norton.*

RELIGION.

Religion is indeed woman's panoply; no one who wishes her happiness would divest her of it; no one who appreciates her virtues would weaken their best security.—*Sandford.*

Earth has nothing more tender than a woman's heart, when it is the abode of piety.—*Luther.*

Reverence the highest, have patience with the lowest. Let this day's performance of the meanest duty be thy religion. Are the stars too distant, pick up the pebble that lies at thy feet, and from it learn the all.—*Margaret Fuller Ossoli.*

No man can either live piously or die righteously without a wife.—*Richter.*

The only impregnable citadel of virtue is religion ; for there is no bulwark of mere morality which some temptation may not overtop or undermine, and destroy.—*Sir P. Sidney.*

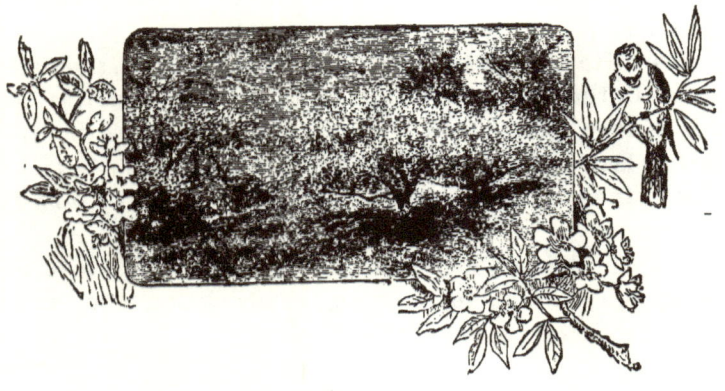

"CURFEW MUST NOT RING TO NIGHT"

BY

Rosa Hartwick Thorpe

ENGLAND'S sun was slowly setting o'er the hilltops
  far away,
Filling all the land with beauty at the close of
  one sad day;
And its last rays kissed the forehead of a man
  and maiden fair,—

He with steps so slow and weary; she with
sunny, floating hair;
He with bowed head, sad and thoughtful; she
with lips so cold and white,
Struggled to keep back the murmur, "Curfew
must not ring to-night."
"Sexton," Bessie's white lips faltered, pointing
to the prison old,
With its walls so tall and gloomy, moss-grown
walls, dark, damp, and cold,—

"I'VE a lover in that prison, doomed this very
night to die

At the ringing of the curfew; and no earthly
help is nigh.

Cromwell will not come till sunset," and her
lips grew strangely white,

As she spoke in husky whispers, "Curfew must
not ring to-night."

"Bessie," calmly spoke the sexton (every word pierced her young heart,

Like a gleaming death-winged arrow, like a deadly-poisoned dart),

"Long, long years I've rung the curfew from that gloomy, shadowed tower!

EVERY evening, just at sunset, it has tolled **the**
twilight hour.

I have done my duty ever, tried to **do it just**
and right;

Now I'm old, I will not miss it.   Curfew **bell**
must ring to-night!"

WILD her eyes and pale her features, stern and
white her thoughtful brow;
And within her heart's deep centre Bessie
made a solemn vow.

She had listened while the judges read, without a tear or sigh,
'At the ringing of the Curfew Basil Underwood
must die."

AND her breath came fast and faster, and her
    eyes grew large and bright;
One low murmur, faintly spoken, "Curfew *shall
    not* ring to-night!"
She with quick step bounded forward, sprang
    within the old church-door,
Left the old man coming slowly, paths he'd
    trod so oft before.

NOT one moment paused the maiden
	But with cheek and brow aglow
Staggered up the gloomy tower,
	Where the bell swung to and fro;
As she climbed the slimy ladder,
	On which fell no ray of light,
Upward still, her pale lips saying,
	"Curfew *shall not* ring to-night.

SHE has reached the topmost ladder; o'er
    her hangs the great, dark bell;
Awful is the gloom beneath her, like the
    pathway down to hell.
See! the ponderous tongue is swinging ;
    'tis the hour of curfew now,
And the sight has chilled her bosom,
    stopped her breath, and paled her brow.
Shall she let it ring? No, never! Her eyes
    flash with sudden light,
And she springs, and grasps it firmly:
    "Curfew *shall not* ring to-night!"
Out she swung,—far out. The city seemed
    a speck of light below,—

THERE 'twixt heaven and earth suspended,

    As the bell swung to and fro

And the sexton at the bell-rope, old and deaf,

    heard not the bell,

Sadly thought that twilight curfew rang

    young Basil's funeral knell.

Still the maiden, clinging firmly, quivering

    lip and fair face white,

Stilled her frightened heart's wild beating :

    "*Curfew shall not ring to-night!*"

It was o'er, the bell ceased swaying ; and the

    maiden stepped once more

Firmly on the damp old ladder, where, for

    hundred years before

HUMAN foot had not been planted. The brave
    deed that she had done
Should be told long ages after —
    as the rays of setting sun
Light the sky with golden beauty, aged sires
    with heads of white
Tell the children why the curfew did not ring
    that one sad night.
O'er the distant hills comes Cromwell. Bessie
    sees him; and her brow,
Lately white with sickening horror, has no
    anxious traces now;
At his feet she tells her story, shows her
    hands, all bruised and torn;
And her sweet young face, still haggard with
    the anguish it had worn,

Touched his heart with sudden pity, lit his
　　eyes with misty light:
"Go! your lover lives," cried Cromwell! "Curfew
　　shall not ring to-night."
Wide they flung the massive portals, led the
　　prisoner forth to die,
All his bright young life before him.　'Neath
　　the darkening English sky,
Bessie came, with flying footsteps,
　　eyes aglow with lovelight sweet;
Kneeling on the turf beside him, laid his pardon
　　at his feet.
In his brave, strong arms he clasped her,
　　kissed the face upturned and white,
Whispered, "Darling, you have saved me;
　　curfew will not ring to-night."